Fierce Love

W. MILLION

STOMILL BOOKS

Copyright © 2025 by W. Million

All rights reserved.

No portion of this book may be reproduced in any form without written permission from the publisher or author, except as permitted by U.S. copyright law.

This book is a work of fiction. The names, characters, and establishments are the product of the author's imagination or are used to provide authenticity and are used fictitiously. Any resemblance to any person, living or dead, is purely coincidental.

Cover Design: Shanoff Designs

Edited by: Red Adept Editing

Tucker Billionaires Series

Temporary Love
Fierce Love
Colliding Love – *Coming Soon*
Reckless Love – *TBA*

To all the girlies with thick thighs and pretty eyes

Chapter One

NATHANIEL

Fourteen years ago

Today will change my life. This marriage proposal has been looping figure eights through my head since I decided a ring was the perfect way to show Hollyn I'm completely committed to making us work, no matter where we live, even if I'm only seventeen.

With no colleges in Bellerive, we have no choice but to go off our small Atlantic island for our degrees. Tomorrow she'll be in New York for art, and I'll be in California taking business, both of us starting our freshman year of college.

And we'll be planning a wedding.

As I come down the stairs of my family's oceanfront mansion, one of my younger sisters, Sawyer, calls out from the main living room, "Mom's on the rampage. She's looking for you. Not sure what you did, but I'd avoid her."

I duck into the open-plan living room, kitchen, and dining room, which takes up almost the entire back half of our massive house and looks out on the ocean. The huge windows are floor to ceiling, and there's a cliff about a hundred meters from the back patio. For some reason, the view catches my attention today when

I'd normally gloss over it. The first time Hollyn was at my house, she said she didn't understand how there were people *this* rich. A lot of the time, I forget that everyone doesn't live like we do. Most people, in fact.

Despite the world I'm growing up in, billionaires are a rarity. Our Tucker family bubble of wealth kept me from seeing the full scope of how everyone else on the island lives, but that bubble burst with Hollyn's family. There's no unknowing what I've seen now.

Maren, my thirteen-year-old sister, pops up beside Sawyer on the white leather couch, and she leans over the back, crossing her arms, tanned from the long summer months spent outdoors. "What'd you do?"

"Nothing," I say. "Mom's just being Celia Tucker." Socialite and social-status obsessed, like always.

If she finds out I plan to propose to Hollyn, she'll be livid, not just because of my age but because Hollyn's family doesn't have two pennies to rub together. She's been living with her aunt for the last ten years while her parents float in and out of trouble. Not exactly an ideal match in my mother's eyes. Or my father's, if he was paying attention. But he leaves us and our troubles to our mother.

In two months, I'll be eighteen, and there will be nothing Celia Tucker or anyone else can do to stop a wedding. I'll have access to the Tucker family trust, and I'll be legally able to do whatever I want. Until then, I just have to ride out her disapproval. Easy enough from California.

"Whenever she gets like this, one of us has done something to damage her social clout. Did you get Hollyn pregnant?" Sawyer asks.

"No!" My response is quick, but if they could read my mind, they'd know I wouldn't have been upset if that *had* happened. Anything that gets me Hollyn forever is just fine with me. But being a teen mother is the last thing Hollyn would want. The first time we had sex, she asked me if I could double bag my dick and go with her to get Plan B, just in case. So yeah—not pregnant.

But if she ever was, I'd parent our kids so differently from how Celia and Jonathan have raised me. I'd give a shit when they succeeded, just as much as when they failed. I also wouldn't tell my kids that I liked them best before they learned to talk—*Thanks, Mom*—which she fully admits is why she had us all so close together.

"Where are you going?" Maren asks, eyeing my outfit.

The jeans I have on are the ones Hollyn loves, and the shirt I'm wearing is the one she bought me. She claims this blueish hue matches my eyes, but other people have called my eyes green too. I never know what to label their color.

"I'm going out. And I'm not telling either of you where in case you sell me out to Mom."

"Sell you out!" Maren scoffs. "What could she possibly offer us?"

"Easy," I say, because they think I don't pay attention to the chatter around the house. As the oldest of five, I used to be the one helping to persuade Mom that the Tucker name could take a hit or two. Until I was the one delivering the blows and she stopped listening to me. "Maren, she could sign the permission forms for you to go on whatever adventure race that teacher has talked you into, and for you"—I turn to Sawyer—"she could let you participate in that sit-in in Tucker's Town over climate change." Excessive exercise and protests are things Celia Tucker finds distasteful and beneath the family.

They both stare at me and then turn to each other, as though they are dumbfounded by my infinite knowledge.

"Exactly," I say, and I point at both of them before grabbing my keys off the table and heading for the bank of garages. The Range Rover is mine, though my parents don't care which of the thirty-odd cars I drive as long as I don't get into an accident. No dents, scratches, or scrapes allowed.

The drive to the campground is short. Nothing in Bellerive is particularly far away—at least, if you've experienced enough of the world to know the difference. An hour's drive from one end of the island to the other, and about the same widthwise, though that's more about the hilly, mountainous terrain the roads have to conquer than the distance itself.

Hollyn is meeting me when she's done with her waitressing shift at The Drunk Raccoon. Tucker's campground overlooks the ocean, prime real estate, just like everything else the Tucker family possesses. Generational wealth is real and prevalent in Bellerive. Unescapable, which Hollyn has reminded me of countless times.

In Bellerive, you're either already ahead or you're behind. The middle class is a myth or such a minority that it feels like a myth—I'm never sure which.

Cal, my distant cousin, best friend, and the son of the branch of the Tucker family that owns this slice of land, meets me at the front gate.

"Does Celia know yet?" he asks, almost giddy, as I get out of the Range Rover, the ring box banging against my leg as I walk toward the spot I've had strung with fairy lights, a blanket, and a bottle of non-alcoholic champagne. Hollyn doesn't drink.

"Fuck no," I say with a laugh.

"Celia will need an enema when she finds out. She'll be constipated for weeks over this."

"Possibly for the rest of her life." But I'm not worried about it, and maybe I should be. My mother can be a force to be reckoned with, but I'm so close to getting financial freedom that her thoughts and opinions are less and less important.

She'd tell me that proposing is rash and impulsive. That believing I know who I want to be with for the rest of my life when I'm seventeen is nonsense. She'd tell me that Hollyn's life and upbringing are too different from mine and that those differences will matter more than I think as we get older. She'd tell me the Tucker name shouldn't be linked to criminals. There's nothing she can tell me today that I haven't heard every day for the last few months—ever since she found out about Hollyn.

It's just that, from the moment I met Hollyn, I've *known* in my gut, in my heart, in my fucking blood, that she's the woman I'm meant to spend my life with. Without question. Without hesitation. The minute her arms slid around me, and our gazes connected that first night, I knew with soul-shaking certainty. Hollyn is mine, and I am hers.

"First love, worst love" and all that trite shit even my dad tried to spew at me—probably after my mom asked him to—doesn't apply. This is forever. Guaran-fucking-teed.

"I honestly can't believe you're doing this," Cal says, and he slaps me on the shoulder. "You're already with her. What's the rush to get married?"

I would have married her the night we met. Or within the first few weeks if she'd let me. But where I'm "Fuck it, let's go all in," she's a lot more cautious. Doesn't think we'll survive our long distance. But once I'm eighteen and have my money, I can fly to her, fly her to me. Transfer schools, even. Making it work might not be easy, but it's far from impossible. Fifty years from now we'll look back and laugh that we ever thought any of this was hard.

"You know why," I say because we've talked about it for weeks. Cal is the one person I trust with everything. He even went with me to check the final ring design. "Maybe you don't get it, but you know."

"To be this sure, though. I just... I don't know. I have a hard time imagining it." He rubs the back of his head and then crosses his arms to take in the scene in front of us.

The sun is setting, and the fairy lights are strung along the rustic wooden fence—older than me—that keeps people from accidentally going over the cliff.

"Think she'll know?" Cal asks.

"Doubtful," I say, and while I'm sure she'll say yes, I'm not sure she'll say yes *right away*. I'm prepared and determined to be convincing. Every possible objection she could utter I've already run through my head, and I've got a rebuttal lined up. Debate club has to be good for something.

"All right, well, I'll leave you to it," Cal says, clapping me on the shoulder again.

I move toward the view, and I splay my hands along the railing, leaning into the rough wood under my palms. The ocean below is calm tonight, as though it also knows that I'm making the right decision.

In the distance, gray misty clouds hang low, threatening to bring rain. Hollyn should be here, and we should have talked everything through before those arrive. Lots of time before we dash to our vehicles, engaged, full of laughter and hope.

As the sun sinks, I check my watch, and then I pat my pocket for my phone before realizing I left it in the Range Rover. If I go get it, I might end up meeting her in the parking lot, and that'll take a wrecking ball to my plan. The mood I want to set is for her to find all this with me *here*, not me walking with her into it.

But if she's running late from work, I might need to be more worried about those clouds in the distance. A rainy proposal gets the job done, but it's not the memory that's been playing on repeat in my head.

Fuck it. I need my phone. Her boss is enough of an asshole that he might have forced her into a bit of overtime tonight. After the third time I called him on his shitty employment practices, Hollyn told me that I had to stop trying to solve all her problems because she'd end up fired, which would lead to more problems. My mother keeps a tight leash on the family funds, or I'd solve *those* problems too.

I dig around the car until I finally find my phone tucked under the driver's seat. There's a missed call and a voicemail, and I click through to play it.

"Nate—it's me. I can't make it tonight. I just..." There's a deep shaky breath. *"Some stuff has come up, and I don't think I'll get to see you before I leave."* Hollyn's voice catches on the last word, and then she's gone. But I'm already climbing into the Range Rover, turning the engine over, putting the vehicle in reverse. Something's upset her, and while I don't know exactly where to find her, I know all the places to look.

As I drive, I click on her name to call her back. When there's no answer, I don't bother leaving a message. I press my hand against the box in my jeans pocket.

But as I drive from her workplace to the apartment she shares with her aunt, to the trailer her parents sometimes use, to all the places that are her favorite thinking spots, she's nowhere to be found.

I've texted her, but she hasn't texted back. In the parking lot to her three-story apartment complex, I sit and stare at the entrance to the building. Worry eats me up in way I never knew it could. The rain is falling in thick sheets all around me, running in rivers down the street.

At the entrance, I huddle tight under the awning and buzz her number—the same way I have countless times over the last few months, the same way I did almost an hour ago when I first tried to find her. Panic swirls in my stomach, and I hit the buzzer over and over again.

Finally, there's static on the other side.

"Hols?" I ask. "Are you okay?"

"I'll be down," Verna says into the speaker, her voice resigned.

She's never spoken to me like that before. Being buzzed up is a given—not once has she made me wait out here—and it's fucking raining tonight. Maybe I'd have to wait in the apartment as Hollyn put on a last coat of mascara or tried to find the purse she really wanted. This doorstep is somewhere I pass through, not somewhere I stay.

I shift on my feet while I wait for Verna to appear, invite me in. But when she gets to the door, she steps out, wrapping her housecoat around her. She doesn't let me in.

"She's gone, Nathaniel. Left early for school."

"What?" I search her face for the gentle teasing I've seen so many times before. Surely, she can't be serious. "I don't understand."

"No, I'm sure you don't." She lets out a deep sigh. "She couldn't do this goodbye in person, so I'm doing it for her." She swallows and doesn't meet my gaze.

"I'll just go see her. I won't fly to California tomorrow. I'll fly to her."

Verna closes her eyes, and when she opens them, her brown eyes are crackling with anger. "That girl is allowed to tell you she's done, that she doesn't want what you're offering. You don't own her, Nathaniel Tucker. You Tuckers can't just do whatever you want with people. You hear me?"

I rear back, shocked at the venom in her voice that feels misplaced, unearned. "I'd never—I wouldn't..." I rub my face, fighting tears. "I don't understand what's happening."

"You and Hollyn are over. That's just the way it has to be."

I want to argue with her, but I don't even know what to say. So I leave without another word, the rain drenching me before I can get inside my vehicle. But I don't stop at home to get new clothes or think anything through. I drive to the airport.

Once our private jet is ready, I run through every possible scenario, everything I could say to Hollyn to convince her that ending things between us is silly, unnecessary. A few years of long distance is nothing when compared to a lifetime together.

But she's not in her dorm room, and when I go to the registrar on the first day of school, they tell me they have no record of her being registered. Her phone number is disconnected, and she never comes back to Bellerive.

She never comes back to me.

Chapter Two

NATHANIEL

My knuckles are white as I grip the steering wheel of my McLaren GT. After Verna didn't show up for her shift in the kitchen at my brother, Gage's, catered family dinner, I agreed to check on her.

Stupid, really.

I've avoided the woman, the whole family, since Hollyn ghosted me almost fourteen years ago. Once the dirt on the grave has settled, hardened, you don't fucking dig it up.

The police car pulls out of the parking lot, Stephen waving to me from the driver's side, and I manage to get one hand off the steering wheel long enough to wave back.

Thankfully, he told me the police are responsible for notifying the next of kin, so my duty here is done.

When I'd arrived, I got the building manager, got into Verna's apartment, and when I found her collapsed and cold, I called 911. Then I waited until everyone was here to get her out, to clean up the scene. Duty done.

But fuck if my heart doesn't hurt at the realization of what Verna's death will do to Hollyn, wherever she is, whatever she's been doing since I saw her last. Maybe she's got kids and a husband, a family to soothe the ache that Verna's absence will leave behind.

If I was feeling generous, I'd want that for her.

But I can't remember the last time I felt generous where Hollyn was concerned.

I rub my chest and stare into the distance. There was a time when I could have called Nick or Brice Summerset, the younger princes in the royal family, who had always been up for a good time in years past. We'd have taken a trip to Vegas, sunk any hint of these unstable emotions threatening to float to the surface with the anchors of gambling and alcohol. But they don't do those things anymore, and I haven't needed that type of amusement in a long while.

Thankfully, I'm done caring about Hollyn and her family problems, so I don't need that type of distraction either. If Verna's death causes Hollyn to crumble, those aren't my pieces to reassemble.

After starting the vehicle, I steer it toward the one place where I know I'm always welcome, no matter the time, the one person who'll understand why I'm so thrown by tonight's events. Finding a dead body is one thing—having that body be Verna Davis is a total mind-fuck.

Cal steps out of his cottage and onto the porch, which rests on the edge of the campground. While his father still technically owns it, Cal is the one who takes care of the day-to-day. Tourists always assume he's just a worker, and he lets them.

"You hear?" he asks. "That why you've come?"

"Hear what?" I ask.

"Verna Davis. Passed away tonight."

"Jesus, the gossip travels fast," I say, taking the glass of gold rush he offers me before sitting in one of the rocking chairs on his porch. "I didn't need to hear. I was there. I found her."

"Fuck off," Cal says, slumping into the chair beside me. "Are you kidding?"

"I wish." I take a deep drink and stare out at the smattering of trailers that are here year-round. Spring isn't exactly high season. With my free hand, I'm flipping my phone from front to back, over and over.

Cal stares at the motion for a beat and then takes a long drink. "Tell me you don't still have it."

"Of course I still have it," I say. "I paid the phone company to let me keep it forever. It doesn't expire."

"Tell me you're not still listening to it."

"Not in years."

"But you're thinking about it now, right? I'm your Hollyn Davis sponsor. The one responsible for keeping you from torturing yourself over things you couldn't change then and can't change now. Just delete it, man. I get that it helped at first—fueled your anger—but that's not what it became, is it?"

No, it's not. Her final voicemail pissed me off for a long time. Made me furious. After everything we'd shared, promised each other, for her to leave me that message and vanish was unacceptable. Still is. But later, listening to it just made me depressed and so fucking sad. Unbearably sad.

I really thought we were something. Everything, actually.

We drink in silence for a while because I'm not willing to admit anything more out loud. Seeing Verna threw me, but I'll recover, and then life will go back to normal.

"Hollyn didn't want the relationship the way you wanted it. And I know that's really fucking hard to hear, man, but I don't want you getting sucked back into this vortex, you know? Where you think if you'd only been a bit better, a bit more, she'd have stuck around. We've talked it out. You know what it was."

She was never all-in like me, and where I thought it was just the social-class stuff, it clearly wasn't. I wanted forever, and she was content with a fling. In hindsight, it felt like maybe I should have seen the end coming. Hollyn wanted to keep us a secret, never wanted a soul to know. Never even said she loved me out loud in the few months we dated. But I felt it. I *know* I felt it.

"I got knocked back a step tonight," I say. "Seeing a dead body—the body of someone you once knew quite well—tends to do that. Doesn't have anything to do with Hollyn." Lies. Big fat fucking lies.

"Right," Cal says, dryly. "Absolutely nothing."

After I leave Cal's, I drive around the island aimlessly. It's not until I'm an hour into my mindless turning that I realize I'm retracing my steps from the night she left, driving past all of Hollyn's old haunts.

Disgust at myself claws at my throat. *Pathetic.*

Wherever my man card went, I need to locate it and brandish it with pride. Drink a beer. Find a woman to fuck. Gamble part of my inheritance. Go shoot something in the woods. None of that's me—not sure it ever was—but I tried on most of it in college. An ill-fitted mask.

I don't fucking care if she's out in the world, hurting at the news of her aunt. My fucks to give expired when Hollyn went out of her way to get rid of me from her life. A conversation was all she would have needed.

Another lie.

Back then, I was obsessed with her. Out of my mind in love. If she'd said no to my proposal, I don't even know what I would have done. Probably worked triple time to convince her we could make a lifetime work. But my love for her couldn't make up for the shortfall of emotion she must have felt in return, and I couldn't wrap my head around that at seventeen. I thought I could love hard enough out loud for both of us.

As it was, I spent a small fortune on a private detective who couldn't find her. At the time, he told me he had a few less-than-legal methods he could go down if I wanted to pay him twice his rate, but I was angry by then and told him not to bother. She didn't want to be found, so fuck it. I'd stop looking.

My phone pings with a flurry of text messages from my sibling group chat, and I realize they've all found out. Other than a tentative text from Sawyer encouraging me to let them know if I found Verna, none of them had messaged me again until now.

In the parking lot of the bar Hollyn used to work at, I open my phone.

Maren: Nathaniel, I just heard. Tell me you didn't find her.

Ava: He found her. Heard from Stephen.

Sawyer: A little compassion, Ava.

Ava: Sorry for Hollyn's loss.

Sawyer: I meant about Nathaniel finding her.

Ava: Oh, right. Sorry you found her, Nathaniel. Would not want to be you tonight.

At least that makes me chuckle. Ava, my youngest sister, is so completely oblivious to how anyone but her feels, and it's oddly charming sometimes. My brother, Gage, used to be like that, too.

Gage: We're on the jet. But I'll head back to the island once I have Em and Nova settled in LA. I can fly Michelle out to pick up the slack. You need me, bro? I'm there.

And that's who he's become. The guy who shows up. My throat tightens at his text. We've never been close, at least, not until recently, and I would have said it didn't matter because I had Maren and Sawyer. I've never wanted or needed to lean on him the way he's leaned on me the last few months, but the realization that I *can* lean on him is a strange comfort. My little brother is finally growing up.

But I don't need them all coddling me. I really don't need some sort of sibling intervention.

Me: I'm fine. Stand down. It was a shock. But I'm handling it fine.

I almost write that I knew Verna in another life, but I know at least Maren and Sawyer won't buy that I feel *that* much indifference toward finding her dead. If I oversell, I'm fucked.

Maren: I'll be stopping by in a few days to make sure that's true. I'll let you know if you need to come home, Gage.

Me: You won't need to come home.

But that night, when I crawl into bed, emotionally and mentally exhausted, I sleep the sleep of the dead, except I dream. Vivid lies. Surreal memories. Hollyn and me. Happy. Together. In love during an endless spring and summer that ended far too soon.

When I wake up the next morning, instead of being angry or upset, I just long to go back to sleep, to live it all over again, one more time.

Two days later, I arrive back from watching a cut of the documentary project I've been producing, on Prince Nicholas and his wife, Julia's, Tanzanian school initiative, to find Maren and Sawyer have made themselves at home in my kitchen. A pot of coffee has been brewed, and they've raided my freezer for the chocolate chip cookies Michelle, the family housekeeper, makes—my favorite.

My penthouse apartment in the center of Tucker's Town is huge—the perks of being wealthy and privileged and coming from old money—but I also own a house outside of the city. This apartment has been in the family for multiple generations, but I'm the current inhabitant. At some point, the roof of the building was raised to create cathedral ceilings, which makes the space feel even bigger than it actually is. It was either done illegally, someone paid a lot of money into a politician's pocket, or the renovation happened before Bellerive made external architectural changes impossible. The Tuckers have always been more of an "ask for forgiveness rather than permission" family.

"What's the occasion?" I ask, eyeing the cookies. "Thawing these without my permission should come with a fine. Michelle is more of a nanny to Gage than a housekeeper to all of us lately. I don't even know when I'll get more." I pluck a cookie off the pile. Which reminds me I might want to hire another person to look after the apartment and vacant house while Michelle is gone to Los Angeles with Gage, Ember, and Nova. "You even warmed these cookies?"

"Your mental health is the special occasion," Maren says, her long dark hair falling over her shoulder, "and warm is when all cookies are best."

"My mental health is fine," I say, stuffing the rest of the cookie in my mouth. I shed my suit jacket on the back of one of the island chairs, take out a cup, and pour myself some coffee. After my first sip, I realize this check-in is serious. They drove across the island for the special coffee blend I can only find in Rockdown—the one that's been my favorite for years. I ran out last week and haven't been motivated enough to make the drive or hire someone else to do it.

"You haven't run into Hollyn yet?" Sawyer asks, her voice gentle. Her blue eyes are soft with kindness.

"I don't think either of us would want that," I say evenly. "It's not like I'm seeking her out." And I knew, in an abstract way, that Hollyn was likely on the island by now. Having my sister confirm that she's definitely here is going to make me search every crowd, wonder if every woman who looks vaguely like Hollyn could be her grown-up self. My mental health was better when I let myself forget what had happened, that anything was happening. Kept Hollyn firmly in the past.

"I don't know," Maren says, tipping up a cookie from the plate and breaking it in half. "Talking to her might help you move on. Get some answers. Get past this mental block you have where women are concerned."

"There's no mental block. I've dated several women."

"And not one of them has lasted beyond four months," Sawyer says. "You never let yourself get too involved."

She isn't wrong. At a certain point, it becomes clear I'm not going to feel enough, that we aren't a good fit, and it seems mean to waste their time. After feeling led on and then ghosted by Hollyn, I'm careful not to do the same to any of the women I date. When we break up, I'm up front about why.

"Every woman you've dated has told me at a party or some other function that *they* thought your relationship was going well. Each time, they're shocked when you break up with them," Sawyer says.

This is news to me—sort of. Almost all the women took the breakups well—even if a bit surprised—and I'm friendly with all of them at social functions.

"You feel what you feel," I say with a shrug. Which, for me, hadn't been a spark. Attraction, maybe, but no connection.

"And I think you don't let yourself feel too much anymore," Maren says. "The pilot light is still on for you with Hollyn, and maybe it's time you snuffed it out."

"There's no pilot light," I say with a huff. "She made her feelings perfectly clear when she disappeared and made it so hard to find her. Message received."

"You won't care at all that she's meeting with Otis Williamson's funeral home, then," Maren says.

"Otis? She went to Otis?" I can't keep the disgust out of my voice. He caters to the rich crowd, and his prices reflect that. There are no deals to be had, and in fact, he's likely to gouge Hollyn for every penny she's budgeted to lay her aunt to rest. "Why wouldn't she have gone to Little John?"

"Maybe she's got more money than sense now," Maren says.

I don't say anything in response, but my mind starts turning over this piece of information. The Hollyn I knew would have never gone to someone like Otis, wasted her money. It's the perfect indication that she's not the woman I remember, and the last thing I want to do is keep talking about her. I'd rather forget she's even on the island. She can go back to being a ghost in my dreams.

"Either of you get the call about being tested as a kidney donor for Mom yet?" I ask.

"I go next week," Maren says.

"Me too," Sawyer says. "What about you?"

"Tomorrow," I say.

The funeral home is on the way to the hospital, and maybe it's worth a quick stop to ensure Otis is keeping in mind the better business practices that are only loosely enforced in Bellerive. Until someone complains, that is.

"Hopefully, it won't come to that," Maren says. "Mom says they're hopeful these treatments will work to stop her kidneys from producing too much protein. There are three or four different courses of treatment they can try before a transplant will be necessary."

"Just as long as the match isn't Ava," Sawyer says with a wry smile. "I don't want to have to try to convince her to be cut open and scar her body."

"She'll do it, though," I say.

"But she won't make it easy," Maren says with a laugh. "Ava never makes anything easy."

"Part of her charm as the youngest," I say.

"Sure," Sawyer says. "That."

I let out a chuckle because Sawyer and Ava have always butted heads, much like Gage and I used to. Maybe they'll figure their shit out at some point, too, or maybe they'll be too different to ever be close.

I settle into one of the island chairs and grab another cookie. "When are you and Brice getting married?" I ask Maren, a smug teasing in my tone. She's probably been asked the same question a thousand times by our mother. Celia

Tucker will want that connection to the island's royal family locked up, a dream come true.

Maren throws a piece of cookie at me, and I catch it and pop it into my mouth with a grin. "You already know when, you idiot." Then the three of us fall into an easy banter for the rest of the lunch hour.

"I should go. I have a client," Sawyer says, glancing at her watch.

"Physio on a Sunday?" Maren says.

"A freebie." Sawyer shrugs and grabs her bag from the island. "You know I can't resist."

"And I suppose you're going back to the office too?" Maren turns to me, eyebrows lifted.

"Still trying to firm up some details on my next producing project. I have a few meetings today with interior designers on the island. Posey is an easy choice for a host for the TV show—late twenties, an interior designer, well-known and liked on the island—but we need someone to bounce off her. The team wants someone who was raised here but in a lower-income area. Silver spoons need not apply. It's been harder than I thought to find someone with that background who isn't overshadowed by Posey's brand of sunshine. We've run a few tests, and they just haven't been right. Nick and Jules had so much natural chemistry on camera—you could feel it through the screen. We need *that* to make this show a success. I had no idea how lucky we were."

"You can't fake chemistry," Maren agrees.

"Ain't that the truth," Sawyer says at the doorway. "Call or stop by if you need me. I mean it, Nathaniel!" Then she flies out the door.

I grab my suit jacket and walk with Maren to the front entrance. After her time working with the streaming giant, Interflix, for her adventure race, she's probably the only one in the family who understands the intricacies of good TV. "No royal duties today?"

"King Alexander always leaves Sundays free if he can. It's his family day. He treats it like it's sacred, which is pretty endearing, really." She gives me a brief smile. "Brice and I are going for a run and then a paddle in an hour."

"Got your next big race lined up?"

"Brice wants a break from the adventure race circuit. We're going to try to get the youth program off the ground more in time for Bellerive's first youth event at the end of this summer. I'm also busy trying to find foster homes for dogs so we can get them out of the shelter. Know anyone who might want one?" She gives me a hopeful look.

"Foster homes?" I say with narrowed eyes. She says that, but I think she means *adoptive homes*. "Nope." We've had this conversation before. There are many things I'll do for my sisters, but taking on a lifelong commitment isn't one of them. At least, not regarding a dog, and that's what would happen. I'd cave and keep it. Besides, I've never had a dog before. I'd be a terrible dog parent.

"We're doing an Ironman Triathlon next, just for fun," Maren says, breezing past my no as though I didn't even wield it.

"Right," I say dryly. "Why not?"

"That's become my motto about pretty much everything," Maren says, patting my chest and straightening my tie. "Why not?"

I can think of so many instances in life where that motto is more harmful than helpful, but I know I'll be stopping at the funeral home tomorrow, inserting myself into something I have no business caring about. Even if this version of Hollyn no longer worries about getting screwed out of money, I'm still the same guy who can't stand by and watch it happen.

Chapter Three

HOLLYN

I've never been able to decide whether it's worse to lose someone quickly or slowly. So far, all my losses have been quick and gut-wrenching, the kind that turn your world upside down in a single phone call or knock on the door. A few whispered words or a strident rap, and my whole life explodes.

Otis, the funeral director, leads us on a tour of the building, showing us where the visitation will take place and where he's suggesting the funeral happen based on projected numbers. The spaces are all neutral creams and browns with comfortable-looking furniture dotted around. Rich, opulent. The sorts of fabrics, brand-name products, and combinations I'd suggest to someone in New York with an unlimited budget.

We follow behind him, and I make noises of agreement as he weaves through rooms and down halls. Beside me, my little sister, Kinsley, says nothing. If I don't dwell on why I'm here, I'll be fine. Except for the design choices, I try to keep my mind blank of any real thoughts, but they creep in anyway.

Quick or slow, the death of my aunt is definitely the worst kind of loss. No comparison. Since I was a little kid, she's been my second mother, and so much better than my first. The person who taught me what it means to mother someone else. Whenever I needed her, she came running. From providing a roof over my head when child protective services seized me to coming to New York for long weekends when she could get the time off, to supporting me when I went after primary care of my sister, she's been my constant. The anchor in any stormy sea.

Losing her is a kind of untethering I didn't even realize could happen to a person. Both my parents, but especially my mother, never tied me to anything but chaos.

My Aunt Verna's death leaves a gaping hole in my chest and a crushing weight on my back. As soon as I got the call about her heart attack, I took a hasty leave from my job as an interior designer, packed bags, pulled my sister out of school, and headed home. Maybe I should have returned years ago, but I rarely felt strong enough to face this place, face what I left behind. *Who* I left behind.

At thirty-two, I'm being forced to confront the choices I made and the decisions that changed my life forever.

Or maybe I can get out of Bellerive again before I have to do any of that. One can hope. God knows I do not want Kinsley growing up here.

"What do you think?" Otis asks outside the final room in the wide hallway. "Will this suit your needs?"

It's the biggest and most expensive funeral home on the island. My aunt's meager life insurance will cover the cost, but her funeral is the first time Aunt Verna will be on equal terms with the people she served most of her life, or the ones whose houses she cleaned for extra cash when I was a kid, desperate for something she couldn't afford. The divide between the haves and the have-nots in Bellerive has always been wider than it should be, as far as I'm concerned.

"I'll e-transfer the money today."

Otis should have had little doubt about what I'd do. I called his funeral home to collect my aunt's body before I left New York. When she was alive, I wasn't able to give her the best, but I was damn sure going to make sure she got the greatest sendoff possible.

"I'll take care of all the details," Otis assures me.

That's another thing about pretending to be rich. People look after you as though you're incapable of doing things for yourself. In this case, I'm happy for him to take control. The minute I have to ponder caskets or urns or flower arrangements, I'm on the verge of sobbing. Otis took my budget, and when I said I didn't feel capable of making sound decisions, he promised me the world.

After having very little most of my life, the world is a pretty great deal, regardless of the cost.

"Your aunt was well respected in Bellerive," he says as he leads us toward the front entrance, and it's then that I realize he's probably around my aunt's age. Twenty to thirty years older than me. Portly and balding but still dignified in a way that only people with money can be. "What are you up to now?" he asks. "Never returned to the island to work?"

"My opportunities were better elsewhere," I say. "I work for one of the top interior design firms in New York." Name dropping would probably be wasted on him.

"Must have gone to a pretty fancy school."

I did. Not at all the school I intended to go to, and my life has been on a trajectory I never imagined as a result. "Hard work pays off," I say. The truth is complicated, and it makes me feel a strange mix of shame and pride. When our backs were against the wall, I did what I had to, and I can't regret that. I won't let myself.

"She's really busy all the time," Kinsley says, a familiar bite to her words.

Her teenage attitude is poking out. At thirteen, she hates how much I work, but living in our shoebox apartment in New York is expensive, and I'm still building my client list. Being in Bellerive is bad for both of those things—paying my bills and keeping my clients happy—but I owe my aunt my time and attention. They're the things I should have given her more of while she was alive too. But I thought we'd have lots of time, so much more time. It seems wrong that my parents are alive and healthy, given the lifestyles they've both led, and my aunt—my sweet, strong Auntie Verna—is gone too soon.

"Thank you for your time," I say to Otis, placing my hand on Kinsley's lower back to move her along.

She leans into the touch. We're both heartbroken in our own way about Aunt Verna's death. I lost my mentor and the woman I wished to call mother, and Kinsley lost the equivalent of a grandparent. Whenever she thought I was being unreasonable, she reached out to our aunt for sympathy or to talk through her feelings. We were a three-wheeled scooter, rushing through life, and it feels unstable to have lost one of our wheels. We're going to have to learn to balance without her stabilizing influence.

We're almost at the high-ceilinged foyer when the front door opens with a whoosh, bringing in a rush of hot air. With the door open and the person lit from behind, all I can determine is tall and broad, but when the shoulders rotate to close the door, a sense of familiarity rushes through me. That movement—it's not the first time it's happened—where I caught a glimpse of a stranger in a crowd and my brain filled in details, made connections that floated away on the wind. But when the suited man lingers with his hand on the doorknob before turning around, I scan his wide back, narrow hips.

It can't be. Fate cannot hate me that much.

Pinpricks dart along my skin.

Oh god.

"Otis," Nate Tucker says, barely sparing me a glance. "I have a few things I'd like to discuss."

Otis lets out a deep sigh behind me, but I can't tear my gaze from Nate's face. *That face.* Everything in me aches, as though I've suddenly caught the worst flu.

"I'm in the middle of a client showing," Otis says, gesturing to us.

"I can see that," Nate says, but he doesn't acknowledge me or Kinsley.

There are laugh lines in the corners of his eyes now—lines he earned with someone else. The realization causes a flood of regret that only makes my physical aches feel watery and less stable.

But I can't stop looking at him, can't drag myself away. From what I can see, he's tanned, as though he still enjoys ample time outdoors. Has he spent most of it with Cal at the campground? Does Cal even still live on the island? He used to be so connected to the campground, to the simple life.

A thousand questions begin running through my head in rapid succession—things I haven't let myself consider since I left here—but when Nate's shuttered gaze swings to Kinsley, I can almost see him adding up the years. I've been told more than once that Kinsley looks like a younger version of me. A twin, if you will.

"And you are?" he says to her, still not addressing me.

"Kinsley Davis," my sister says, holding out her hand. At least *her* manners are on point.

His very deliberate avoidance should probably annoy me, but I'm grateful for the reprieve, the chance to study him without his piercing gaze undoing me.

Because in all these years, I somehow managed to convince myself that seeing Nate would be hard but not gut-wrenchingly difficult. Standing here, mere feet from him, it's devastating to realize all these years passed between us and I never got a chance to see any of these subtle changes, have no sense of what happened to create the reserved man he's obviously become.

My Nate was fiercely protective but also giddy with young love. Whenever we were together, it felt like we were walking on clouds. Nothing could touch us.

Until I crashed back down to earth, alone.

"This is my sister, Hollyn," Kinsley says, gesturing to me when Nate doesn't make any move to introduce himself. Why would he? But Kinsley doesn't know that, doesn't know much about my childhood in Bellerive. For good reason.

"We've met before," Nate says.

That might be the greatest understatement I've ever heard uttered in person. "Met before" as though we weren't once everything to each other. His comment would be laughable if I wasn't glued to the spot, unable to move, barely able to breathe.

He seems to drag his gaze off hers to meet mine. His reluctance is clear, but it doesn't change what happens once we're face-to-face, and the sharp knife of remembrance slices through me. Can he see the truth, like a stain, coating me? I'd loved him, almost more than I'd ever loved anyone. Romantic love has never been the same—in ruins for anyone else who has come into my life after.

Electrical currents zip through the air between us, alive with our past and all the things we've never said, will never say. Out of the corner of my eye, I notice his hand flex, clenching and unclenching at his side. The same way he used to clench the sheets beside my head as he tried to hold on a little longer, bury himself a little deeper.

My stomach drops at the memory.

"We knew each other a long time ago," I whisper, but I can't stop staring at him. Right now, "a long time ago" feels like forever and just yesterday. My memory didn't do his blue-green eyes justice—they're stormy when all I remember is how brilliant and bright they used to be. A teasing glint never absent for long. Looking at him now, I can't imagine where that boy went, replaced with this intense manliness. Unfamiliar but still wildly attractive.

His hair is deep brown, much shorter than before, but still has a glossy sheen that makes my fingers twitch with the desire to weave through their former playground. I spent hours toying with the soft strands as we laid in bed talking, daydreaming, hiding from reality. A few months that felt like lifetimes.

God, we were so naïve.

"We were just leaving," I say, hating how husky my voice sounds.

"Of course," Nate says, stepping to the side. "I wouldn't want to hold you back."

I close my eyes briefly, and I open the door, tugging Kinsley along behind me. While I wait, she closes the door, and I cover my face, taking a deep breath, hoping Nate didn't see me but not caring enough to pretend. My emotions are a mess right now, and I might have to choose which feelings to hide from Kinsley.

At thirteen, she doesn't deserve to feel the kind of weight I used to get offloaded onto me from the grownups in my life.

"Are you okay?" she asks, her voice small.

"Yeah," I say, closing my eyes again for a couple more deep breaths before squaring my shoulders. "It's just a lot, but I'll be fine."

She laces her fingers with mine and leans into my shoulder, a comfort and a responsibility I never take lightly. No matter what choices I've had to make, they've been to ensure Kinsley gets the life I always wanted. One run-in with Nate Tucker isn't going to make me question the path I chose.

Chapter Four

NATHANIEL

Acting without thinking is something I did a lot in my youth. If I wanted something or someone, I leapt in with both feet. After Hollyn left, I changed. Heartbreak does that, I guess, though I've never put my heart at risk again to test that theory. Maybe it's only the first one that slices you open, never quite able to heal.

Going to the funeral home without an appointment is the old version of me—the one who leaps first—and I'm already regretting it.

Seeing Hollyn was like being pummeled in the kidneys. If it's possible, she's even more beautiful. Where she'd been worryingly thin as a teenager, she's filled out in adulthood. Lush and full. She's poised and polished without seeming artificial. Leaving the island doesn't look like it's disagreed with her.

Her naturally wavy auburn hair was tamed today and fell just below her shoulders, unlike the short bob she had in high school. Every detail of her appearance kept getting slotted into place over the old version the longer we stood staring at each other. Redrawn in my memories.

Pity those gorgeous hazel eyes are the same. They held my gaze like *I* wounded *her*, making the whole encounter worse. She ghosted me. Whatever ache she still feels is her own doing.

Perhaps I'm reading too much into our brief encounter, wishing to see what I feel reflected. Maybe the look wasn't even about me. Maybe it was about what a shithead Otis Williamson is.

He's sitting behind his desk, and I'm leaning against the wall, not even bothering to sit down. This won't take long.

"It's customary to make an appointment, even when you're a Tucker," Otis says, linking his hands together on top of his desk, trying on the tough-guy persona that he doesn't really possess.

"I caught wind of you overcharging some clients," I say. "I wanted to let you know that I'll be going to the Better Business Bureau of Bellerive with a formal complaint tomorrow."

"Did a client complain, or is this a Nathaniel Tucker complaint?" His tone is dry, as though he already knows the answer. My reputation is well-known and earned.

"Any complaint is worth investigating. The rich-poor divide on the island is already concerning. There's no point in exacerbating that by inflating your prices based on what you *believe* people can pay instead of having a firm price list." His lack of consistent pricing is legendary. Whoever comes to him from the island knows what they're getting, but Otis banks on his prestige, on the illusion that anyone who uses him is too rich to care that they're being ripped off.

"Who do you believe I'm overcharging?" he asks.

I ease my hand along my jaw, hesitant to answer truthfully. If I hadn't run into Hollyn, I would have used her name freely, but Otis saw how stiff we were with each other. It's not believable that we're friendly enough for her to have shared his rates.

"The people who came to me asked for confidentiality, but I can tell you it is one of the clients you have coming up. Not a past client," I say.

He grumbles as he flips through the appointment book on his desk, and when he looks up at me, I can tell he's mulling over his options.

"I'm not bluffing," I say. "If you don't adjust your prices and create some consistency, I'll be at the bureau every single day until they sanction you—heavily—for every infraction I can find, not just this one complaint."

"Fuck you, Nathaniel," he mutters. "I don't understand why you're so opposed to other people making money. The Tuckers are billionaires, for fuck's sake." He moves between two pages in the book. "Does adjusting over the next two weeks cover this current complaint?"

"Seems reasonable," I say, pushing off the wall. A funeral home can't possibly be booked much further out than that, can it? "A pleasure, as always." I duck out the door before he has a chance to respond. He's pissed off, and I get it, but I need to get to the hospital for my kidney testing. Bigger, scarier things are weighing on my mind.

As I walk toward the entrance, I fire off a text to Sawyer and Maren.

Either of you hear about Mickie Davis having a baby just after Hollyn left the island?

The message delivers, but neither of them responds right away. Hollyn's sister's age has been nagging at me. Hollyn didn't seem nervous for me to meet her or like she was trying to keep me from talking to her. But the timing...

Yes, Sawyer replies, *I had to ask someone, but yeah. Apparently she was visibly pregnant at her trial, the one that sent her to jail.*

I wondered too, Maren says, *if your brain went where mine did, Nathaniel. Must have been a shock to see her.*

Since I'd deliberately avoided any news about the Davis family in the years I was at college, in the years after Hollyn left, seeing Kinsley was definitely a surprise, and for a minute I wondered if Kinsley was the reason Hollyn had vanished. But even if Kinsley was mine, it wouldn't have made sense for Hollyn to disappear. Before any baby's birth, I'd have had my part of the Tucker trust. We would have had ample wealth and resources. Hollyn wouldn't have had a reason to hide a baby from me, and even if I hate the way she left, it's impossible to imagine Hollyn hiding a pregnancy from me when she already knew *I'd* be happy about it.

She's not mine then, right? I type out. *That's what we're agreeing?*

Hollyn went after full custody when Kinsley was five. Caitlin says the court documents have been sealed, but her office handled it, so someone had knowledge. Sawyer sends another message right after the first. *Once Hollyn got out of school, maybe?*

That would make sense, Maren agrees.

As far as I know, Hollyn never actually went to college, and the rest is none of my business. As long as Kinsley isn't mine, I can stop obsessing about the past. Our cousin, Caitlin, is a very good lawyer, so she'd be able to access all the right details. There's really no reason to dig more up.

You okay, Nathaniel? Want us to stop by? Sawyer asks.

I'm good. As long as I'm not a surprise baby daddy like Gage, I'm completely fine.

I just had Caitlin double check Bellerive's birth records to be completely sure, and Mickie and Niall are listed as the parents. All seems to be on the up-and-up. No surprises—other than that you didn't realize it happened. Sawyer sends a hug emoji at the end of the message.

My phone buzzes with a reminder from my mother about the hospital appointment. Thirty-one, and my mother takes more notice of what I do now than she did when I was a kid. Of course, these tests could directly impact her life, so I suppose it makes sense. If more than one of us is a match, we'll have to rock-paper-scissors to see who goes under the knife.

A joke, mostly.

As the oldest, if I'm a match, I'll be the one to give our mom my kidney. I haven't discussed it with my siblings, but that's the way things have always been. If there's a sacrifice to be made, I'm the one making it.

I climb into my car in the parking lot and turn toward the hospital. Hollyn Davis needs to get out of my head. With my mother sick and this new TV show to produce, I have bigger things to worry about than whether my teen crush is back on the island. We knew each other for a few months, and I have to finally let the past go. I rub one hand along my face.

For the next week, I just need to avoid any places Hollyn would logically go or visit, and then she'll be off the island again, back to the life she built when she left here. I can return to mine, content never to think of her again.

Chapter Five

Hollyn

Fourteen years ago

The Drunk Raccoon is packed with tourists, since the cruise ships start arriving in droves at the beginning of May. It's the closest bar to where the ships dock—smack-dab in the middle of nowhere. You'd think the island would have built up some tourist things here, but it's just us, a scooter rental place, and a tacky tourist shop for shirts, keychains, and other things you probably have five hundred of already.

We're everyone's first and last stop, and we just reopened for the season two weeks ago in mid-April.

"You alright?" Franny asks as she slides her round tray beside mine at the edge of the bar and then rattles off her drink order to the bartender when he comes over, sliding some of the drinks I need onto my tray. Two more to fill, and then I'm back out in the weeds.

"They'd better tip well," I say. "If one more guy grabs my ass, I can't guarantee he won't get a drink dumped on his head." Though, I've always been more talk than action. Besides, the tips have to supplement my scholarship to art school next year. The art degree wasn't my first choice, but I couldn't turn down the full tuition offer.

"They *are* a grabby lot," Franny agrees. "Worst ones we've had so far this season."

The ship docked right now is due to leave in the morning—only the fifth cruise ship departure I've worked—and this one seems to have been carrying a boatload of frat boys or maybe even a bachelor party. A few have tried to talk to me, but it's so loud I can barely hear them. Every one of them seems to believe they are irresistible, and they're looking to lay their pipe in a foreign girl before they go home.

"Did you see who was here, though?" she asks, glancing over her shoulder into the crowd.

"Everyone?" I suggest with a laugh, not even following her gaze. The place is wall-to-wall people.

"Callahan Tucker." She splays her hand over her chest and leans over a little, like she can't catch her breath.

"Ugh," I say with a grimace. "A Tucker? Please." I roll my eyes. "I avoid anyone with that last name—which is half the island and definitely all the rich people. But any time I *have* run into one, they've been shitty humans."

"He used to come into the bakery I worked at last summer to grab the stuff they sold at the campground, and he's *not* a typical Tucker. His two older brothers fit the mold, but Cal doesn't."

"If you say so," I say. "Anyone can pretend they're a good person in short bursts." My parents are excellent short-term actors. Some of the best. I've learned to never accept anyone at face value or first meeting.

"Order up," the bartender says, practically in my ear after I don't grab the tray immediately when he sets down the last two drinks.

I glare at him and slide the tray onto my palm. As I wade through the crowd, the tray balanced above my head, hands are all over me, as though I'm an object to be fondled on the way past. The soft touches I can pretend are accidental, but the ones who squeeze hard are asking for the tray to be dumped on their head. If Franny wasn't here tonight, I'm not even sure if I'd feel safe.

After I've given out the drinks to the booth at the back, I check on my other tables to see if anyone else needs an order. The night continues on like that—orders, waiting, fondling, delivering, repeat.

When the last call is nearing, there's still a few groups of people huddled around. Most of them are men, which causes a little frisson of worry to snake down my spine. Men and alcohol are rarely a good mix, and if the tips at The Drunk Raccoon weren't legendary, I'd never have vied so hard for this job.

As I circulate, one of the frat boys loops his arm around my waist and draws me in close, his lips close to my ear. "What are you doing after this?"

"I'm going home," I say, keeping my voice light, and I don't try to wiggle free, even though his grip is firm and annoying. Sometimes it's easier to play along.

"Ship doesn't leave until dawn. Come take a tour."

"No, thanks," I say, throwing him a smile. "I've got plans."

"Change them," he says, a sloppy grin on his face that's probably meant to be charming but comes across as creepy.

"Can't. Sorry." I twist away from him to head behind the bar to ring the bell for the last call. As the *clang, clang* echoes through the rooms of the bar, most of the people start to leave or come to order one last drink.

Ship guy and his friends are lingering, and I wonder if he told them I was up for what he proposed. Drunk guys are the worst for understanding when a "no" is firm, as though their brain can't process the word. He starts to swagger toward the bar, and I scoot around it to the group Franny has been serving all night—the ones who look like they came from the campground.

I only hesitate for a beat before I press my hand into the lower back of the one closest to me, a touch too intimate when I don't know him. He's tall and lean but broad shouldered with shaggy dark brown hair under a ball cap. When he turns at my touch, his blue-green eyes are stunning—the kind you can't stop staring at. He meets my gaze, and the air around us is charged in a way I've never had happen before with a stranger. Very slowly and deliberately, he leans down, his lips near my ear, the brim of his cap skimming my shoulder. But unlike the last time, a shiver of pleasure races across my skin. The difference in my reaction is so stark that I can't help sucking in a surprised breath. He smells like fresh air and cedar blanketed by bourbon, and I've never smelt anything so good.

What the hell is happening to me?

"You okay?" he asks, his voice rumbly and deep. "Do you need something?"

"The guys over there don't seem to understand I'm not on the menu," I say.

"Want me to go talk to them?" He leans back, his gaze traveling over my face. He lifts the arm that's holding his drink and flexes his impressive bicep, the T-shirt stretching across his skin, tanned from the sun. "I could take them."

I grin and shake my head. "No! Don't do that. Just... can we pretend we're together?"

"Like I'm your boyfriend?" His expression lights with genuine amusement.

"If you want a label for this role-play..."

"To be in character, I need to understand the assignment. The details matter."

"What might help you?" I ask, finding I'm enjoying the light flirting.

"Lean into me a little more. Yeah, that's right. Tuck in there." He slings his arm around my shoulders, and I wonder briefly whether Elmore, the owner, will be pissed that I've paused my last-call hustle.

"What's your name?" he asks, and he runs his callused palm along my arm and down to my fingers, linking them together.

"Hollyn," I say. "You?"

"Nate," he says, and I could close my eyes and listen to the timbre of his voice forever. There's something about it that just nestles into me, warm and comforting. He peers over my head and then spins me around so my back is pressed to the bar, his body shielding me from whatever is behind him. He's caged me in, but I've never felt safer. "Not sure they're buying us. I might need to break out the biceps."

"No bar fights. I can't get fired." On impulse, I say, "Kiss me."

A slow smile spreads across his face, but he doesn't ask if I'm serious or if I'm sure. Instead, one of his hands leaves the edge of the bar, turns his ball cap around, and his thumb sweeps across my cheekbone. "You're really fucking pretty," he says, and then he slides his hand into my chin-length hair, and he kisses me.

His lips are gentle at first, soft and tentative, as though he didn't ask for permission with words, but he's asking with actions. With a slight slant of my head, I deepen the kiss, and then I can't help myself. I slip my hands around the back of his head, fiddling with the silky strands under the brim at the nape of his neck, drawing him closer, tighter. Even though we've just met, our lips move in sync, as though they've done this dance before. I've never had a kiss feel so wildly passionate and so precisely practiced at the same time. He kisses in a way I'd never be able to describe but feels perfectly balanced, just for me.

When we finally break apart, we're both breathing hard, and Nate's forehead is pressed to mine. "Marry me," he says on an exhale.

I laugh. "What? We just met."

"In this life, sure. But that wasn't a first kiss. First kisses are exciting, but they aren't *that*. That kiss was... that kiss was born out of lifetimes—hundreds or thousands of them."

"You have to be drunk. What are you talking about?" I laugh again, but there's a tingle down my spine, as though some part of me agrees with the nonsense he's spewing.

"I've had a few drinks." He grins, but he doesn't seem drunk, at least not on alcohol. "As your official boyfriend for the night, I can give us any backstory I want."

"So you're going with past lives?"

"It was either that or we're a couple that's been dating for years. Ever since we knew what dating was. We've always been serious about each other—right from the first kiss. Now we're headed off to college, and I've decided it's now or never. And I want all my 'nows' with you. Forever."

He's so earnest when he says it, so persuasive that I can almost picture his rewritten history. "Except we just met," I whisper.

"Did we? Convince me." His tone is teasing, and there's a playful glint in his eyes. "I like my version of history better."

"That's not how the world works, though," I say, but my heart is pounding because there's a part of me that wishes history could be rewritten that easily.

Silence hangs between us for a beat, and I realize the bar has mostly cleared out. The lights are on full strength, and the music is off. "I should go. I'm going to get fired."

Nate backs off, glancing around as though he's coming out of a trance, just like me. Somehow we ended up in our own bubble, but it's burst now.

"Nate," a sandy-blond-haired guy calls from the door. He's just as tall as Nate but a little more muscled where Nate is leaner. "We gotta go."

"Go out with me?" Nate asks, stepping away. "Whenever. Wherever. Name the time and place, and I'll be there."

"Good night, Nate," I say with a laugh.

"I'm serious," he calls out to me as his friend tugs him out the door. "I'll be back."

"Oh my god," Franny says from beside me, watching the two leave together.

"Yeah," I say, unable to hide my wistful tone.

"You know who that is, right?" She peers at me, surprise clear in her gaze.

"Nate. He must work at the campground? Or a backpacker or something? His hands were callused." I stare down at my hand, the one he linked with his at some point. His palm pressed against mine is still fresh in my memory. Another shiver dances along my spine, sending a rush of goosebumps down my arms.

"I doubt he actually *works* at the campground. Not in the way you and I work."

I give her a quizzical look.

"That was Nathaniel Tucker. As in Celia and Jonathan Tucker's oldest kid. He's Callahan's cousin. The two of them are tight—like brothers."

My eyes widen, and I press my fingers to my lips. "Oh my god. No!"

She lets out a cackle as she starts moving around the bar, tidying bottles and glasses. "Only *you* would be offended to have made out with a Tucker."

While she loads her tray with empties and takes it to the bar, I do the same.

"It's not like he's a troll," Franny says. "It's really unfair how beautiful all the Tuckers are. You shouldn't be disgustingly rich and disgustingly handsome."

On top of that, he's a good kisser. That kiss was the best I've ever had, not to be repeated. If there is one thing I know with absolute certainty—the Tucker family is trouble, and I already have enough of that in my life.

Chapter Six

Hollyn

The funeral is well attended, and from behind one-way glass, I survey the crowd with my sister by my side. As a kid, everywhere I went on the island, it felt like someone knew my aunt. She worked for countless wealthy families as an employee in some capacity or worked beside so many of the people in our neighborhood that I shouldn't be surprised. Unless she was incredibly sick, she never missed a shift, never let anyone down.

I loved her with my whole freaking heart.

Giving her eulogy is going to be like ripping my heart out of my chest and showing it to everyone in the room. No matter how many drafts I've gone through over the last couple of days, I can't seem to get the sentiment exactly right. Nothing I can say will ever effectively convey how deep my bond ran with my aunt, but I owe it to her to try, to tell all these people how wonderful she was. What I've got will have to do.

Maybe if I was sleeping better, writing it would have been easier. Distorted memories—some distant, some not that long ago—have been eating chunks of my REM sleep every night since I got the call. I thought staying at a hotel, devoid of anything personal, might have been easier. No such luck. Between seeing Nate and my aunt dying, I'm a mess, barely holding my emotions in check.

At the door to the observation room, there's a kerfuffle, and I half turn, wondering who's trying to burst into the room. When it finally swings open, I realize I shouldn't have been surprised to see my mother and father, frazzled, their appearance grizzled by poor care. I'm sure they've been to my aunt's apartment, but we're not staying there.

Kinsley presses closer to my side. I doubt she remembers them, and they look like hardened criminals. Which they *are*. Prone to drinking or taking drugs when the mood suits. Volatile.

"You're not welcome here," I say as Otis leaves, probably to get security. I already told him that my parents might try to crash the funeral.

"She was *my* sister," my mother says, pointing at her chest, as though that makes all the terrible things she's done forgettable in this moment. I don't even know what their sibling relationship has meant to my mother. From the outside, it looked like a means to emotionally manipulate Aunt Verna.

My mother can't guilt me into anything anymore. I'm numb to her efforts, but I still possess a healthy amount of fear. Mickie has a mean streak that's almost unmatched.

"Aunt Verna wouldn't have wanted you here," I say.

"Yes, she would have. You poisoned her against me. Just like you've probably poisoned my poor, sweet baby girl." She tries to touch Kinsley, and my sister shrinks into me.

"All right." A tall, dark-haired police officer enters the room, his voice booming. He's got thick arms and thighs, and he's pretty freaking intimidating, and *I* haven't done anything wrong. He looks familiar, and I try to place where I might have seen him before. Maybe we went to school together. "Mickie, Niall, you gotta get out of here," he says, slinging his thumb over his shoulder. "Otis doesn't want you here."

"Stephen," Mickie says, turning toward him, her bottle-blond hair swinging around her shoulders. "Verna would *want* us here. She loved me."

"Officer Foster, Mick. That's how you address me. We've talked about this," Stephen says, leading her by the arm out of the room. His hand makes her arm look like a twig. "We're not buddies, despite how many times I've detained you for drunk and disorderly conduct and listened to you rant behind bars."

My father drops into one of the seats in the room, his graying reddish-brown hair falling into his eyes. Officer Foster turns back to him after pushing my mother somewhat gently out the door.

"We're not fucking doing this, Niall," he growls, his tone pissed off. "Don't make today harder on your daughters. For once in your life, do the right thing. You've been told to leave, now leave."

My father glares at me and then at Kinsley, but he pushes off the arms of the chair and ambles out of the room behind the police officer. I don't know what kind of magic Officer Foster possesses, but that was impressive. Every time I've had a confrontation with my parents without my Aunt Verna present, it turned violent quickly. Maybe they've mellowed in their old age, or maybe the officer's tree-trunk arms intimidate more than just me.

No sooner are they gone than Otis comes hustling back into the room, a thin sheen of sweat on his forehead. "Thankfully Officer Foster was in the area, and he's very familiar with Mickie Davis and Niall Thompson."

The last names are a reminder that my parents never married and that, for a reason I either never asked or can't remember, we are the Davis girls, not the Thompson ones.

"I bet Officer Foster is *very* familiar with my parents," I mutter, and there's something about Stephen that's nipping at the back of my brain. Was he at the hearing for Kinsley a few years ago? "You'll be regretting that first-time-client discount you gave us this morning."

"I would have regretted the alternative more," Otis says with a tight smile.

His discount is the only reason I can afford to stay at the hotel for a few more days while Kinsley and I clean out Aunt Verna's apartment. Otherwise, I would have been forced to sink into those memories, that old life, for longer than the few hours a day we'll spend sorting through the things Aunt Verna held dear. The more distance I can keep between the person I've become and who I was, the better.

Otis peers through the one-way glass. "We believe everyone is settled. We'll have the music you selected play, and we'll escort you and Kinsley to your seats at the front. We have someone reading a poem based on the theme you selected, and a few other people from the community came forward asking to say a few words. You'll be the last to speak."

"Okay," I say as he presses a program into my hand and leads us to the side door, which will take us out into the service room.

Kinsley squeezes my hand, and I squeeze hers back.

As the music is drawing to a close, Otis opens the door and leads us through. We pass by the crowd, and I can't help searching the sea of faces for any that are familiar from my childhood. I'm not surprised by the ones I find. Just as I'm about to sit down, the back door opens, and my heart freezes.

Nate stands for a second, framed in the doorway, and then he slips into a seat at the end of the closest aisle. I press a hand to my chest, and Kinsley's worry radiates off her.

Why would he come? After the awful way I left, after our stilted conversation the other day, I can't understand why he'd come.

"You okay?" Kinsley whispers to me as we sit down, our backs to the crowd.

"Yeah," I whisper back. "Just so many familiar faces from my childhood."

"Can we talk to some of them later?" she asks.

"Oh," I say. "I'm sure some of them will come to the reception, but there's no need to get too comfortable here."

Kinsley sighs, and I try to ignore the obvious disappointment in the sound. She doesn't understand how severe the class differences are on the island, and I'd prefer she never realizes it the way I had to.

The service starts, and it passes in a blur of me mostly trying to keep myself from crying too long or too loud.

When it's my turn to speak, Kinsley squeezes my hand before releasing me, and the papers I took out of my purse shake. I smooth them out on the lectern, and I adjust the microphone, stalling while I get myself together.

Once I'm ready, I look toward the back of the room, an old public speaking trick. No eye contact but looking forward. Except at the back of the room is Nate, and I expect to tense up again at the sight of him. We aren't on good terms. We don't know each other anymore.

Instead, some long-buried instinct takes over, and my body remembers that he used to be a safe landing place, that I once felt safer with him than I ever had with anyone. The memory of those months settles over me like a weighed blanket, a shield against what I have to do next.

And when I start to speak, I don't look at anyone but him. The page and then him, over and over until I finish. Somehow, I don't cry, and I don't stumble. The speech is smooth and practiced, as though I didn't bawl my eyes out every other time I tried to say it to the end.

There's no clapping when I finish, just a long impossible silence. As I leave the lectern, Nate rises to his feet and slips out the door. As soon as it clicks shut, it's like whatever was propping me up, whatever got me through the speech, leaves with him, and I practically fall into my seat.

Otis directs everyone to the reception area in another part of the funeral home, but I stay seated with Kinsley by my side.

"Are we going?" she asks, glancing behind us.

"Is everyone gone yet?" I ask. "I just need a minute before we go in there." Because once we leave this room, I have to pretend to be okay, even if that's the last thing I feel.

"Yeah," Kinsely says. "Everyone is gone now."

I'd tell her to go ahead without me, but that wouldn't be fair. Some of those people, I remember well, and others are hazy memories, but either way, Kinsley will be a curiosity to most of them. We haven't been back to the island since I took Kinsley to New York with me.

I smooth down my hair that I straightened this morning, and I rise to my feet. Once I'm through today, there's only a few more hard things left to do. For Kinsley, I can hold my emotions together.

With more confidence than I feel, I follow one of the funeral home workers to the reception. There, finger foods and drinks are being served by wait staff that are milling around. I can't help thinking that my aunt could have easily been one of the servers.

I grab a glass of water off the tray, and I down it in three gulps, pretending it's something much stronger. Kinsley takes one beside me and sips at it, gazing around the crowd.

It doesn't take long before people start approaching, telling us stories of how they knew my aunt or when they knew me as a child. Some of the stories are nice, heartwarming, and others are strange, as though the person hadn't been sure of what to say and then proceeded to insert their foot into their mouth.

A few times after someone leaves us, Kinsley leans over and says, "What the fuck?"

Normally I'd laugh with her, not caring about her phrasing, but the day has been overwhelming, and so I chastise her for swearing instead. It's not the time or the place, and I'd hate for anyone to overhear, to think we're just like our parents.

"Hollyn?" A tall, lithe woman, maybe a bit younger than me, approaches with her hand outstretched. Her brown hair is pulled back, bouncy and shiny under the light. "I'm Posey Jensen. Your aunt was the sweetest, kindest woman. I was so unbelievably sorry to hear she'd passed away. I live in an apartment down the street from the deli she worked at for years. I loved her. Really, really loved her."

There's something so genuine in her demeanor that I can't help feeling a little comforted by her words. "She was one of the best," I agree. "This is my younger sister, Kinsley."

They shake hands, and Posey doesn't miss a beat. "She talked about you and your sister a lot. She was so proud of you, Hollyn, for being the first in the family to get a college degree. Interior design, right?"

"Yep," I say feeling a rush of warmth for Posey and her keen memory. Aunt Verna had somehow cobbled together enough money to come to my graduation. I still remember seeing her beaming in the crowd.

"I'm also in interior design, so I always thought it was funny we had that in common." She gives me a sunny grin. "She said you'd gotten a scholarship to attend school, which is amazing. You must be a hard worker."

"She is," Kinsley grumbles beside me.

But I shift on my feet, antsy at the mention of the scholarship. It's true and untrue, and the only person other than me who would ever understand the intricacies of my college journey is gone.

"She works at a fancy firm in New York City," Kinsley says. "Maybe you've heard of it," Kinsley continues in the tone of voice I use when I'm about to name-drop. "Reyes and Cruz?"

Posey straightens, and she eyes me with curiosity, but she doesn't ask if it's true. "That's impressive," she says. "Really amazing. Such an opportunity."

On someone else, those comments might seem disingenuous, but it's the opposite with Posey. She comes across as the type of person incapable of bullshit, as though it would tarnish her shine. She talks like someone raised with wealth on the island, but not like everyone else is beneath her. Definitely an art not many rich people on this island possess.

When I first arrived in New York, I'd loved how big the city felt, so different from anything in Bellerive. Bellerive's population is the same as a midsized city. New York felt like a whole new world.

But lately my life has become dominated by people who care more about how things appear than how they actually are. Maybe that's the price of climbing the ladder in the company. Many of the people I meet are screwed up in some way by extreme wealth. Not that far, after all, from the wealthy in Bellerive. Just took me longer to see it.

Bellerive's rich-poor divide should have prepared me for those clients, but other than the brief time I spent with Nate's family and friends, my interactions with rich people before taking the job at Reyes and Cruz had been limited. Even in college, I seemed to naturally gravitate toward others on scholarship or financial assistance.

"Look," Posey says, digging into her purse. "I know now isn't the time, but I wanted to chat with you about something. Maybe we could grab lunch? When do you head back to New York?" She passes me her card.

I took all the bereavement leave I could—which was only a few days—and I paired it with all my banked vacation. In theory, I could be on the island for weeks, but I didn't intend to stay that long. My clientele in NY would collapse or be consumed by another designer if I stayed too long. Not enough people know who I am yet to make up those lost commissions with ease.

"Next week," I say. "We're leaving next week."

Kinsley slumps beside me, as though she'd been hoping for another answer.

"Tomorrow?" Posey suggests. "I can come to you, wherever you are." She smiles again, as though she realizes it has magical properties.

"We're at the Eastgate Smith-Wesley hotel. What about tonight?" I turn the card she gave me over in my hands, happy for the momentary distraction, the focus on what comes next.

"Seven? I can meet you in the lobby, and we can find somewhere to go. You're welcome to come, Kinsley," Posey says. "I'm sure it's been a hell of a few days. Excellent food and strong coffee are good temporary Band-Aids."

"Hollyn doesn't cook much, so anything other than mushy mac and cheese sounds great to me." Kinsley brightens for the first time all day.

"Mushy," I say with a scoff. "You try making it."

"I do." Kinsley's tone has a touch of sharpness. "You're just not there to see it."

Posey lets out a little laugh. "I have a sister." She flicks her finger back and forth between us. "So I get this."

I wish I did. Lately it feels like I can't do anything right, and I'm not sure if it's teenage angst from Kinsley or if I'm really a terrible replacement parent.

Someone hovers at Posey's shoulder, clearly waiting their turn, and I try to place them before another awkward conversation starts. "I'll see you tonight," I say as Posey steps back and the other person steps forward.

"I like her," Kinsley whispers before we fall into more introductions and reminiscing about the past.

Chapter Seven

HOLLYN

I've met enough rich clients to recognize when I'm being wined and dined, when someone is trying to win me over for some reason, which is the impression Posey is giving me without doing any of the rich-people moves I'd typically expect.

The mom-and-pop diner she's taken us to is in the middle of Tucker's Town—a tourist-heavy area and likely extraordinarily expensive for rent. But the prices in the place aren't outrageous, and the staff doesn't look stressed or run-down despite how busy it is in here, even at seven at night on a weekday. It's like she somehow found a little pocket of happiness in the almost nonexistent middle class.

If my aunt and I had ever been able to afford to eat out, this would have been the type of place we'd have gone to.

Kinsley stares around in wonder, and when she looks at me, there's a hint of a smile on her lips. "It feels like home in here. Isn't that weird?"

"Part of the charm," Posey says with a wink. "It's like magic. Everyone who walks into the place never wants to leave. It helps that the coffee is always hot and the food is always exceptional. I love eating." She opens the menu.

I scan her figure, and I can't help questioning her claim. She looks like a dancer, not someone who gorges on gourmet food. Me, on the other hand? My thin days are long gone, and for the most part, I'm not even upset about it. I've escaped the ache of starvation, the need to hide my hunger so my aunt didn't spend more money on groceries when we had other bills to pay. And if I've gone a bit too far in the other direction, so what? I'm not going to begrudge my body storing some fat in case there's another famine. My body and my mind both understand how unpredictable life can be.

The waitress takes our orders, and with the menus gone, Posey plants her elbows on the table and grins. "I have a good feeling about you."

"Thank you?" I can't help a confused answering smile.

"I'll cut to the chase about why I wanted to meet with you. King Alexander and the Advisory Council of Bellerive have decided they want to invest in Bellerive television productions. As you probably know, most of what's on TV now is foreign made. This shift, for me, is a dream come true." One of her hands presses against her chest while the other tucks stray strands of hair behind her ears. "One of those productions is being called *Redesigning Home*. The premise is that two interior designers compete to transform a home for a couple or family who is down on their luck—essentially a lower-income property. Each host uses the space and budget in a different way. The family picks the winning design, and then the two hosts work together to create the fairytale for that family."

"Okay," I say, my brain already clicking over all the various areas and families in Bellerive who would have benefitted from this concept when I was younger. "I'm not sure I understand why you'd want to meet with me about that? I don't live here."

"The producers really want someone who grew up here. Someone who is familiar with all aspects of Bellerive," Posey says.

"They want someone who grew up poor," I say, the pieces clicking at the same time the words are coming out of my mouth.

"Disadvantaged, yes," Posey says. "The great part about the job—well, there are lots of great parts, I think—but the best part is a real work-life balance."

"Sounds like a great opportunity for you," I say as the waitress drops off our drinks. Kinsley elbows me, but I ignore her. I know how these shows work, and it's not something I want any part of, even if that is what Posey is trying to offer.

"I'd like it to be a great opportunity for *you*, actually." Posey picks up her latte and takes a long sip.

"I have a job."

"I know Reyes and Cruz. It's impressive that you've managed to make a career there while raising your sister, but I can't even imagine the sacrifices you've had to make. They're all commission based, right? This show is good money. Really good money, even by Bellerive standards."

"But then what?" I ask, even as I can feel Kinsley's eyes boring a hole into the side of my head. "In a few months when the show is done filming, I no longer have any clients in New York, and a hard job becomes an impossible one again."

"You'd have enough clout on the island that you could easily start up here, if you wanted."

"I don't want to live on the island." It's a knee-jerk reaction, and I take a minute to examine it before deciding it *is* true. When I left, I never intended to come back.

The food arrives, and we eat in silence for a moment before Kinsley says, "Hollyn, would just get the job? You're offering her the job?"

"It's not really *mine* to offer," Posey says. "We'd have to do a chemistry test in front of producers. Make sure the two of us are compatible on screen. But I wasn't lying. I have a good feeling about this partnership. Everyone else they've tried to put me with has been a bust."

"I think you should try," Kinsley says, pushing her food around her plate with her fork. "I want you to try."

"Even if I wanted the job," I say, "I don't like how these shows operate. The people, in this case, poor people, have to pay for everything—every design choice costs them money."

"Remember when I said there were lots of great parts to this job?" Posey says, a twinkle in her eye. "The show is one hundred percent funded. From our salaries to design choices to on-set catering—it's all taken care of. Show participants pay nothing."

"How?" I ask.

"Government grants and rich partners is the short answer," Posey says. "I've also been told that Interflix is interested in possibly picking the show up for their streaming service, which would obviously be huge for Bellerive, and for us, personally." Posey sets down her fork and takes a sip of her latte before giving me a sly smile. "Reyes and Cruz would be lucky to have you back, if you wanted to return. Rich people want famous people. They love the power of having a famous person working for them."

She's not wrong. A few of my colleagues are famous in certain design circles, and they never lack for wealthy clients. But the opportunity she's dropping in my lap still feels like a huge risk. Right now, my life with Kinsley works in New York. I'd never say that it works *well*, but we're not drowning in debt, unable to eat. Kinsley hasn't been forced to get a job just to help us keep our heads above water. I've committed myself to working unsustainable hours so she doesn't have the upbringing I did.

If the producers like me, if the show is picked up, if it somehow catches on in America... if, if, if... and if not, then I could be giving up the stable life we've built to chase something I don't even want.

But I can tell from the energy vibrating off Kinsley beside me that she *wants* this chance. I don't know if it's the island calling to her or the carrot of a work-life balance that doesn't exist for me right now, but she's probably literally biting her tongue to keep from begging me to take a chance. She doesn't understand what's on the other side of risks that don't pay off or pay off in ways you never anticipated and definitely didn't want.

"How long?" I ask, swirling the last bite of my food around on my plate. "How long is filming?"

"Three to six months. We're guaranteed six shows, but they'll stretch it to twelve if the first few episodes test well with audiences."

For the first time, I turn my attention to Kinsley. "You'll be away from your friends. For *months*. You'll have to attend high school here. You won't know anyone."

"I don't care," Kinsley says in a rush.

"We'll have to move apartments. I can't afford to pay rent here and there."

"You could probably negotiate that into a contract," Posey says. "They haven't been able to find anyone. You've got the upper hand, if they like you."

"Right," I say, trying to digest that information. Power, any kind of power, isn't something I'm used to holding. Normally, I'm grateful for whatever comes my way, not demanding more. "I'll keep that in mind."

Hope shines out of Kinsley's eyes, and I feel a twinge of guilt that leaving everything behind is preferable to returning to our life in New York.

"All you ever tell me is that 'we can't, we can't, we can't.' But maybe we *can* here. Even if it's just for a little while," Kinsley says, a hint of pleading in her voice.

Her argument hits me right in the heart. While I haven't given her the upbringing I had—financial instability, absentee parents in and out of jail—I'm suddenly uncertain about whether I've given her something better. *We can't* is a phrase I say far too often, and most of the time, what I actually mean is that *she* can't. That I don't have the time to spend with her, to get her to the activities she'd like to do, the events she wants to attend.

As a kid, what I wanted more than anything was money. Money seemed like the key to happiness. Maybe that was a false desire because even though I have some money now, it never feels like enough. I don't even know what *enough* is. But in my pursuit of it, it's becoming crystal clear that the one thing Kinsley would do anything for is my time.

"Okay," I say to Posey. "I'll audition or whatever it's called. When?"

"No time like the present," Posey says. She grabs her phone off the table, and her fingers fly across the screen. "I've got two out of three producers who can meet in thirty minutes."

"Thirty minutes?" I pick up my phone and I text one of my aunt's best friends, Shannon. At the funeral, she offered to help out in any way she could, and she lives only a few blocks from my aunt's apartment building. "I'll have to drop Kinsley off first."

"Drop me off?" Kinsley says, a touch of panic in her voice.

"At Shannon's," I say as the answering text comes through agreeing to keep Kinsley for a few hours. "Aunt Verna's best friend. You met her at the funeral home. I've known her since I was a little kid. She's good. I promise."

"I want to stay with you," Kinsley says.

"I need the space to concentrate," I say, glancing at Posey, who is now talking quietly on the phone across from us. The reality is that I'm worried I'll be pressured into saying yes on the spot if they offer the job and Kinsley is there. I need to be sure that this job, this opportunity in Bellerive, is the best one for her but also for us.

There are things on this island, people, I'd rather not face. Staying here might solve one problem, but it could create a whole host of others.

"You'll come get me right after?" Kinsley says.

"Right after," I say.

"We're all set," Posey says. "I can't get the one producer to answer, but we'll record the chemistry test for later viewing. Two out of three will work." Posey slides out of the booth. "How'd you get here?"

"Public transit," I say.

"I'll drive," Posey says. "Come with me. I can take you wherever you want to go."

I just hope I end up wanting to go where both Kinsley and Posey so badly want me to end up. When faced with a sure thing or a risk, I've rarely been one to take the leap into the unknown.

Chapter Eight

NATHANIEL

The cold from the ice is penetrating the thick glass in my hand, the chill seeping into my skin. Instead of taking that as a sign that my brain isn't functioning on high, I set down my glass on the kitchen island and mix myself another gold rush. Drunk seems like the best idea, really. Why not? No one except me is going to care if I'm hungover tomorrow.

Besides, cold hands are better than the shaky ones that gripped the steering wheel earlier, the funeral home in the rearview mirror. I had to get out of there. Going in the first place made me the stupidest person on the island, possibly the planet.

But last night, I dreamed of the funeral, Hollyn collapsed at the front, and it was so vivid that I couldn't shake the feeling that something was going to go wrong. In my dream, I picked her up. She curled into me and sobbed against my chest, clutching on to me like I was the only tree strong enough to withstand her own personal hurricane. When I woke up, my arms still felt heavy with the weight of her, of her grief, as though it was possible for my subconscious to still remember, even after all these years, the shape of her, the feel of her pressed against me.

After my dream, I had to see her. No matter what happened all those years ago, I could never know she was in that much pain and do nothing. Before I arrived and saw her, standing tall at the front of the room, my heart was a mangled mess, sure that my dream was some sort of premonition, sure that Hollyn needed *me*.

Then at the funeral, it felt like she delivered the whole fucking eulogy just to me, and I hadn't been able to look away. Enthralled. Trapped, once again, in Hollyn Davis's spell. Or maybe I never really got out of the original spell, which is what Sawyer and Maren keep telling me.

Magic is really the only way to explain her effect on me. The connection to her has never made sense, but I didn't care about sense in high school. Had no need for it. I loved her, and she loved me, and the rest of the world could go fuck themselves if they thought they had any part in that equation.

The first time we met, her hair reminded me of the rising sun—like I was waking up for the first time—a splash of deep red across the sky. Breathtakingly beautiful.

The wake-up call wasn't a blessing. It was a warning, or it should have been, of what was to come.

Danger, Nathaniel. She'll rip your fucking heart out without a second thought.

No matter what, I'm not giving her a second shot. Her hazel doe eyes and the vulnerability I still see in her won't crack my resolve.

Thank god she'll be leaving the island soon so all this stirred up angst over the past can get covered over again. No matter what my subconscious or unconscious or whatever this nagging sensation is, wants to believe, Hollyn doesn't need me, and I sure as hell don't need her.

I take another long gulp of my drink as my phone lights up on the island. Posey's name and picture are on the display. For a beat, I consider answering it. Two drinks ago, I would have. Now? I'd probably make no sense and say something I'd regret. It's not her fault she's calling while I'm wallowing in emotions I shouldn't even feel anymore. She'll be calling about the TV show, and I don't feel like having another conversation about how we could press to make the concept work with just her as host. My voicemail picks up the call, and I wait until a beep signals that someone left a message.

I pour myself another drink and swirl the contents of my glass around, staring into the melting ice, contemplating whether I should have gone to work out instead of getting drunk. That would have been the healthier, more productive choice. It's been a while since I let myself sink this deep into my feelings.

Not for the first time, I pick up my phone to search whether it's possible for hypnosis to erase a person from your mind, your memories. I scan the results. Still a no on that, apparently.

The one time I went to see a hypnotist, they said we'd have to tackle each memory individually to change my thought patterns, and nothing would be erased. Despite how short our relationship was, I have so many fucking memories of Hollyn. Going after each recollection to figure out which one has caused this lingering ache in my chest seemed harder, more painful than drinking or working out each time a memory surfaced. One way or another, I could dull the pain, even if I couldn't vanquish it.

Luckily, as with anything, the further I've gotten from the night she left, the less the memories float to the surface. Or that was true until I found Verna on the floor of her apartment, and whatever dam I'd built in my mind, around my heart, cracked. Now those memories aren't just floating passively in the depths of my subconscious. They're surfacing, creating waves, crashing against my resolve to keep the past in the past.

My phone pings on the island, and I finish another drink before setting down the glass and trying to read the message. The font is blurry, and I squint, trying to decide if I'm that drunk or I suddenly need glasses.

Probably drunk.

I open the message, and it's a video from one of the producers, Felipe. Another message arrives before I can start the video, declaring that they've found their second host. With a frown, I click the video to have it play at maximum size on my phone screen. Posey starts on camera first, and it's the same script I've seen what feels like a thousand times. Bold banter that no one but Posey seems able to carry with any believability once the camera starts rolling.

But when the second figure comes into frame from the right, my stomach shoots to my feet, and I have to brace both hands on the island.

No fucking way.

With clumsy fingers, I stop the video before it even gets to the part that must have swayed the others. Then I try to type a reply, but I keep garbling the letters, and the autocorrect is on makes-no-sense mode. A second squint reveals that I cannot send anything I typed. After deleting all of it, I send a voice memo asking where they're at and telling them I have thoughts.

Then I send a second voice memo to Bill, one of the drivers the Tucker family employs, to see if he can pick me up. He's quicker to reply than Felipe is, and I tell him I'll be waiting in front of the apartment.

Felipe replies while I'm waiting for Bill. At least they're all still together at the studio, trying to hash out some contract points, and nothing has been promised that we can't rescind.

The logical thing would be to wait until tomorrow to sort this mess out, but I'm at least three drinks beyond logic penetrating my brain in any actionable way. Instead, I'm running on pure emotion, and while I can recognize that going to the studio might be a bad idea, I'm not sober enough to stop myself.

At the studio, I take the elevator to the boardroom they've all convened to, and I try to get my raging emotions under control. There is nothing I want more than to have Hollyn Davis off this island, and if we give her this hosting job, not only will she *not* be off the island, but she'll be in my face every single week for months. If my worst enemy devised a method of torture, they could not have come up with something more gut-wrenching. I would face a mountain of physical pain over revisiting the emotional turmoil Hollyn put me through. Cut off my limbs, but leave my damned heart alone.

The double doors to the boardroom are closed, but I know on the other side is a spacious room with a killer view of the downtown core of Tucker's Town, even if it'll be too dark to see anything but bright lights.

Before I can overthink it, I open the door and step inside. Everyone looks up from the papers they've been discussing, and Posey comes around the table, a grin on her face.

"Can you believe it? What a stroke of luck, right?" she says.

But I can't focus on her, because Hollyn has also risen from her chair, and our gazes are locked. I hate the simmer of emotion threatening to bubble up inside me, scald me again. Whatever hold she had on me is still there, and I resent it.

"You're the other producer?" Her words are tinged with the panic I felt when I saw her on my screen less than an hour ago.

"Yes," I bite out, unable to say anything else when faced with those doe eyes that make my stomach twist with longing.

"I can't take this job," she says, and her wide eyes turn to Posey. "Yeah, this isn't... this won't work."

"No," I agree. "It won't."

"Whatever is going on here," Felipe says, still seated, wiggling his pen at me and then Hollyn, "unless it involves something illegal, the two of you need to get over yourselves. She's got the experience and feel we need on camera beside Posey, and you," he says, trying to catch my gaze, "have the money. Don't tank this project because the two of you have history."

I *wish* this thing between us felt like history. It would be so nice to look at her and feel nothing but nostalgia.

"If she stays," I say, "I go." Ultimatums have never been what I reach for first, but in this case, it's self-preservation.

"I'm not staying," Hollyn says, avoiding my gaze as she gathers her things. "If I'd known, I wouldn't have come."

"Wait," Posey says, stretching her arms wide in a stopping motion. "I don't know what's going on here, but we can figure out a way to make this work. We can. Creative thinking is all we need."

"I have a job. I have a life. It's not here," Hollyn says, slinging her purse over her shoulder. "I'm sorry I wasted your time."

She steps around the table and gives me a curt nod on her way past, as though our act of agreeing that we couldn't exist in the same space has put us on the same team somehow. What a joke. She's almost out the door of the boardroom when the scent of her apple shampoo arrives, having drifted behind her. Against my will, I close my eyes, and I remember what it was like to have her naked, pressed against my side, my nose buried in her hair. My chest is unbearably tight.

"Are you drunk? This isn't like you," Posey hisses from beside me. "What's going on with you?" She's searching my face, and I honestly have no idea what she'll find.

"I think I'm quitting this project," I say.

"Nathaniel." She breathes out my name. "Without you, it doesn't move ahead. The government grant isn't enough to cover all the costs. We'd have to charge the people for their own makeovers."

"Maybe this is a sign that the show shouldn't run at all when the only person you can find as your cohost is the last person on the planet I'd be okay with."

"You don't hold grudges, and you don't dislike anyone except your cousin Hugh, so I don't…" Then she tilts her head, and understanding lights her eyes. "Oh my god. It's the opposite of that, isn't it?"

"I don't know what it is," I say, suddenly weary. "And I've got no desire to find out."

"If you find someone else," I say, loudly enough for the other producers to hear, "I'll come back on board. If you really want her, you need to find another money guy. I'm not it." At their protests, I merely throw up my hands, rotate on my heel, and leave the boardroom.

As I exit the elevator, I catch a glimpse of red hair ducking into a cab, and I hate how my feet urge me forward, as though they have a mind of their own.

Bill is waiting at the curb, and I climb into the back. We sit for a moment, with him waiting for me to give him some direction. Going home seems even more depressing than being in the back of the car.

"Just drive around for a bit," I say.

"That, I can do," Bill says, shifting the car into drive and pulling away from the curb.

As I look out the window, the city zipping past, an idea—not a good one—forms. My alcohol-addled brain latches on to it, and before I can second-guess myself, Bill is headed in a new direction, one that's sure to lead me straight to hell.

Chapter Nine

HOLLYN

Fourteen years ago

It takes him a week to keep the promise he shouted from the doorway of the bar before he left. In the days in between, I convinced myself that he wouldn't show up or that, if he did, I wouldn't even notice. But the minute he enters The Drunk Raccoon, it's like something inside of me *knows*, as though the energy in the room shifts with his presence.

Unlike last weekend, there's no departing cruise ship—that's tomorrow—so the bar has a steady stream of people without being too crowded. He swaggers to a table, loose-hipped and confident in a way only criminals and rich people are, and I wonder how I missed all the signs of privilege the other night.

The camp attendant's outfit and his callused hands threw me off. Even today, his worn jeans and soft flannel shirt suggest the rugged outdoors more than fancy dinners and Rolex watches.

The confidence, though—there's no disguising that.

Lots of guys are cocky for no reason, and maybe I just assumed his kissing skills were his source of confidence. The Tucker family have lots of reasons for their inflated egos, and most of those are not good.

He's chosen one of my tables, and I wait as long as I can before Elmore's glare from behind the bar tells me that I can't keep ignoring a paying customer.

"Hollyn Davis," he drawls with a grin when I approach his table. I hate that his lips are full and kissable, that the memory of them pressed against mine is still so fresh. "I told you I'd be back."

"Nathaniel Tucker," I say with a falsely sweet smile. "What can I get for you?"

"Nate. My friends call me Nate."

"We're not friends, so Nathaniel it is."

"I've been thinking about that this week, actually." He gives me a pensive look, brow furrowed. "Since you're my future wife, do I risk being temporarily friendzoned despite that amazing kiss last week? Friendship is a viable route. I think I'd be able to swerve out of that lane eventually. Or do I go after what I really want, even if I'm worried you might think I'm too much too soon?"

"Guys never get the 'too much' or 'too soon' label," I say, my pen poised over my notepad. "That privilege is exclusively given to women."

"My sisters would disagree with that."

"That's because they have a different kind of privilege that allows them to do that. Maybe even to be taken seriously when they feel something is wrong or unjust. I wouldn't know. Drink?"

His gaze travels over my face for a beat, and awareness prickles across my skin. His handsomeness is annoying in its genuineness—bright eyes, messy hair, casual clothes. He's not glossy or polished, and I almost wish that he was. Polished would be easy to bat away, to ignore. Polished would never understand the complications in my life, my past. Polished would never even get a glimpse at my heart.

There's an energy between us that I've never felt before, and I cannot decide if I should allow myself to be exhilarated or if I should force myself to run. Either way, when our eyes lock, I know I can't deny its existence.

"I'll have a gold rush," he says, his gaze still locked with mine.

"You aren't eighteen," I murmur. "I can't serve minors."

"My ID says otherwise." He tries and fails to smother a charming grin. "Did you want to see it?"

"Everyone knows who you are," I say. "There's no way a fake ID works on this island."

"I didn't say it was fake," he says, reaching into his back pocket and removing his wallet before setting it on the table, unopened. "That must mean you knew who I was the other night when you pressed your hand to my back."

Heat rises into my cheeks, swift and ferocious. I'm not sure which admission would be more damning—the truth or a lie?

"I didn't," I admit.

He slips his ID out of his wallet and sets it on the table, and when I look down at it, I see I *was* right. His birthday is in the fall, and it's only late spring right now. "You're not eighteen."

"I'd still get served if I took it to Elmore," he says.

"Because you're a Tucker," I say, and I can't keep the bitterness out of my voice.

"I'm just saying you won't get in trouble." He tries to catch my eyes. "You'll be a Tucker one day too."

"No, I won't." I tap my pen on the edge of my notepad, but I don't write down the gold rush he requested. The other night, I knew he was drinking, and his alcohol consumption didn't bother me. For the first time in my life, the smell of alcohol on a guy's breath hadn't been completely repulsive, but I don't like that he's here by himself ordering a drink.

"When did you turn eighteen?" he asks, his voice quiet, but his eyes on me are intense, searching.

"A few months ago."

"When, exactly?"

"Why?"

"It's my favorite day of the year. I can't have someone ask me for my favorite day and then not know the date."

I shake my head and stifle my smile. "February first."

"Missed it by a mile this year. I won't make that mistake again. Can I buy you a birthday drink now?"

"I don't drink."

"Me either," he says, slipping his ID back into his wallet. "Just quit today. I'll have a Coke. Probably shouldn't be drinking when I'll be driving you around the island after your shift anyway."

I let out a laugh. "Driving me where?"

"Wherever you want to go, as long as you're in the passenger seat beside me."

Our gazes meet again, and he holds mine, his sincerity clear, so I try to make mine clear too. "Look, if you're hoping to hook up with some starry-eyed poor girl for fun, you've come to the wrong bar. Or at least the wrong waitress. I don't do random hookups with bored, rich guys."

His lips tip up in an almost smile, and he sits back in his chair, arms crossed. "If I was a bored rich guy, I *might* be offended." He sets his phone face down on the table. "Your claim isn't very convincing anyway." There's a teasing glint in his blue-green eyes. "I mean, you were the one who asked me to be your boyfriend the other night. Asked me to kiss you. And you certainly looked a little starry-eyed *after* our kiss, so..." He raises his eyebrows and gives a little shrug like I'm the problem, not him.

There's no easy comeback or brutal honesty I can drop on him, because he's right. All of it happened exactly as he says, and there's a part of me that really wants to give into whatever he's proposing. Heat rushes to my cheeks again, and I'm sure I'm bright red with embarrassment.

"I didn't come here looking for a poor girl or a random hookup. I came here looking for you. Just you. Rich or poor. Hookup or friendzoned; I don't care. Whatever I felt the other night, whatever *this* is right now—I want more of it. As much as I can get for as long as you'll let me have it."

A web of cracks streaks across my hard heart at his earnest delivery. His private school education has certainly given him the gift of persuasion. "You're a Tucker," I say, the words falling out of my mouth before I can stop myself. "I'm a Davis. A Thompson. Do you understand what that means? What I'm coming from?"

"You're Hollyn," he says. "And I'm Nate. And I don't care who's a Tucker or a Davis or a Thompson. None of that matters to me."

But it'll matter to other people, and he won't be the one facing their wrath, looking over his shoulder. Agreeing to go anywhere with him is a field of potential landmines, given my family.

"I don't know," I hedge.

"Give me one night. Tonight. If I can't convince you that this is worth whatever comes our way, then I'll figure out how to let it go. I promise." He extends his pinky finger toward me, and he holds eye contact as I hook my finger around his.

"One night," I say.

The stars dot the sky, an incalculable number, impossibly bright. Nate eases one hand under his head while his other points out another constellation. Then he takes my finger and traces the stars across the sky. Beneath us, the floor of the boat is cool, even through the blankets. When we arrived at the campground, Callahan met us with the keys to a boat. We'd gone down the narrow cliff face path to a sheltered dock, and from there, Nate had taken us off the island on the biggest boat I've ever been on to the middle of nowhere. There isn't any artificial light for miles.

The ocean rocks us, lulling me into a false sense of peace.

"Constellations are rich-people education," I say, and Nate's laugh beside me is gentle. Everything about the night has been dusted with magic.

"Everyone can see the stars."

"Not everyone has time to see the stars and research constellations and memorize them."

"It's a personal interest. Not everything about me is because my family has money," he says.

"Maybe that's true. I can't believe a *campground* is your favorite place in the *world*."

"You're never going to get over that."

"Never. After all the places you've told me you've been, *that* is where you'd most like to be?"

"Right now, *this* is where I'd most like to be." He glances at me, the moon casting a glow across his features. Painfully handsome. "I love it there," he says. "Splitting wood with Cal is the highlight of my week. They need a lot of it for the summer campers, and I find the work strangely satisfying."

"Hence the calluses on your hands."

"Hard work comes at a cost," he says, and the same teasing tone is in his voice.

"You could just buy your own campground."

"Maybe. I don't know. Might just be Cal's parents' place that makes me feel this way and not any ol' campground, you know? Can't buy anything until I'm eighteen anyway. After that, I'm out from under Celia Tucker's iron fist."

"You don't get along with your mom?"

"It's not that."

He's quiet for a long moment, and I wonder whether, despite all the money, he has as complex a relationship with his parents as I have with mine. Is that even possible? At least he still lives at home, never has to worry about rent or his next meal. Even the fact he's had the time and energy to study stars and constellations means he's never had the same worries as me.

"We just care about different things," he says at last.

For the hundredth time since I slid into his Range Rover after work, I'm surprised at how easy conversation is between us. We've shifted between topics as though we restarted a conversation we've been having for years, not hours. At the bar, he sat and nursed his Coke while scrolling through his phone, waiting for my shift to end. From the minute I stepped out the door of the bar with him, I've had this fizzy sensation bubbling inside me, but the feeling doesn't make me anxious. I'm just happy—and it's strange to realize I'm happy *with him*. Being worry-free is a novelty.

"You've lived with your aunt since you were seven?" he asks, shifting onto his side to face me.

"She saved me," I whisper into the dark. "I'm just so glad my parents never had any more kids."

"Do you still see them?"

"More than I'd like. My aunt's too forgiving. Mickie and Niall aren't good people. They'd stick a knife in her back if it saved their own."

"You don't think it would have been nice to have someone else who understood what you were going through? A sibling? Sawyer, Maren, and I lean pretty hard on each other sometimes. We spend too much time looking after Ava and Gage, though." His tone is rueful.

"When I was little, I wanted someone, anyone, but once Aunt Verna got me out of there, I just..." I close my eyes and take a shaky breath. "I wouldn't want anyone to face the same years, the same problems, I did."

He eases my hair off my cheek with his fingertip. "I'm about to be too much," he whispers.

"Be too much," I say, meeting his gaze. "I dare you."

"Hearing you talk about your past makes me wish I could throw enough money out into the world to get a time machine, and I'd go back, and I'd stop any of that from happening to you."

Tears prick at my eyes, and I'm surprised at the warmth flooding my chest, the chill streaking behind it. Even if he doesn't mean it, can't possibly mean it when we've only known each other such a short period of time, his words are comforting. I like the idea of being cared for that much, but I don't know how I'd ever learn to trust it.

"Have you always been such a hopeless romantic?" I ask. "Cinderella only gets the prince in the fairy tale, you know. That's not real life."

"There's nothing hopeless about my romantic notions," he says with a slight smile. "Or at least, I hope not." He takes my hand and kisses the palm. "All of this is real."

"Is it?" I ask. "It's so fast, and I just..." He can leap, but I can't. The depth, the dimensions, the safety net—I need all the details to take a risk, and by then, is it even still a risk? The only times I leap without enormous calculation are when I don't feel like I have any other choice. Jump or die.

"We can slow it down." A slow smile spreads across his face. "Give me more than tonight. Easy."

"None of this makes any sense, does it?" I ask.

"I don't need how I feel to make sense for me to trust it. I just know you're it. I *know*."

In the distance, another engine roars across the silence, and we're hit with a bright light, waves jostling the boat, yanking us both out of our private bubble.

"This is the coastguard," a female voice blares out of a speaker across the water. "We had reports of a drifting boat. Are you in distress?"

With a huff, Nate gets to his feet, and he heads into the cabin, where the radio is located. I tug my phone out of my pocket, and I'm shocked at the time. The lights of the coastguard boat flash and then they peel away.

"We have to get back," I say to Nate when he comes out. "I don't have a phone signal, and it's the middle of the night." My Aunt Verna will be beside herself. Hopefully, she hasn't called the police.

We rush full speed to the campground and then into the Range Rover to get me to the apartment I share with my aunt. At the door to the building, Nate frames my face and stares down for a beat.

"So, best friend," he says with a small smile, "are we the kind that kiss?"

We've been touching each other all night, casual brushes or caresses that never went any further but shot electricity through me with each contact. Now that I'm home, my sense of urgency to get here, to get in the door, is gone. Instead, I'd rather stand out here with Nate's hands on me, his handsome face mere inches from mine.

Jump or die. God, it feels like I might die if I don't jump.

"I might need another taste before I can be sure which way it should go," I say, breathless.

"Easy," he says, and he tilts my chin before his lips brush mine, unhurried, far more practiced than I want to consider.

But he's right. It is easy. So easy to slip into the rhythm from the other night, to forget about my waiting aunt, the massive social-class gap, all the ways this decision could bite me in the ass. None of it matters as his lips move across mine. All I can think is *Nate, Nate, Nate*.

When we break apart, I punch my code into the building, and he holds my hand until he can't possibly hold it anymore.

"I'm coming back," he says through the glass, and I smile, unable to hide the joy that's bloomed in me.

"You'd better," I say, and then I rush up the stairs to the apartment, slot my key into the door, and shut it, collapsing against the wood with a sigh.

"Where in the world have you been?"

Aunt Verna's voice makes me jump at the same time my phone finally gets a signal and begins vibrating with messages. Probably messages from her, and I know guilt is seeping in, but it hasn't reached me yet.

"I met a boy," I say before I can think it through. Everything inside of me is buzzing. It makes me wonder if this is what it's like to be drunk or high—it's a feeling I can see people chasing, longing for, constantly wanting to replicate.

"A boy?" Aunt Verna's tone shifts quickly from concerned to amused. She comes out of the kitchen, a mug of something warm in her hand. Steam rises off the cup.

It's the middle of the night, but I knew she'd be awake. Even if I'd messaged to tell her what I was doing, she would have waited up, but I'm surprised she isn't mad. With everything my parents have done, I try to be good at telling her where I am, what I'm doing. Disappointing her or letting her down makes me anxious.

"I don't think I've ever seen you look so..." She smiles. "Happy. Do I know him?"

"Nate," I say. "Well, Nathaniel. Tucker. He's a... he's a Tucker."

"Hollyn." Her expression darkens, and she shakes her head.

"He's not like the rest of them. He's not like the ones you've warned me about."

"I'm sure he doesn't seem like it. They never do." She rubs her face. "But it's not *that* I'm worried about. You've always been good at looking after yourself, protecting yourself where boys are concerned." She gives me a look loaded with a meaning I can't decipher. "Mickie and Niall are going to think they've hit the jackpot. Their daughter dating a Tucker? One of Celia Tucker's kids? Whew." She sucks on her teeth. "I hope you're ready."

"They've got nothing to do with who I go out with. Who I'm friends with." I straighten against the door.

"Oh, sweetheart. I'd think you'd know better by now." And that's all she says before she wanders down the hallway back to her bedroom.

Chapter Ten

HOLLYN

"Just drive," I say to the cab driver, barely able to get the words out around the constriction in my throat.

Part of me knew Nate would be angry with me. Our meeting at the funeral home hadn't exactly been sunshine and roses, but it hadn't been terrible either. Then when he'd come to Aunt Verna's funeral, when I'd felt so much inner calm at his presence, I tricked myself into believing he would have felt that way too. That maybe, despite what I did, how things ended, we could be okay.

That meeting in the boardroom just now was the opposite of okay.

I dig around in my purse until I find my phone, and I call Shannon. But it's not Shannon who answers the landline. It's Kinsley.

"Did you get the job?" she asks, her voice brimming with excitement. "It sounded like you were going to get it."

"I can't take it, Kin. It's not a good fit." My voice is husky with regret.

"*Can't* take it?" Her anger pokes through. "I *can't* go back to New York. Not if things are going to be like they were. I hate it there. I hate everything about it there."

"Kin," I say, trying to suppress my own scattered emotions to reason with her. But I don't get the chance to say anything else when the phone goes dead in my ear.

A dropped connection, or did she hang up on me? I'm not sure it matters. Calling her back will only escalate the fight. We've been in enough of them lately that I know that much.

Even if I wanted to take the job—and I'd been prepared to accept it until Nate walked in the boardroom door—Nate made it clear he didn't want me hired. The bank account always gets what it wants, no matter what anyone else in the room thinks. Before he arrived, Posey and the other producers told me the third producer was the one covering the majority of the shortfall from the government, the one who'd been so adamant about giving lower-income families this opportunity at no cost. I'd been touched that someone had considered the impact on families and used their own money to solve the problem, and I'd been feeling a little bit of pride that I'd be involved in an initiative that would make a difference for neighborhoods like the one I came from.

I will never admit it to Kinsley, but staying here seemed possible, at least in the short term. Then it all collapsed around me when the boardroom door opened. One way or another, Nate was always going to be one of the reasons that staying on the island didn't—couldn't—make sense.

"Have you decided on a destination yet?" the cab driver asks, eyeing me in the rearview mirror. The meter ticks over at the front of the vehicle. I'm wasting money I don't have to spare.

The last place I want to go is to Shannon's to pick up Kinsley and have her either give me the silent treatment or try to attack me for not doing what she wants.

"Yeah," I say, and I give him the name of the last place I ever thought I'd want to return to.

When I open the door, stale beer and spilled tequila greet me like an old friend. It's strange to hate a place and love it at the same time. The months I spent working here when I was eighteen were some of the best of my life, but the job had very little to do with my intense happiness.

I avoid making eye contact with the few people in the bar, and I head for a table near the window. It's too dark to see the ocean view, but knowing it's out there brings me a familiar comfort.

It's only after I've set my purse on the table that something inside me pricks to attention, as though an invisible tuning fork has been hit, sending out pitch-perfect vibrations meant just for me. Years have passed since the last time I felt this sensation, but I'd recognize it anywhere.

Nate Tucker is *here* somewhere.

My skin tingles with awareness, and I stare at the scarred tabletop, afraid to look anywhere but down. What are the chances I came here on a whim and he is here, too, hating me with enough force that I can feel it?

With a shake of my head, I grab my purse, and I'm just about to leave this table, exit the bar—god help me, exit the island—when a thick glass slides onto the table's surface. Cold strawberry-mint tea, a favorite when I worked here, sloshes over the side, creating a little puddle on the wood.

Startled, I glance up, and my gaze connects with Nate's.

"Hi," I breathe out before I can catch myself, realizing how silly I sound.

For a long beat, he searches my face, and I can't help categorizing his, wishing he'd somehow gotten ugly with the years instead of more handsome. The boyish fullness of his face has been replaced with rugged angles that only seem to highlight the pretty color of his eyes. Eyes that no longer have the teasing, playful glint I once loved.

He yanks out the chair across from me and sits in it, as though I asked him to and he resents it. "Painfully long day for you, I imagine," he says, his speech thick with alcohol.

Tears spring to my eyes. Despite his body posture, those words are the Nate I remember. The one who'd been able to read me so much better than anyone else, who seemed to understand me in ways no one else did. The reminder that

I walked away from that, from him, makes my chest feel like it's on the verge of caving in.

"Yeah," I whisper, barely able to get the single word past my lips. I take the glass he set on the table, and I hold it between my palms. "Thanks for this."

"Probably not as good anymore," he says. "Apparently, Elmore sold this place a few years ago."

I take a sip, and I try not to think about why Nate decided to sit with me, why he's acting like him being at this table isn't weird and uncomfortable despite how comforted I actually feel. My subconscious that took over at the funeral is doing it again. *Nate is safety.*

"It's not the same," I admit. "A bit more minty than before. But it's just as good."

He lifts his glass to his lips and takes a long draught of his gold rush. Some things don't change. At seventeen, that was his drink of choice, but I'm surprised he's still drinking it at thirty-one, that he didn't outgrow the taste.

"You live in New York now? Work for Reyes and Cruz?"

"Yes."

"You're raising Kinsley there by yourself?" he asks.

I let out a shaky laugh. "Raising? I'm pretty sure she'd tell you I'm 'ruining' at this point."

"Why's that?" Nate takes another long drink, and then he lifts his hand, and a waitress materializes out of nowhere, another glass of gold rush at the ready. Another indication of the man he's become, the attention he draws to himself without even trying too hard.

"It doesn't matter," I say, running my fingers through the condensation on my glass. We're not old friends, and it's weird that we both seem to be trying to act as though we are.

"Looking after a sibling. Not a job you ever wanted," he says.

"And yet one I would not change." I struggle to hide my frown. "Not enough hours in the day, that's all."

"Posey tells me your sister was really set on you getting the network job, on staying here for a while."

I tear my gaze off my glass to meet his. This version of Nate, the one who'd throw himself on the sword to make my life easier, is still recognizable, familiar. Tears threaten again. *What did I do?* I don't understand how I ever found the strength to not just walk away but to stay away.

"You don't want to work with me, Nate, and I don't blame you."

"It's Nathaniel," he says.

"Nathaniel," I whisper. "Sorry." I clear my throat. "I just... I have to say that I think what you're trying to do is... it's admirable."

"Some experiences, some *people*, change you, and no matter how much you might wish to be unchanged, you can't go back."

"Still no time machine," I say, though his words are both a painful stinger and the calamine lotion to soothe it. His comment is loaded, which makes me believe it's about me, but if that's true, it's hard to be hurt if the change is him caring about the class divide on the island, him actively working to make people's lives better.

"Not even sure what I'd reverse time for anymore," he says, setting his empty glass on the table.

Ouch. That comment lands, as I'm sure he intended. His efforts to make my life better when we were teenagers were the first time anyone had ever put me first. Aunt Verna took me in as a kid, but I always felt like I was competing for her heart with my mother. Aunt Verna could never let Mickie go, and even though I understand that sisterly bond better now, part of me resented her for it back then. Mickie could have led Verna straight to hell, and she'd have gone if it meant Mickie suffered a little less.

"Your resume says you went to the East Coast School of Interior Design, but that summer before you left, you had a scholarship at Pratt for art?" He raises his hand, and another drink appears, as though the waitress is waiting for her cue to deliver. I was never that attentive to anyone in this place. She must make a killing on tips.

"I got a last-minute offer from ECSID which included my housing, so I took it." The half-truth rolls off my tongue, practiced and familiar.

"How last-minute?"

"Very." There's nothing I can say to him that'll change what I did, the choices I made. At eighteen, I did the best I could, and I've tried to make peace with that. Rehashing anything when I'm going to be leaving the island in a few days is pointless. Our wounds might have become uncovered in the boardroom, but I'm not going to pick them until they bleed.

"You were going to California for a business degree, but you've ended up in television?"

"Cut my producing teeth in documentaries."

We stare at each other across the table, and I wonder if he's slotting all the ways we're the same and different the way I am.

"When you graduated, you went after custody of Kinsley?"

"Yes," I say, though the answer is a little more complicated than that.

"Your aunt didn't want to raise another one of Mickie's kids?"

The way he says it is a poke in my side, but I ignore it. "She would have," I say, "but I didn't want Kinsley growing up here."

"And now?"

"I still don't," I say. "Kin seems to think the grass would be greener here, but I suspect the grass is exactly the same as it's always been." Burnt.

"You were going to turn down the job?"

I let out a little laugh, realizing how contradictory I'm going to sound. "No, I was going to take it. She hates me right now," I say, and I fight back the tears that come into my voice, "and I'm not sure I've been a better parent than Mickie and Niall would have been."

Nate's expression softens, and he leans his elbows on the table, invading my personal space in a way that should bother me. Intimacy, warm and familiar, seeps across the space between us. Gone is the edgy, angry man, and in his place is the Nate I remember, and god, my fucking heart crumbles into dust, flies away on the thin breeze between us, and reassembles at his fingertips, whole and needy.

"I guarantee you're better than Mickie and Niall. You were better at eighteen, and I know that any mistakes you've made would have been done with good intentions."

"Good intentions don't make people hurt less," I say, and my heart pounds at the double meaning in my words. "Doesn't make Kin hurt less. Good intentions haven't tucked her into bed at night or gotten her to dance classes when I was too busy working."

"New York is an expensive city," Nate says, his words laced with kindness. "Your childhood here was a hell of a lot worse than some missed dance classes and some late nights." His thumb skims across the scars on my wrist, and I shiver at the contact. "If those are her biggest complaints, I think you're doing okay."

Every single fiber of my being is focused on the brush of his thumb against my skin, the rhythmic comfort that's blossoming into something fuller, heavier. When we were younger, it was like this—the briefest, gentlest touch could inspire a storm of lust that clouded and obscured everything else. Franny called me "dickmatized" that summer—so enamored with Nate that I couldn't see or hear anything that didn't have something to do with him.

I would have gladly spent the rest of my life lost in that haze. It was the sole reason I couldn't let myself see him the night I left. If he'd been within fifty feet of me, I never would have been able to get on that plane. Never.

Right now, the idea of ever leaving this bar is holding less and less appeal. The longer he touches me, the less anything else matters.

When I glance up, our gazes connect, and I see exactly what I'm feeling reflected in his expression. Desire. Confusion. Longing.

He lets go of my wrist like it's burned him, and he leans back in his chair, runs his hands along his face in quick motions that look almost painful.

"I have to go." He stands, a little unsteady on his feet, and makes his way with intention toward the exit.

I rise from my seat, grabbing my purse off the table.

"I hope he's not driving," I mutter as I make my way through the bar.

"He's not." An older man is hovering near the exit door, the waitress next to him with a pay machine. "I'm driving him. Not to worry."

"Oh," I say, stopping abruptly. "I guess it... I mean, it wouldn't have been like him to drink and drive."

"One of the more reasonable and responsible Tuckers," he says, glancing over his shoulder before shifting his attention to me. "Usually." He holds out his hand to me. "I'm Bill, one of the drivers the Tuckers employ."

"Hollyn Davis," I say, taking his hand.

"Oh," he says, and the edges of his lips tilt into something that's not quite a smile.

It's pretty obvious he's heard of me, and I'm not sure what to make of that, but it also means that Nate is outside, waiting in a car.

I stand for a beat, unsure of what I should do. There's still something there between us, and I want to seek it out like a source of heat in the dead of winter. The intensity that unfurled between us when he touched me feels necessary and real, unavoidable. As though the string connecting us is made of the strongest steel, not delicate and fragile like I assumed. Despite the years, despite how badly I let him down, Nathaniel Tucker is under my skin, nestled in so deep that I didn't even realize he was still there.

But tonight has made it even clearer that I can't stay on this island for even one more day. Tomorrow, I set everything in motion to get us back to New York.

Chapter Eleven

HOLLYN

Anger surrounds Kinsley like a living, breathing thing. A dragon in the room. But I'm too busy purging my aunt's history, as though I'm literally on fire, to take much notice.

I cannot stay on this island, and I was a fool to think it was possible, even for a second. Letting myself sink a single toe into the quicksand that is Nate Tucker was a massive mistake.

Last night, I kept dreaming of him, over and over. Each time I woke up, I'd reassure myself that it couldn't possibly happen again, only to find myself trapped in some forgotten memory warped by my subconscious. If the dam of my Bellerive history had cracks in it before, it's a full-blown crisis now. The flood is coming, and I need to get to the higher ground of New York before I drown.

Even if Nate still desires me after what I did back then—and I think that's possible given what pulsed between us last night—our history is so much more complicated than a simple ghosting. With my aunt gone, one string has been cut in the web, but I don't know what wrath will fall on my head if I tell Nate everything.

"Shannon said I can stay with her for a few weeks if I want," Kinsley says.

"Shannon shouldn't have said that, because Shannon has no legal authority," I say, dumping one of my aunt's drawers onto the bed and sorting through the contents. "You need to go back to New York and back to school."

"As soon as I'm eighteen, I'm taking charge of my own life," Kinsley says.

"Wonderful."

"I'm serious."

"So am I, Kin. I'm not being held hostage by your bad attitude. The job didn't work out. I have a job in New York. We have a life there, even if it's not ideal right now. If I could have taken *this* job, I would have, but I can't. Your pouting isn't going to change the facts." After last night, I'm more relieved than anything that I can't take the job, that Nate put down his foot and said he wouldn't work with me.

From under the pile of mostly clothing, my phone rings. I dig around until I find it, but I don't recognize the number. It's likely a telemarketer, but between talking to a pouty Kin or speaking to some stranger trying to scam me, I'll take the scam.

I click on Accept, and I hit the speakerphone icon.

"Hello?" I pick up a shirt, examine it for stains, refold it and put it in the donation pile.

"Is this Hollyn Davis?" a male voice asks, one with a Bellerivian accent.

"This is she," I say, a frown creasing my brow, and I try to remember if Aunt Verna had any outstanding bills that I haven't taken care of yet.

"It's Felipe Sousa calling. We spoke last night about the television series. I'm one of the producers."

"Oh, right, yes." He's probably called to apologize for how epically bad things went with Nate.

"I wanted to apologize for how things went last night. It was less than ideal."

"I completely understand Mr. Tucker's feelings," I say in my most professional voice. There's no point in making Felipe feel bad. We put him in an awkward situation last night and then put ourselves in an even more awkward position at The Drunk Raccoon. Best to forget the whole thing.

"Well, it appears that Mr. Tucker's feelings have changed, actually. He's now quite happy for us to move ahead with negotiating a contract with you." Before he finishes his sentence, I'm scrambling for the phone, trying to get it off speakerphone, but I don't make it until his final word.

Kin appears on the opposite side of the bed, and she's staring at me, hard. She knows exactly what she heard, and if I turn the job down now, I'm pretty much guaranteed to ruin my relationship with my sister forever.

"He changed his mind?" I manage to squeak out.

"Yes," Felipe says, a hint of a smile in his voice. "Stewart will be the producer you'll deal with most often. Nathaniel's decided to stay involved but take a more hands-off approach to the project."

"I can hear him," Kin says, pointing at my phone. "Even without it on speaker."

I push the volume button with my thumb while I try to process what he's just said. "Nate—Nathaniel won't be part of the production?"

"He'll see cuts of the episodes, might provide some notes, but he won't be a visible presence."

"Right," I say. "Okay." My brain is stuck on *processing*, and it can't seem to move forward.

"Say yes," Kinsley says in a harsh whisper.

"I know you were hoping to have a lawyer look over your contract last night, and you wanted to speak to Reyes and Cruz about your position there. I can email the contract to you, and you can take that to your lawyer," Felipe says.

"Say *yes*," Kinsley hisses.

"Please send me the contract," I say, suppressing a deep sigh. "When do you need an answer?"

"Yesterday," Felipe says. "We're already behind with all our timelines. The sooner we can get you signed off, the better I'll feel."

"The amendments we discussed—"

"Already added to the contract I'm sending you now," he says, and my phone vibrates with the arrival of an email.

I took Posey's advice, and I negotiated hard last night for the things that were important to me. Firm hours of work. Salary. Bonuses for a second season or if Interflix picks up the series. Payment of my aunt's apartment rental for the duration of our stay, which lets me keep our place in New York and take my time cleaning out my aunt's things. None of the producers flinched or balked at anything. Made me wonder if I should have gone after even more.

"Thanks, Felipe," I say, turning away from Kinsley's expectant expression. "I'll let you know as soon as I can."

"I'm really looking forward to working together," Felipe says.

My heart sinks at his words. While a part of me wanted to stay last night, after spending time with Nate again, I've realized how quickly and easily things between the two of us could get out of control.

"Me too," I say, and after we say our goodbyes, I hang up the phone.

"If you don't take this," Kinsley says, her voice tinged with frustration, "I'm never speaking to you again."

"If you're going to make a threat, Kin, at least make it a realistic one."

She storms out of the room, and from across the hall, my old bedroom door slams. Looks like I've come full circle, from being the one to slam the door to the one listening to it shudder on its hinges.

I sink onto the bed, my phone cradled in my hands, and I wonder whether staying in Bellerive will make things between us better or worse.

Chapter Twelve

NATHANIEL

The wood cracks when my ax connects, the two equal pieces falling to the ground, and I roll my shoulders. The campground has extensive woods behind it, including a patch of scotch pines that Cal has been trying to turn into a place for Bellerivians to get a homegrown Christmas tree. From the looks of it, his efforts are finally taking hold in a way that might make that venture profitable soon. Historically, neither of us has been good at giving up on things we want when all it'll take to achieve our goal is a bit more effort. Most of the time, that feels like a good thing.

A little way from me in the clearing, Cal pauses his more delicate kindling work to take me in, a pile of wood shavings beside him. The thin slices of wood require more patience than I have today. On the ground not far from him is a heavily pregnant lab cross that Maren convinced him to take in as a foster. She's a loyal little thing—toddling after Cal all over the campground. I won't be surprised if he keeps her.

"Been a few years since you were out here chopping wood," Cal says.

"Still feels good." *Mostly*. Tomorrow I might not make the same claim. We've been chopping wood for hours, and I'm slowing down. But I've been grateful for the mindless routine of the swing and slice. Cal still does this regularly, and he's faster and stronger than me. He hasn't complained about my silence or slower pace.

"You want to talk about her yet?" he asks before resting his ax against the stump and putting his hands on his hips. We both ditched our shirts during the heat of the afternoon, and while he looks comfortable with the glistening sweat drying on his skin, I'm worried that the sinking sun signals an impending chill.

"I don't know what to say." I lift my hat, push back my hair, and flip it around so the brim shields my face again. "I care. All these years, and I still care. I care too much, and it pisses me off."

"What do you think she feels?"

"I wouldn't even want to guess." Though I've spent a lot of time *trying* to read into what happened between us at The Drunk Raccoon the other night. Made me wish I had fewer drinks so my judgment wasn't in the toilet.

After Posey texted me about Hollyn's tense relationship with her younger sister and then sent me her resume, I couldn't help wondering if I was being selfish to keep Hollyn from the cohosting job. Hearing her confess her problems with her sister to me at the bar determined my course of action.

The next morning, I told Felipe and the other producer to give Hollyn any financial clauses she wanted, whatever she needed to be able to say yes. I've got the money to pay her what she's worth, and Hollyn always used to undervalue herself. She was never going to ask for more than we could afford. Or rather, what *I* could afford. At least, not in terms of money.

"Are you going to ask her what happened that summer? Now that she's staying?"

"No point," I say. "She left. We both moved on. Looking back doesn't do either of us any good. I've arranged it so we can avoid each other, even while working on this project."

"Working directly with the families is what got you excited about this project. You're not going to be the hands-on one anymore?"

"No." I shake my head and then readjust my ball cap again, pushing my sweaty hair off my forehead. "Strictly the money guy. Might review a few early cuts of episodes and give my opinion, but I'd honestly rather not." I can't watch her in person or on screen and pretend to be indifferent, impartial. We slipped so easily into what we once had the other night that I've felt rattled, not quite stable, since.

"Who's the hands-on producer now?" Cal asks, having heard me talk enough about my newest career avenue to be curious.

"Stewart Laidlaw," I say, and I anticipate Cal's reaction. "He was the one willing to step in."

"Stew?" Cal questions with a huff. "You're not going to be happy with that."

"I won't be there. And I'm confident Hollyn can handle herself." Hollyn used to be good at pushing back against men—maybe because her own father was the weaker figure in her parents' relationship.

Cal looks at me like I've lost track of reality, but he doesn't call me on my bullshit.

I set down my ax, and I roll my shoulders again. They're starting to tighten up. After this, I'm going back to the apartment to sink into my hot tub that's perched on the spacious balcony overlooking the city and let the aches of the day work themselves out. "I'm not micromanaging this project." Even I don't believe myself.

"Fuck off," Cal says with a laugh. "One *hint* that he's being a dick to her, and you'll micromanage the shit out of everyone. You step in to help people in Bellerive you don't even know very well. I'm surprised you even agreed to do this project with him."

Stewart was a late addition after Heather Sommer dropped out, and since I was going to be the hands-on producer, his involvement didn't bother me. But with me reluctant to keep that role—not just for my sake, but for Hollyn's too—that left the job to Felipe or Stewart. Felipe has his hands in several projects in America, so he didn't want to commit himself too heavily here.

"He knows my reputation," I say, picking up another piece of wood, setting it on the stump and swinging hard, cracking through it like slicing soft butter.

"You think that'll keep him in check?"

"He knows what's at stake. He was at her screen and chemistry test. He's a hotheaded asshole, but I've never heard anything beyond that." Or at least nothing physical with anyone—male or female. He prides himself on "telling it like it is," which is just code for not caring about other people's feelings. "What have you heard?"

"He's an abrasive prick. Whether he tries to lay an unwanted hand on Hollyn or he simply hurts her feelings, we both know you're not going to stand back and let it happen more than once."

"She's survived fourteen years in New York, so I'm sure she can handle one dickhead producer." I set up another piece of wood, and I crack it in two. "My role in this TV production is clear, and it has nothing to do with her."

"Right," Cal says with a laugh. "You keep telling yourself that."

We have enough money that my mother could pay for almost anyone on the island to take her to her treatment appointments, but she's decided that these appointments will be shared equally among her children. While she's not in danger of dying anytime soon, this health scare seems to have made her reevaluate her relationship with her adult children. One can hope it'll make her more productively involved in her granddaughter's life too. Though I'm not sure how much of my mother's brand of help Gage and Ember would want in raising Nova.

In the past, Celia hasn't wanted much to do with any of her children unless the interaction benefitted her in some way. If we're making her and the family look good, we're on a pedestal, and if we're not, well, she'll claim we've been put on this earth to test her resolve. Resolve over what, I've never been sure. Social climbing? Maintaining power and influence on the island? Nothing any of us has ever done has put either of those things in serious jeopardy, despite the claims my mother has made.

"How's your TV thing coming along?" my mother asks, peering at me from the passenger seat after we've just been sitting together for over an hour, mostly in silence, while she receives the newest treatment meant to shock her kidneys back into working properly.

"Fine," I say, shifting in my seat, not at all eager to get into the details, for once.

"I heard something interesting the other day, and I wondered whether you were going to tell me," she says, clearly fishing.

"What's that?"

"Hollyn Davis is going to be the cohost? I'm surprised that's been something you'd support."

"Like any job," I say, "you want the best person for it."

"And she's that person?"

"My coproducers believe so, yes."

"Ah," she says, relaxing back into her seat, "so *you* don't agree with that assessment."

"I saw the audition reel," I say, not willing to admit that I've now watched the whole thing several times. "She's deserving."

"I don't like that she's involved," she says.

"Yes, I'm aware you've never been a fan of hers," I say, unable to keep the bitterness out of my tone. She never missed an opportunity to tell me that getting involved with a Davis-Thompson was a terrible idea. "We'll have very little to do with one another."

"That's not been the case with your other producing projects."

"Different productions require different roles," I say.

She shifts, sinking deeper into the leather. "Good. The hold she had on you back then was unnatural, and it was a lucky escape the first time."

There's no point in me saying anything since we won't agree. I didn't escape; Hollyn did. "How many more treatments do you have?" I ask.

"Five," she says. "Spread out over the next few months. But I'm feeling much more optimistic now that I know both you and Ava are a match for a transplant."

"To be clear," I say, "a transplant is a last resort and maybe months or years down the road, according to your doctor. There are still three or four other treatment options, correct?"

"Yes, yes," she says, waving me off. "And in the meantime, I get to bond with my children through these moments. It'll be nice, won't it?"

I murmur something that I hope sounds like agreement.

"I really need my family right now," she says, and the hint of vulnerability in her voice takes me by surprise.

When we've really, truly needed her—failed relationships, hospital visits, financial loss—she's come through for us, but not always in the way we want. As selfish as she can be, she's never been completely oblivious to our lives. She's been the best parent she's capable of, and maybe I've finally gotten to an age where I don't need more than she's able to give.

"We're going to stand by you, Mom. Whatever you need, we'll be there for you." I squeeze her hand, and she squeezes mine back.

After dropping my mom off at home, I'm late to the production meeting. Stewart and Felipe are already deep in conversation when I enter, a storyboard on the oversized TV in front of them. The director, the person in charge of wardrobe, and our two writers are also seated at the table.

"I know she tested well and we're all signed up, but I'm having second thoughts," Stewart says, rocking back in his chair as I take my seat.

"Second thoughts about who and what?" I take out my computer and set it up on the table. My focus turns to the boards in question as Felipe clicks through them for our first episode.

"We're having trouble locating clothing designers on the island willing to work with someone Hollyn's size," Twyla, the show's costume designer, says.

"She's tall, but—" I start.

"It's not her height," Stewart says, stepping in. "She's not even close to a sample size. A pretty face, but she's overweight. With the camera adding even more weight, Posey is going to look normal sized, and Hollyn will look supersized in comparison."

"Stew, if that's your perspective, then you're not the right person to be doing the day-to-day work with Hollyn and Posey," I say, and inside, my blood is boiling. The last thing I'm having is this prick making Hollyn feel insecure from inside the show when we don't have a clear idea of how the public will react to her outside our bubble.

"I think Hollyn is great," Tariq, our director says. "Part of the government funding is for highlighting Bellerivian talent throughout the whole production, but we can do that in lots of other ways. Doesn't have to be clothing for Hollyn."

"I'm not saying Hollyn isn't great," Stewart says, raising his hands. "I said she had a pretty face. What's her size, like a quadruple-extra-large or something?"

"A North American eighteen," Twyla says, and I can tell by the way she says it that she's not impressed with this conversation either, even if it was her job to bring it up to production.

Every time Stew opens his mouth, my mood darkens. Defending Hollyn's beauty feels like crossing a line, but I can't leave his remarks alone. "Hollyn Davis is more than a pretty face. At least a third of the people in Bellerive will identify with Hollyn based on body type alone. Highlighting diversity, in all its forms, is important to this production." Not to mention that I think Hollyn is one of the most gorgeous people to ever exist, no matter what size her body is. From the moment she touched my back at the bar, she's owned a piece of me that no one else has ever been able to claim. She was beautiful to me when we were teenagers, and seeing her now, she's just as exquisite.

I know what her extra weight means. Stability. Regular meals. A chance to indulge in a way that was denied to her as a kid. The privilege of aging—one of many things that used to sit heavily on Hollyn when we were younger. Life expectancy on the island, when broken down by socioeconomic status, isn't pretty. I'm sure she doesn't begrudge her metabolism slowing down, because it means she's made it this far.

But saying any of that in this room reveals a lot more than I'm comfortable discussing at this point. Half of it doesn't even feel like mine to tell when it's so closely connected to Hollyn, a woman I don't even know anymore.

"Do I need to throw more money at these designers, or what?" I ask, pinning Twyla with my gaze.

"I doubt it, but you can try. They all told me they didn't want to get into the plus-size market and they didn't want to give Bellerive, and the world if it's picked up by Interflix, the wrong idea." Twyla repositions her computer in front of her.

"Fuck 'em," I say. "We'll source clothing from elsewhere for Hollyn."

"I believe that's my call," Stewart says from the other side of the table.

"Not anymore," I say, staring him down. "I'm the money guy, and the money guy gets what he wants, and I don't want you anywhere near the day-to-day when your discrimination is so blatant. Neither of our stars are going to quit or feel diminished in any way because of something happening within our crew. I won't allow it."

"Hollyn signed to the show with the understanding that you—" Felipe starts.

"I'll talk to her," I say, cutting him off. The thought of seeking her out sends a shot of adrenaline down my spine, and I try to ignore it. Fucking Cal was right. Stewart was a dick, and I couldn't handle it. Cal will fall on the floor with laughter next time I see him. "I'm not worried about working together." Which is, possibly, the biggest lie I've ever told.

Chapter Thirteen

HOLLYN

When the apartment buzzer pierces the quiet of Aunt Verna's apartment, I'm surprised at how much the noise takes me back to my childhood. For years, the buzzer was attached to a box by the door, and you'd talk to the person trying to gain entry.

Like almost every other aspect of life, things have changed in the last fourteen years. Now the voice box has been replaced with a display screen, and on it, clear as day, is Nathaniel Tucker, in all his six-foot-plus glory.

It's criminal how attractive he still is with his hands shoved into the pockets of his suit pants, and when he stares up into the camera, as though he can sense me even through the technology, a shiver races down my spine.

Some part of me, some deep, deep part of me, still wants him, still remembers what it was like to have his big hands exploring my figure, bringing me to life in ways I didn't know someone else could do. That summer, he'd known my body almost better than I knew it myself. No man since has taken so much care in exploring every inch of me, memorizing every curve and crease, using every moan and sigh to guide the next brush of his fingers—rough or firm or featherlight. Unbelievable to have *that* at eighteen and not again since.

Instead of hitting the talk icon, I stare back at him for a few beats, scanning his features, taking in the familiar and noting the places where time has left its mark. It's not the first time I've stared at him since I returned, but I can't seem to help searching his face for something, but I don't know what I'm trying to find.

I don't know exactly what he might feel toward me, but it's apparent that what I feel is going to be a problem. The obsessive love I once felt for him could so easily take hold again, and the smart thing to do is ignore him right now. He doesn't know I'm home or even here. Seeing him alone in this apartment is a bad idea. I bite my lip and stare at his image for another beat while my heart races up into my throat.

I buzz him up without a word. It wouldn't matter what he said about why he's here. Now that I've seen him standing there, I can't turn him away. Which was my problem with Nate from the first night we met. Denying him anything was always a mountain I didn't want to climb, an ocean I didn't want to swim across. Whenever we were together, it was so much easier to bask in the glow, the warmth, of him, of us—to say yes to it all.

I turn from the screen and take in Aunt Verna's apartment.

Oh no.

I've been so busy decluttering and sorting through my aunt's things that the place is a mess. Clothes and old bills and knickknacks are strewn everywhere. She'd be mortified to know I allowed anyone into this apartment with it looking like this. Frantically, I start gathering things up, shoving papers and trinkets in any drawer I can find, any bag I can reach.

Luckily, Kinsley went to a free dance class with another girl her age from the apartment complex. To my sister's credit, she's thrown herself into this new life. Bellerive is a country that feels like a series of small towns—everyone knows everyone—and I'm less wary of letting Kinsley go places with other families. Everything across the island has six degrees of separation, and when I called Shannon to check on the girl's family, she assured me they were good people.

That sense of the island as one big family is a perk I completely forgot about in the years I've been away, and I'm not sure my teenage self would have considered everyone knowing everything a perk back then. There have to be some positives to counter the negatives of staying here for an extended period of time.

Like the negative of this man about to reach the apartment at any moment. No sooner has the thought gone through my head than I hear the briefest brush of knuckles on the door. I scan the main room to find that it's barely presentable. The love seat is clear of clutter and little else. He can sit. I'll stand. I can stand.

I send up a silent apology to my aunt, and I swing the door back.

I'm barefoot, and although I'm tall at five-eight, it still feels like Nate towers over me. But for the first time, I'm a little self-conscious of every pound of the one hundred I've gained. Most days, I'm good with my body. It does what I need it to do, and I've never had any complaints from the men I've chosen to be with. But it took me a long time to be with anyone after Nate, and my hungry-thinness was in the distant past by then. He can't possibly look at me and still feel the same as he once did.

But when I glance up, I realize my initial thought about him was wrong. Nate could never be a negative in my life. Even if he hates me. Even if he no longer finds me remotely attractive. Even if we'll never be what we once were to each other. Even if his eyes no longer spark with loving delight when he meets my gaze. He's a fountain of care and good intentions, and even if those things aren't directly aimed at me anymore, I can't put him, as a person, in the negative column. He'd never deserve to be lumped in with my parents.

I want to force him into the negative column because of the choices *I* made, but that wouldn't be fair.

"Can I come in?" he asks when it probably seems like any form of speech has left me.

"Oh, uh, yeah," I say, stepping aside and cringing internally at the mess he'll soon discover.

"Is Kinsley here?" he asks.

"No," I say as I close the door behind him. "She's making fast friends in the apartment complex."

"I've heard Bellerive can feel very cliquey to an outsider, so I'm glad to hear that."

I'm sure the upper echelon of Bellerive isn't as easy to break into. Cal and Sawyer were the only ones in Nate's circle who were welcoming in high school. The working poor have always held out a hand to help others up—at least all the people I've ever known. Well, except my parents' associates, but I'd hardly call what they get up to "work," though I'm sure they'd disagree.

"I didn't think we were starting until next week," I say, gesturing to the remnants of my aunt's life lying around the tiny apartment. "I was hoping to get all this sorted out before then." Even if the sorting is painful and forces me to switch off every feeling that threatens to surface. The clear-out requires practicality and logic, not sentimentality. Ever since I was a kid, I could compartmentalize aspects of my life with ease. I had to in order to survive the chaos my parents had following them like their own personal hurricane. But when Nate blew into my life, that skill abandoned me. I went so all-in with him that no aspect of my life went untouched. I've never made that mistake again.

"That's correct," Nate says, scanning the room. "Next week." He purses his lips. "Do you want help with this? It seems like a lot for you to handle alone."

"Kinsley's helping," I say, which is a lie. She's avoided the whole thing. She has no emotional compartments, and anytime I've asked her to pitch in, she's burst into tears and fled to her room the minute something sentimental or meaningful lands in her lap, unearthed. "You obviously didn't come here to help me clear out my aunt's apartment," I say, trying to steer the conversation back into safer waters. It would be so easy to take his help, sink back into the familiar rapport.

"Right. Yeah." He takes a deep breath. "There's been a necessary change in producers, and I wanted to tell you in person that I'll now be the one overseeing the day-to-day production decisions. The other two will offer notes and guidance, but they won't be as heavily involved."

He can't meet my gaze for some reason.

"Do you want to sit down?" I ask, not sure where to take this conversation now.

He nods and settles into the love seat. I stand awkwardly in front of him, not taking the obvious second seat beside him.

"Do you want me to quit?" I ask, trying to read what's going on with his awkward reluctance. "If you want me to quit, I'll quit. I can still go back to New York."

"Do you *want* to quit?" he asks, which isn't an answer to my question. "Because if this won't work for you, I can try to find another producer to replace me. It'll delay everything, but I can... I can do that."

My legs feel shaky, and I'm not sure if it's from the idea of working closely with him or having him quit so I can keep the job. I sink into the seat beside him, and when I turn toward him, there's so little space between us that I almost believe I can feel his body heat radiating off him. Sitting was a bad idea, but now that I'm here, I only want to inch closer, not further away.

"I don't want you to quit," I whisper.

"I don't want *you* to quit," he says. "We've been looking for the perfect person to bounce off Posey for months. Losing you would be..." He shakes his head, and when he meets my gaze, I wonder if we're still talking about the production. "You're impossible to replace."

"Nate—"

"Nathaniel," he corrects quietly but firmly.

"Old habits," I say.

"Long gone," he says, but he takes a strand of my long hair and twists it around his finger. "Things change."

Some things don't change enough, because the heat between us on this love seat is stifling. My breaths come shallow as he loops my hair around his finger.

"Sorry," he says, letting the piece slide off in a twirl, back out of his reach. "*That was unprofessional.*" A hint of a wry smile touches his lips. "Muscle memory—an uncontrollable reflex. It used to be so short."

"Running your hands through my hair is an uncontrollable reflex? Should I be alerting HR?" I raise my eyebrows, but I can hear the flirty tone in my voice.

"One lock of hair is hardly a sin," he says, and when our gazes meet, there's heat behind his words.

What sins would he like to commit? Because certain parts of my body—a lot more than a few strands of hair—are game to get involved in whatever ideas are running through his mind. And I *really* should *not* be having these thoughts.

"Are we agreeing to work together?" I ask, my voice breathless.

"I think we are," he says, searching my expression. "Do you think we can handle it?"

Not a chance. One of us is going to crash and burn, and I definitely don't want it to be Nate, but I don't want it to be me either. The smart thing would be to quit the job or ask him to walk away. There's still too much bubbling under the surface between us. So much is unsaid, unknown.

"No problem," I say. "A fresh slate, right? All work."

"Right," he says, and clouds brew in his eyes. "That's what you want? A fresh slate?"

"Wipe it clean," I say, and really that's to my benefit more than his. If we pretend the past never happened, I don't have to reckon with my choices.

He licks his lips and then takes a deep breath. "I can do that." He stands and then immediately sits back down. "I promised myself I wouldn't do this, but if we're wiping it all clean—pretending none of it ever happened—I'm going to ask this once and let it go. Whatever you tell me, consider this the end of it, okay?"

I swallow and nod. Unease washes over me. There's no way that his next question is going to be simple or easy.

"Why did you leave so suddenly? Why did you leave me one voicemail and then disappear?" His voice is gritty by the end, and I can't tell if it's anger or hurt making it sound so raw.

I close my eyes to block out the sight of his hurt—the coward's response—but it's the only one I know where he's concerned. Tuck my tail and run. "We were too different. We were deluding ourselves. I needed a clean break." I almost tell him that Celia Tucker would never have let us work out, which is true, but it's not the whole truth. Being unable to tell Nate the granular truth is the price I paid to get what I wanted, so it's best to keep the past buried. I might not be the poor girl I once was, but I'm still the daughter of criminals, still not fit to be a Tucker. "In your mind, our breakup might have been this big dramatic thing." I swallow again, desperate to keep any emotion out of my voice—I have to sell this. "But in mine, this was the way it was always meant to go. I ripped off the Band-Aid."

His jaw tics, and he rises to his feet again. He scans my face for a beat, and I wonder whether I've given the truth away—that it was nothing like what I'm telling him. There's a grain of reality in my words and nothing more.

"Consider the whole thing erased," he says. "I suppose we're more strangers than anything anyway." He heads for the door, and I rise to my feet to follow him, fighting the urge to tell him to wait, to let the real events spill from my lips.

But I made promises, deals that got me to where I am now. Nate was my sacrifice, and even if I told him everything, I don't see how even he could forgive me for the choices I made. Now that I'm faced with the damage I did, I find it hard to forgive myself.

He's out the door before I can get there, fleeing the scene of my crime. I press my back against the door and fight tears. How is it possible that the price I paid years ago *now* feels too high? Back then, it felt high but necessary. Hindsight and age make me wonder whether I was just too young and inexperienced to see other options.

The past is such a tangled web of coincidences and lies and sacrifices that it's impossible to untangle it all in my mind. One change would have had massive repercussions for me and others. Luckily, Nate has vowed to let his questions go, and he's not the type to go back on a promise.

But I might be.

Secrets have a way of rising to the surface, especially ones that did as much harm as good.

As a teenager—despite my better judgement—I hadn't been capable of staying away from Nate, of keeping either physical or emotional distance. He was the sun, and I bloomed under his attention. Grew in ways I didn't know I could.

And as much as I wish that particular truth didn't still hold true, it appears it does. He's back in my life, and my world already feels brighter and warmer than it has in years.

The past can't just be erased by declaring it so.

Chapter Fourteen

HOLLYN

Fourteen years ago

At my insistence, we've stayed in areas of Tucker's Town and the island that make me most comfortable. We avoid the rich areas. We also avoid the places my parents and their associates hang out. Whatever this is can't last, and I'm happy to keep shunning reality, all the reasons we can't work. We both know what this is—a summer fling.

For a fling—so far, a sexless fling—he's been very committed. From the minute he showed up at the bar the second time, there's been no cooling off, no game-playing to see if I'll chase him instead.

I've seen him every night for the last two weeks. If he's not sitting in the bar while I work and then driving off with me at the end of the night, he's at my apartment door, begging me to come out with him. He has absolutely zero shame in literally begging through the speaker when my aunt isn't home, and it's probably the most adorable thing any guy has ever done for me. Any hint of cautiousness on my part only seems to make his behavior more extravagant. He thinks I'm trying to hide us, and I am, but not for whatever reason he probably thinks.

Tonight, we're headed to a coffee shop that's open twenty-four hours in the heart of the working poor neighborhood where I live. I've tried to avoid any place where people might be familiar, might notice me with Nate. My aunt was right—if my parents see him, realize that I'm with him—I might lead myself into trouble I don't want.

It's late enough after my shift at the bar that the coffee shop is mostly empty. Nate holds the door open for me as I enter, and while we're standing in front of the counter, reading the options, Nate says, "I'm going to start calling you my girlfriend. Just so you know."

"No, you're not," I say with a laugh of disbelief, and then I step up to the counter to order a bagel and a coffee.

He orders a coffee and a donut, and he hands over money before I can get mine out. I don't argue with him because being here is an extravagance I don't normally allow myself. I could get the same things for far less from a grocery store. We take our food to the table that's farthest from the counter.

"I knew if I asked you, you'd say no, so I'm telling you instead." Nate takes a seat across from me.

"That's not how labeling a relationship works," I say, sliding right back into the conversation.

"You agree that we're in a relationship then."

"Maybe no one ever told you before, but you're not supposed to make your hookups your permanent side chicks."

"You're not a side chick." His neck flushes with the heat of his frustration. "You're the *only* chick. You're it. Just you."

"That's not smart, Nate." I poke out the glob of cream cheese stuck in the middle of my bagel, but I don't take a bite. "It's better if we don't make a big deal about whatever this is." I gesture between us with my index finger. "We're a 'just for now' thing, and that's okay. I'm not offended. You're at the private school, and I'm a public-ed kid. You could have five girlfriends at school and then me on the side. I'm not asking questions."

"Ask me any question you want, but if you think there's anyone but you, you're delusional. I spend every single free minute I have outside debate club and lacrosse with you. You're it. There is no one else. There will never be anyone else. It's wild to me that you'd even say that it's possible for me to be with anyone else. What haven't I told you that you need to hear? Once school is out for the summer, I'll be totally focused on you—no other distractions."

"Not a good idea," I say with a shake of my head. "I'm going to school in New York, and you're going to California. We'll be on opposite coasts. It doesn't make sense for us to be together."

"Once I turn eighteen in October, I'll have access to the family trust. I can fly to New York on the family jet, or I can book myself a ticket. I can book you a ticket to California, or we can both fly home. Your distance reason is bullshit, and I'm not accepting it." He takes a big bite of his donut and throws the rest down on the plate for emphasis.

"High school relationships don't survive college."

"Says who?"

"There's lots of examples." Not one will come to my mind, but I know it's a thing—high school relationships and college don't mix. It's a known fact.

"None of those people were us." He meets my gaze with determination. "I've never been more certain of anything in my life than I am about my future with you. I won't let anything come between us."

Everything inside of me turns to mush, and then butterflies, somehow, sprout out of the goo to flutter around my stomach, up into my throat, making it hard for me to speak. "Nate," I whisper, my throat closing up and tears filling my eyes. No one has ever put me first, put me so far out in front of their lives that I'm the number one priority above all else.

"I know you've wanted to keep us quiet, but I'm tired of it. I want to shout about you from the roof, across the city, out into the ocean and see if I can make my joy felt all the way over in America or Europe." He slides back his chair and stands on top of it before glancing down at me and stepping onto the table. "Everyone! Everyone! Can I have your attention, please?"

I'm too embarrassed to look around the coffee shop to see who's entered, but I get out of my chair, and I tug on the hem of Nate's shirt. "Get down," I say.

"I, Nathaniel Jonathan Tucker, love Hollyn Noelle Davis with my whole fucking heart. I'm going to marry this girl one day. Anyone else who thinks they might have a chance will have to come through me. I'm not giving her up."

There's a smattering of whooping and cheering, but I refuse to look at anyone but him. My face is on fire, and I cup my cheeks, hoping the coolness of my hands will bring some relief. But my heart is warm and glowing. Did he really just do that?

When he steps down, I grab his hand and head for the exit, keeping my head down and tugging him along behind me.

"Nathaniel Tucker," I say as soon as we're out the door, "what in the world—"

His mouth is on mine, and his hands are in my hair, and he's backed me up against the cool brick of the building. I slide my hands up his back, and I kiss him back with the same intensity. No one has ever done anything like that for me before, and all the warring feelings inside of me might burst out if I don't keep my lips and mouth engaged in something else. I can't fall in love with a Tucker, no matter how wonderful he might seem. I'm a realist, and nothing about this relationship is real or permanent.

"I love you," he says when we break apart, his fingers gentle along my jawline, his forehead pressed to mine. "I love you so fucking much, Hols. It feels like I was always meant to love you."

Instead of saying it back, I tug him into another kiss, wrapping myself around him, trying to pour all the feelings I refuse to say into the movement of our lips, the close connection of our bodies. I've always known my aunt loved me—that's not even a question—but her love is complicated by her loyalty and love for my mother. Aunt Verna's love is unconditional, but that love has always felt inextricably bound to my mom. She loves me as much because I am Mickie's daughter as because I'm Hollyn, and that reality has never sat easy on my shoulders. But I still owe Aunt Verna every ounce of happiness I've ever felt—all those moments are connected to her.

What Nate is offering me, what he's giving me without asking for anything in return, is something I've never had. Joyful love. Love without strings. Love without a painful history. A love that can exist outside my warped family structure. The chance to be loved completely and totally because of who I am and not whom I belong to.

And as much as I don't want it, as much as I think I'm a fool to even consider it, I might already be in love with him too. The thought is terrifyingly big, a song whose lyrics are being sung at full volume in my heart as our kiss goes on and on. *You're the one. You're the one. There will never be another one.*

Meeting him that first night was a lightning bolt straight to the core of my being, and I fear I'll never be the same again.

Chapter Fifteen

NATHANIEL

"She's lying to me," I say to Cal as I watch him pour my coffee from my spot at his kitchen table.

Gage leans against the counter, cradling his own cup of coffee. He's supposed to be in LA with Ember and Nova, but he literally jetted home to check on me because I didn't text him back yesterday. He flew through the night, worried about me. He never used to be the one in the family who showed up when you needed someone—that was always Sawyer, sometimes Maren—but here he is. I'm not even sure I need his support, but the gesture isn't lost on me. Whatever he's discovered with Ember and Nova has changed him profoundly and for the better.

"Want my advice?" Gage asks, lifting his cup to his lips.

I'm not sure he's changed enough to be the advice giver here. But he was already at Cal's when I arrived, as though he suddenly knows what I'll do before I do.

I lean back in my chair and throw my arm over the back. "Let's hear it."

"If it was me, and if it was Ember, I'd take her confession at face value."

"Just let her go?" Cal says, skepticism rich in his voice as he slides into the seat at the head of the table, his own coffee in his hand. "Your brother has been pining after her for years."

"Pining?" I scoff.

"Exactly. She didn't give you a *real* reason for her behavior. Or, I don't know, maybe she gave you a reason that makes sense when you're eighteen. All I remember of eighteen is alcohol, women, and surfing."

"You've lost me," I say. This is what I get for suggesting he can give advice—utter nonsense.

"Go after her. You want her. Go after her. Fuck her bullshit reason. At thirty-one, thirty-two, her reasoning is a nonissue. Who cares if you come from different backgrounds? And you're old enough that you can make any situation work if you really want to."

"I'm her boss now," I say. Any attempts at reconnecting on my part bears the weight of off-kilter power dynamics.

"Gage has a point," Cal says, sitting forward and putting his elbows on the table. "If her reason was the Tucker name or your intimidating-as-fuck mother. Hell, maybe even Jonathan was intimidating to her back then. You're both old enough to handle all that now. Her reason *is* bullshit, or at least it is now that you're older."

"It might be bullshit, but it's pretty clear she wasn't willing to fight, or even *try*, to make us work. Why would I want someone like that back in my life?" My emotions have been all over the fucking map since she claimed what we'd had together was always destined to fail. There are a lot of things in the world that are hard to control, but how much effort you put into something you want isn't one of them, and it pisses me off that she gave up without even talking to me about it. Would I have been reasonable about her desire to call it quits? Absolutely not. In hindsight, I sure as shit would have appreciated the conversation. It would have been a hell of a lot easier to let her go than deal with being left in the dark.

"Before Ember, I didn't get it. I'll admit that. Longing for some woman for fourteen years? Never gonna be me." Gage takes a long sip of his coffee before continuing. "Now? I'd move heaven and earth for that woman. No question."

"You've been pretty tight-lipped," Cal says, pointing his cup at me. "When you're with Hollyn, does it feel like there's still a connection?"

Definitely still a simmering fire. Whenever I'm within touching distance, I want to touch. The thought of getting to taste her again makes me immediately hard. As much as I don't want it to be true, her hold on me is, potentially, just as strong as it once was. Which is fucking terrifying for all kinds of reasons.

Judging by her breathing last night on the love seat, at least the sexual chemistry is mutual. Anything else? I've got no idea.

"There's something," I admit reluctantly. "Doing anything about that is so fucking risky." I massage my temples before drawing my hands down my face.

"The power dynamics aren't ideal," Cal says with a shrug. "I'm confident that if she gives you a firm 'no,' that you're capable of letting it go."

Good thing one of us is confident. If I let myself go down this path, I have no idea whether I'm capable of obeying the signage along the way. At seventeen, being with her was the only road I could see—the very definition of tunnel vision—and I'd like to think I'm mature enough to handle those emotions now. But the truth is that I'm out of practice. I haven't allowed myself to feel them since Hollyn, so in that sense, I'm still a rookie. Untested. And Cal is really only seeing the risk related to our mutual job.

"What's the worst that happens?" Gage asks and then his brow furrows, and I wonder if he's going in all the *Oh shit* directions my mind has been wandering. "Actually, I don't know how you survived that heartbreak the first time. I honestly think it would kill me if Ember or Nova walked out on me."

"One foot in front of the other," I say, staring into my cup. "The same way you survive anything."

"You've always been one to go all-in," Cal says. "The rich-poor divide in Bellerive, learning how to produce movies and TV shows, looking out for the underdog. Are you really going to let the one thing—the one person—you've wanted the most slip through your fingers because you're afraid?"

"We don't know each other anymore. Hollyn is basically a stranger," I say, but my heart kicks in my chest in denial. My heart knows what my brain wants to deny. I'd know Hollyn anywhere—across space and time and other lives—there is no reality, no version of the world, in which I don't know Hollyn Davis. To me, it's impossible.

And so I guess that's my answer.

"I know what I'd do," Gage says. "I'd pursue her exactly how you wanted to, how you would have fourteen years ago if you could have found her. It might break your heart again, but at least you'll fucking know. You won't spend the rest of your life wondering if you'd have it all if you'd just risked it all."

He's right. No matter how much I hate the reason Hollyn gave me for her disappearance, we aren't kids anymore. The objections she had then aren't realistic to throw up between us now. Even if there's something she's not telling me—and part of me strongly suspects there's more to the story—pursuing her might dig that up, force it to the surface too. We'll either get past our history, or my tactics will drive a permanent wedge between us, but at least this time I'll understand why. I'll feel like I played a real part in how events unfolded.

We were just kids the first time around. I didn't have the resources or skills I have now, and I intend to use every single one to win Hollyn back, to make her mine.

Chapter Sixteen

HOLLYN

Outside the Tucker Millennium Hotel, I stare at the fancy gold and limestone exterior, and I text Posey again. She and her fiancé, Brent, are already inside after having checked into the spa. She's never done a TV show before, so she couldn't tell me if the request to come here was normal or not, but an internet search turned up several examples where producers or directors organized bonding events to help increase cast chemistry.

But as far as I know, it's Posey, Brent, me, and Nate. The four of us. Like some kind of warped double date. At the most luxurious spa in Bellerive. Obviously, the double-date vibe wouldn't be one Nate—Nathaniel—is trying to create, but it's in the back of my brain, nudging me, just the same. Why would Posey's fiancé be here?

Of all the places we could have built some chemistry—a bowling alley or laser tag or rock climbing—why would the production team choose a spa?

I didn't ask Nate any questions when he texted with today's date, time, and location. If I seemed reluctant, he might think I'm going back on the decision we made to forge ahead, to pretend like our past together is nothing.

The last thing I want him to know or suspect is that I can't honor the fresh slate. That, for me, there's no reality in which we can forget what happened—not any of it—no matter how much I might want some of it to have never happened.

I weave my way through the massive hotel, following the signs for the spa. Clearly, I parked in the wrong lot, but I've never even stepped foot in this hotel, let alone considered booking myself in for a spa treatment. There are no prices on the website, so I can only imagine how much production is paying for this bonding day.

Posey was delighted. And of course she would be. I bet she looks stunning in a teeny-tiny bikini. Whereas I've brought the most practical, no-nonsense bathing suit I own—the one I use for swimming laps at the YMCA—not the one I'd ever use if I was trying to impress someone.

Which is what I keep reminding myself as I turn corners and open doors. Nate Tucker and Hols Davis are old news. Just like our nicknames. Whatever chemistry I still felt on the love seat the other day was probably completely one-sided, and even if it wasn't, I cannot let myself go down any roads with him.

This shapeless suit is the best defense I have today. No sexy thoughts will be happening for Nate with me in this suit. And if that makes me a little sad, I try to ignore that twinge as I open the final door and step into the dimly lit spa reception. A platonic, sexual-tension-free relationship is smarter than injecting angst and confusion. I know what happened and why and the reasons we can never be together again.

The reception room is all warm-brown tones and pale-pink flowers, and I approach the desk with a false confidence I honed in a variety of situations in New York. It's the same confidence I laid over my normal persona for the screen test with Posey. Most of the time, it works well enough to get me through, sometimes even brings me success.

Imposter syndrome is just fear trying to hold you back. Embrace it. Step into the discomfort. Don't care about what others think. Be you. All these mantras play on repeat in my head as I give my name. They're phrases I've had to repeat as I tried to rise through the ranks at Reyes and Cruz. If you let people keep you down, they will. Know your own worth. That's a lesson I learned the hard way in Bellerive. Or maybe it was know *what* you're worth. Learned that one too.

The receptionist gives me a canned response on all the amenities of the spa, the services we can take advantage of because production has rented the whole facility for the afternoon.

I stare at her for a beat, dumbfounded. "The whole spa is rented?"

"That's correct." She checks her screen. "You're slated for a massage at one thirty and a facial at five fifteen. In between treatments, you're welcome to go in any of our pools, the sauna, hot tub, or any of our other specialty rooms." She passes me a brochure.

"How many people are here?" I ask, suddenly wondering if I got it wrong.

"Four now, including you. Tariq Covington and his partner, Marshall, came down with a bug and had to cancel at the last minute. The rest of your party is already in the spa."

So Posey brought her partner, Brent, and Tariq would have brought his. That means Nate must not have anyone special in his life, and he must have either assumed I didn't or asked Posey. Knowing his status, and the thought of him asking Posey, even if it was just transactional, makes my pulse climb.

In the women's locker room, I organize my clothes and other items longer than necessary while I wait for Posey to text me back, uncertainty thrumming through my veins. I check the time on the wall clock and realize I've dawdled fifteen minutes away, afraid to leave, which is a waste of this experience. I square my shoulders, tighten my robe, and head for the exit to the indoor facilities. Maybe Posey is in a pool by now, wondering what's taking me so long.

Nate and I agreed to pretend, and I can do anything I set my mind to for a few hours. Even pretend that Nathaniel Tucker doesn't still set my pulse racing.

On the deck, I scan the area with trepidation, but I don't hear any voices. Quiet meditation-style music plays over the speakers, and I contemplate what to do first. With all of us having preset treatment times, I'm probably stressing for nothing. Nate and Posey and Brent could all be in the middle of a service. It would explain why she hasn't responded. That thought lets me release my breath, and when I spot the steam room beside the locker room exit, curiosity gets the better of me.

With Reyes and Cruz, I've had high-end experiences, but most of those were restaurants or being in a box at sporting events or concerts. A spa is a luxury I'd never give to myself, and so even if Nate is here, even if it feels like a weird double-date scenario, I'm going to enjoy myself. Experience it all. Take no prisoners. Bond with Posey and Brent. Avoid Nate like he's infected with a deadly disease. Perfectly reasonable behavior.

I hang my robe outside the door, relieved to see mine is the only one there, and I open the opaque door, slipping in as quickly as I can to avoid letting the steam billow out.

For a beat, I stand still, letting the plumes of steam swirl around me, moisture dampening my skin, and then I let out a deep sigh. Being alone with my thoughts might not be the best idea, but it's better than the alternative.

"That bad, huh?" a deep voice says from somewhere in the thick fog.

I jump, startled to realize that not only am I not alone, but the one person I don't want to be alone with is in here.

"Seems you might be in need of a day to relax and unwind," he says, still a disembodied voice in the room.

His voice, even detached from the intense physicality of him, still does strange things to my insides. My stomach flips, and heat pools low in my belly. His deep rumble reminds me of all the hours we spent on the phone, hushed whispers in the middle of the night, breathing in sync, a constant longing for each other that never seemed to subside no matter how close or far apart we were.

"I'll come back later," I say. "I didn't realize anyone else was in here." I put my hand on the door handle, but before I can leave, his big hand lands on mine, a gentle cage. I don't even understand how he approached without me sensing it. His chest, slick with sweat, presses against my back. My heart stalls and then revs, threatening to drive full speed out of my chest. Nathaniel Tucker is a shot of adrenaline, right to my heart. Fight-or-flight isn't what's happening, though. No part of me wants to run. My body, my traitorous, traitorous body, aches to sink into his embrace, back my ass up against his hips, see whether he feels what I feel. The best worst idea I've ever had.

"Don't go," he says, his breath stirring the wisps of my hair that aren't secured in my high ponytail. "There's plenty of room for both of us."

We stand there, breathing in short, quick breaths. Asking him what he's doing is on the tip of my tongue, but part of me doesn't want to break this spell that's been spun between us. It's deliciously familiar, and no other man has ever had the ingredients to make desire rise in me this quickly.

"Is there enough room in here? Feels a bit tight," I say, and I haven't turned around. The air is heavy around us. He's got me pinned to the door, but I don't feel trapped.

"Snug, not tight. Hot and sweaty," he murmurs. "I hear it's a good stress reliever."

"Yes," I say, my voice breathy. His words coupled with one of his hands covering mine, the other pressed against the door beside me, might be the hottest thing that's ever happened to me. Every point of contact is wild and alive. "Stress relief is so good."

"It's bad for you to keep it bottled up," he says, his lips so close to my ear that I think I can feel them even though I can't. Even though I want to.

"So bad," I murmur.

"You probably need that." His voice is smooth and deep and so close. "Some relief. I was hoping to help."

"You were?" I'm drunk on his proximity.

"Yes." His tone is now rough with want.

When I rotate to face him, the cool glass of the door brushes against my back, and my lips part with a little gasp. His gaze gets stuck on my mouth for a beat, and time slows to an unbearable pace. If it's possible, the air grows thicker, steamier between us. His thumb skates across my bottom lip, and I consider drawing it into my mouth, letting my tongue swirl around it.

Then he's scanning my face with that familiar intensity, as though he can't get enough of the sight of me. And I want to let him sink into me so badly. It's a physical ache, thrumming through me. My body is begging for what I remember he can give me, what I'm sure he could give me again.

"You're still so fucking pretty," he says, and his knuckles brush my jaw before his palm settles around the back of my neck. "Tell me no. Tell me to walk away. Tell me you don't want any of this."

"Nate," I say, my tone pleading, but I have no idea what I'm pleading for. Mercy? And I'm not even sure what that would look like, whether it would mean fucking me here in the steam room or turning and walking away. The smart choice is obvious, but I've never been smart with Nate, and that's always been my problem.

"Tell me," he says.

"You don't want this," I say, suddenly desperate to keep what little space still exists between us. "You don't want me."

"Don't tell *me* what I do or don't want," he says, his voice like gravel. "What I *want* is for you to tell me you still feel *this*." And the way he says the word, he might as well be slipping a hand inside my bathing suit, separating the folds, finding me hot and ready.

My brain almost short-circuits with how badly I want him, but a tiny voice from my subconscious wonders whether Nate is the type to play games now. I hurt him; he hurts me. Maybe getting me to admit I still want him, that I'm the one who couldn't let go, is what he needs so he can reject me, get revenge for how I abandoned us.

"If you don't want this, you need to tell me now." His thumb makes slow circles on my neck, distracting me, making me want to arch into the contact. "Otherwise, I'm coming for your heart, Hols. And I won't stop until you're Hollyn Tucker, and everyone knows you *were* always, *will* always be *mine*."

A chill races across my skin at his words, like someone doused me in cool water. I'll never be Hollyn Tucker, and I sealed that fate when I left last time. The air around us is stifling, hard to breathe.

"I can't," I say, my voice cracking, gasping for air. "I can't." I shove him away, and he stumbles back, far easier than I would have expected. But he doesn't say anything, doesn't try to stop me.

Head down, I slip out the door, grabbing my robe and tying it tightly, before disappearing back into the women's locker room.

And I fear the only thing this day will bring is a desire for things I'll never have again.

Chapter Seventeen

HOLLYN

After I gather myself in the locker room, I head to the outdoor pool, hoping some fresh air might restore my balance. There, I find Posey sipping a blue cocktail on a lounger.

"I wondered where you were," she says, and she presses a button on the side table where her drink rests. There's no sign of her phone, which might explain why she didn't text me back.

A waiter dressed in black-and-white emerges from the double doors farther down the patio. He comes straight for us as I settle into a lounger beside Posey.

"Would you like a drink, Ms. Davis?" he asks with a polite smile.

"Bellerive sweet tea?" I ask with a hopeful note in my voice. Most places on the island don't make it the way my Aunt Verna used to, but if anyone is capable of a superior version, I figure this place will be it.

"Of course," he says with a nod. "Anything for you, Ms. Jensen?"

"I might as well order another one—save you a second trip." She raises her Bellerive Blue.

After he leaves, I let out a sigh. "I used to miss all the Bellerive-branded things when I was in New York. Some places try to imitate our more popular stuff, but it's never the same."

"Agreed," Posey says, sliding her glass back on the table. "I had one good restaurant near Northern University that I could go to that had authentic stuff, but that was it. Homesickness was real." She eyes me for a beat. "But I heard you didn't come home much at all."

"I didn't," I agree with a tight smile. "Just to get my sister, that's it. My aunt visited me in New York a few times. We'd go around the state, exploring little towns. I always told myself I'd outgrown Bellerive."

"I guess it's possible to outgrow a place," Posey muses. "When I left Northern University, I knew I was done. Satisfied with the experience but ready to move on." She shoots me a grin. "Or move home. Brent's ready to be done with the Olympics too. The next one is his last. His schedule is... it's a lot."

"You two have been together a long time?"

"Longer than I ever thought possible," she says with a laugh. "I was not a relationship person before I met him. But we just—I don't know—we work. We have a lot of respect for each other's hopes and dreams. We're proud of each other, and I'd never had a real partner before. But he is—he's my partner. He's the first and last person I want to talk to, every day."

It's been years since I've let myself think of Nate, of what we had, when someone mentions how great their relationship is, but that's where my mind goes now. The ache that blooms across my chest and zips down into my stomach is a reminder of why I've kept such careful control over any thoughts of him. When you throw away the best thing that's ever happened to you, it's hard to face that day in and day out.

Posey and Brent's relationship is exactly what I think I would have had with Nate if it had been allowed to flourish, if we'd been able to keep growing together in the same direction.

Maybe we wouldn't have, though. Maybe we'd have grown apart. How many people actually make it all the way with their high school love? There were a lot of obstacles back then, even if Nate brushed them aside like they were a mirage only I could see.

But what happened in the steam room earlier has me spiraling with deep, introspective thoughts that'll probably never have a concrete answer.

I made choices, and this is where we've landed.

"We're getting married at the end of production in September. Everything is all planned, so make sure you stick around for that. You're invited," Posey says. "What about you? Do you have a plus-one for the invite?"

"Not for a long time," I say with a shrug. "Relationships haven't really been my thing either." In fact, I got quite good at playing games and avoiding commitment in New York. Work and Kinsley kept me as busy as I could handle, and any man who managed to wiggle into the cracks was squished out without much fanfare. "My priority has been taking care of my sister."

"Hopefully your time here will be good for the two of you," she says as our drinks arrive, and the waiter sets them on the tables.

"Should we tip him?" I ask as he leaves us.

"All taken care of," she says with a wave of her hand. "Nathaniel made sure everything was included."

"Right," I say with a nod, and then I take a tentative sip of the drink. Immediately, I'm transported back to my childhood, to sitting at my aunt's worn kitchen table, anticipation bubbling in me for my favorite drink. The tea always had to rest long enough to finally be drinkable, but I could never get a straight answer on how long was long enough, which might be part of the reason I could never replicate the taste. The drink in my hand is as close as I've ever had anyone else come to my aunt's blend. It fills me with sad nostalgia.

"I worry about my sister being here," I say without thinking, the words tumbling out at the visceral reminder of my childhood.

"Why?" Posey finishes her first drink with a long gulp.

"My parents are master manipulators. They had my aunt wrapped around their finger. They were always trying to lead my aunt down the wrong path."

"You haven't had much to do with your parents while in New York?"

"Nothing," I say. "Kin hasn't seen them, other than the other week at the funeral, since she was really little. She was in foster care for a few years before I could get custody."

"Your aunt couldn't take her in?"

"No." Kin's foster parents were friends of my aunt's, so that part wasn't so bad, I don't think. I *hope*. Kin doesn't remember much about any of that. I didn't want my sister to have the upbringing I had. A tie between my aunt and my parents, as well as a source of guilt and stress. I didn't want Aunt Verna to take Kin out of the system because I knew I'd do it as soon as I was done with school. And that's what I did. "I took over responsibility for her when I could," I say, "and I ran far away from my parents."

"I would say it's only for a few months and how much damage could they do, but I don't tempt fate like that." She lays back in the lounger and closes her eyes to the sun. "My family is pretty chill, mostly, and so is Brent's."

That reminds me of how not chill Nate's family is. His siblings were often okay, but his parents... they were a much different story.

"I don't know how I would have turned out if I'd been raised in the Tucker family. It's a miracle Nathaniel and most of his siblings are good people. My mother is a force to be reckoned with," Posey says, splaying her hand across her chest, "but Celia Tucker is in her own realm. When that woman wants something—look out."

Truer words have never been spoken.

"Still," Posey says, "it's a shame about what's happening to her now."

"What do you mean?" Tension rises across my shoulders. My feelings about Celia Tucker are incredibly complicated.

"She has some sort of kidney disease or sickness? It's not cancer, but I don't know what it is. Basically, she might need a kidney transplant."

I digest the news slowly while I sip my drink, trying not to appear overly invested even though my heart is pounding and my brain is rapidly firing questions that I haven't let leave my mouth. "A transplant is serious."

"Very," Posey agrees. "Luckily, Ava and Nathaniel are a match, so the family has options. She's not going to die from whatever this is."

"Nathaniel would give her his kidney." It's a statement of fact. There's no world in which he'd let his mom die, let *anyone* die.

"Ava would too—though she didn't get the martyr gene." She grins over at me. "Despite their upbringing, they're all pretty close now, I think. The kids and the parents."

"Nate—Nathaniel and his mom are close?" When we dated, I got the impression that I was part of the wedge between them, so maybe it makes sense that after I was gone, they returned to normal—whatever that was.

"The siblings are taking her to her treatment appointments, and they've all rallied around her." She presses the button for another drink and then angles her body on the lounger to get a better look at me. "Is it weird being around Nathaniel now? Did Celia know you two dated?"

"She knew," I say, trying to make the words sound normal instead of strained. "Went about as well as you can imagine." I close my eyes to the sun and rest my head back on the lounger, pretending nonchalance. "And no, being around him now isn't weird." An absolutely massive lie. I've pushed what happened in the steam room to the back of my mind, but I know later tonight, after Kin is asleep, when I'm alone, I'll replay that scene with a very different outcome. I can't even remember the last time I was that turned on by so little.

Just then, as though to mock me, Nate and Brent wander out of the double doors. Every single muscle in Brent's body seems to pop, as though someone carved them out. Nate, by comparison, seems softer. Athletic and fit, and I find I'm genuinely attracted to that softness more. Brent's level of fitness doesn't seem real, whereas I can imagine myself leaning into Nate, resting my head against his chest, sliding my hand along his flat stomach, placing open-mouthed kisses in the hollow of his neck, which used to make goosebumps rise across his flesh... and then I realize my gaze is trailing over him as though he's a snack I'd like to devour, and I avoid meeting his eyes before lying back on the lounger again. I really hope he wasn't watching me the way I was watching him.

"Not weird at all," Posey murmurs beside me. "We'll have to get into how *not weird* it is later." Her tone is teasing, as though I've just opened the story of Nate and me, placed it in her hands, and asked her to read every page.

Chapter Eighteen

HOLLYN

Just like when we were kids and it took him a week before he returned to The Drunk Racoon, Nate's behavior after the spa is the opposite of what he claimed. And it confuses the heck out of me.

In the two weeks we've spent leading up to filming our first episode, Nate has been the consummate professional. He's so firmly cruising between the boss-employee lines that I've almost convinced myself I dreamt the way he veered so far off course in the spa. On the eve of filming, I'm sure I've completely misread Nate's intentions.

Which should make me happy, but his behavior has merely set me on edge, made me irritable with Kinsley, unable to completely focus on set, and I need to focus.

Once filming starts, we'll be zigzagging all over the place. We begin a project, work on the design plans for another, and film the result of a third. At any time, there will be multiple people, multiple spaces, to consider. Not only are Posey and I in charge of creating the design, but we're overseeing the implementation. I've redone rooms in people's houses before—even several rooms or spaces—but I've never remade a house from top to bottom. With the way the show works, if my designs are chosen over Posey's on a consistent basis or vice versa, we could end up extremely busy or feeling very inadequate, maybe even questioning our skills. The closer we get to the start, the more I'm second guessing my decision to stay here and take part in the TV show. At least in New York, I knew what to expect.

Twyla has given me one last outfit to try on for this week's wardrobe, and I've just taken it into the changing room, which is located inside the warehouse where everything is being stored for production. Getting ready to film has been a weird mix of bare bones and extravagance, but I have no idea if that's normal.

I'm wiggling into the skirt when my phone goes off. The message is from Kin saying that Shannon is taking her to the Youth Adventure Race Club so she can try it out. Turns out, after all these years of complaining she couldn't do dance lessons, she doesn't like dance anyway. Not jazz or tap or contemporary or ballet or hip-hop—she's tried them all the last couple of weeks. One class after another. Each one a firm "no."

I guess that's one less guilt trip I'll need to suffer when we go back to New York.

"Everything okay?" Twyla asks. She's come to interpret my silence from the other side of the changeroom door as dislike, which is often true. When I like some piece of an outfit, can see that it flatters the figure I've developed, I can't help oohing and aahing over it. But when an outfit makes me stare at myself in the mirror, wishing I was at least fifty pounds lighter, I barely say a thing.

"Just a text from my sister," I say, replying to Kin with an okay and zipping myself into the leather skirt, feeling my whole body suctioned in with the fabric. I don't even have to look in the mirror to know the silhouette will present my curves in a way that's inaccurate. "I don't know," I say, coming out of the room, focused on the skirt, running my hands over my hips, "I think people will call me a liar in this outfit."

"I think they'll call you stunning," a deep voice that is not Twyla's says.

I jerk my gaze up, and Nate is the only one there. Heat creeps into my cheeks, and I search the room for Twyla.

"She went to the bathroom," he says. "Why would anyone call you a liar in that outfit?"

"It's nothing," I say, tucking my hair behind my ears and looking over his shoulder for Twyla. Every nerve ending in my body is on high alert to have him so close and for us to be alone. In the last two weeks, if he's been close, other people have been around. Whether by luck or design, we haven't had a chance to be alone. There's always someone somewhere with an opinion or a question about something that demands his input, and the lack of one-to-one time has been frustrating and a relief, depending on the day. Being around Nate takes some mental fortitude, and it's exhausting to be constantly braced for an impact that never happens.

"Seriously," he says, stepping close enough that I catch a whiff of cedar and fresh air—scents that take me back to another time. Was he at the campground today? "I'm not going to let *anyone* be mean to you."

That causes a smile to rise in me, and I stare up at him, my lips quirked. "Oh yeah? Nate, I don't know if you've noticed, but the internet is full of mean people, and I'm going to be on a TV show. I'm practically asking for people to tear me down."

"No, you're not," he says, his brow furrowed. "No one asks to be torn down."

"There are probably a lot of reality TV stars who'd wonder if they did ask given their experience and the reaction from the public. Have you ever read the comments on some of those articles and social media posts and just... everywhere? Because I have. All my favorite reality stars have been trashed. I'm preparing myself."

"This show is about houses and renovations and decorating. It's not about whether a skirt makes you look like a fucking Greek goddess." His voice has grown husky. "And it does, by the way, make you look like a goddess."

Heat explodes across my cheeks, and I give my head a little shake. "False advertising."

"I don't see anything false." His knuckles skim my cheekbone. "Why does it feel false to you?"

Because you said you were coming after me and you haven't done a single thing since. I shouldn't want him to. Having him back in my life is already complicated, and throwing that door wide-open would be a mistake. The choices I made are likely unforgiveable to him. I'd be going back on promises I made.

Still, even though it's not smart, a part of me has wondered whether he changed his mind because not only are we different people on the inside, but I'm not thin and young anymore. The insecurities that I can keep at bay in New York are starting to poke holes in my confidence. The Bellerive stage with Nate and the show is big enough, but the fact that Interflix appears to be seriously interested in picking up the series off the back of the Prince Brice and Maren Tucker adventure race saga only increases the stakes. Part of me worries I won't be able to slip on the mask of cool confidence that I perfected in New York when it matters in Bellerive—with him or the show.

"I just think I need to be really careful about how I present myself," I say, trying not to give too much away. We don't need to become confidantes. That's a slippery slope that I've already gone far enough down.

"I'm confident people are going to love you." He inches closer and tips my chin to meet his gaze. "How could they not?"

I'm wondering the same thing about him right now. How is he still single? There's no doubt in my mind that women across the country—hell, probably the world—would do all sorts of incredible and terrible things to get a chance with Nathaniel Tucker. I had my chance, and I squandered it. Knowing what I know, it's not right to pursue anything with him, even if it really seems like he'd let me walk back into his life.

His proximity has enveloped me, and his aura of care and concern is the softest, gentlest blanket slipping over my shoulders. There's always been something about Nate that felt both unbelievably safe and yet incredibly thrilling. Even now, as my heart beats out of tune, frantic and flustered in my chest, I know he'd never hurt me, never do anything to put me in harm's way, would do anything to keep me safe. That's just who he is.

I'm not sure there's a mask that I can slip on that'll keep me from falling back under Nate Tucker's spell. If he wants this to happen, I doubt I'm strong enough to say no.

"I don't think this is a good idea," I whisper.

"Give me one legitimate reason," he says, brushing his nose against mine, his lips so close I can imagine how the mint of his breath would taste.

"I already gave you lots of reasons."

"Those were reasons an eighteen-year-old might have," he says, skepticism clear in his tone. "Nothing a strong, confident thirty-two-year-old would worry about."

Heels click in the hallway. "Oh my god, I'm so sorry," Twyla calls, just before she reenters the room.

Nate and I jump apart like her voice is an electric shock, zapping some sense into us.

"I'm not feeling well. It came out of nowhere." Her eyes are glassy, and her tanned skin has taken on a yellowish tinge. "I think I should go home, and I know I promised you a ride—"

"I'll take her back to the apartment," Nate says, cutting Twyla off. "That's not a problem. Go home. Get some rest. We've got Monday morning. We don't meet the first family until the afternoon to start shooting."

"Sorry," Twyla says. "So sorry."

"It's okay," I say.

"I love that skirt. We're keeping it," she says, grabbing her bag and pointing to my leather outfit. "We just need a better shirt to pair with it."

I give her a tight smile, unwilling to detail my insecurities in this room. "I'll see you Monday morning."

Once she's out the door, Nate and I stand staring at each other. The tension that temporarily left the room when Twyla entered returns tenfold.

"All your reasons are bullshit, Hollyn, and I think you know that."

"We don't know each other anymore." I search for something else. "And you're my boss. How would that look?"

"I'm *a* boss. Tariq runs the set. I just make sure everyone is happy, we're on budget, and general production runs smoothly." He searches my face for a beat. "If the answer is no, just say that. I can treat you exactly as I have the last two weeks. Completely professional."

I take in a shaky breath and press my fingers to my temples because I know deep down—actually, not even that far down—I don't want to be just his colleague.

Whenever he's in a room, I'm hyperaware of where he is and who he's talking to, and I have no claim to him.

"We don't know each other anymore," I try again, the same argument that I know he can brush aside. The solution is easy and obvious.

"You said you *can't* at the spa, not that you *won't*. Maybe we don't know each other, but we both know that's laughably solvable. The only real obstacle to us trying again is if you don't *want* to."

His rich-boy confidence is out in full force. I loved it when we were teenagers because so few people in my life were confident with good intentions, and Nate's intentions were always good. But sometimes I loathed his execution. He often put me in sticky spots with other people in my life without even realizing it. He's doing it again right now.

"When the show is over, I'm going back to New York. I don't want to stay in Bellerive. I don't want to live here."

"You want to put a ticking clock on us, is that it?"

"I want you to understand what this would be." Because anything I agree to has to be temporary and as far from public as I can make it. There are consequences, beyond his feelings, that I'd like to avoid.

"And see, I think you're the one who doesn't understand what this is. What it's always been." His tone is challenging, like he's daring me to contradict our connection that's so strong it's made the air in the room thick and heavy.

"Nate, I—" My phone chimes from inside the changing room, and I take the opportunity to break the tension between us by striding into the changeroom and closing the door. I scoop up my phone and see texts from both Shannon and Kinsley. The Youth Adventure Race Club ran around Victor Tucker's campground, and now some dog on the property is having puppies. Kinsley wants to stay to watch the puppies being delivered, but Shannon needs to get to work.

I poke my head out the door and find Nate running his hands down his cheeks, wearing a beleaguered expression. He looks how I feel—worn out by our conversation. We're going in circles, and we both know it.

The solution—to give in—feels easy, but it's the opposite of that. Giving in comes with so many complications Nate isn't even aware of.

"Any chance you can drive me out to the campground instead? I can catch a cab back to the apartment later."

"Cal's place?" A furrow appears between his brows. "Why are you going there?"

"A dog is having puppies, apparently?" I flash my phone at him. "Kin is out there running with the adventure race club, and she wants to be there for the puppies being born."

"I'll drive you," he says without hesitation.

The last thing we need is more time alone, but a little thrill goes down my spine at the chance to be with him a little longer. "Thank you," I say as I close the changing room door.

Chapter Nineteen

NATHANIEL

I can count on one finger the number of times I've wanted something and not gotten it, where money or perseverance hasn't given me the result I was after.

Initially, I planned to pursue Hollyn whether she agreed or not, but as I let that idea percolate for two weeks, I couldn't get it to filter properly. There are people I will railroad into doing what I want, but the truth is that pursuing her relentlessly didn't work out for me the first time. Ignoring her objections didn't get the result I wanted, and I have to be mindful not to make the same mistakes.

When I was a kid, I was content to be the one who could see a clear future together laid out before us. I always thought she'd catch up—one day, she'd wake up and realize what I already knew—but instead, she woke up and realized she wanted out completely. Even now that she's told me why, her reasoning refuses to fully settle in my mind or my heart.

This time, if I'm going after her, I want her to be choosing me too. She doesn't have to want our future together the way I do—not yet—but I don't want to convince her we're worth another shot. I want her to acknowledge what I already know. There's something undeniable between us. Turns out years, distance, and truckloads of hurt feelings changed nothing. Not for me, and I swear to fucking god, not for her either.

Instead of pressing her for an answer when we get to my car, I let us ride in silence for a few minutes. The air is dense with tension, with the things we're not saying, the truths we're not quite giving.

I remember when we first started dating last time, what a delicate balance it felt like in the beginning. Pursue her but not so hard that I'd put her off or scare her away, and that's what I'm feeling now. If I push harder than she's comfortable with, she'll tell me no. There's steel underneath her that wasn't there when we were kids. Back then, she was too used to bending to other people's whims and wills. To survive in her family, to keep her job, that's what she had to do. A true people pleaser, at least with everyone else.

I've seen the change in her the last couple of weeks while we've worked together. She's learned to say no and to be firm in her opinions, to trust her gut instincts. I'd rather circle around a yes than draw a straight line to no.

"There never used to be any animals at the campground," Hollyn says, staring out the window as the ocean scenery passes us by. "How long have they had a dog?"

"It's recent. Uncle Victor was against animals on the property, but since Cal has taken over, things have changed. He has some chickens, a couple of goats, and some bunnies in a small petting zoo–type area. Campers love it. The dog came from my sister."

"Which one?"

"Maren. Her newest charity project is the animal shelter, rescue, whatever you want to call it. She tried to talk me into taking one of the animals too. Get them out of the kennels and into a home. Make them more adoptable."

Hollyn's lips twitch, and it feels like she's trying to hold back a comment.

"Say it."

"You'd be a terrible foster parent," she says with a slight smile.

"What?" I splay my free hand against my chest while my other continues steering the car. "I'd be an *incredible* dog parent. You need to explain yourself."

"Maren wants to make them more adoptable? By whom? You? Once a dog is in your house, it won't be fostered. It'll be adopted. So you're right. You'd be an incredible dog parent, but a much less successful foster dog parent." She laughs. "Rescuing wounded things is totally your thing."

Even though I know she's right, I press back. "Name one time."

"I can name several times." She raises her five fingers and starts to count them off. "One time, you rescued an injured pigeon from traffic in the middle of downtown Tucker's Town. A *pigeon*. To be fair, watching you do that was probably one of the funniest things I've ever witnessed. For an injured bird, it was pretty spry."

"I couldn't just let someone run over it." But she's right. For a bird that couldn't fly, it was alert and agile and fucking hard to catch. If I close my eyes, I can still remember the sound of her laughter floating out my vehicle window while I tried to outwit the thing. "I suppose that's one."

"I'm not done," she holds up her hand. "Anytime you saw a homeless person, you gave out gift cards to Donuts and More, the biggest coffee-and-food chain on the island. Like the cards appeared magically in your wallet, but you obviously went out of your way to make sure you always had some." She pauses for a second and then says, "The reason you started chopping wood at the campground was because Cal broke his arm one summer and couldn't do it. Instead of Victor hiring someone, you took over the job. It wasn't like Cal's dad couldn't afford to get help."

I can feel her searching my profile while I'm focused on the road, even though I could drive the route to the campground in my sleep.

"You organized a clothing and toy drive to support all the women's shelters across the island before I even met you. I found that out from Aunt Verna."

"That was a Tucker family initiative." But it was my idea—mine and Sawyer's, and I was the one who pitched it to my parents. A goodwill gesture that would benefit a lot of women and children. My parents only appreciated charity endeavors that raised their profile.

She takes a shaky breath. "And then there was me."

"You were *not* wounded," I say, a reflex.

"I was. You know I was. In so many ways. In ways you never heard about, in ways you did. I survived in Bellerive, but I never thrived."

"You were my Helen of Troy, Hols. I would have waged all the wars for you." I can't keep the husky emotion out of my voice. "The people who pushed you around, tried to manipulate you, I would have stood at your back and let them know there was a brick wall they couldn't cross or scale or knock down." I let out a whoosh of air. "If you'd let me, I'd have done it even more than I did."

"Ironic, isn't it?" She's staring out the window again when I glance at her. "You tried to help me, and you were also the only person I could say no to."

"I like to think I was the only person you knew you could say no to. That I wasn't going anywhere. I would never punish you for saying no."

"I made so many mistakes," she whispers.

"We were young. We were bound to make mistakes. But our older selves don't have to keep paying for those mistakes. We can move past them."

"Can we?" When she looks at me, there are tears in her eyes.

"We can." I keep my voice firm, but her tears are making my heart expand in my chest, make me want to pull over the car and soothe all her hurt. I want to tell her that whatever spooked her back then is long gone. But I'm worried if I remind her too much of the past, she'll dwell too closely on why she left. And I want her in the present, in this moment, where the air between us is filled with sadness, but also possibilities. We're on the cusp of something.

"I just don't see how you can forgive me," she says, her voice thick with unshed tears. "Not this easily. It doesn't make any sense. I ruined everything."

"Not ruined," I say, and I pull over to the side of the road so I can face her fully. The balance here is delicate, and I need to give her my full focus. "Delayed, not ruined."

"There are things..." She visibly swallows. "There are things that happened back then that might change your mind."

I take a beat to search inside myself for what could have possibly happened that would cause me to believe we were ruined. There's only one thing. "Was there someone else?"

Hollyn goes pale in the bright sunlight streaming through the window. "What?"

"Did you leave because you cheated on me?"

"No!" Her eyes go wide, and she looks genuinely shocked. "No. Never. I can't... Even after I left, there was no one for a really long time."

I want to tell her it was the same for me. That she ripped my fucking heart out and I was never able to give it to anyone else the same way again. But a guilt trip isn't going to get me what I want. Whatever she's not telling me left a deep wound in her, the same as it left in me. At some point, maybe we'll talk about those wounds—we probably have to—but I need her to trust me again first. I need her to understand that I'm not going anywhere.

Maybe it's rash and sudden and completely ill-advised, but I'm *in* this, as deeply as I was the first time. She's still in my blood, and while this feeling might have lain dormant for years, it's back raging through me again. The last two weeks, it's been painful to pretend we're merely colleagues. I can't just let her walk away a second time.

Her phone rings in her bag, and she digs through it, sniffing. "It's Kin," she says to me, a hint of apology in her voice. "Hello? Yep. No. We're almost there."

With reluctance, I put the car back into drive and signal onto the highway.

"No, no, I'm fine," she says, but I can hear the wateriness in her voice, the same thing Kinsley must hear or sense. "Allergies, probably." She listens for a few minutes, but she's shaking her head as she does. "We're going back to New York in a few months. We can't keep a puppy. It would be miserable in our apartment." She listens again for a beat and presses her fingertips to her forehead. "Yes, we *are* going back. Look—we can talk about this when I'm there, okay?"

She hangs up, and heaviness settles between us again. We haven't resolved anything, but we can't move forward unless she wants to.

"Maybe the clean slate should be erasing the hurt but keeping the connection," I say.

It sounds so simple, and right now, on the edge of something new with her, I think I can let go of the past. If there is more to why she left and she never comes clean, I won't care enough to seek out the truth. Why would I prod that wound? But if I really let myself consider that, it's naïve to think I never will, but I also have no desire to head in any direction that puts a second chance at risk. I want her. I want what we once had so badly that I'll negotiate anything. If she wants me to pretend the past doesn't matter, that her reason for leaving doesn't matter, I'll grit my teeth and do it.

As I pull into the parking lot of the campground, Hollyn's wounded eyes see right through me. "There's no world in which you can just erase hurt, Nate. Hurt can't be ignored. Maybe you think you can set that aside, but I know from past experience that hurt coats everything, even when we don't realize it." She opens her door and leaves before I can say anything else.

Chapter Twenty

NATHANIEL

"I haven't seen you look at a woman like this since the last time I was in a room with you and Hollyn Davis," Cal says as he takes his place beside me, leaning against the kitchen counter, watching Maren, Kinsley, and Hollyn tending to the black lab and her puppies on the other side of the room. Mom and her litter are tucked into a secure corner in a baby pool with the three women fawning over the tiny pups.

"Fucking pathetic, right? After all this time to be right back where I started." I cross my arms, but I don't stop soaking her in. Sometimes, I can't quite believe she's back, that I could have another shot at getting the future I once wanted more than anything.

"Makes my stone-cold heart question whether I've done the right thing staying in Bellerive. Maybe my version of whatever *that* is exists out in the world somewhere. Someplace I've never been, will never be."

"Want to hear the kicker? I told her I could forgive her for anything if she'd just give us another shot. And I'm pretty sure she turned me down." The thought causes my voice to get raspy at the end. To have her this close, to know she'll be this close for months, and to have the answer to my question be a *no* is almost intolerable. "You ever considered becoming a TV producer?"

"No," Cal says with a chuckle. "I don't work for other people, in case you haven't noticed. That's why I like it out here. I decide who I interact with and when. Got people hired for all the rest." He gives me a side-eye. "You must regret telling Stewart to go fuck himself."

"I can't regret that," I say and release a deep sigh. "He would have been an asshole to her, and no matter what does or doesn't happen between us again, I could never knowingly hurt her or see her hurt." The black dog is panting her way through more contractions. "But I don't know how to be around her and not want more."

"Still the same bullshit holding her back?"

"Sort of. But I think it might be more that she doesn't believe we can get past our old hurts."

"Our? What'd you do to *her*?"

I scratch the back of my neck and try to formulate a coherent thought. "I don't know," I say, feeling my way through my response. "But it definitely feels like something bigger happened. I can't explain it. She thinks I'll be mad, but she didn't cheat."

"I'd have been shocked if she had," Cal says, going to the fridge. "Beer?"

"No, I gotta drive them home."

"I'm sure Maren would."

I just stare at him, and he laughs.

"Forgot who I was talking to," he says, popping the top off the bottle and taking a swig. "She thinks you'll be mad at her..." His expression gets pensive, and he shakes his head. "I got nothing."

"She never wanted me to get involved in her family drama. Was almost desperate to keep me away from any of it. Part of me wonders..." But I don't even want to think it, let alone say it.

"If she was in legal hot water when she left?" Cal frowns. "Wouldn't you have heard?"

"Maybe not? I went pretty far down the private investigator route looking for her. In hindsight, my eighteen-year-old ass must have hired the world's worst PI.

She was still in New York. She got a fucking degree." I drag a hand through my hair and wish I'd said yes to the beer.

"A lot of fun things about being eighteen. How dumb we were and how smart we thought we were wasn't one of them."

"I didn't look into anything *on* the island. If she made a bad choice, one she thought I wouldn't like, that might make things hard for me, legally..."

"She'd have wanted to protect you from the fallout," Cal fills in. "The same way you'd do for her. Again with the being eighteen and thinking we know it all."

"If whatever happened would have put her in jail, I'd have moved heaven and earth to take the fall for her."

"And Celia Tucker would have moved heaven and earth to keep you out of jail. Look what she did for Gage."

"Yeah, well..." I sigh. "Not sure Gage would say that Mom was helpful in that situation. I love her, but her help comes with strings, always."

"You did wonder whether Celia ran Hollyn off the island back then," Cal reminds me. "Did you ever work up the nerve to ask?"

"Mom said she didn't. *Promised me* she didn't." I run my hands through my hair. I'd needed liquid courage to ask my mother back then. One too many gold rushes, and I was grilling her, determined to get to the truth, even if it meant my relationship with my mother was fractured forever. "And why would Hollyn think I'd be mad at her if my mom was to blame for her leaving? That wouldn't make any sense."

"The easiest way is to press Hollyn to tell you."

"No," I counter, "the easiest way is to let it go. As long as whatever took place back then isn't going to happen again, none of that matters. She wasn't unfaithful, and that's really the only thing I couldn't have stomached, would have struggled to get over."

Cal raises his eyebrows and takes another long sip of his beer. "We'll see how long that certainty lasts. Curiosity, man. Even if you can get past the hurt, you'll always wonder why."

"As long as I've got her again," I say, "I don't need to understand why." And despite what Hollyn said earlier, I'm almost sure that's true.

By the time the last puppy is born, it's the middle of the night. Kinsley and Maren have made plans to get Kinsley out to the runs, hikes, and paddles around the campground for the rest of the week, with Maren playing coach and taxi driver.

"Since I'm already going to be out here," Kinsley says, eyeing Cal and then the ten black puppies nestled into their mother, "maybe I could help look after the puppies each day after training?"

"No," Hollyn says without a moment's hesitation. "Maren's a busy woman, and I don't have a car to come pick you up. We're not inconveniencing her."

"My schedule is pretty tight some days," Maren admits, but I can hear the reluctance in her voice. She's already said she thinks Kinsley is a strong runner, and there's nothing my sister loves more than tapping into potential. She won't want to deter Kinsley from training in any way.

"I can play Uber driver," I say. "My schedule is flexible. I can pick her up or drop her off. She can stay longer and help Cal here at the farm—I mean, campground." I wink at Cal, and he rolls his eyes. The last thing he'll want is regular company, but I also know he won't break Kinsley's heart just because he enjoys his solitude.

"Really?" Kinsley's tired but delighted gaze meets mine. She reminds me so much of a younger, less jaded version of her sister. I might have disagreed with Hollyn in the moment, but there had been a certain wary, wounded quality to her when we were teenagers.

"Really," I say. "Assuming it's okay with Hols." I nod toward Hollyn, trying out one of my old nicknames for her.

Kinsley's gaze tracks between me and Hollyn, as though she's finally catching on that there's history between us. "What do ya say, Hols?" She lifts her eyebrows at her sister, a challenge.

Hollyn bypasses Kinsley and meets my gaze for one of the first times since we left the car. "You don't have to..."

"I know," I say, letting my response sit between us for a beat. "She reminds me of you, though, so it's hard not to."

Hollyn flushes, and Maren and Cal pretend to gather up things to get us all out of here. I'm done holding my cards close to my chest. It's not who I am, and it's not how I feel.

"It's fine, Hollyn," I say, again. "As long as you're okay with it."

Hollyn nods, and Kinsley lets out a squeal of delight, rushing over to the mom dog to give her a gentle pat and to speak quietly to her for a moment before gathering up her things.

"You can come play with the puppies too," I say to Hollyn as we walk to my car.

She shakes her head. "I don't like getting attached to things I know I can't keep."

Her comment is heavy with meaning, but if she thinks I'm one of the things she can't keep, she's dead wrong.

Chapter Twenty-One

HOLLYN

Fourteen years ago

So far, being more open about our relationship has yet to bite me in the ass, but I keep waiting for the sting nonetheless. We get side-eyed when we go anywhere in his rich realm, but no one has said anything to my face. Around my neighborhood, everyone loves Nate, treats him like a son, and every time someone speaks to him like he belongs here, in my world, it warms my heart.

I'm sure it's because he's riding the high of his acceptance in my neighborhood that he's decided I should formally meet his family. I've met his sisters and brother in passing a few times, but his parents have remained aloof and out of the picture. Up until now, I've been grateful. None of the stories about Celia and Jonathan Tucker are flattering.

I'm rushing around the apartment, putting the final touches on the dress, shoes, and jewelry Nate bought me to meet his parents. He didn't say it, but I know he's trying to conceal just how poor Aunt Verna and I are. He was very careful with his words the day when he took me shopping in downtown Tucker's

Town, as though he thought I'd object to his efforts or be offended by his money. To be fair, in my neighborhood, I *am* both of those.

But I don't want to be a source of conflict between him and his family, and I can already sense it brewing under the surface. I know what it's like to be attacked from within, and I wouldn't wish it on anyone.

A key slots into the lock on the apartment door, and I check the clock on the wall. Aunt Verna should still be at her shift at the café. If she got fired or she's sick, I'll need to pick up extra shifts at The Drunk Racoon to make sure our rent and bills get paid this month.

Instead, in waltzes Mickie, as though it's my mother who lives here, not my aunt.

"What are you doing here?" I ask, and terror creeps into my throat. Aunt Verna told me she took back the key from Mickie, didn't give her the new entrance code to the front door.

"Came to see my daughter. Heard you had a special event tonight." She throws herself into the worn couch and grins at me. Her blond hair is cut into a short, straight bob. The wave in my hair comes from my father's side of the family. "Talk all over the neighborhood how you landed yourself a Tucker. My baby!" She exclaims with a laugh. "God, you've done good, and without me to teach you."

I can't speak, afraid to set her off. She's prone to throwing things, dragging me across a room, screaming at the top of her lungs, using her razor-sharp nails like knives. I can't smell any alcohol from here, which is good. She's so much worse when she's been drinking.

She eyes my figure in the navy dress and low heels. Her gaze sticks to the necklace around my throat, the one Nate bought me for tonight. Even in the dim lights of the apartment, the small sapphires and diamonds are probably twinkling—they were in the bathroom mirror when I put it on.

"You ditch the birth control yet? Getting that boy's seed in you is the best ticket to a good life. From what I hear, he's not like his dad. He'd actually look after you and the kid, not let his baby mama and bastard run all over Bellerive, the rest of the world, as though they were nothing to him. Or *force* you into *other* options." The way she says it makes me think there's a story there, but I'm not digging.

I shake my head. "It's not like that."

"You're not fucking him? Bullshit." She gives me a disgusted look. "I've heard about the two of you, fucking horny as hell all over the neighborhood. Heard he stood on a table and declared his love for you." She makes my relationship sound dirty, as though there's nothing real about it. "If you're not fucking him and you got that declaration"—she eyes me again—"good on you, I suppose. But you really should not waste this opportunity. Nailing a *decent* Tucker is like winning the lottery in Bellerive." A small smile plays on her lips. "Is he decent?"

I bite my lip and scan her face, trying to determine her mood, what might come from any admission or denial. If it seemed like the best way to handle it, I'd make Nate look bad to her, awful, even. But I just can't tell what she's after. She can't force me to get pregnant.

"He's decent," I admit, thinking that's the biggest understatement of my life.

"Perfect," she says, planting her hands on her slender thighs and rising to her feet. She sashays to me, a walk that probably lures in men but only makes me tense with impending trouble. My mother is always most relaxed before she lets loose. "Your father and I have a new investment, but we need some capital."

"What does that mean?"

"It means I need you to ask good ol' Nate for a cash donation to the Thompson-Davis bank. An investment, if you will, in our newest venture. He's so keen to be part of the family, so he might as well drop some cash into the well as a goodwill gesture."

"I'm not asking Nate for money," I say, the words spilling out of me before I can consider their full impact. I should have lied, told her I'd ask. Or admitted that Celia still controls *all* the purse strings.

Her hand snakes out, grabbing a fistful of my hair, the careful waves I just finished crafting before she arrived crumpling. "You fucking will, you little whore. I need fifty thousand dollars, and that's a drop in the bucket for your boy. He's probably got that sitting in his personal bank account right now." She tightens her grip, making me cry out.

"No," I say, tears springing to my eyes. Nate is the one good thing I have, and I'm not tarnishing it for her.

"He bought this for you, didn't he?" Her other hand seizes my necklace. She pulls hard, and when the necklace doesn't break, she spins it around and unlatches it with a deft flick of her fingers. When it drops to the ground, she brings me down with her, her fist still firm in my hair. "Probably worth a couple grand." She measures the weight of the gold and jewels in her hand, and then she forces me to meet her gaze. "You don't want to see what I'll do to get what I want."

I've seen it plenty of times.

The buzzer on the door sounds to signal Nate's arrival to pick me up, take me to his parents' house. Except I've started crying, my makeup smeared, and my hair will have the indent of my mother's hand.

"If you get pregnant, you won't even have to ask him for the money. It'll be your money too."

"Stop," I whisper. "Please stop."

She lets go of my hair, flinging me back onto my ass. My dress hiked up my thighs. "Best get yourself cleaned up. Don't want the pretty boy thinking he's slumming it."

"He'll ask about the necklace," I say as she heads toward the apartment door, leaving me sprawled on the floor.

"Tell him you gave it to me as a push present, for giving you life." She faces me, her lips quirked up into a half smile, her hand on the door. "And then ask him for my money. You won't like what I do to get it otherwise."

My phone starts ringing in the clutch Nate bought me, the one resting on the coffee table. He's probably wondering what's taking me so long. I just hope Mickie went out a side door and not past him at the front.

Taking a deep breath, I go to the buzzer, and I ring him in without a word. My throat still feels tight with tears. I leave the apartment door unlocked and head to the bathroom.

"Hols?" Nate's voice echoes through the apartment as he enters.

"Out in a minute," I say, injecting false brightness into my tone. In the bathroom mirror, I frantically fix my makeup and try to wrangle my hair back into the careful waves I constructed.

Then I stare at myself, take in my whole face, still a bit unsteady from the confrontation with my mother, and I know in my gut that I'll never drag Nate into this mess, that I'll do anything to keep him safe from them, even if that means I have to let him go.

Chapter Twenty-Two

HOLLYN

Fourteen years ago

"I've never lived in a house," I say as we drive down the long laneway to his place that's perched near ocean cliffs.

"What would your dream house be?" Nate asks.

He asked about the necklace when we got in the car, after he commented on my bracelet and earrings. When I told him the clasp broke, he offered to get it fixed. I asked for the receipt, said I'd do it myself, and the whole time I was sure he'd realize I was lying, think I'd pawned the necklace for money or that I didn't value what he'd given me. But so far, he hasn't detected anything odd in my behavior, hasn't sensed my frazzled nerves.

"There's a house near Victor's Campground," I say. "On the other side of the national park."

"The gated two-story with the ocean view?"

"It doesn't look like much from the road because it's so far away with so many trees, but when I saw it from the water..." I trail off, unable to adequately explain how much I loved it. The house reminded me of photos I'd seen of antebellum houses in the United States. "The double balcony and the huge pillars—every time I look at it, I just think it looks like home." I let out a self-conscious laugh. "Why would I even think that? Stupid, right?"

"Why would it be stupid?"

"I would have to win the lottery to afford that house in my lifetime." Which reminds me of the comment my mother made, and I shake my head, realizing I need a new topic. I'd never want Nate to think he was my lottery. "I'm sure your house is also amazing. Have you always lived here?"

"As the story goes, my mother didn't like the original Tucker home that was here, so she had it torn down. Built this instead. That was back when my father ascribed to the 'happy wife, happy life' mantra. He outgrew that real fast, by all accounts." We emerge from the tree cover to loop into the circular drive, and I can't help drawing in a sharp breath. It's the biggest house I've ever seen up close. It's probably a mansion or a palace or something much grander than *house* by definition.

"That's what one hundred thousand square feet looks like, which is technically bigger than the palace... according to my mother." He shrugs and parks his car next to the other high-end vehicles sitting outside the spacious garages. There are six garage doors. *Six.* The front entrance looks like an expensive, luxury hotel, not a house.

Other than when we went shopping, this is the first time Nate's level of wealth has felt truly staggering. We spend so much time in my neighborhood or at the campground that I'm not sure I fully realized how much money his family has. Of course, I *knew*—everyone on the island *knows*—but that's not the same as understanding.

Staff greet us at the door, warm and friendly to Nate, assessing me. I never asked him if he's brought a girl home before, but their behavior makes me wonder.

Once we're in the entrance, they take my clutch, and I peer past the wide staircase to the ocean beyond. The ceilings are extremely tall, and the windows are expansive and all-encompassing. As soon as we pass the staircase, cliffs and ocean dominate the view.

"I can't believe you live like this," I say, almost breathless with the beauty of the house and the land and the fact that Nate is growing up here. "I don't think I'd ever leave."

He lets out a tight chuckle. "The view is spectacular, and the house is huge."

Heels click on the marble floor, and I turn to see Maren and Sawyer coming toward us in pretty summer dresses, their hair and makeup done.

"Mom insisted we dress up. Calista, the newest nanny, is still upstairs trying to wrangle Ava and Gage into something other than pajamas," Sawyer says with an eye roll. "Both of them have decided that today is opposite day—whatever my mom wants, they'll do the opposite. Dinner should be fun."

"At least it'll keep Mom distracted and gritting her teeth over them instead of anything else," Maren says, a false bright smile on her face. "Since they're being such little devils, Calista will be forced to eat with us, too, so Mom can shoot daggers at her for being unable to control Gage and Ava instead of at other people."

Nate slides his hand into mine and squeezes, and I realize he's nervous. Despite everything he's told me the last few weeks about his mom's bark being worse than her bite, that stories about her are exaggerated, despite the comments his sisters have made when we've run into them, this is the first time I've doubted him.

"All right," a female voice says from the top of the staircase, her tone echoing through the space below. "I don't care what you have to do to get clothes on those children, but it needs to be done. No one is going to the dinner table in pajamas. Tuckers don't do that."

Heels click across the floor, and the three siblings exchange a loaded glance that I can't quite interpret.

"Mother," Nate says, turning toward Celia Tucker, "this is—"

"Hollyn Davis," Celia drawls, and one edge of her lips tips up, which reminds me of the expression my mother wore earlier. Two women used to getting what they want, whatever the cost. "It's lovely to finally meet you." But her tone doesn't make it sound lovely.

"Thank you so much for having me," I say, confused for a beat about whether I should be curtseying or something similar, like I would for the royals. The way she carries herself is so different from Nate, who seems so normal in comparison.

Jonathan appears from the bar area with a tumbler in his hand, and I wonder if he was there the whole time.

"There you are," Celia says, a hint of exasperation in her tone. "Go upstairs and sort out your children."

"My children?" He raises his eyebrows. "You wanted them."

"I wanted babies. These preteens are a nightmare. Children should come with warning labels."

Jonathan approaches me and extends his hand. "Jonathan Tucker. Apologies for the chaotic start. Our two youngest aren't well trained."

From what Nate has told me, it's unlikely they ever will be. Nate says they inherited a version of the "don't give a fuck" gene that skipped Nate, Sawyer, and Maren. According to Nate, the three oldest know where the lines are and generally keep within them, but the two youngest gleefully run straight through the lines as though they don't exist.

"Oh, it's..." I give Nate a quick glance, unsure how to answer. "Families are complicated."

"Yes," Jonathan says, sipping his drink. "I'm sure you'd have learned that lesson well by now."

"Dad," Nate says, his voice tight.

"No point in avoiding the obvious, son. The Davis sisters have been well-known around this island for a long time, and while Verna might have settled down, I think Mickie's only gotten worse."

There's nothing I can say to that. He's not wrong.

"Dinner is served." A woman in a black-and-white uniform appears out of nowhere, and I wonder where dinner is being served. The table overlooking the ocean doesn't seem to be it, and the open-plan kitchen to our right is dim and empty.

"There's a formal entertainment area," Nate says, his lips suddenly close to my ear. "Follow me."

A formal entertainment area. Makes sense. What else do you do with one hundred thousand square feet of space?

We cross the kitchen, living room, and family-sized table into an adjacent room that's been set with formal place settings. The table is angled so that everyone can have an ocean view, and the sun is just starting to set. It's breathtaking.

"Oh wow," I whisper.

"Best time of day," Nate agrees, letting me take in the view for a beat while everyone else finds their seats. The table is huge, but it looks like only one section of it, the one with the best views, has been set.

He draws me over to two chairs looking outside, and I slide into the one beside him. There's a clatter from the other room, and two dark-haired younger children practically fall into the room. They aren't in pajamas, but Gage's dress shirt and Ava's dress look as though they've been through a war, wrinkled and disheveled. A young woman follows behind them, out of breath, and Celia glances at her, disdain clear in her expression.

"We'll need to work on that before we host another dinner." Her tone is directed solely at the nanny, which seems unfair to me.

For the rest of dinner, Jonathan and Celia mostly ignore me, talking to each other, admonishing Ava or Gage over something, or commenting on an event one of the other children are involved in. The meal, a lamb roast with vegetables I can't name, is the best food I've ever tasted, and I wish, more than anything, that I had a big-enough appetite to eat more than one helping or that it was possible to ask for the leftovers. Do they even eat it or throw out the excess?

After dinner, Maren and Sawyer take phone calls and disappear from the table, Calista practically drags the children back toward the staircase, and Jonathan tells Nate he needs his opinion on something in his office for a minute.

"Are you going to be okay?" Nate asks. The table is empty. His mother has disappeared somewhere as well.

"I'll go out on the balcony. Take in the view. I'll be fine."

He squeezes my hand and then rises to follow his dad. I wander out the huge sliding doors that are thrown wide to the ocean breeze. There isn't a lot of backyard before the cliff face, and I wonder whether anyone ever worried about the kids going over. There isn't a fence.

"Don't get too comfortable," Celia says from behind me, and I jump, startled. "A summer fling isn't the type of girl someone like Nathaniel is meant to marry."

Much like when my mother comes after me, my voice leaves me. Instead of defending myself or defending *us*, I say nothing.

"You don't think you're the first girl Nathaniel's brought home that he wanted to save, do you? My son does love wounded things, and you can't get much more wounded on this island than a Davis girl, now, can you?"

"I don't know," I whisper, and I genuinely don't. I'm sure, based on my neighborhood, there are people who have it rougher than me. I've got Aunt Verna, and some people don't even have that.

"He has such a big, open heart. Falls in and out of love so easily."

Unlike my closed heart that's never let any relative or boy or friend in too far—my Aunt Verna is it, and even the love I feel for her is conflicted by her close connection to my mother, whom I hate.

"I just wouldn't want you to think this is something it's not. His father and I are tolerating this dalliance because girls like you never last, and with him going to California for school, and you to New York on a scholarship... not exactly destined to last, is it?"

She must not know that Nate already floated the idea of changing schools after his first year. California is a family tradition, but Nate said he'd break it for me. Assuming his mother isn't lying and Nate hasn't said something similar to every other girl he's dated. I close my eyes at the notion, unable to believe it's true, even as a grain of uncertainty sneaks in.

"He'll go off to college, and he'll meet a girl who shares his values, who'll suit this lifestyle, who'll understand him in ways you never can." She spreads her arms wide. "I bet you can't even fathom this life."

I *can't*. But this life doesn't quite feel like Nate either, at least, not the Nate I know.

And maybe that's the point. How well do I know him after a few weeks? How long can you occupy a corner of someone's life and feel like you know the whole person? We've avoided confronting his wealth, which makes me wonder if he knows, deep down, that we can't work, won't work.

"Clinging on to a dream that'll never happen isn't good for anyone," Celia says.

"I think Nate feels like it will happen," I say, gathering the tiniest bit of courage.

"Oh, he might," she says with a little laugh. "He *is* a dreamer. But you and I? We're more practical. We live in *this* world, and part of that is realizing that everyone can be bought, has something they deeply desire." She smirks as though my agreement is a given. "The Davis family have *always* had a price. When you've got yours, you know where to find me."

"Everything okay out here?" Nate asks from behind us, his tone cautious, and I can tell he must not have heard enough to be sure.

"Fine," I say, giving him a half smile. "I was just saying goodbye to your mother."

"It was so lovely of you to join us," Celia says. "A truly unique experience."

But from her tone, I can tell she means for me to take the opposite from her comment—that these dinners are routine, that girls like me come and go often.

A little later as we're leaving the mansion, Nate's hand slides along the small of my back, and I resist sinking into the feeling, drawing closer to him.

"Is everything okay?" he asks. "Did my mother say something terrible?"

"No," I say, shaking my head. "I'm just tired." And that's true, at least. Exhaustion settles over me, a blanket I can never completely remove.

"I'll take you home," Nate says without criticism or hesitation. He takes my hand and draws it to his lips, and I savor the feel of him, close and secure.

The minutes tick between us on the drive back to my apartment, and I try to live in each one because after tonight, I know our time together is limited, slipping away with this endless spring and summer.

Even if I'm not one of a string of others, his mother's other points are valid. I could never live the life Nate does—I wouldn't even know how to. And if I could, I'd constantly be looking over my shoulder for my parents, for their outstretched hands, their schemes leaking into the crevices of our life. If I didn't poison his life, they would.

He can't help who he is, and neither can I.

Chapter Twenty-Three

HOLLYN

Nate keeps his word to make sure Kinsley gets back and forth to training for the next week as the production schedule grinds to a standstill. We were supposed to start shooting the first episode, but the Bellerive network behind the show didn't think there was enough drama in the outline and told production to hold until they were satisfied the content would draw viewers.

Nate said it wasn't a big deal, but Posey seemed a little concerned that the network didn't understand the vision behind the program. If there's one thing *I* understand from being in New York, it's that profits trump vision every time.

I'm not sure how Nate manages to give the impression he's capable of being everywhere at once, but that's how it feels. The minute anything shakes my sense of belonging or causes me to doubt my choices—a wardrobe fitting, a questionable line of dialogue the writers run past me, Kinsley's attitude—Nate is at my side, helping me adjust without sacrificing any of my strength. A gentle, solid presence.

Somehow, I forgot what a good listener he is, but when he's within hearing distance of a conversation I'm having, he seems to be filing the details away, helping to smooth out any rough roads behind the scenes. And it's hard to know, given how little experience I have, if that's literally his job or if he's doing it for me, specifically. I haven't had the guts to ask Posey if he's doing it for her too—I'm not sure what I'd do with either answer.

On top of that, each time he picks up or drops off Kinsley, he seems to sew her a little more firmly into the fabric of Bellerive. This week, she's been brimming with Bellerive facts, little known stories of the island, and a few well-placed nuggets about teenage me that Nate let slip. None of his memories are embarrassing, but the specifics surprise me.

On Friday, we've all assembled into the conference room to find out whether production is a go for next week, when Nate comes in last, rubbing his face. He slides into a seat beside Tariq. Felipe and Stewart are also here today, so I'm wondering if the news is bad.

I try to remember what my contract said if the show doesn't even get off the ground. My bigger worry is Kinsley. She won't take a cancellation well.

"One of the key ways the network can make money early is through product placement," Stewart says, clicking through the slideshow on the supersized screen. "Since this is one of the first large-scale Bellerivian-sourced and run productions, and we're anticipating being picked up by Interflix, we've had a lot of interest in products that range from Kale's Fried Chicken to Riccard's Heavy Equipment. They've all asked for placement." He pauses the slide on a long list of products and then clicks to a second, equally as long. "And the network said yes to all of them."

Posey gasps. "*All* of them? How do we maintain the integrity of the show?"

"They didn't agree to a verbal pitch for many, so it's literally a placement in a scene for a set amount of time. Tariq has a list of requirements and which episode we've agreed to use a certain product." Steward nods at the director. "The verbal pitches will take some finagling, and some of them specifically asked for either Hollyn or Posey to be the one speaking about their product."

"Are any of them design related?" Posey asks.

"A few, which is why we've brought everyone here. This might mean that you can't get your first choice of product for something if we have a sponsorship or placement deal. We didn't anticipate this much interest from this many parties, and we certainly didn't expect the network to agree to all of them—no matter how unrelated." Felipe sighs. "The dialogue might take some finessing, but the writers are aware of what needs to be done to make everything *feel* natural, even if you're saying unnatural things."

"We can make it work," I say with confidence, and when I meet Posey's gaze, I give her a little nod. "As long as we're free to alter the dialogue a bit whenever it feels stilted, I think we can improv things to make them feel natural." Posey and I already have a good rhythm to our conversations, and she's naturally witty. I just have to be able to keep up.

"I like your attitude," Felipe says. "Sometimes you gotta roll with the punches. We want to get the show up and running, and then we can try pushing back on some of the more absurd requests."

Rolling with the punches used to be my specialty, and while I might have gotten a bit out of practice with being hyperflexible—I learned that giving in only gets you so far in life—I have faith in Tariq, Nate, and Posey's direction, even if these other people don't instill as much confidence.

"If we want the Interflix pickup, we need to knock these first few episodes out of the park. Expect reshoots, multiple takes of the same scene, different angles explored on the competition between Posey and Hollyn. Anything that we can afford to run multiple ways, we will until we hit on a formula that seems to yield the highest interest"—Stewart glances at Posey—"while maintaining the integrity of the show, of course."

"Of course," Posey says, but even I can tell by her wry smile that Stewart tacking that on at the end didn't soothe her initial worries.

This conversation is making me wonder whether either of us will even want to do a second season if it's offered, even if Interflix picks it up. The only thing I'm not sure I can stomach, what I'm sure won't benefit my career in New York, is being embarrassed about the product we put out. Something kitschy and unrealistic will make my life harder in every way.

"We have a green light for Monday, so let's make sure we bring our A game and our flexibility to set. For the first few episodes, you'll get to walk through the house before we shoot so your design ideas are at your fingertips when you talk to the camera," Nate says. "The network has come in hot in terms of their involvement, which we weren't anticipating." Nate doesn't say that's because he and the government fronted most of the money, but I'm sure that's what he's thinking. Without a network to deliver the program to the masses, the endeavor means nothing, so I understand the push-pull he must be feeling. "Enjoy your weekends."

When I rise with everyone else, Nate stays seated for a beat, a pensive expression on his face. "Hollyn, can I see you in my office for a minute?"

He's been friendly and professional with me all week, and the only time we've slipped beyond work colleagues is when he has picked up or dropped off Kinsley. Even then, we're cautious with each other, as though we're balanced on the edge of quicksand.

"Sure," I say, smoothing down my skirt and following him out of the conference room.

Once we're in the office, he tips his head at the door. "Close that, will you?"

I do, suddenly a bit worried. What if I'm getting fired before we even start?

Nate's removed his perfectly tailored suit jacket, a look I've admired so many times in the last week. There's something about grown-up Nate, in command, sure of himself, that causes a flame to flicker in my core.

He comes around to perch on the edge of his desk, facing me, and rolls up his sleeves to reveal his tanned forearms. His lack of eye contact is worrying, even if my brain is focused on each roll of his shirt material that bunches just beyond his elbow. Desire and nerves form a confusing concoction in my belly. I don't sit down.

"Is it bad news?" I ask. "Or do you not want to deal with Kinsley anymore? Because I can sympathize."

He lets out a light chuckle and shakes his head. "No, I'm just measuring my words—trying to figure out the best recipe for success."

"You do that?"

"With you? All the time." Our gazes lock, and my stomach flips.

It's really unfair how attractive he is. Those eyes can sear my soul without an ounce of effort on his part. Looking at him is physically painful sometimes. We were together for such a short amount of time—one summer—but the emotions were infinite, unending, heart-wrenching. God, I loved him with my whole fucking heart. Loved every inch of him, inside and out.

That's really the problem with being around him now—even if Nathaniel lost all his hair, gained five hundred pounds, became hideously disfigured, he'd still be *Nate*. The fact that he's maintained his gorgeous exterior is just karma's way of rewarding him while laughing at me.

"You don't have to watch how you deliver your words with me," I say.

"Yes, I do," he says, and his eyes light with amusement.

"Try me."

"I want to fly you and Kinsley to New York this weekend on the family jet. Kinsley told me she's a huge fan of Mia Malone, and I can get us tickets in a private suite in New York for Saturday."

"Oh," I say, rocking back on my heels.

"Yeah—see?" He gestures toward my stunned expression. "I can't just say what I want. My wealth freaks you out sometimes. It always has."

"Kin is a MiaMite," I admit, still processing what he's said. "Obsessed would be an understatement."

"She mentioned that you'd promised her tickets months ago, but then obviously you accepted the job here... and those tickets are hard to come by, apparently."

I can't even imagine the strings he had to pull to get us tickets at short notice. Her tour has been sold out all over North America. Mia Malone looks similar to Ariana Grande, sings like vintage Mariah Carey, and has the star appeal of Britney Spears or Taylor Swift at the height of their fame. And Kinsley *loves her*.

I'd promised the tickets knowing I'd have to land a big design contract to pull off the price, and then with Aunt Verna dying and getting the job here, the concert slipped my mind. Kinsley wouldn't have wanted to mention it to me in case I suggested we return to New York permanently.

"You're going to steal my sister's heart," I say with a half smile.

"It's not *her* heart I'm aiming for," he says without missing a beat. "What do you say? Whirlwind trip to New York? You can check in on your apartment,

Kinsley can see a few of her friends, maybe you two can grab anything you might have wanted to have in Bellerive that you never thought to bring..."

That would also appeal to Kinsley. Her stuff *and* her friends.

"Does Kinsley know?"

"Give me some credit," Nate says with a scoff. "I knew you had to say yes first. *She's* not going to say no, is she?"

"The three of us?"

"I secured four tickets, so Kin can bring a friend from here or from New York. I figured it would be more fun for her than hanging out with just us."

"And we'd leave..."

"Tonight. The New York apartment is available, so we can stay there. Maximize our time tomorrow before the concert."

I want to ask him if his mother knows he's doing this for me, for Kinsley. It's one thing for him to fund a TV show I'm part of, but it's a whole different vibe to whisk me and my sister off to a weekend in New York on the family jet and to stay in the Tucker family apartment.

Except, there's nothing going on between me and Nate. He's doing this for Kinsley.

Which, if I'm honest, is also for me because I'm the one who promised and wasn't going to come through. Nate saving my relationship with my sister one over-the-top kindness at a time.

"You know I'm not staying in Bellerive once our show wraps. Kin and I are going back to New York. So, if you think... I don't know... I just want to make sure that's clear."

"I know what you've said," Nate agrees easily, eyeing me. "And I know that we're adults and that New York isn't on another planet. It's one short flight from Bellerive. My stance hasn't changed, Hols. You don't want us, you don't want us. But if you think you *can't* have us, you're wrong."

Sometimes you don't understand you can hate someone for something they've done until you're confronted with the crime. *I* hate myself for the pain I caused Nate. Necessary, maybe, but unforgiveable.

"I get to pay for all our meals, including anything we buy at the stadium," I say.

Another amused expression floats across Nate's face, and I know that even if he agrees, he'll find some way to thwart my efforts. The number of times he let me pay for anything when I was a teenager, I could count on one finger. Of course, I couldn't really afford to pay for anything, but my pride wouldn't let me stop trying. He was the master of slipping someone his card when I wasn't looking or prepaying before we even arrived.

"Deal," Nate says. "Shall we shake on it?"

He extends his hand, and I eye it for a beat, nerves zipping up and down my spine. As our palms make contact, a shiver cascades across my skin, a familiar sensation. He has calluses, and I wonder if he still cuts wood with Cal, ball cap backwards, skin glistening in the sun. The thought causes my own cheeks to heat.

With a gentle tug, he draws me between his legs, and he releases my hand to run his thumb along my cheekbone. Gentle and intoxicating. Our gazes are locked, and there's a part of me that wants him to lean in, brush his full lips against mine, slide his hand into my hair, angle his mouth over mine, deepen the kiss, make me forget all the reasons I can't let us happen.

"I can't believe you're here," he whispers. "Every time I see you across a room, standing in front of me, literally cradled in my hands, I question everything. Do you know how often and how long I wished you were here?" His voice is gravel, scraping across my heart.

"Nate," I breathe out. I never let myself wish for him because I knew wishes were futile. I used up all my wishes on something else.

"I'm in no rush, Hols. I've got time, but I'm not letting you go without showing you that you don't *need* to leave. Not this time."

And then I do the thing I know I shouldn't, that'll only lead us into something that'll break both our hearts. I grip the back of his neck, and I kiss him.

Chapter Twenty-Four

NATHANIEL

Victory shoots through my veins, followed closely by intense desire. My body is so present, so fully engaged, that the powerful emotion would be unnerving if this wasn't Hollyn, if this wasn't how it was between us from first contact. I forgot how hard the sense of rightness hits me the minute we're skin to skin. Every inch screaming the same claim.

Mine. Mine. Mine.

Without pausing to question why she's kissed me, I angle my head, deepening the kiss, seeking a fuller experience. God, with her, I long for deeper. Nothing is ever deep enough, connected enough, close enough to satisfy whatever exists inside me that's so inextricably entwined with her.

The kiss is wild, unleashed. Passion races through me as though we've uncorked a shaken bottle of champagne, and the spray is soaking the room in anticipation.

I dip my tongue into her mouth, and she responds in kind. Her fingers are rough in my hair, as though she's fighting with herself, but I don't fucking care. We're doing this. Free-falling back into something. For weeks, I've been tiptoeing around her, hoping she'd come to me.

Now that she has, now that she's made the first move, I intend to make her glad she did.

I clutch her ass cheek and spin us so she's pressed against the desk. Then I've got my hands under the hem of her skirt, pushing it up her thighs. Her hips arch toward my body, seeking contact. This urgency, this need, is even stronger than when we were younger, as though it built up in the years between, as though I never quite released the full force of my yearning with anyone else. Or maybe this intensity only existed with Hollyn. Maybe we were made for each other, can only ever be *this* together.

Hollyn moans as I lift her onto the desk and step between her spread legs, leaning against her, letting the heat of my desire rub against her core, and the simple friction is almost enough to bring me to my knees. She gasps, clutching the back of my neck and my arm that's braced against the desk, and I swallow the sound.

There is no greater discovery than this fire, burning, the realization that I can still make her whimper, crave more. She's shaking with need, body primed and ready for whatever I'm willing to deliver.

I slip a hand between us, cupping her sex, and now it's my turn to groan at how soaked she is, so ready for me that my cock strains against my pants at the thought of sliding into her wet heat.

A tiny part of my brain knows I shouldn't be fucking her in my office on my desk as a way into a second chance.

The rest of me doesn't care what that part of my brain thinks.

She's *here*. For weeks—hell, maybe years—I've dreamed of this moment, where she'd come willingly into my arms. There are no brakes. I'm full throttle to the finish line.

I shift the edge of her panties to get better access to the bundle of nerves that'll have her panting and clinging and finally crying out my name. God, I used to love hearing her beg for more, the release, the connection.

When I dip my fingers inside her, making them slick with her need, she breaks the kiss and presses her forehead to mine, her breaths coming quick. Her nails dig into my arm, and these tiny sounds of desire keep passing over her lips, as though she's never wanted anything more than my hand in her panties, my fingers rotating slow, firm circles right where she wants them most.

It takes a herculean effort to keep the pressure steady and not rushed, to keep my mind focused on her and not on the overwhelming urge to drop my pants and let my cock seek her heat, delving into her sweetness once again.

"Oh god. Oh, Nate." The words are garbled, and she's clutching on to me like I'm a lifeline. "Oh fuck. Don't stop. Please," she whimpers, "please don't stop."

I scan her expression, so turned on by how into this she is. Giving Hollyn pleasure is a drug I'll seek forever.

"I'm..." Her head tips back, her auburn hair cascading down her back, and as she lets out a little cry, I slide my fingers inside her, feeling her squeeze around me as I pump in and out of her in slow, leisurely strokes.

Watching her come brings me an immense rush of accomplishment, as though I just won an Olympic medal. As soon as she starts to return to earth, all I want to do is create that rocket ship for her again.

"That was—" Hollyn starts to say.

Knuckles rap on my door, and Hollyn is off the desk like a shot, fixing her panties, tugging down her skirt, and I'm adjusting myself, already realizing I'm going to need to sit behind the desk.

"Nate, are you still here?" Posey says from the other side of the door, and the handle jiggles. Thankfully, whenever I close the door, it automatically locks to anyone coming in.

"One moment," I call. "Just finishing a meeting with Hollyn. I'll be out in a minute."

Hollyn's wide eyes meet mine as I round my desk, rotating a stapler and some papers back into place. I gesture to the chair behind her to get her to sit and act normal, but she puts her head in her hands instead, not sitting.

And there's the regret. Which, if I'd been capable of thinking with the right head, I would have seen coming. Her sudden acquiescence should have been a red flag.

"Hols," I say, my tone gentle.

"What was I thinking?" she whispers.

"I don't think we were," I say. The only thing I was thinking about was how fucking good she felt, how incredible she smelled, how her whimper still sneaks into my dreams some nights, soaking my sheets.

"We're in your office, and we work together," Hollyn says. "We aren't teenagers who can't control ourselves."

I mean, apparently, we are, but I'm not agreeing with or denying her statement.

The only good news about her obvious horror and disbelief over getting off in my office while people are in the building is that my raging erection has been reduced to the normal semialert "Hollyn has entered the room" position.

"Don't overthink it," I say, "there's no point—it happened, and we move on." I flick off my computer and brace my hands on the desk. "I need to talk to Posey, and then I'll drop you off at the apartment while I pick up Kin. She can train with Maren, Brice, and the team before we fly out. After practice, she can shower on the plane."

"There's a *shower* on the plane?"

"On the one we're taking, yes. It's new." Purchased by my father, who is in league with King Alexander in trying to lure a professional sports team to the island. The latest bid is for a professional ice hockey team that needs new owners or a new home.

"I'm having second thoughts," she says, twirling the bracelet on her wrist.

"No need," I say. "The plane is huge, the apartment building is even bigger, and the suite at the stadium will be packed with people. If *I'm* your second thought, you can tuck it back where it belongs."

"I don't want to give you the wrong impression."

"If I don't have to watch my words around you, you don't need to manage my emotions or expectations. I'm an adult. Deal?"

"You really think this trip is a good idea after what just happened?"

"I'll find Posey," I say, rounding the desk and grabbing the door. "Make sure you're ready to go when I'm done."

Then I leave the office before she can try to talk me out of what I know is inevitable, and it's a lot more than just this trip.

Chapter Twenty-Five

HOLLYN

The plane is absolutely gorgeous, modern and spacious with more seats than our small group would ever need. I'm deeply grateful that Kin decided to bring a friend from Bellerive rather than someone from New York, because it means that while Kin is in the shower, I'm not alone with Nate.

Unhinged tension must be radiating off me, and I feel sorry for Kin's friend, Indy, who, even at her age, must sense there's something off. Nate and I are sitting at opposite ends of the plane, as though we've never shared space in the world.

Whereas I'm stewing, unable to focus on anything, hyperaware of how my body was singing for him earlier, he's on his computer doing billionaire things as though he wasn't seconds from losing his sanity right along with me in his office.

Am I bitter about that? Maybe. A little.

If Posey hadn't knocked, I probably would have begged Nate to slide more than his fingers inside me.

Part of me can't help but wonder whether this is Nate now, whether what happened in his office doesn't mean anything to him. He was so casual afterwards—it happened, we move on—as though I was threatening to get too attached. Some clingy girl who doesn't know how to adult.

He's the one who keeps saying he wants me and then backs away like he doesn't mean it. Gameplaying 101.

His comment depicting me as someone hung up on something I can't have sets me on edge. It's valid, and I hate it. I can't stop thinking about how I basically ground myself against his hand. On his desk. Less than three hours ago. Desperate for him. God, did I really say "please"? Beg him not to stop?

My exact wording is a blur, but if I close my eyes, I can vividly picture the dark desire in his blue-green eyes, the way his breath came hot and quick on my cheek, the feel of his calloused hands guiding me right into the rough waves of pleasure. I can't even remember the last time I came *that* fast or hard.

Every time I look over at him, those moments in his office are all I can see. I don't even know how I'll go into his office again and not turn crimson with embarrassment.

But I also don't know how I'll stop myself from wanting to do it again.

We learned ourselves and each other during that spring and summer together—how to tease and taunt, make each other plead for release, every touch and caress that could leave us breathless with need. We fostered a connection that felt as necessary as breathing—and now that I've had even this thin slice of him again, it makes me feel slightly ill that he could have ever done any of that with someone else. It feels *wrong*. As though I've spent the last fourteen years in some parallel dimension and I'm just realizing I've been tricked into living a second-class life.

The bathroom door flies open, and Kin is in such a haze of excitement that she doesn't even notice I'm being weird when she starts talking to me, her mind already in New York. She's dressed in her favorite leggings and a Mia Malone T-shirt, and she quickly leaves me to collapse into the seat beside Indy, the two of them immediately consumed by giddy chatter. Nate was right to bring a friend for Kinsley—she's over the moon, and I can't adequately match her energy.

The rest of the trip to the Tuckers' NY apartment is an anxious blur of oscillating emotions, from frustrated and angry at Nate's detached politeness to lustful with an edge of hopefulness every time our gazes connect, even for an instant.

But anger and frustration are safer.

At the apartment complex, we take the elevator to the top floor, and when we step off, there's a door on either side of the hallway.

"We own the whole floor—two apartments," Nate says with a hint of apology as he unlocks one door.

The two girls pile into the foyer with high ceilings, overnight bags slung over their shoulders. There's an audible gasp from Kinsley as they get deeper into the space and then squeals of excitement. I'm sure it's bigger than any apartment Kinsley has ever seen, and I linger at the entrance, that faint hopefulness wafting back into my emotional landscape. I spent the ride in the elevator wondering how I could hide from our connection for the rest of the trip or smother it somehow, and now I'd give anything to have him stay for a few more minutes. This emotional seesaw is getting old, but I can't seem to get off it.

"The key," Nate says, dropping it into my palm. Then he removes another from his pocket. "This one opens my apartment"—he nods toward the door across the hallway—"where I'm staying, in case you need a break from their teenage moods."

"You know Kinsley well," I say with a small smile.

"I'm working on it. She's important to you, so that makes her important to me."

I don't even have to fight the urge to correct him—it barely rises. He leans his shoulder against the doorframe, as though he's waiting for me to either invite him in or dismiss him, but I can't work up the mental willpower to make that choice. I want him to stay even if I know it's better for him to go. He holds my eye contact.

"It's late," he says.

"It'll be a long day tomorrow," I agree, willing him to make the choice to stay or go.

"I'll see you in the morning," Nate says, a hint of a smile playing at the edge of his lips as he pushes off the frame and strolls to his door. I can see him from where I'm standing, and at his doorway, he glances back at me, and even from this distance, the air hums between us.

"Hollyn," Kinsley yells from inside the apartment. "Come see this!"

Reluctantly, I shut the door and wander into the open-concept apartment with high ceilings, tall windows, and expensive leather furniture. I clock all the brand-name furniture strewn around—tables, lamps, chairs, art—in almost-new condition. It seems like such a waste to spend so much money on a space they must not use very often.

Then I focus on Kinsley and Indy, who are strutting around the room, lanyards dangling from their necks.

"What are those?" I ask.

"Backstage passes," Kinsley squeals. "We're going to *meet* Mia Malone."

"I cannot even believe this," Indy says, hugging Kinsley. "This is going to be the best weekend of my life."

"And this apartment," Kinsley says, twirling around. "We could fit like ten of Aunt Verna's apartments in here. There are five bedrooms. *Five*!"

"And they all have their own bathroom," Indy says.

"The kitchen has all our favorite snacks," Kinsley says. "There's even a bottle of that Bellerive sweet tea you like—the one from that hotel—in the fridge."

I cross the room to the kitchen, and I open the fridge. Sure enough, my favorite sweet tea is there, and my mind ticks through how long Nate has had these concert tickets and how heavily he banked on me not being able to say no. As I open other cupboards and drawers, I find foods I've been eating at work as snacks or that I've mentioned having a craving for in passing during casual conversations the last few weeks.

"Wow," I whisper, and Kinsley's at my shoulder.

"Right? And he left us Mia Malone concert merch too. Like stuff people only get from the VIP packages we've seen people open on TikTok, and not like *some* of the stuff—I mean *all* of it."

When I glance back at the kitchen table, I see what she means. There are T-shirts, tote bags, stickers, pins, signed headshots, and I can't even see what else. It's an explosion of Mia Malone.

"There are three sets," Kinsley says as Indy sifts through everything and keeps holding stuff up for me to see from where I stand. "You get it too."

"You can take it to school," I say. "Give it to your friends." I like Mia Malone's music, but I'm not one to collect or fawn over fan apparel.

"Can I take some of it too?" Indy asks. "My little sister was so jealous I was coming here this weekend."

"Sure," I say. "Just divide it up." My heart is slow-thudding in my chest, and I can't decide if I need to leave the apartment or sit down. "You girls should get to sleep," I say. "Tomorrow will be a long day."

They grab their things and go from bedroom to bedroom, finally deciding on one that has bunk beds that look like pods built into the wall with an actual staircase to the top bunk and bookshelves stacked with books.

I hover at the door for a beat and then make a decision. "I'm just going to pop over and thank Nate for all this," I say.

Kinsley barely spares me a glance as she gathers her things for the en suite bathroom. "Sure. We'll see you in the morning."

"You're okay, Indy?" I ask, feeling a little uncertain about leaving them alone, even if I'm only going across the hall for a minute.

"Yep," Indy says. "Better than good," she says as she practically hops into the bathroom behind Kinsley.

I hesitate for one more beat, battling with my urge to be overprotective and questioning the wisdom of going to Nate's apartment. One close encounter today was enough.

But heaven help me, I'm not sure *enough* exists where Nate Tucker is concerned.

The girls are oblivious to my struggle, chatting to each other while brushing their teeth.

I slip out of our apartment, and I stand at his door. The key he gave me, presumably so I didn't need to knock or ask permission to enter, is in my hand. Without letting myself overthink it any longer, I slot it into the lock and push open the door.

"Nate?" I call into the open space. Unlike the first apartment, there's no entryway here. I'm into the open living room and kitchen immediately. The layout seems a little smaller than the other apartment—still high ceilings, expensive furnishings, but slightly cozier, as though people actually *use* this apartment. "Nate?" I call again, making my way deeper into the apartment.

I check the time on my phone and realize it's late. Maybe I should have just texted him. Maybe he's already asleep. I poke my head into the first bedroom, but there's no sign of him. Two bedrooms later, I hear a noise from across the apartment, and I head that way.

"Nate?" I call, tentative.

There's a set of double doors flung wide, and Nate's overnight bag is open on the floor, and then the sound of the shower finally registers. I turn to leave, realizing I should have texted instead of letting myself into his apartment like a creeper, when I catch sight of him through the partially open bathroom door. The shower stall is huge, and the big glass panels give a clear view of him, naked.

He's under the showerhead, one of his hands braced against the wall while the other is running up and down the length of his long, thick cock. Water flows over him, little rivers everywhere. My stomach flutters. And I know I should look away, that I shouldn't stand here, frozen and transfixed. I should back up to the bedroom doorway and call his name loudly, announce my presence. My heel rocks back on a tentative step when Nate moans, "Fuck, Hols," and I freeze again.

The tempo of his hand increases, and his head drops, mouth slightly agape. Heat pools in my belly and spreads lower.

"Oh, fuck," he says. "Hols, god," he groans. "Hollyn."

My heart races, and I know I should go, but I can't make myself move.

Then he must sense me or someone, and he glances toward the door. Our gazes connect, but his hand never slows. "Fuck," he mutters, but there's no edge of anger. "Hollyn," he murmurs, and then he shudders with his release, curling in slightly on himself, hand still pumping.

My eyes widen at the realization that I've been caught, and heaven help me, I *liked* what I saw. "I'm so sorry," I say, automatic.

He shuts off the water, grabs a towel, and steps out. He slings the towel around his waist, and he saunters over, his lean frame on display, not an ounce of outward embarrassment. At the doorway, he leans his shoulder against it, and his gaze sweeps over me, and I'm not sure if the desire I see in his depths is old or new.

"I shouldn't have just let myself in," I say again when he doesn't speak.

"That's why I gave you the key," he says. "So you could let yourself in."

"Obviously you didn't mean for me to see *that*."

"Did you enjoy it?" he asks, a mischievous light in his eyes. "I loved having a hand in you coming apart in my office earlier. Only fair for you to see me lose control at the mere *thought* of having you."

"I..." Words fail me.

"I've been getting off to your image in my head, your name on my lips, for years, Hols. None of that's new. I just got some updated material today, so I had to try it out. Watching you come, seeing how much you wanted it, how much you enjoyed it, might just be my favorite reel."

I close my eyes and press my palms to my belly. My insides are turning to mush, and I don't know if I'm going to be able to stay on my feet. I take a deep breath, trying to still my racing heart, the surge of desire that's threatening to overrule all common sense. "Nate," I breathe out.

When I open my eyes, he's right in front of me. He sweeps wispy tendrils off my cheek and behind my ear. His lips press a gentle kiss on my forehead. "We could have it all," he whispers. "There's no reason we can't if you want it too."

I give my head a little shake, and I step back. "I just came to thank you for everything, and I should have... I shouldn't have just barged in here. It's late. I'm... I should go."

"Hollyn," he says, grabbing my arm when I turn to leave. "How long are you going to run from me?"

"I'm not running."

"Bullshit. If this isn't running, what do you call it?"

Self-preservation. "I'm being a professional. We work together. Maybe if that wasn't the case..."

He laughs and lets my arm go. "You're hilarious. I don't even know where to start with that. Professional? What happened in my office today, what happened now—that's your version of professional?" He stares at me. "Is that what professional looked like for you here, in New York?"

I don't know what to tell him. Nothing about what I feel for Nate is professional. The truth will only make everything worse.

"If we didn't work together, if you hadn't taken the opportunity Posey offered, you'd have fled Bellerive without even seeing me. You've been running for fourteen fucking years, and I've been hiding from the fallout, trying to pretend your disappearance didn't wreck me." His jaw hardens. "I can forgive you for anything, Hols. *Anything*." He holds my gaze. "Because the fucked-up thing is that I think the only thing that'll fix me, the only thing that'll heal me, is having you again."

Tears pool in my eyes, and I shake my head. "There are so many—"

"Just go."

I stare at him for a beat, dumbfounded.

"You're just... just go." He flings his hand toward the door in frustration. "Obviously, you're not ready to be honest with yourself or with me."

Instead of doing the mature thing, I do what I've done best since we split—I flee. I run out of his apartment, into the other one, and I close my bedroom door and lock it before collapsing on the master bed in floods of tears.

I should never have taken this job, agreed to this trip. He might not hate me now, but he will.

Chapter Twenty-Six

NATHANIEL

The nice part about having two excited girls with us is that the whole morning has been filled with their chatter.

Hollyn and I aren't speaking.

Barely a word has passed between us since I went to their apartment to pick them up for the day of sightseeing and visiting their old haunts.

We ride in the car to their old apartment with the girls talking to the two of us or to each other, but we've frozen one another out, a thick layer of ice between us. As though both of us decided last night that we aren't going to start something but instead draw it to a close.

This stop and start with her is painful, torturous.

When we were teenagers, we were full throttle from the moment we met. I never had to put up with any back-and-forth, and even once Hollyn decided we were done, she didn't lead me on, drag it out. We had a clean break, which I hated at the time. Loathed more than anything that had ever happened to me. Her complete lack of caring broke something in me—I wasn't lying about that—and I think the only thing that'll heal that wound is to have her choose me. To have her decide that I'm worthy of the *forever* label I so desperately want.

As much as I long to chase her, I need to know she's choosing me. I'll woo, but I won't chase.

"When we're done here, I want to meet some friends for coffee," Kinsley says as we pull up to their apartment building.

"Coffee?" I ask, surprised, trying to hide my sour mood, not wanting to spoil Kinsley and Indy's day. "You drink coffee?"

"I do here. Everyone does." She glances at her sister, looking for approval. "It's one of the things we do together when Hollyn's not working. Which, like, isn't a lot, but still..." She seems suddenly uncertain, as though she might be giving too much away. "We have a coffee shop down the street that I meet my friends at when Hollyn is working."

"If you want to hang out with your friends, that's fine with me," I say.

Hollyn is staring out the other window, lost in thoughts I can't access.

A bright smile splits Kinsley's face, and she jumps out of the car, dragging Indy behind her. Hollyn leaves behind them. I tell our driver to find somewhere to park and I'll let him know when we're ready. I follow the three of them into the entrance and up the stairs to the second floor.

The building is older but not as ratty as I feared. Hollyn must make fairly good money at Reyes and Cruz. Once we're at the apartment door, Hollyn bites her lip and glances at me over her shoulder. Her long auburn hair falls across her cheek.

"You can just wait here if you want," she says.

If she thinks I'm missing a chance to see what her life has been like, who she's become, she's dead wrong.

"I'll stay out of the way," I say, not exactly agreeing with her suggestion.

As soon as the door is open, Kinsley drags Indy into the apartment, but they don't get far before they stop. The square footage is tiny—even smaller than her Aunt Verna's in Bellerive.

"This is where you've been living," I say, and I can hear the judgement in my voice, and I silently curse myself.

"Yes," Hollyn says, her tone bristling. "New York is an expensive city."

"I didn't mean that—"

"Look," Kinsley says, pulling down what appears to be a cupboard to reveal a single bed. "I sleep here, and my sister has the bedroom. Feels like so long ago already."

While Kinsley shows Indy where all her clothes are hidden in drawers and closets that should probably hold other important things, I trail Hollyn to her bedroom.

"You've been happy here?" I ask, drilling into the ice between us, testing its depth.

"Happier than I ever was in Bellerive," she says, and it comes out so quickly and smoothly that I know she means it. She spares me a glance from the edge of her shoebox closet. "I didn't mean... that wasn't meant to be..."

A dig. Still a hit, intended or not.

Maybe trying to pursue her *is* a lost cause. I can't seem to break through long enough to leave an impact. The thought causes a stone to drop into my stomach. Maybe I'm fooling myself to think whatever is between us is enough to overcome the past, the trauma of her upbringing, whatever sent her running and has kept her from stopping. I drag a hand down my face and turn away from her, going the few steps it takes me to be back in the main room.

Kinsley has another backpack slung across her shoulder, and drawers are flung open. "I'm never coming back here," she says to me and Indy.

I'm tempted to tell her that I agree, that the idea of the two of them living in this tiny apartment is depressing as fuck, but Hollyn might literally murder me if I fanned the flames of Kinsley's discontent.

"Some of my friends are meeting us at Kaelin's Coffee in twenty minutes," Kinsley calls out to Hollyn. "We're leaving."

Hollyn appears behind me. "I didn't say yes to this."

"He did in the car," Kinsley says, pointing at me. "It's not my fault if you weren't listening. Besides, I go to the coffee shop all the time by myself when you're working."

The claws are out, and they are sharp. "I shouldn't have said yes," I say, holding up my hands. "Your sister is right—that wasn't my place."

"She wasn't listening," Kinsley says. "The minute we're back in New York, it's like"—she waves her palm up and down in front her face—"the wall goes up and she's not listening."

I cannot comment on that, but I have a hard time believing Kinsley is being fair.

"An hour," Hollyn says. "You get an hour, and then you need to be back here."

Kinsley leaves with Indy, slamming the door behind her. Pictures on the wall rattle, and I raise my eyebrows at Hollyn, but I don't say anything.

Instead, I settle into one of the two armchairs that have a small coffee table between them. There's no kitchen table or even any discernable space for one. The place is crammed with storage and, if I didn't think Hollyn would object to me poking around, memories that I'd love to uncover. She's this puzzle that I can't stop trying to solve even though I know I might never have all the pieces.

Hollyn sighs, and when I glance at her, the toll that fighting with Kinsley has taken on her is obvious. Though Kin had a point about Hollyn not listening to her this time, I also understand how frazzled Hollyn might feel, 'cause I'm all over the fucking place with my own emotions.

"She'll be thankful for you someday," I say.

"Sometimes I think I should just sit her down and tell her in detail how much worse it could be. What her life could have been." She runs her fingers along her wrists where scars are either a faint outline or clearly visible. I haven't consciously clocked them like I did when we were teens.

Mickie Davis was a monster, and I fucking hated her before I ever met her. At one point, I even considered trying to sic my mother on her. Celia isn't altruistic, but I would have been willing to manufacture something my mother would care about, frame Mickie in a way that would make my mother respond.

But I never did because as terrible as Mickie Davis was, Hollyn's feelings were always conflicted because of her aunt's connection to her mother. Hurting her mother hurt her aunt. The worst tangled ball of emotion that left Hollyn, sometimes, unprotected.

"Other than 'because they can,' why does the Tucker family have two massive apartments?" Hollyn asks, toying with the shirt in her hand.

"My parents stayed in one, and all of us kids stayed in the other with a nanny." I give her a slight smile. "As you know, my parents ascribed to the whole 'seen but not heard' mantra as far as their children were concerned. And 'seen' was only when they felt like it."

"I heard you and your mom are closer now?" She's twisting the shirt, and she hasn't fully entered the room, despite the tiny size of the apartment, as though she's most comfortable close to an escape.

And the whole time I'm looking at her, there's an ache in my chest, this intense desire to minimize the awkwardness, recapture what we once had. Maybe I'm a fool for thinking it's possible after fourteen years apart.

"We are closer, I guess," I say tapping my fingers on the arm of the chair. "I grew up. Realized Celia Tucker did the best she knew how. Could have been worse." My gaze slides to Hollyn's wrists, and she twists the shirt around her hands and wrists, shielding them from my gaze. "She's got a protein issue with her kidneys, which could mean a transplant if they can't get it under control. The first step in the treatments they can do to kick-start her kidney into functioning properly isn't working yet, but the doctors have a pretty extensive plan of attack."

"You're not worried?"

"Ava and I are both a match for a kidney, so Mom shouldn't die from this, but I think it's definitely shaken her. She's not immortal and untouchable after all."

"Softened her?" Hollyn asks, and there seems to be a hint of hope in the question.

"I wouldn't go that far," I admit. "I'm still not sure it would be wise for anyone to cross her."

"I'm just going to finish getting some stuff together in my room," she says, and she takes the few steps back until she's out of sight again. After a few beats, I hear movement, rustling of clothes, opening and closing of drawers.

The briefest thaw in the ice between us hardened, too thick to penetrate, in the blink of an eye. It's so impossible to be sure if I need to push more, if I'm pushing too much, or if we're truly a lost cause in her mind. If only she'd tell me what she wants, not just what she doesn't think she can have.

We spend the rest of the day buffered by the girls and their excitement, and it's the only saving grace in what might otherwise feel like a descent into darkness. I'm starting to think I'm fooling myself to believe Hollyn will come running to me, embrace the reality of us. A few stolen kisses in an office might be the peak. I've made my feelings clear, and they just seem to create more barriers between us, not less.

The concert is loud and chaotic, but the private suite makes it bearable. I managed to get us into a suite with other studio and television executives, so this is as much a work opportunity for me as a kindness for Kinsley.

Instead of sitting with Hollyn, Indy, and Kinsley in the seats in the open area of the suite, reveling in the music, I'm back at the bar area, mixing and mingling, trying to drum up more investors in some of the projects people are pitching me in Bellerive. *Redesigning Home*, the show Posey and Hollyn are fronting, has cracked open the interest in reality-style television in our limited streaming-focused community. So many Bellerivians now believe our country is the ideal backdrop. Convincing others who reside outside our island is the trick.

Once the concert ends, we're swept up by people from Mia Malone's crew and taken to a separate oversized room where other fans with the same lanyards are already mingling. The meet and greet is militant in its organization, and as soon as we're in the room with Mia, she's bubbly and personable despite just doing a two-hour show. Indy and Kinsley only seem to fall more in awe and in love with her. The only moment that isn't joyous is when Mia's mother enters to usher us out, and a blend of annoyance and exhaustion seems to descend over Mia before she can conceal it.

Then we're back in the car on our way to the apartment, ears ringing from the concert, the girls high on adrenaline. Hollyn's been quiet all night, and I've compensated by talking to the girls or mingling with other industry people I recognized. I can't seem to find my footing with her, no matter how badly I might want to.

In the hallway between the apartments, the girls float in their door, elevated by the whole experience.

"We need to meet the car at eleven in the morning to get to the jet in time," I say, walking backward to my door. The whole day has been rife with tension, and I'm exhausted.

Up until this weekend, I felt determined, like patience and perseverance were the keys to getting her back, but I'm not so sure anymore. She's sealed herself off.

"Okay," Hollyn says, and she gathers her long hair into a fist and then lets it go. "Thank you, Nate. She'll remember this forever."

I nod, and I slot my key into the other apartment's door, feeling more defeated and unsure than I've been in a long time.

Chapter Twenty-Seven

NATHANIEL

I'm staring at the ceiling, debating whether I should get up and take a sleeping pill. After Hollyn came back to Bellerive, I went to the family doctor to get them. One week of sleepless nights was enough to tell me the insomnia that plagued me when she first disappeared had returned. For whatever reason, no one has ever impacted my heart and soul the way Hollyn Davis does. Invades my dreams, seeps into every crack and crevice of my psyche.

There's a sharp knock on my door, and I drag on the sweats beside my bed before jogging to the front entrance, my heart pounding that something is wrong. It's three o'clock in the morning.

I throw open the door, and Hollyn is in the hallway, a short, silky pink wrap hugging her curvy frame. Long, full legs go on for days below the hem, and I'm equal parts turned on and worried.

"Is everything okay?" I ask, forcing my gaze back up to meet hers.

She searches my face, and the tension radiating off her feels familiar, as though we're on the cusp of something I dare not name.

Then she reaches for me, hand around my neck, body arching into me, lips meeting mine.

For a stunned minute, my brain can't register if this is a dream or reality, but when she tries to pull back and I hear the tiniest noise of embarrassment escape, I wrap my arms around her and slot her tight against me, deepening the kiss.

"Don't go," I murmur against her lips that taste like mint and sweet tea.

"Is this what you want?" she asks between kisses, and I can sense the anxiety in the question.

"I want it all," I admit, "but I'll take whatever you'll give me." Any determination to hold out for everything I want went out the door the minute she came to the threshold. I can meet her where she's at. I'll meet her anywhere.

"I don't want to run from you. I've never wanted to run from you," she says.

I kick the door shut, and I spin her against the wall, caging her in with my body. I'm not in the mood to question or second-guess her claim. Forward momentum is enough, and god, I'm fucking aching for her.

Lights from the street and other buildings filter through the open windows, curtains thrown wide in the living space as I undo her dressing gown and let it drop to the floor in a puddle. Her negligee is the same color as the robe. It barely covers her figure, and I love it.

"Every inch of you is mine tonight," I say, trailing kisses along her neck, sliding my hand up her thick thighs to find she's not wearing any panties. "You're so wet. You've been thinking about this, have you? Fuck, that's hot. I love the feel of you."

Was she lying in bed, unable to sleep, knowing that I was just a knock away, that I could ease the restlessness inside her with my tongue or my fingers or both, over and over again? God knows I've been longing for her to ease mine.

With my free hand, I tease and taunt her breast, my thumb skimming her nipple before coming back to run the bud between my thumb and forefinger. Then I bend my head, kissing and licking her peaks through the silky material of her negligee.

Part of me wonders if I did take a sleeping pill—if this is just a dream, my subconscious on overdrive—and I'll wake up to soaked sheets and deep disappointment.

I palm her flesh, sliding my hand along her warm skin. If this is a dream, it's the most vivid one I've ever had. Her hands are in my hair, urging me closer, her body responding to each light or firm touch as though she's desperate for what only I can give her.

And I want to lay claim to every inch of her again, mark her with my teeth and tongue, leave behind a residue of my presence so thick that she'll never be able to scrub me out again.

On some level, I know that's not the right way to feel, that I shouldn't want her this violently, this completely and without compromise.

I urge her onto the heavy marble table near the entranceway, and once she's perched on it, I drop to my knees, eager to taste her. But I need to slow down, or it's going to be hot and fast and not at all how I want us to be. Or at least, not this time.

Hot and fast can come later.

So instead of burying my head where I want to, going where I know she wants me to be, I test my memory. I circle my index finger around her anklebone, and then I kiss a line up her leg, getting to her inner thigh, where I nibble and tease. She's squirming and whimpering, and as soon as I'm close enough, her hands are in my hair.

I abandon her again to repeat my teasing line on her other leg, and then I rise to my feet, drawing her negligee over her head. She watches me, intent.

"I don't look like I used to," she whispers.

"I'll never complain about having more of you," I say, cupping her cheek and kissing her, long and deep. "Right now, I'm the luckiest man alive." Then I kiss along her neck, in the spot behind her ear that used to make her moan, and she clutches at me, tries to wiggle closer.

"Please, Nate," she gasps.

"Hearing you say my name like that—I fucking love it." I drop to my knees again because I know what she wants, what she needs. At the first taste of her on my tongue, I groan. "Just like I remember. You taste so fucking good," I mutter, and then I press the flat of my tongue against her most sensitive area. I swirl and lick, the way she likes to be brought to the edge coming back to me in fractured memories.

"Oh, Nate," she breathes out, rocking against me. "Oh god, yes."

Then she's arching into my tongue, crying out so loudly that I have a brief moment of worry that she'll wake the girls in the next apartment. I lap her up, loving the feel of her contracting in pleasure. And then I kiss a line up her body, not sure if I'll get another freak-out or she'll be completely okay with her choice this time.

"I want to feel you," she murmurs, drawing me into a kiss. "I want to feel all of you."

"I have—" I start to say, keenly aware of what she used to need.

"I have an IUD. Please," she says, her voice needy. "I just want to feel you." She slips her hand down the waist of my sweats, and I let out a strangled noise at the contact.

"Are you sure?" I ask as she's pushing my sweats down with one hand while her other hand has a firm and assured grip as she works the length of me.

"Yes," she says, guiding me toward her entrance. "Are you?"

"Never been more sure of anything."

And we both watch as I enter her, and when I glance at her, double-checking that this is actually okay, she puts both her hands on my ass, drawing me deeper. I close my eyes against the sensation of her warm, wet heat. Bare like this is a first for me, but I can't say that, can't make this more than she's willing to let it be.

I open my eyes to watch my cock slide in and out, and then I wrap my arms around her, tilting her a little more off the table, so I can get deeper. She gasps and then moans at the tight fit. I sneak one hand between us, and I use my thumb to draw circles over her clit, seeing if I can drive her to a second orgasm.

She clutches on to me, and I kiss her, angling my head to keep us as connected as possible. Her breasts brush against my chest, and I press kisses along her neck.

"You feel so good," I murmur into her ear, licking her earlobe. "I never want to be anywhere but here."

"Nate," she cries, need in her voice, "I think I'm going to come again."

"Not yet," I say, slowing the swirl of my thumb. "We're coming together this time."

Then I shift us so I can brush against her with each thrust, so that each time I get closer, so does she.

"I don't know…" She shakes her head, clearly in the throws of passion. "I don't know…"

"Hold on for me, Hols. Be a good girl and hold on for me."

She whimpers into my ear, and I draw her so tight, we're doing little more than rocking together, the table banging into the wall with each movement.

"Please," she whispers. "Please."

"Oh, fuck," I mutter as everything inside me tightens. "Come for me, Hols."

She cries out, and I push as deep as I can as my orgasm rushes out of me, the two of us coming hard together.

I get a warm cloth from the bathroom, and I press it between Hollyn's legs, sweeping up the mess we caused. Even as I wash her, taking care to be as gentle as I can, I want more. Hollyn's always been a drug, and being with her like this is a complete and total relapse.

When she slips her negligee over her head again, I try to draw her into the bedroom.

"I should go back," she says. "I'm not just responsible for Kinsley on this trip."

I scan her face, trying to figure out if this was anything other than her trying to scratch an itch. Accusing her of that won't get me far, but I'm also not sure where else to step.

"I can't just forget this happened," I say, trying to tread lightly. "I don't want to."

She bites her lip and seems to think for a minute before responding. "When the TV show is over, I'm still going back to New York. No matter what."

"You've said that." I try to keep the irritation out of my voice. Where she lives is so far from a deal-breaker for me that it's comical. She could live on Mars, and I'd build a rocket ship. But for some reason, she doesn't want to hear that. "What do you want this to be, Hols? Because I can't have it be nothing."

I don't say the rest—that it would wreck me all over again, that I've made my intentions clear, and if she came for a one-night stand, I'm not the guy. But I wouldn't want anyone else to be the guy, which is the real mind-fuck. Don't treat me like shit, but if you're going to treat anyone like shit in the way you just did, pick me. Pretty fucked up.

"I don't want to hurt you, Nate."

"Just tell me what you want, Hollyn. What you actually want. No filter."

"I want you," she says, but I can see the conflict in her eyes, the sense that she shouldn't have said it with so much certainty. "For as long as I can have you. But I don't want anyone to know. I just want whatever this is to be for us. No one else."

"No one else?" I can keep work professional without any problem, but it seems impossible to keep whatever this might be from my family, from her sister.

"No one," she says. "You have to promise me. Just us."

I step toward her, and I cradle the back of her head with my palm before pressing a kiss to her forehead. "Just us," I agree.

Whatever gets me her, whatever gives me a chance for more, I'll seize it with both hands. She places a soft kiss on my lips, and then she slips out of my grasp, sweeping her robe off the floor before disappearing out the door.

She might see this as ending between us when she goes back to New York, but I don't. That's not how I see us at all. I'll go where she goes—all she has to do is ask. Then there'll be a ring on her finger. My child inside her—eventually.

And that's just the beginning of what I see happening, what I know to be true. I just have to hope that these next few months give us enough time for her to see it too. I can't chase her. I won't. But I don't know how I'll ever let her go either.

Chapter Twenty-Eight

HOLLYN

Somehow, Nate and I managed to get on the plane and back to the apartment on Sunday without Indy or Kinsley being any the wiser about the shift in our relationship. It helped that the two girls were still absorbed in their concert experience and all the merch they needed to dole out to friends today.

"I'll see you after school," Kin says, dropping her breakfast plate in the sink. She breezes out the door, her stuffed backpack over her shoulder. Other than a bit of attitude on Saturday over her coffee shop visit with friends, we had a good weekend.

As much as it pains me to admit it, being in Bellerive has been good for her and for me, and it's definitely healed our relationship, at least a little bit.

I polish off my second piece of toast and then head back to my bedroom. I tug on a loose cotton dress and run a brush through my hair before gathering it into a ponytail. Even though Nate and I agreed to keep us a secret, I don't know if I can get my head out of the clouds to sell professionalism. Between going to his apartment and finding him climaxing while obviously thinking about me to receiving two orgasms to having him inside me bare for the first time, the last few days are a lot to process. I never let myself consider I could have any part of Nate again. Because no matter how great this moment is, these last few days have been, the dark clouds of my past are just beyond the horizon. They're there, waiting to cause a life-altering storm. The only way to keep the storm from ruining everything is to keep Nate and me quiet and, god help me, less serious than last time. Somehow.

We might have unearthed emotions in New York, but so many other things need to stay buried, for both our sakes.

Staring at myself in the mirror, I take a deep breath. We're filming today, and I was told that hair and makeup would be done once I got there. "Fresh-faced and ready to be primped and pampered" was my directive from Twyla before I left the office on Friday.

The door to the apartment opens. "Kin? Did you forget something?" I ask, coming out of my bedroom. My steps stutter to a stop.

"I think *you* forgot something," my mother says, a key dangling from her fingers. "I kept expecting you to change the locks."

My father wanders into the apartment behind her, and my pulse skyrockets.

I'm a grown adult. They can't hurt me the way they once did. Keep calm and levelheaded.

"You shouldn't be here," I say, and I cast a furtive glance toward the kitchen. If I was closer, I'd grab a knife.

"We have a key," my father says with a chuckle. "We've got as much right as you. You don't *own* this apartment."

Reasoning with him about rental agreements and my aunt's will won't help.

"Where's my stuff?" my mom asks as she gazes around the space.

"Aunt Verna didn't leave you anything," I say. "There's nothing here for you."

"We came looking for it a few times—money, papers—she was keeping it safe for me. Where the fuck is it, Hollyn? What'd you do with it?"

"I never found any money, and if you don't leave, I'm calling the cops."

"Ah, right," my father says with a tsk. "She's got the cops in her back pocket now that she's hanging out with a Tucker. Just like last time."

"I don't know what you mean," I say.

My mother has been scouring the room, and now she's getting closer than I'm comfortable with. They're like circling lions, ready to pounce.

"TV shows, VIP concert tickets—those things don't come cheap. What kind of vagina hooks have you got that you managed to reel him back in a second time?"

"That's not..." The denial dies on my lips. "How do you..." Then I remember a few times I came home and things in the apartment felt different, like stuff had been moved, but I could never place what. Her words from when she entered register. "You've been here, trespassing."

"That's a big word," my father says. "One I'm not sure you understand the meaning of. We've paid money toward this apartment. We've got a legal claim here."

"I don't know anything about that," I say.

"Kinsley seemed overjoyed about the concert," my mother says, sly as she weaves her way closer.

"How would you know that?" I ask.

"We follow each other," she says with a little shrug. "Besties."

Kinsley can't know it's Mickie on the other side of whatever profile our mother is using. I refuse to believe Kin would have gone behind my back to befriend Mickie. Curiosity, I can understand, but Mickie is implying an actual relationship.

"It makes her really angry that you work so much, you know. I always tell her she's right to be angry. Justified. After all, her sister stole her from her rightful parents—the ones who should be raising her. The ones who would have raised her here, given her everything."

The courts took my sister. I just swooped in and removed her from government care. But I know that tone in my mother's voice. She's a viper, waiting to strike, and I'm not handing her any provocation. I can deal with whatever has been happening between her and Kinsley with my sister—who is, funnily enough, the rational one in this situation.

"I want my shit," my mother says, "and I'm not leaving until you hand it over."

"I don't have anything," I say, flinging out my hands. "Whatever you're after isn't here."

"Nah, it's here somewhere. Verna would have wanted me to have it all back. So either you're looking for it right now, or I am," she says.

"Neither of us are. I have to get to set." And when I see the time on the clock, a little bit of panic sets in. If I don't take some brave steps here, I'm going to be very late on my first day of shooting, and Nate already explained to everyone that being late is money and time lost. "You need to leave."

"Fuck that," my father says. "You get your mother's things, and then we'll leave."

"I'll call the police," I say, taking my phone out of my pocket.

My mother lunges and tries to grab my phone, but I cling on, instinct taking over.

"No!" I shout, trying to hold it away from her.

With the hand that's not trying to grab my phone, Mickie swings at my face with a closed fist.

The blow lands, and I stumble back, letting go of my phone. Younger me might have cried or been shocked that she hit me so hard, even after all the episodes of violence before. No matter how many times it happened when I was a kid, it always felt like a new betrayal, a wound I'd never forget. My cheek throbs from the blow, which used to cause me to close in, fold in on myself, want to be small enough she wouldn't strike again.

But I realize I don't have to be the kid who backs down anymore. Being small never stopped her. Fear isn't what's surging through me; it's indignation and rage. She's got my phone in her hand, a smug smile on her lips, and I dig my hand into *her* hair, and I twist, just the way she used to do to me. It's the movement that always buckled my knees, caused my eyes to water, made me pliable.

"You're going to get out of my fucking apartment," I say, practically dragging her to the door, adrenaline surging through me.

"Let your mother go," my father says, hands up. He's always let her do the dirty work, perfectly content to watch with glee as she ruined me.

"Get the fuck out," I rage, pointing at the door with my free hand.

He backs out, and I practically throw my mother out the door behind him. She spins and hurls my phone at me, aiming for my head, but I duck, and it skitters across the apartment floor.

"Don't come back," I say, slamming the door.

Fists pound on the other side, the same rage I just felt mirrored in her. I hate that I've inherited the ability to go there, to be that person, even if it's in response to her.

"You think I'll just take that? I'm not you, Hollyn. I don't take shit like that from *anyone*. If you don't give me my stuff back, I *will* kill you." There's venom in her voice.

Bluster, probably, but her threat still causes my heart to kick.

"And if I can't get to you," she says, her voice pitched low against the door, "I'll pay you back through Kinsley instead."

My eyes widen, and my stomach drops out.

One last boom of a fist resounds on the door, and then their step retreat, my mother cursing loudly and yelling more threats as she leaves.

Instead of going to the set like I'm supposed to, I grab my keys and head for Kinsley's school. Looks like she's getting a day off until I figure out how to fix the mess I created.

Chapter Twenty-Nine

NATHANIEL

"I feel like I need to tell you to sit down," Posey says when I answer the phone.

"I'm driving, so I suppose I already am," I say, signaling a lane change.

"Hollyn just called and said she's going to be late getting to set because she's going to pick up Kinsley from school."

"Okay," I say, my mind working. "Is Kinsley sick?"

"No," Posey says, and she takes a deep breath. "Hollyn was crying. She said her parents came to the apartment and threatened to kill her and Kinsley. I just… is that like, hypothetical? Or real? I know the Davis-Thompson family is rough, but are they murderers?"

I skid onto the shoulder of the road, wheeling around to do a U-turn in the middle of the highway. Other cars honk at me, but I've been going the wrong fucking way if Hollyn needs me.

"Where was she last time you talked to her?"

"Is this a real thing?" Posey asks, a hint of panic in her voice. "Do I need to call Stephen?"

"Just tell me where she is!" I burst out.

"She was just picking up Kinsley—had just pulled up to the school."

I press my foot down harder on the gas, confident I'm headed the right way. "I'll call Stephen, and you let Tariq know Hollyn won't be filming today. Hollyn and Kin will be with me until I can get a restraining order and some security measures in place." Without waiting for a response from Posey, I hang up on her and immediately dial Stephen.

"You working?" I ask when he picks up. I'm never sure if my mother has a deal with Stephen, if Ava has a deal with Stephen, or if the chief of police has a deal with my mother, but Stephen is our family's go-to for all police-related matters.

"What do you need?" he asks, alert.

"Mickie and Nial Davis threatened to kill Hollyn and Kinsley. I need an immediate police escort in Tucker's Town."

"You'll have one. I'm in Rockdown, but I'll get some people to respond. Location?"

"East Pembroke Academy," I say, weaving in and out of traffic. On the outside, I probably seem collected, but on the inside, fear and anger are at war. First, I need Hollyn and Kinsley safe, and then I'll make Mickie regret ever having that threat cross her lips.

When I pull into the school's parking lot, two police vehicles with officers are already there talking to Hollyn and Kinsley. Before I'm out of the car, I notice the red, swollen mark on Hollyn's cheek.

The inclination to commit murder has never been so strong.

"We need a restraining order," I say, coming up beside Hollyn and the male officer.

"Nate, what are you doing here?" Hollyn's surprise is evident. Her eyes are puffy and swollen, but it's the red mark on her cheek that I can't stop seeing.

"Posey called me." I stare at her for a beat. "*You* should have called me." I'm not going to like her response, so I turn to the officers. "Restraining order? Warrant for Mickie and Niall's arrest?"

"We've documented the evidence," the one officer says—I think his name is Marcus, "and Ms. Davis is welcome to come down to the station to press charges."

"Which you're going to do," I say, swinging my attention back to Hollyn.

"I just need a minute," she says. "I just need a minute to figure out what makes the most sense."

"They assaulted you, and at least one of them uttered threats," I say. "What's there to think about?"

"You don't know her," Hollyn says, glancing at Kinsley, who's within earshot with another officer. "I have to figure out what won't make this worse. It's not just me I have to worry about."

"If you don't want to press charges and you're concerned about the threats," the officer says, snapping his notebook shut, "you should consider whether there's another place for you to stay. You should definitely get the locks changed."

"She has a key?" I ask in disbelief.

"My aunt must have given her one at some point," Hollyn says, her tone weary. "I think they've been in the apartment before when I wasn't there."

My blood pressure rises along with my level of concern. "Are you fucking kidding me?"

"Nate," she says, and when she meets my gaze, I see exactly what this morning has taken out of her.

"I'm not helping," I say, running a frustrated hand through my hair.

I know how I can help, but it makes me nervous to even suggest it. Offering her another place to live will show all my cards—not that I have been holding many back, but there'll be no doubt how obsessively I've thought of her over the years.

"Whatever you decide to do," I say, trying to even out my tone, "you'll need protection. I know a place you can stay. Gated, with security." Of course, right now it's only electronic surveillance and security. I'll need to make some phone calls to get human security too—both the kind Hollyn will see and the kind that'll subtly trail Hollyn and Kinsley around Bellerive until I've managed to neutralize Mickie and Niall.

"We're leaving the apartment?" Kinsley asks. The female officer is beside her as Kin steps into the little circle we've all formed.

"You can't stay at the apartment after this," I say, and my focus latches on to the bruise blooming on Hollyn's face. I want to eviscerate Mickie Davis.

"We can change the locks," Hollyn says, rubbing her forehead.

"I know of a house," I say. "It's empty. Mickie and Niall won't know where you're staying."

"Well, they might," Hollyn says, giving Kinsley a pointed glance. "Mickie follows your social media. Didn't we talk about adding people you don't know?"

"I didn't know I added her," Kinsley says, her cheeks flushing with color. "I don't even know who she's pretending to be."

"Cal's brother, Weston, is in IT. I can have him figure out which of your followers is Mickie in disguise," I say. "And his other brother, Owen, just left Bellerive's military to start his own high-profile security company. He can consult on what we need to make the house as safe as possible."

"I've never lived in a house before," Kinsley says.

The male officer rips a page out of his notebook and passes it to me. "Officer Foster says to call this judge, and you'll be able to get your restraining order."

Hollyn has her face in her hands, and I run my palm along her back in slow circles. The motion used to soothe her when we were kids and something her parents or her aunt had done caused her pain. For all the neglect I experienced as a child, my parents never deliberately hurt me. Hollyn can't say the same.

"I just don't know what to do," she whispers. "This is why I didn't want to stay." She drags her hands down her face and looks at Kinsley. "I never wanted you to see this."

"I'll delete her," Kin says. "I'll be more careful about who I add. I promise. And I think..." She glances at the police and then at me. "I think you should press charges. She shouldn't be allowed to do this."

Hollyn and I both know exactly how much Mickie got away with before anyone put a stop to it when she was a kid, but Kinsley must not.

"You're not a kid anymore," I say to Hollyn, careful to keep my tone soft. "And you're not facing this alone. You're not alone, Hols. I'm behind you. I'm beside you. I'm wherever you want me to be. I won't allow anything bad to happen to either one of you." I don't tack on *no matter what I have to do*, but I hope she knows there's nothing I wouldn't do to protect her and Kinsley.

We lock gazes for a beat, and I can almost see her assessing how much I mean that statement, as though she's weighing whether she really can put that kind of trust in me again. But just like her, I'm not a kid anymore either. There are things I can do now that would have felt impossible at seventeen. And while I'm not normally one to straddle the line between legal and illegal, I'll happily not just walk that tightrope but fall right off in the wrong direction if it means Hollyn and Kinsley are safe.

"You really know somewhere we can stay?" Hollyn asks.

"Yeah," I say with a small smile. "I think you'll love it there."

Chapter Thirty

HOLLYN

We make the turn down the long laneway, and my mind ticks over. The trees have grown bigger and obscured the house more, but I'd know this place anywhere.

"You know who lives here?" I ask, wondering if he remembers.

"No one lives here," he says. "I know who owns it, and it's empty. Or empty-ish—it has some furniture."

At the gate, he rolls down his window to punch in a code.

"This is so fancy," Kinsley says, even though she's been to the royal palace with Brice and Maren and she understands what *fancy* really is now.

"I'll hire security to patrol the property," Nate says.

"I'll pay for that," I say.

"We can discuss payment," he says, and his gaze sweeps over me in a way that suggests my payment plan won't be in money.

As soon as we get close to the circular drive, my breath catches. It's a two-story white colonial house with wraparound balconies on the first and second floors. It overlooks the ocean, and Nate and I used to drive past it in his boat when we were kids. It was my dream house, the place I coveted most out of anywhere on the island. It's also, probably, ten thousand square feet of living space, which, now that I'm older, I understand is more than two people could ever need. Kinsley and I survived on little more than six *hundred* square feet in our New York apartment.

"This is probably too much," I say, my voice hushed. "Can they rent out the rest of it to someone else?"

"There's no need," Nate says. "It's just sitting empty anyway."

At the front door, he parks the car, and when I climb out, I cling to the edge of the car door, completely in awe that I'm going to be living in the house of my dreams. Life is wild sometimes.

"We're going to live here?" Kinsley says with a laugh of disbelief. "I'm never going back to New York."

"Yes, you will," I say, my tone sharp. After our parents just threatened us, we can't stay. Even before that, I didn't want their influence creeping into Kinsley's life.

"Let's take a look around," Nate says, ever the peacemaker. "I can arrange to have someone pack up your essentials from the apartment, or I can have security accompany you. Owen can handle it."

I want to tell him that he's taking my parents too seriously. They wouldn't really hurt their children, but my mother has hurt me far too many times in far too many ways for me to ignore her warning. While Nate's suggestions might seem extreme, I'm not going to turn them down.

Nate uses a code to unlock the double front doors, and when they swing back, I'm stunned by the grandeur. The ceilings are incredibly high, and the artwork that's still on the walls is modern and, strangely, almost exactly what I'd expect to see.

I've been to a lot of nice apartments and houses in New York, and when Nate and I were together, we were in quite a few beautiful places. Almost every one of his friends lived in what I would have considered a palace.

But stepping in the doors to this place feels like coming home, and it's the strangest sensation—as though the house has been waiting for me.

Kinsley has been let loose, and she calls out comments from different rooms, deep in the house. I'm still grappling with this overwhelming feeling in my chest, like I want to cry, but I wouldn't be able to articulate why.

"What do you think?" Nate asks, hands in his pockets.

My throat is tight, so rather than answering him, I move past the grand entrance and into the bones of the house. The ceilings are high throughout, and the décor is neutral, as though the place might be mostly abandoned but it hasn't been allowed to become outdated.

The back of the house is a gigantic open-plan kitchen, living, and dining room. Views of the ocean are visible through the floor-to-ceiling windows. I open one of the sliding doors and step out onto the bottom level of the wraparound porch, and I gulp in the salty sea air. My equilibrium is wobbly, as though I've put a rip in the space-time continuum by being here.

"I saw this place so many times from the water..." I say to Nate, not turning around. He's been quietly following me, watching me in silence since we got here. "That it feels like I already know this house. Isn't that weird?"

"Maybe you were meant to be here," he says.

It *does* feel that way, which I'm not saying out loud.

"You said I'd be happy," I say with a little laugh.

"I said you'd love it," he says, as though it's not the same thing. "Living here will make you happy?"

"It's incredible, Nate," I say, turning toward him. "I honestly can't believe this is happening."

"Knock knock," Maren calls from the front entranceway. "I thought you were worried about security. The front door is wide-open. Jag, Brice's security guard, came with me just in case."

Maren appears on the porch, an imposing guy following behind her.

"Want me to talk to Owen?" the guy who must be Jag says to Nate.

"Please," Nate says with a nod. "We need someone here consistently, and I'd like a tail on both Kinsley and Hollyn."

Again, I feel the urge to protest, but I keep my mouth shut. I'm not taking any risks with Kinsley's life, and I already know Nate won't let me take any risks with mine.

"I'll get that set up for you," Jag says, nodding at Maren. "I'll be out front."

"I figure if Kinsley's not in school, you two have a lot to sort out. I can take her off your hands for the day. She'll be safe at the palace, and I've got Jag." Maren glances around. "Where *is* Kinsley?"

"Warming up with a run through the house," Nate says, glancing behind him. "Every once in a while, she calls, 'Marco,' and we pretend to mutter, 'Polo,' so she doesn't get lost."

Maren and I both laugh at Nate's dry wit. He's so rarely let me see it since I returned to the island. It feels like we're both sinking back into the people we once were, which is dangerous for so many reasons.

"I love this house," Maren says, staring out at the sea beside me. "Nate, I never understood—"

"Don't you have somewhere to be?" Nate asks.

"I never understood," Maren says, giving him a pointed look, "why you lived in Tucker's Town at the boring family apartment when you could have lived out here."

"Lived out here?" I say with a little laugh. "Was it for sale?"

"Yes," Maren says, and I can see Nate running a hand through his hair in frustration behind her. "Ten years ago. When he bought it."

"You *own* this?" I say, unable to hide my surprise.

"It was a good deal," he says, and he's closed up again, as though admitting anything else is too much.

"A good deal," Maren says with a scoff. "Whatever you say, big brother. Kinsley!" She turns and calls into the house. "We're pulling out in five."

Kinsley's feet are loud on the stairs, echoing through the rooms and out the door to us. "I'm here!" she says. "I don't have any of my stuff, though. They picked me up from school."

"We have extras at the palace. Brice is busy today with royal things, so it's just you and me until practice later. Should we stop in to see the puppies on the way home?"

"Definitely! Can you teach me how to do that leap on the rock wall?"

"Leap?" I ask, my heart kicking.

"Everyone's harnessed in," Maren says, guiding Kinsley toward the door. "Totally safe."

"And amazing to see," Kinsley calls over her shoulder. "You should see Maren climb!"

Then they're out the door, and Nate and I are left alone, standing on the porch. We're staring at each other, and I don't even know what to say first.

"Maren really is a great climber," Nate says as though that's the most important thing in this moment.

"You bought this house. My house. The house I loved from afar. The house I once told you I'd genuinely murder someone to possess."

He purses his lips, and he gives a slow nod. "I bought the house."

"Why?"

He gives a little shrug, but he doesn't respond.

"No," I say stepping closer. "I need you to say it."

"What do you want me to tell you, Hollyn? You knew how I felt about you when you left. I never hid how serious I was about you."

"But I left," I say. "And the way I left..."

"Was fucking awful and deeply unfair, yeah. I think we both know that." He glances away. "And when this house came up for sale, I couldn't let it go. I needed to own it because it reminded me of you, because part of me hoped you'd come back someday." When he meets my gaze, his expression is tortured.

It sinks in that Nate bought this house for *me*. Even though I trampled on his heart, betrayed his trust, ghosted him in the worst way, he never gave up hope that I'd come back, that we'd figure things out.

I close the space between us, throw my arms around his neck, and I kiss him, pouring every emotion I can't reveal, every word I can't say into the physical expression of those feelings. Maybe I still can't keep him, but I'm sure as hell going to give him as much of myself as I can while I can.

He meets my kiss without an ounce of hesitation, and then he lifts me onto the wide, thick stone-and-concrete railing of the porch and steps between my legs. My loose cotton dress is around my thighs, inching up with each kiss.

When Nate's thumb skims my cheek and I involuntarily flinch, he steps back, examining the bruise that's formed.

"I'll never let them hurt you again," he says. "Whatever I have to do, they'll never get to you again."

"This isn't worth you getting into any trouble," I say.

"Getting out of trouble is a Tucker specialty."

Never have truer words been spoken, but I just shake my head. "I'm not worth you getting into trouble."

"You still don't get it," he says gently. "You're worth *everything* to me, Hollyn. There is nothing and no one above you. My life, my fortune, they're nothing without you in it."

One way or another, I'm bound to break his heart again, and if I let myself dwell on that, we'll both be miserable right now. So I drag him into another kiss. I run my hand along the waistband of his pants, and he shudders at the contact, deepening the kiss.

Right now, with the day I've had—my parents' assault and threats, finding out about this house, knowing that I can never have all this long-term—I need a solid connection with him. I need to feel him around me, inside me.

"I want you, Nate," I murmur.

"Here?"

"Yes. Right now."

He groans into my mouth and then falls to his knees to push my dress up, tug my panties to the side. Without hesitation, his tongue sinks into me, and I lean back, bracing myself on the edge of the railing. His lips and tongue and the barest hint of teeth sweep me out of my head and into this moment, where I'm somehow back with Nate, where we're in sync like I've never been with anyone else.

If I thought about it too much, it would make me want to cry how much I've settled since I left Bellerive, how much I lowered my expectations for men and sex and relationships. Or maybe, deep down, I just knew no one would ever measure up, no one would ever slot into my heart and soul the way Nate did when we were teenagers. I loved him so deeply, so completely, that I'm not sure I was ever able to dig the roots out, kill the feelings. And god knows I tried to poison it all.

"Please," I say, almost unable to take the unbearable pressure he's been building inside of me with his persistent assault on my senses.

"Please what?" he says, chuckling against my thigh. "Tell me what you want."

"I want you inside me when I come," I say, barely able to get the words out with the amount of pleasure that's cascading through me. I'm so close, but I don't want it to end yet.

He leaves between my legs, and I almost cry out at the injustice even though I just asked for it. Wiping his mouth, he urges me off the railing and then spins me around, planting my hands on the edge of the wide railing. He tugs my panties down so they pool around my ankles, and then he lifts my dress.

The sharp sounds of his belt buckle and zipper makes me feel like I might explode in anticipation. He draws me back, and then as he slides in, he hisses, and I glance back to see the look of pure ecstasy on his face.

"You're so wet. So ready," he says, stroking slowly before bringing his hand around to swirl against my clit.

"Nate," I murmur, caught up in feeling once again.

"Look out," he says, his voice thick with desire. "Look out and know that you were once out there with me, wishing to be here, and now you're here with me. Always with me."

The notion brings tears to my eyes, that if I'd made different choices back then, there might not have been years and so much pain between the two moments. But I'd have avoided my pain and his only to cause an equal amount for other people.

"Tell me," he says against my ear, causing a shiver to race through me.

I know what he wants me to say, what he used to love hearing when we were together. I glance at him over my shoulder, hoping my tears aren't visible. "I love the feel of you inside me. I love it so much."

He searches my face, and I can see the war in his expression, between wondering what's going on in my head and giving into the pleasure we're both drowning in.

"Are you okay?" he says, concern for me overtaking his desire.

"I want this," I say. "I want you. Faster," I say, bracing myself. "Please."

"Hols..."

"Please," I say, breaking eye contact to look out at the ocean, letting myself drown in the intense physical connection rather than suffer at the rocky shore of the emotional one.

He does as I ask, and the edges of my vision start to blur out, my orgasm just out of reach.

"Can you come? God, I'm barely holding on."

"Keep going," I say, focused on the horizon.

Then his hips jerk, and he groans just as I crest the wave and catch it. I let out a moan of relief, clutching on to his hand, stilling its rotation on my most sensitive parts.

He kisses my neck, his breath ragged like mine. His hips jerk, driving him deep inside me. It takes us both a few minutes to come down.

"Just a second," he murmurs near my ear. "I'll get a cloth."

He pulls out, and I want to cry at the loss of connection. It's like there's a part of me that's terrified I'm going to lose him again, even if I think that's the only logical outcome to this whole thing.

He returns with a warm cloth, and he gently cleans me up, sliding my panties back up my legs and into place. He leaves again, and when he comes back, I still haven't turned around.

"You said you wanted it," Nate says in a gentle voice, "so why does it feel like you didn't?"

Tears spring to my eyes, and I keep my back to him. "I did," I say, my voice thick. "I did."

"Talk to me, Hols. What's going on with you?"

"I'm terrified to let you in again," I say. "And every time we're together, it feels like you're unlocking doors I've bolted and kept shut just to survive."

"Maybe we forgive each other one bolt at a time," he says, his hand on the base of my neck.

"Forgive each other?" I say with a scoff. "What'd *you* do?"

"I gave up. I stopped looking. Even though I was sure what we'd had was real, I didn't keep pushing to get you back. Instead, I locked all my doors, boarded up my heart. Maybe if I hadn't let hurt and pride get in the way, we would have worked things out sooner."

For him to say that when he doesn't even know why I left, what I did... I just... I shake my head. "You have nothing to be sorry for. And we said we were going to leave all that in the past."

"Hard to do that," he says, his tone wry, "when you can't let it go either."

A heavy silence sits between us, and then Nate says, "I want to move in here, too, if you'll let me. I can't imagine being in Tucker's Town and wondering if you and Kinsley are safe. Security is great, but I want peace of mind."

"We said we'd keep this just between us."

"The house is ten thousand square feet. If we don't want to see each other, we don't have to. But I won't sleep at night knowing you're here, wondering if you're *truly* safe."

"You don't think people will wonder about us if you're here?"

"I'm going to have a bodyguard with you constantly, and I'm going to get Owen to get permission from Kinsley's school to do the same there. Because of the connection to Owen, people are probably going to assume, rightly, that I've done that. We work together already." He takes a deep breath. "And a lot of people on the island already know I own this house. It's just that *you* didn't."

Finally, I turn to face him, and his gaze is laser focused on the bruise on my cheek. As long as that visual reminder is there that my mom can get to me, that she can hurt me, Nate will find a way to stay close. I can make that hard for him, or I can make that easy.

But in making that easier for him, I'll be forcing myself to confront some of my past I'd prefer to keep buried. If he's right and people will make certain assumptions—correct ones, for better or worse—then I'm sure I'll have someone knocking on my door, reminding me of choices and promises I already made.

"As long as we're in separate wings of the house," I say. "Is that possible?"

"The master suite is on the main floor. You can have that. I'll sleep upstairs on whatever end Kinsley doesn't want."

"We just need to be careful around Kin," I say. "While other people in Bellerive might assume certain things, I can't have Kinsley thinking we'll be staying in

Bellerive. I don't want her to believe that whatever is going on between us changes whether we return to New York."

"God forbid," Nate says, a hint of annoyance in his tone. "Whatever you want, Hols. I just want you safe."

Then he leaves me standing on the porch alone as he strides back into the house.

Chapter Thirty-One

HOLLYN

The thing about knowing there's a guillotine poised above your neck is that everything in life becomes just a little bit harder. Going to work, going to sleep, delivering a line of dialogue—even deciding what to eat for breakfast—the mental load is increased just enough to make some of those pieces feel impossible.

We've filmed two episodes while I've been waiting for the sharp slice across the back of my neck. I'm actually surprised it hasn't come yet—from my parents, from the network because I'm not a good cohost, or from Celia Tucker.

The only bright spot has been Nate, but even his presence in the house and in my life hasn't been enough to counter all those other variables hanging over me.

With a break in production today while Nate and the other producers meet with the network to discuss the episodes that have been completed and the upcoming ones that have been storyboarded, I've decided I have to get at least one shadow off my neck.

I can't quit my job, and there isn't much I can do about my parents that I haven't already done with the restraining order. It's just that the third one makes me feel like there's already blood trickling down my throat.

Somewhere behind me is a security detail that Nate is paying for, and I try not to think about that as I drive toward the Tucker mansion. This conversation could go in a thousand directions, but the one thing I'm sure of is that Celia probably already knows everything *I'm* about to tell her. Truthfully, I'm surprised she didn't come knocking first.

But that's probably always been her strength. She's never the desperate one.

I ring the doorbell when I arrive, and a butler answers. It seems so old-fashioned, but that's a Celia trait. If people would expect someone with money to have it, she has it. Her children—with the exception of Ava—appear to have grown up to be completely different.

"Can I help you?" he asks, and he even has a British-sounding accent. I'm tempted to ask him if he's seen Bruce Wayne, and if I wasn't so nervous, I might just do that.

"I'm here to see Celia Tucker."

"Is she expecting you?"

"Probably."

"And you are?"

"Hollyn Davis."

"A Davis?"

"Yes."

He closes the door in my face, and I stand waiting on the front step for longer than I suspect Celia keeps people with more power or influence. Now that I'm older, I can clock the games she plays, the way she exerts her power and privilege in ways that are unexpected or almost invisible.

The door swings open again, and the butler steps out, closing the door behind him. "She'll see you on the back patio. Follow me."

I don't even get to go into the house. She knows every way to make someone feel small, because I know it's a straight shot right through the center of the house to get to the back patio. Walking all the way around the house to get to her makes a statement.

When we finally get around, the hot sun has caused me to sweat, and I'm no longer looking my best nor feeling as mentally strong.

Celia is in a lounger in the shade, reading on her tablet. When the butler approaches with me following behind, she doesn't even glance up.

"May I present Hollyn Davis?" He steps back and practically runs in the back door into the air-conditioning.

"What are you doing here?" Celia asks, flicking her finger on the tablet without looking up.

"You don't know?"

"I have ideas about *why* you'd be here, but I want to know why *you* think you're here."

"I thought you might seek me out to remind me of our deal, considering who I'm working with, who I'm living with."

"Why would I need to do that?" Celia sets the tablet on the table beside her and finally looks at me.

There are no other chairs near her, so I'm still standing, and the shade is more behind Celia than in front. In order to face her, I've had to stay in the hot sun, squinting.

"You're not worried I'll break our deal?"

"Of course not," she says, waving her hand dismissively. "If Nathaniel knew what you did that night before you left the island, it wouldn't be *me* he'd be angry with, now, would it?" She shakes her head. "As soon as he realizes how little you valued him, how easily you tossed him aside, anything that's started up between you two is done. You were never stupid, Hollyn, just a poor girl from a criminal family."

I can feel myself getting smaller. Just like my mother, Celia's always been able to make me shrink into myself, and while I gained a lot of practice in New York at keeping my back straight when I'm challenged—old habits die hard. With my mother, I had rage on my side, but with Celia, all I have is shame.

"You know," Celia continues, "the women Nathaniel's dated since you left the island have all been from rich families. Women who fit into this world, who understand his family and his lifestyle. Lovely, lovely people. The thing that *my* Nathaniel has learned is that you can fuck the help, fuck the criminals, but marry them? Build a life with them? Never. You just can't. And that's something idealistic young boys learn when they become men."

Words bubble in my throat, but I can't get them to form coherent sentences. It's like she's sewn my mouth shut.

"Besides, the minute Nathaniel discovers the truth—the way you left the island, the deals you made—he's not going to forgive that. If you don't feel like just the help right now, you will again then." She rises off her lounge chair, and she gives me a patronizing smile. "You never did understand your place."

"He won't let me go again," I say, pushing the words out past my natural resistance.

"He won't?" Celia laughs. "Well, it's a good thing you'll go anyway. Because staying on this island for longer than this television season would break our deal. And you don't want to see me when someone crosses me, Hollyn Davis. I've been quite docile with you. Don't make me get rabid."

"You don't understand—"

"No, *you* don't." Celia steps toward me. "My son likes to take care of people, but I'd like to think you've been well taken care of. Have you not?"

I stare at her, silent. In all the ways *she* cares about, I'm sure she'd consider anything other than a yes to be a lie.

"So anytime he's inclined during a post-coital moment to suggest something temporary could become more permanent, you find some of that fierceness you drummed up the night we made our deal. Have your fun. But remember the limits *you* already put on that."

"As long as I leave…"

"You won't suffer any consequences for the pieces of our deal you've *already* broken. I'm not completely heartless. See yourself out."

She steps past me and walks into the house, but I can see her lock the door behind her. Clearly, I'm meant to go all the way around again.

The notion that Celia's supposed grace isn't heartless is laughable. She's essentially telling me that I can get as close to Nate as I want in the next few weeks and months, but none of it will matter. The decision I made at eighteen under extreme duress still stands.

I wipe the sweat off my forehead and start the long walk back around to the front. Some of the things she said, I should have pushed back on, but my brain short-circuited when she said Nate would be so angry with me that he'd never speak to me again. It's like she looked inside my head and heart to reveal my biggest fear.

Maybe I walked away from him the first time, but part of me has always been terrified that one day, he'll look at me and he'll wonder what good he ever saw in me in the first place. He'll finally realize the time he spent with me then, the years he spent missing me in between, and whatever we manage to eke out here, were really just a waste of his time and energy.

That would truly break my heart.

All those memories I've clung on to for years would become irrevocably tainted.

I came here to figure out a way to diminish the shadow threatening to cut off my head, and instead, Celia Tucker planted a bomb in my life that's already started ticking.

Chapter Thirty-Two

HOLLYN

Fourteen years ago

"I'm really not sure about this," I say to Nate when he picks me up to take me to the mall in Tucker's Town where all the rich people shop. I've never been inside the doors of the place, much less actually purchased anything there.

"About going to my prom with me or going shopping?" He steers the car onto the highway.

"Both," I admit.

"We're all just people," he says.

It's such a rich-person thing to say that I'm not even sure how to respond, and that's the problem sometimes between us. He has all this privilege, and he doesn't see or understand how that's shaped him.

His parents aren't great people, but they haven't truly denied him anything. He has multiple roofs he can put over his head, multiple cars he can drive, siblings he can rely on, strained family dinners, and some form of love, even if it's not the ideal kind.

He's never gone hungry or worried about whether his mother would break into the apartment he shares with his aunt and steal any cash they haven't hidden well enough. He doesn't have to listen to his aunt explain away the terrible things his mother has done—physical, mental, or emotional.

I'd never tell him that the neglect he's experienced doesn't count. Being raised by nannies isn't the same as having your mother and father involved—and I know that. But just like he can't really relate to what I've experienced, I can't really relate to his either.

On paper, Nate and I shouldn't work. The rational, reasonable part of me knows that. We don't make sense.

But when I'm with him, it feels like we're the only thing that does.

Being with him is like getting my first big breath of clean air and realizing I've been inhaling toxic chemicals my whole life. Stunning and surreal. He loves with his whole heart, and my heart feels so beaten up that I've been afraid to tell him he has it, that it's his. I think he knows, but I haven't been able to say the words, as though they're stuck in my throat, my last line of defense against free-falling into this with him.

At some point, we'll stop floating in this alternate version of Bellerive where our vast difference in social status doesn't matter, and he'll wake up and realize that being in love with me is foolish. I believe that in my bones.

He grabs my hand and kisses the back of it. "I'm glad you said yes."

As anxious as I am about walking into that mall, picking out a dress that Nate will buy, I can't deny that I'm also glad I said yes. Despite everything, the idea of Nate going to prom with anyone else—even as friends—would rip what's left of my heart right out of my chest.

When we get to the mall, Nate takes my hand and leads me around from one designer store to another. He tells me not to look at price tags but to just look at colors and designs. What do I want to wear?

The thing is, I'm not even going to the prom at my own school. I've avoided everything about it throughout May and June, and when Nate asked if I wanted him to go with me, I pretended like we didn't even have prom. He either didn't realize it was a lie, or he decided not to call me on it. This dress—the one he's buying me—will be worn exactly once. I'll never go to another event fancy enough again.

When I try on the first dress, a slinky low-back number that makes me feel too old and too young all at once, Nate gives me a broad smile.

"You look amazing but deeply uncomfortable. I don't think that's a winner. Do you?"

Instead of going back into the dressing room, I cross the space and wrap my arms around him, kissing him. His ability to read me so quickly and accurately constantly surprises me.

When I step back, he goes to another rack and pulls out a dress I touched on my rounds, but when I caught a glimpse of the price tag, I didn't pick it up. It's seafoam green with a fitted bodice and a slightly billowy bottom from the waist down. It's the kind of dress I could see a princess wearing or a famous person.

"What about this one? It seems like you?" He looks back and forth between me and the dress.

"I'd never have anywhere to wear it again." Even the dress I have on right now is so expensive that it made my stomach hurt to try on.

"You will." His eyes light with amusement. "You can wear it to our rehearsal dinner when we get married."

When I seem to hesitate, he continues, "Or any of the charity things we'll have to attend when you're my wife."

He says it like it's a fact, and I've stopped trying to correct or question him. He told me once that every single part of him believed we'd get married, that even if I didn't love him with the same intensity that he loved me, that I'd learn to trust him and us.

But I do love him like that. I just can't seem to say the words, so I've stopped telling him no because every part of me wants to say yes to it all.

"I guess I could try it on," I say, taking the hanger off his outstretched fingers.

In the dressing room, it slips over my body as though it was made for me. There'd only been one size of this dress left, and it just so happened to be mine. When I stare at myself in the multiple mirrors of the oversized changing room, I can't help being amazed.

For the first time, maybe I can see a glimmer of what Nate says he sees when he looks at me. Except it's not all there yet for me—just potential. The notion that maybe, with enough money and time, I *could* fit in.

When I step out, Nate looks as though he's forgotten how to breathe. His palm flattens against his chest, and after he's looked me over from head to toe, he meets my gaze.

"I mean..." he says.

"Yeah," I agree with a self-conscious laugh. "It doesn't even look like me."

"It does," he says, and he steps toward me and tucks my hair behind my ears. "It's *exactly* you." He frames my face and gives me a soft kiss. "But how do you feel?"

"Beautiful," I admit, my throat tight. The prettiest I've ever felt in my life.

"Then it's yours," he says.

"It's really expensive."

"I can charge it to my card. No one will even blink."

My stomach rolls again at the cost, at the groceries I could buy, at the rent payments I could make. But it's not my money, and if this is how Nate wants to spend his, then I can give him this. There's so little I *can* give him.

I make Nate take my dress to his house to keep in the closet in his room until prom night. Something that expensive in the apartment is asking for trouble. Even if my mom hasn't been around for weeks, she has a habit of turning up when you least want to see her.

When I let myself into the apartment, Aunt Verna and my mom are sitting on the couches. My mom has money in her hand, and I'm sure it's come from my aunt. Seeing the two of them together is like having a rock settle in the pit of my stomach, heavy and uncomfortable.

"Hollyn," my mother says, a slight smile gracing her face. "Where have you been?"

I'm so glad I made Nate take the dress. If she'd spotted it, she'd have wanted to sell it, or she'd have come back to steal it. Aunt Verna has never denied me anything I earned or bought with my own money, but she is also terrible at saying no to my mother.

"Working," I say since Nate picked me up from the lunchtime shift at the bar.

"Verna tells me you've got a scholarship to go to school."

I eye my aunt warily. Giving my mother details is something she's not supposed to do. Somehow, my mother always finds a way to twist even the best things into something terrible.

"Yes," I say.

"Does that come with any cash?"

"No," I say. The scholarship covers my tuition and housing for the first year, but I'm responsible for food and book costs. It's part of the reason I've been working so many hours. Although, sometimes I tell my aunt I'm working longer than I am, and then I spend the night or day with Nate.

My mother stands up and saunters toward me, and I hold myself very still, try not to appear afraid. For whatever reason, my mother never touches me when my aunt is home. I don't know if my aunt has made that a hard line between them or if my mother just senses that my aunt wouldn't put up with it, but when we're all together, she doesn't grab a fistful of my hair, or slap me, or run her razor-sharp nails along my arms, thin streams of blood trickling down to the floor.

"Thanks for the loan, Verna," my mother says over her shoulder. "I'll see you both again soon."

Once the apartment door clicks shut, I glare at my aunt. "You gave her money?"

"She was about to be kicked out of her apartment."

"I bet that's a lie. I bet she's using that money for all kinds of bad things." I storm past her toward my bedroom. "I'll never understand why you let her in the door."

"Of course you don't," Aunt Verna says, her anger spiking. The one thing we fight about is my mother. "You'll never understand what it means to be an older sister. To work your ass off to protect them. To feel the full weight of responsibility for them because your parents never felt *any* of that weight."

And as I slam my door, I know she's right. I thank god all the time that I'm an only child, that my mother couldn't seem to get pregnant again. I wouldn't wish Niall and Mickie on anyone, and like my aunt, I can't imagine what I'd do to keep another person from having to experience them.

Unlike my school, where prom is in the gymnasium in June, Nate's prom is at the palace in July. Different months. Different worlds. Nate goes to high school with the princes, and he tells me that the royal family agreed to host prom every year they have a child in the school.

Walking into the ballroom after having my hair and makeup done with Nate's sister Sawyer at some fancy salon, my arrival feels like a true Cinderella moment. People are staring at us, and for the first time, I'm not sure if they're wondering why Nate's with me or who I am. When I looked in the mirror before we left Nate's mansion, I didn't even recognize myself.

I try not to look with my mouth open, but it's hard to take in the grandeur without emotion. The ceilings of the ballroom are impossibly high, and there are people circulating in Bellerive blue with trays of drinks.

"Is that alcohol?" I whisper to Sawyer, who's stuck close to my side. She came with one of Nate's friends as his date, but she said they aren't dating or anything.

"No," Sawyer says. "The Royal Summersets are pretty strict. Alex—you know he's the oldest, right—is super by the book, but Nick and Brice are a little wilder."

"You know them?"

"We all do," Sawyer says with a little laugh. "Bellerive is big and small all at the same time."

"Can I have this dance?" Nate asks, appearing in front of me and giving a cheesy bow that makes my whole chest explode with love.

"You may," I say, matching his grin.

He twirls me onto the dance floor, and my gown billows out around me. Then he settles me into his arms, and we sway to the music. "Having a good time?" he whispers into my ear.

I take a beat to reflect on how it's been since we arrived, and if it wasn't for Sawyer staying so close, I'm not sure if the answer would be yes. Nate's been good at checking in, but I don't think he really understands how out of place I still am. I look the part, but I don't feel it. Not yet.

"Yeah," I say, and when I draw back, he searches my expression before kissing me.

"There's an after-party at a friend's house. Are you okay to go to that?"

"Do you want to go?" The idea makes my stomach swoop low.

"I'd like to, but if you hate the idea, I'd rather be with you."

But I've seen with my own eyes tonight how much people enjoy Nate, love his company. We've barely been alone since we arrived. There's always someone who wants his attention to tell him something or show him something. He's well-liked at his school beyond his social circle, which isn't a surprise but still feels like a revelation. We spend a lot of our time just the two of us, so I don't fully understand the life he has beyond me. Maybe I can get a sense of that tonight.

"I think we should go." Bravery takes hold in my spine. I can do anything for one night. Even if it's terrible for me, it's a memory for Nate.

"You're sure?"

"Yeah," I say. "I think it'll be fun."

The mansion isn't as imposing as the Tucker estate or the palace, but the after-party is filled with drugs and alcohol. While the Summersets might be strict, the rest of Nate's circle seems to be pretty liberal.

It doesn't take long for most of the crowd to be drunk enough to start giving me the eye when I wander through the crowd. Given what I've seen drugs and alcohol do to people, I don't touch them.

Sawyer is there for the first hour, but her date drinks too much too fast, and she ends up having to drive him to another friend's house where their parents are doctors.

That leaves me without an anchor. Nate's been swept up by his guy friends, and I go in search of him, eager to leave if he's not desperate to stay.

When I pause near a hallway, searching the crowd, I hear Nate's name, and I shift in that direction, wondering if he's down the hall. I peek around the corner, and there's a small crowd of girls, one of whom is crying.

"Why her?" the crying girl asks.

"Just be thankful he's getting it out of his system in high school," one of the other girls says. "That's what my mom says about the whole situation. Be grateful he's fucking the help now and not later."

"Let's be honest," another says, "he's not going to marry her. Celia Tucker would *never* allow it."

"And it's just not done," another says. "Can you imagine her at a charity function? We'd be fundraising for her relatives." She lets out a snarky laugh. "Literally, the people she lives with would be getting our charity."

"Nate isn't stupid," the crying girl says. "He told me he loved me."

Oh god.

"He's not stupid," the first girl agrees, running her hand down her friend's arm. "We're all going to college, and she'll get left behind. Next summer, Nate will be yours again."

My heart squeezes at the notion that he's someone to play with, someone to trifle with, a prize to be won. What they've said about me should bother me, but it's what they've implied about Nate, that his personal worth is tied to his financial worth, that hits me square in the heart.

The fact he told her he loved her, though... Hearing that makes my stomach cramp. It's not that I expected I was his first; I knew I wasn't. But I never anticipated being faced with another version of the world, one in which he belonged to someone else.

"Nate's the type to rescue a stray dog and end up adopting it," another one of the girls says.

Are they comparing *me* to a stray dog?

"He's not going to want to show off the mutt in public. He'll soon realize he needs a purebred. Give him a bit of time. He's just too kindhearted."

Her comment lands like a concrete block on my shoulders, and I almost bow under the weight. Unlike the others, she seems to understand Nate a little more, and I wish I'd left thirty seconds earlier.

"Hey," Nate says from behind me, and I jump, startled.

The girls in the hall whip around, and their faces would be laughable if I felt like laughing at all.

"Ready to go?" Nate asks, wrapping his arms around my waist and tugging me back against him, his nose nuzzling my neck as he breathes me in.

Tension fills the air, and he seems to sense it.

"You alright?" he murmurs, and then he must look up. "Ladies," he says to the group of girls. There's another beat, and he says, "Sienna."

"Nate," the crying girl whispers back, offering a watery smile.

"Let's go," he says to me, taking my hand and leading me toward the front door.

"Who was that?" I ask, glancing back over my shoulder.

"We used to date," Nate says.

"How long ago?"

"A while ago. Not sure what she's crying about, but I'm sorry to see it."

You, Nate. She's crying over you.

"Did you have fun?" he asks.

"Yeah," I say, though it's not true, and I couldn't explain how the night had been even if I wanted to. For now, he's mine. So even if the girls are right, even if his mom is right, and this fierce love from him is going to burn out, I'm going to bask in every bit of warmth while I can. The other option—me leaving him—is impossible to consider.

Chapter Thirty-Three

NATHANIEL

The first four episodes are done, and even though the network is happy with the content, they're coming in hot on other things they now want. Obnoxious product placements aren't enough. Their goal seems to be to mess around with episode storylines to elevate the drama. We're a fucking home-reno show. It's not supposed to be high drama—at least, not in the way they're trying to create it.

I read the long email they've sent with what they're hoping for, and I sigh. If only I had enough money *and* clout to bypass their input completely, I'd tell them to go fuck themselves. But I need a few more shows under my belt before I can go that forceful.

My phone buzzes on the desk beside me in the office, and I glance at it. Ava has started sending the family voice notes like she's starring in her own podcast and we're her captive audience. Today, she's sent a long sequence of notes about the various investor contacts she's been mining through Dad's associates. Old men with old money.

Our father has been too preoccupied with the bids he and King Alexander have been putting together to bring a World Hockey League franchise team to the island to pay much attention to Ava's escapades. Last I heard, they had a chance at a hockey team the WHL wanted to move from California. Alex and my father would then be able to justify the sizeable arena that's been greenlit by the Advisory Council and has already broken ground.

If I didn't already have enough on my plate with the threats to Kinsley and Hollyn as well as keeping this production on track, I'd be inserting myself into Ava's drama before she gets herself in over her head. She might think she knows everything—including how to manipulate a man rather than being manipulated herself—but Dad's golf buddies aren't to be trifled with.

I flip my phone over so I'm not distracted by Ava, but it doesn't take long for other thoughts not linked to work to draw my attention.

I've spent the last four weeks abiding by Hollyn's wishes. At work, we act like we barely know each other. No special treatment, no lingering glances—or at least, I try not to linger—and we haven't directly mentioned that we're sharing a house.

Bellerive is a whole country, but it often acts like a small town. There are probably people involved in the production who know exactly what's happening between Hollyn and me, but I'm counting on their professionalism to match ours.

Kinsley's been training like mad for her first youth adventure race, which Bellerive is hosting at the end of the summer. Hollyn reluctantly agreed to let Kinsley participate. Production on the show should have wrapped by then, and they could go back to New York. It gave me a spark of hope that she agreed, but Hollyn's emotional distance isn't doing much to turn that spark into a flame.

I get her body when we're alone in the house together—in any way I want, whenever I want. But unlike in high school where I felt like I also had her heart, even though she never said the words, I'm not as sure this time. That uncertainty could be my instinctive caution. Who wants to have their heart crushed twice? Or she really could be holding back or maybe not even feeling the same old emotional and physical intensity that I do. Sometimes I think she does, and then she closes up, hard to read again.

It's impossible to know without asking, but that's equally dangerous. It wouldn't take much to send Hollyn running, and I'm determined that if she leaves the island at the end of this and we're not together in any capacity, I have to let her go.

It'll fucking kill me, but I can't cling on to her anymore if she doesn't want me. I've wasted years half-assing my other romantic connections because I knew what I'd had. To be happy, I was sure I needed to be swept away like I was with Hollyn. Hot. Intense. All-consuming. Maybe that's not realistic or even healthy. When I'm with her, I can't see anything or anyone else.

But I can't be the only one who believes in us, who wants this. We have to fight for it together, and I'm not sure I'll ever get there with her.

I pick up my phone and ignore the flurry of messages in the family group chat to text Posey and Hollyn to come to my office.

Their laughter floats through the door before I see them. The sound sends a shot of warmth through me. Getting a laugh out of Hollyn is rare, but Posey seems to be able to do it more often than most. The number of takes that have been ruined by the two of them cracking their TV personas to burst into laughter should make me frustrated. But I love to see the friendship they've formed, the ease Hollyn has around Posey when she used to be so guarded.

They arrive at the door at the same time, and Hollyn's smile is still wide when they both enter and slip into the seats across from me.

"Problems, boss?" Hollyn asks, arching a brow.

Definitely getting her to call me that later, maybe in a breathy voice as I bend her over some piece of furniture. The sight of her is an instant turn-on. It's amazing I get any work done around here at all.

"Network problems again?" Posey asks, probably when she notices that I can't quite drag my gaze off Hollyn.

"Yeah," I say, leaning back in my chair. "They say that Interflix wants a more dramatic episode before they'll consider picking it up. Realistically, I think the chances of Interflix picking up the series before we've done all the episodes and we've started showing them in Bellerive is slim, but I'm relatively new to all of this." I spread my hands wide.

"What kind of drama?" Hollyn asks. "At this point, it doesn't even feel like reality TV. Or at least not what I *thought* reality TV was. Situations are edited deceptively. We work really closely with the clients to ensure we have a vision they'll support before we even film. Even which one of us will 'win' in an episode is often predetermined. Nothing seems to be left to chance or circumstance."

"As long as they're not pitting us against each other," Posey says. "I'm happy to bring the drama."

I wince. "Not exactly *against* each other. But they do want one of you to be out of touch with what the client needs or wants one episode. Really far out of touch."

They both stare at me in silence, and I can tell, at least from Hollyn's expression, that she's working out what that might look like.

"They want a villain," Hollyn says.

"I wouldn't put it that way," I say. "But they do want one of you to be really off and for the other person to..." I call up the email to try to remember how they phrased it.

"Give them a reality check?" Posey suggests.

"Something like that," I agree, scanning the email. "Or exactly like that."

Hollyn and Posey exchange a long look, and then Posey says, "I think it should be me."

"Why?" Hollyn asks. "I'm probably better suited to be the villain."

"There was an article about you living in Nate's mansion today," she says and hesitates before continuing, "and speculation that you two are together." She waves her hand between us. "It was a blind item, but..."

Bellerive gossip is something I've lived with my whole life. Any time I've dated anyone since I've returned from college, I've been the subject of multiple blind items. When I moved into producing television and movies, I also got hit with the gossip machine, and I've learned to live with it. Ignore it, mostly. People are going to believe whatever they want. But I can tell from Hollyn's expression that she's deeply uncomfortable.

"All the misogynistic assholes are going to think I slept my way into this job," Hollyn says.

"Which is why I think I should be the one who gets it wrong," Posey says. "Besides, I was raised next door to the palace. Nick, Brice, and Alex are practically my brothers. If anyone would be out of touch with reality, it would be me."

"Except anyone who's met you would know that's not true," Hollyn says.

"As you already pointed out, the show is far removed from reality," Posey counters. "If the show gets picked up internationally, we just need a small grain of believability. It's there, trust me."

"What do you think?" Hollyn says, turning to look at me.

The truth is that I'm a little worried about how Hollyn will be received by Bellerive in general on the show. She's from a family of known criminals, she left the island for America, carved a place for herself in a world-famous interior design company, and returned to star in a television show. We selected Hollyn because her poor background might make her relatable, but there's little about her life after she left Bellerive that fits the bill. Leaving here brought her success and turned her into an outsider.

"I think Posey is the wiser choice," I say.

"Why?" Hollyn counters, and there's an edge to her voice, as though she's pulled my thoughts out of my brain and read every one.

"Subvert people's expectations," I say. "If we want drama, we go with the less obvious choice, and we can craft something believable about why Posey might be so off base with these particular clients. Root it in Bellerive history or culture somehow." I scan them both for signs of discontent, and while Hollyn doesn't look thrilled, this request was never going to make anyone happy. "Am I good to push this out to the writers and other production staff?"

"Yes," Posey says, and she takes Hollyn's hand and gives it a squeeze. "Let the trolls try to come for me."

And I'm grateful that Posey seems just as determined to protect Hollyn as I am. Hollyn has grown up, and she's certainly not the fragile teenager she once was, but there's something delicate under Hollyn's surface, as though the wrong people could still cause her to bend in ways I'd never want to see.

"If you both think that's what's best," Hollyn says.

Production has booked an evening shoot for Hollyn and Posey, so I agree to pick up Kin from Cal's campground, where she's been helping to look after the puppies in between training and school. I could have had security drive her home—which sometimes happens with Hollyn because she doesn't have a car—but everyone seems to prefer to have whoever is tailing Kin to be mostly invisible.

When I arrive, the puppies are bounding around the open-plan living room, dining room, and kitchen. There are puppy pee pads scattered around, and Kinsley is frantically running around with a roll of paper towels and cleaning spray.

"This looks like chaos," I say as a puppy barrels into my legs, backs up, growls, and then barks at me. Almost all of them are black, but a few have white feet or a streak of white on their chests, and a couple have brown slashes on their ears or faces. The mother was definitely a black lab cross, but the father truly feels like anyone's guess.

"They've gotten too big for the baby pool," Kin says as she cleans up another puddle of pee. "Cal has a pen for them, and they're supposed to pee in the pool before they get the run of the area." She lets out a deep sigh. "They suck at it today."

"Are they ever good at it?" I glance around the area for Cal, but he's nowhere to be found. We're entering high season for camping in Bellerive, so he's probably out doing chores around the campground. Of all my relatives, he's probably the one closest to earning an honest living off the land. He's never embraced the trappings of the billions we have some access to.

"I wasn't very patient tonight, and I let some of them out of the pool before they went pee," Kin says as I point to another puddle. "Now I'm paying for it." She sets down the bag of soiled paper towels and starts plucking up puppies to deposit them back in the makeshift pen in the corner of the room.

I scoop up the one at my feet that's still pretending to be far tougher than it is. He licks my hand as I take him over to the pen. When I glance inside, I see that Cal's laid plywood down over the tile floor.

"They poop a lot," Kinsley says, dropping two back into the pen. "The plywood saves his floor."

"Right," I say as though I've ever had a puppy. Celia Tucker did not approve of pets when we were kids. Too messy. Too much responsibility.

Kinsley puts them all in the pen except one of the black ones with white on its chest that follows her around as she cleans up the messes. When it pees on the puppy pad, it glances over at me as though looking for approval.

"He's the only smart one," Kin says, using a high-pitched voice to praise the little male dog, and his whole body goes into a full-on wag as he waddles back over to her. She gives him a good rub before scooping him into her arms. "I love him so much." When she glances at me, there are tears in her eyes. "People are coming tomorrow to pick puppies from the litter."

"They're ready to go home already?" They seem so tiny.

"Not quite, but they've had a lot of applications." Her voice is shaky. "So they're putting colored collars on them to send them home with their new families soon." The unshed tears make her voice thick. "Or at least, that's what Cal said."

"That's the one you'd pick?" The tears she's trying so hard to hold back remind me far too much of her sister. The resemblance does funny things to my chest, as though she's a window to the past. "Hollyn's still not interested?"

"We can't take him back to New York," she says, giving him another cuddle before setting him into the pen with the rest of them. "If they get as big as their mom, it's probably not fair."

"Where is the mom?"

"She follows Cal around now that the puppies are eating real food. I think he's keeping her."

I try to memorize the markings of the male she set in the pen. "Do any of the others look like him?"

"The white on his chest almost looks like a heart." Kin stares into the pen. "None of the others have the heart."

"How's adventure race training going?" I ask as Kin gathers her things.

"Good," she says. "The running is no problem, and I'm getting better at keeping my momentum up big hills on the bike. My climbing is still so-so. Did you know your sister Sawyer is running now?"

"No," I say, and I remember the thread in the family chat that I haven't read yet.

"Maren says it's because of some guy, and she seemed pissed off." Kin glances at me, but I'm not going to call her on her language. Hollyn only corrects her when she thinks there's someone around who'll care.

"Some guy?" I slip my phone out of my pocket and check my notifications. There are at least a dozen voice memos from Ava. If Sawyer is dating someone and I don't know about it, it makes me question how deeply I've let myself get sucked into the production, my life in the house with Hollyn and Kinsley. "I should call her."

"You should," Kinsley says, stepping out of the house in front of me.

"What do you know?" I ask.

"His name starts with a D, and I think he has something to do with government?" Kinsley shrugs. "Maren said he's charming, which shouldn't be an insult, should it? She didn't seem to think that was a good thing."

Maren's feelings about charming men were definitely complicated. Her first marriage had been to a charming man who'd used his charm in all the wrong ways, but her second marriage is to an equally charming man who loves her to pieces.

"A charming man with a D name," I say with a little laugh. "Could be anyone." I exit out of the group chat and fire off a solo message to Sawyer and another to Maren.

"Is charming an insult?" Kinsley asks, peering up at me as we reach the car. Another car sits on the edge of the property, lights off, and I give a wave to whoever is on duty.

"It can be," I say. "If someone is using their charm to convince other people of things that are harmful or to hurt people for their own gain."

"I think Hollyn would call *you* charming," she says, sliding me a sly glance before getting into the car.

"She didn't tell you that." I settle into the driver's seat.

"She'd never admit it," Kin says as I start the car and navigate us down the road. "But have you ever noticed the way she looks at you? It's like…" She takes a deep breath and stares out the window.

"Like?" I prod, trying not to seem desperate for some insight.

"Like you're the last rays of a summer sun, when you know it's going to get cold and you can't quite bear it."

"That doesn't sound like a good thing."

"She wants to linger, you know? Or stay in the warmth. Seems like a good thing to me."

Except for the wistful way Kinsley describes Hollyn's look makes it seem like she's preparing for the frost even as she's basking in the sun. And to me, that doesn't seem good at all.

Chapter Thirty-Four

HOLLYN

We're in the studio prepping our designs for the sixth show, Posey next to my shoulder, her own design program up on the screen for me to peer at. The trick is usually to make our designs different enough to present a real choice while also adhering to whoever was "supposed" to win and keeping in mind what the family wants. A lot of balls to juggle.

Most of the time, I really enjoy how this job sparks my brain. Each time I formulate a new house plan, I feel lit up, brimming with possibilities. The challenges and roadblocks are exciting most of the time, rather than frustrating. Every single episode, I've learned something new about Bellerive, about the family we were helping, about sourcing materials on the island, or about someone involved in the production.

Had anyone told me I'd like this job when I'd taken it, I probably would have disagreed. I took the role for Kinsley, but it has turned out to be good for me too.

"Eight episodes," Posey says beside me with a sigh while she plucks out high-end finishes to put in her inspiration board. "Why not the full twelve? Doesn't that seem like they lack confidence in the show?"

"It's two more than what we were supposed to have for the base," I say.

"I know. But this job is my dream—one I never thought I'd get to fulfill while staying in the country, so I'm just bummed that we might only get eight episodes in total. If we don't get twelve episodes ordered, I'm nervous we won't get a second season either."

"Eight to ten episodes by streaming standards is pretty normal." And I haven't let myself think beyond this production. I haven't even given Posey a firm RSVP to her wedding in September. With the youth adventure race at the end of August, I shouldn't really stick around for another two weeks after that just to watch Posey get married when I'll need to get back to work at Reyes and Cruz.

But she's also become a really close friend. Flying back for the weekend is financially impossible.

"There's no bachelorette party, right?" I click on another element and add it to my design, changing the color as I go.

"The Summersets threw us bachelor and bachelorette parties a long time ago. Been there, done that." She lets out a little laugh. "Honestly, I think it was just an excuse to go to Vegas for a boys' weekend, but whatever. Brent had fun there, and I had fun on the island. As a bonus, it means we just cruise right into the wedding now."

"How early?"

She looks pensive. "Before Amelia was born. Brent and I waffled on the date at first, and then we finally committed to doing it just before his last Olympics."

"Timing can be tricky, I guess."

"Speaking of timing, you and Nathaniel seem to have gotten close," she says, waggling her brows. "Again."

I drag some furniture around the screen in front of me, trying to decide what to say. She's been good about not prying, even though I'm sure Nate and I have been more obvious than I'd like to believe the last few weeks.

It's impossible to switch off the sexual chemistry when it's happening constantly all over our shared house. The minute Kinsley is gone somewhere else—training, off with a friend, looking after the puppies—Nate and I are all over each other. The dickmatizing that happened when I was a teenager has come back in full force. And if the circumstances around the two of us were different, that might be a joy. Whenever I think about what we're doing, all I feel is anxiety about the end.

Which might be another reason I haven't told Posey a firm yes or no for the wedding. I hate thinking about leaving, but with my parents and with Celia, staying is impossible. I can't protect Kin or myself from the fallout that staying would bring. At least in New York, none of those people are factors.

"Nate and I come from opposite backgrounds," I hedge.

"Do you think that matters when you're in your thirties? I could see when you were kids that it would have mattered a lot. But now?"

"We just think about things differently."

"Doesn't everyone? We're all a product of our environment, and even two kids raised in the same house don't take the same lessons from their experiences."

"You and Julia?" I ask.

"Yeah," she says with a little laugh. "Or, you know, we become traumatized by our older sister's romantic trauma and take years to extend our own heart." She slides a couch into a different position from where I've put mine and changes the color on the walls on her screen to bright pink in the living room. "Now that I'm older, I can see that Jules and Nick's biggest problem was getting out of their own way. Communication is vital."

"What if the thing you need to communicate would fundamentally change the way someone looks at you?"

Posey clicks on a few other things, switching between screens before hitting save. Later, we'll export our designs to the iPad, which is what we use to show them on-screen to our clients. The designs are also turned into a video file by someone else, and that gets slotted into the episode. All these logistics, most people never consider when they watch a show.

She turns toward me. "You're afraid to tell Nate something about why you left the island as a kid? Do you want to tell me first? Maybe it'll help to talk it through."

There are three people who know the complete truth, and one of those people is no longer here to tell it. The idea of unleashing all of it on Posey is strangely appealing, but I know I can't. Part of the deal I made, the one that both saved me and damned me, required me to keep my mouth shut. Forever.

"I can't tell anyone," I say.

She gives me a pensive look. "Then it must have something to do with Celia Tucker. She'd be the only one who'd demand absolute silence."

That's a speculation I'm not going to bother confirming or denying, instead I turn back to my computer and try to focus on the design for the next episode. Posey's design can be outlandish, but mine needs to be on the money.

"You don't think Nathaniel deserves to know his mother ran you off the island?" Posey's voice is gentle.

"She didn't run me off the island. I went willingly." Then I pin my lips together, determined not to let anything more spill out. Celia is just as dangerous as my mother when crossed.

"That could mean all sorts of things where she's concerned," Posey says, her tone ominous, and it's clear she's familiar with Celia Tucker's modes of operation.

But I don't blame his mom for what happened; I only blame myself. She didn't put a gun to my head or hold me over a barrel or any of the other metaphors I could dig up to make her at fault for my choices. I'd love to lay it all at Celia's feet, but I can't. Things got fucked up, and I tried to fix it, and in fixing it, I fucked things up in a different way. Nate was the price I paid, and I don't think he'll ever be able to forgive me for that.

"If the past is actually what's holding you back from being with Nathaniel more permanently, from signing on for a second season if we get one, from saying yes to my wedding, then maybe you need to reconsider what's most important *to you*."

The thing is, I already weighed those scales fourteen years ago, and there's no way to go back and rebalance them. And despite how much the truth hurts, I'm not even sure if I would.

Chapter Thirty-Five

NATHANIEL

Owen, Cal's brother who owns the security company, has every piece of damning evidence he and his crew have gathered on Mickie over the last four weeks laid out on the kitchen island of my apartment. It's substantial—drugs, money laundering, illegal gambling, physical abuse, and torture—but I don't know what's admissible, what we can use to take her down. Hollyn got the restraining order but decided that formal charges would only enrage and embolden her mother. Maybe she was right, but it hasn't stopped me from doing everything I can to get Mickie Davis out of Hollyn and Kinsley's life.

Hollyn hasn't said it, but I feel like any chance I have of convincing Hollyn to stay on the island when production ends is at least somewhat tied to her safety. She can't go around with a security detail for the rest of her life. I hate that she has to have one now.

"Can we feed this to Stephen Foster or someone else in the police force?" I ask.

"I can get it into the right hands," Owen says, brushing back his dark-blond hair from his forehead before planting his hands back on the island to survey all the printouts, "but you have to be sure this is the path you want to take. With her prior convictions, this will be a life sentence for her."

"You didn't get anything on Niall?"

"You asked for the focus to be on Mickie, so that's where I planted my people."

Niall would be a bonus, but he's been Mickie's sidekick in everything, rather than the instigator. The scars still lightly visible on Hollyn's arms come from her mother, not her father. He was the cheerleader, and while I'd love to take him down, too, Owen is right that Mickie is the priority.

"And none of what you've gathered could be considered entrapment?"

"*I* don't think so," Owen says, "but that's not my part of this process. We give it all to the cops, and we see where the chips fall."

"I wish a company like yours had been around when I needed a private investigator."

"We don't normally do surveillance like this," Owen says. "Not unless it's tied to a specific client—stalking or some other crime that requires it. This is the cousin's special." He gestures to the pages. "Satisfied?"

"Yeah," I agree, stepping back. "I just hope it's enough. If it's not, I'm going to keep going for her. I don't care how long it takes or what I have to do. I'll get her out of Hollyn's life."

"When did you hire a PI?" Owen asks.

"A long time ago." *Fourteen years ago.* "Hired some guy in New York City."

Owen squints in thought. "You remember his name?"

"No, but he must have been ill-qualified. The person I was trying to track down was literally *in* New York City."

Owen sweeps all the printouts and photos back into the envelopes he brought with him, and he seems lost in thought for a beat. "Your mom has a lot of ties to a lot of people."

"Yeah, I know," I say with a sigh.

"Do you really know, though?" He stops what he's doing to look me in the eyes. "She's got her fingers in a lot of pies across the island."

"Her currency is gossip."

"Maybe that's what you thought it was as a kid, but her currency is *lives*, man. Your mom makes and ruins lives. That's not even an exaggeration." He shakes his head. "You and Sawyer and Maren are out there trying to make people's lives better, and your mom is out there covering up some things, digging up other things. A dog with a bone that she's constantly burying or revealing. It's fascinating to watch and scary as shit. I would not want to cross her."

"Sounds ominous," I say, though I'm not as surprised as I wish I was. She's always been one to trade in information, but I don't think I ever really thought enough about the consequences of that—who gets helped, who gets hurt. Much of what she does has never touched me, and in cases like Gage, where he got into trouble with the government, her ability to wield information often proved helpful to the family overall. At times, I've even gone to her, knowing she'd get something done that I'd find distasteful or that I wasn't sure how to approach. Less now that I'm older, but there were definitely times when I asked for help and didn't question how she solved my problem.

"I suppose that's why Celia and Jonathan are still together," Owen says. "I bet she knows all the skeletons in his closet." He lets out a little laugh. "I wouldn't even be surprised if she was the one who buried them all there."

"She's never deliberately set out to hurt any of us kids. Neglectful, in a lot of ways. Self-absorbed sometimes. Since she got sick, she's been a bit better." I shrug, but I wonder whether I should be looking into exactly whose lives my mother has been making and ruining. It's not a path I've ever wanted to go down, because I'm afraid it'll fragment our family, but it's also the height of privilege to be able to ignore whatever she's doing. Not exactly a great feeling to realize that maybe I'm not as far removed from my rich, entitled upbringing as I'd like to believe.

"When are you turning all that over?" I ask.

"I'll talk to Stephen to figure out the best way to get it into the right hands. I want to make sure they can use as much of it as possible. You want her nailed to the wall, right?"

"That's right," I say, "and I don't want any possibility that she can hang those nails on a cross. Mickie is not the victim here."

"Fair enough," Owen says, tucking the files under his arm before slapping me on the shoulder. "It's been good to be out of special forces and back on the island."

"Business is going well?" I ask.

"Palace has hired some of my people for the princes and their babies. We've got celebrity clients coming to the island looking for local security. My bodyguard and security guard training programs are up and running, and my brother Weston built all the tech for the company to keep us secure and state-of-the-art. Things are ticking along. Can't complain."

Then we stand around talking for a few more minutes about producing television, working with Interflix, and the hit documentary my company put out about Prince Nicholas and Julia Jensen, which was picked up around the world.

When there's a knock on the apartment door, Owen excuses himself just as Maren enters with a small dog carrier.

"Kinsley is going to bawl her eyes out when she sees he's gone later," Maren says, setting the carrier on the island. "You have to give him to her before then."

"I'm picking her up from school," I say, "so telling her won't be a problem."

"Telling Hollyn?" Maren says, raising her eyebrows.

"Might inspire a fight," I admit. "But he seemed like a good dog, and I couldn't take Kin's tears."

"Your little marshmallow heart," Maren says, patting me on the arm.

"Hey, what's going on with Sawyer? I texted her. She's dating Dalton Worthington?"

"Yep," Maren says, her expression tightening. "He's running for the Advisory Council, just broke up with his wife about six months ago. There's something about him that rubs me the wrong way."

While I love Maren, she can be a little prickly sometimes, particularly with men, so it's hard to know whether her gut feeling is accurate or a knee-jerk reaction to a political figure.

"I haven't heard anything about his divorce," I say. "Good or bad."

"Me either," Maren says. "I'm tempted to ask Mom, but I don't want to drag her deeper into Sawyer's life if I can help it. He *is* charming, and he does seem to be well-liked at the palace. Brice, Nick, and even Alex, speak highly of him. Fair, funny, personable—which should all be good things."

"So..." I hedge. "Maybe it's just you?"

"Maybe it's just me," Maren says with a sigh. "Why am I like this?"

"Your ex-husband," I say. "Ruined your trust. Brice has been working on restoring it, and you're just not there yet."

"And I thought my radar was warped when I married Enzo," Maren says, and the puppy whimpers in the carrier. "Apparently, that 'bad guy' radar still might be off-kilter."

"What do I do with him?" I ask, gesturing to the puppy. Once I've got Kinsley, I'm taking her to the pet store to get everything we'll need. I'm letting her lead the way, but until she's with me, I'm a bit fucked. I've never owned an animal, let alone a puppy.

Maren reaches into her bag and pulls out some folded material. When she sets them on the island, I recognize what they are.

"He'll pee on those?" I ask, skeptical even though I've seen it.

"He's a pro," she says. "Honestly, the best pup in the litter. Kinsley has good taste." She pats me on the chest. "I need to go oversee all the other pickups. Videotape Kin's response, will you? I'd love to see it. Ten dollars says she bursts into tears of gratitude."

"I don't want her crying!" I call after Maren as she heads to the door.

"Too late, brother. You're going to make her heart too big for her chest with your infinite kindness."

When the door clicks closed, I put the pee pads down, and I stare into the carrier. For as long as Kinsley is on the island, this little guy will be hers. And if they really do leave us both behind, well, he'll become mine.

Chapter Thirty-Six

HOLLYN

When Posey drops me off at the house after we're done shooting for the day, Nate greets me outside the circular driveway, and immediately, all my insides tense up. He's more the type to be in the house watching sports or on his computer rather than outside when I arrive.

"Is everything okay?" I ask as I shut the door to Posey's car, and give a quick wave to her as she drives away. The security that's constantly tailing me sits at the end of the long driveway, and I clock the other security person who often patrols the exterior of the house coming around the corner at a leisurely pace.

Nothing unusual about any of that, and I relax a tiny bit. Nate's expression doesn't look worried either. But there's definitely something off.

"Yeah, fine," he says with a slight head nod. "I just wanted to talk to you in private before you went in the house."

"Did something happen to the house?"

He bites his lip and stares at me for a beat, and I can tell he's measuring his words again.

"You can just say it," I say.

"Kinsley fell in love with one of the puppies, and I adopted it. It's in the house."

"*You* adopted it?"

"I did."

"Without consulting me?"

"Since *I* adopted it, and we're not technically a '*we*,' I didn't think I had to."

There's a hint of challenge in his voice, which I wasn't expecting, but he's also correct. We're not a "we." Sometimes I forget we can't be more than we already are when we're all in this house together. A brief prick of sadness threatens to penetrate and spread. If he wants to adopt a dog—even if it's a thinly veiled gift to my sister—I can't really say much.

"Congratulations on your new puppy. I hope the two of you are very happy together," I say before trying to step around him.

"Hols," he says, grabbing my arm. "I'm keeping him, so there's no pressure on you to take him with you or stay here with him. It's a neutral thing."

"Neutral? You think adopting *this* dog is neutral? Have you met Kinsley? She already loves the dog. What do you think another few weeks or months is going to do? She'll be attached, and I'll be the horrible, terrible, worst sister ever—again. Which is how I was hoping to have my time in Bellerive end when I have to leave—right back where I started." Two hearts breaking for different reasons.

"You don't *have* to," he says, quietly.

I stare up at him, and I wish so badly that were true—that I didn't have to be the bad guy in any scenario, that I didn't have to leave the island, that consequences for actions didn't reverberate years after a decision was made. If only I could live in *that* world.

"Let me go, Nate," I say, keeping my voice equally quiet. I don't want to fight with him, not when the clock ticks between us, making our time together limited and finite. I've got a second chance, and even if it doesn't look the way I want, I won't spoil our time with bitterness and anger.

He releases me, and I step around him into the house. He doesn't follow.

As soon as I enter, I call out for Kinsley, but instead of my sister, a little black dog with a white splotch on his chest and the biggest feet comes plodding toward me, his tongue lolling out of one side of his mouth. I deliberately stayed away from the puppies the last few weeks because I was afraid I'd fall in love too. A dog isn't practical with our life in New York, but I can't deny this little guy's cuteness.

I drop my purse on the floor, and I fall to my knees to embrace his rambunctious puppy wiggles and licks. Kinsley stands in the light, deeper into the house, and I can tell she's hesitant, probably because Nate didn't come back inside.

"Are you mad?" she calls out.

"He's Nate's dog," I say, keeping my tone airy. "How could I be mad?"

"I got to name him and pick out all his stuff."

I survey her from a distance as the puppy gives me enthusiastic slurps on the face. "I want to be happy for you, Kin, but I need to be sure you understand that *we* can't keep him."

"I know," she says. "I already told Nate that." She comes closer, and I can clearly see her face now.

"You've been crying."

"I lost it when Nate showed up at school with Henry."

"That's what you've called him?" I scoop him up under his front legs and hold him aloft, scanning his face. Strangely, it suits him.

"It means a lot to me," Kin says, and I can hear the emotion in her voice, "that Nate adopted him. It might be..." She takes a shuddering breath. "It might be the nicest thing anyone has ever done for me."

My heart aches at how hard she's trying to keep her tears at bay, and the creak of the door behind me signals Nate's return to the scene of his crime, but I don't even try to stir up anger.

Like always, Nate's been able to see what lies in someone's heart to deliver their deepest desires right to their feet. His thoughtfulness, his generosity, is unmatched. Given that I remember what it's like to be on the receiving end of that, how can I begrudge her this?

The sadness will come—it has to. But for now, we can both bathe in the happiness we've started to carve out in this house. Maybe I can't keep Nate or this dog or this life, but it's mine for now.

"Anybody hungry?" Nate asks from behind me. "I can order in."

"Sure," I say, half turning toward him so he can see that even that brief desire to murder him for his impulsive kindness is gone.

His lips tilt into an almost smile, as though he can read my thoughts.

"Kin?" he asks.

"I didn't know I was getting a puppy today, and I made plans with Indy. Can I take Henry with me?"

"As long as Indy's family is okay with it and you take something to keep him penned up in case he's running a bit wild."

"He has a crate." Kinsley glances from me to Nate and back again. "And since it's Friday, maybe I can sleep over at Indy's place?"

"*With* the puppy?" I ask.

"If her parents say it's okay?" she asks.

I look at Nate, as though seeking a second opinion, and he shrugs. "You can ask."

Twenty minutes later, Indy's parents, Indy, and her sister are all in the driveway, making a big fuss over Henry with his sparkly purple collar and leash. Since Kinsley is spending the night, I explain about the security detail and, not for the first or likely last time, apologize for the fact that my parents are horrible people.

Just before the car pulls away, Kinsley sticks her head out the window. "Nate!"

He turns and gives a wave.

"Can you send me the video you took?" she asks, holding up her phone.

"Sure," he says with an easy grin, and the car heads off down the lane.

"Video?" I ask.

"Maren asked me to take a video of Kinsley realizing she was getting Henry—" He hesitates for a beat and gives me the side-eye. "I mean, that *I* was getting Henry."

"Of course," I say, unable to resist winding my arms around his middle now that we're alone except for our own security detail. "Can I see it?"

"You'll cry too," he says, wrapping his arm around my shoulders as we head into the house.

"I'm not a crier," I say with confidence. As a kid, when I cried, my mom hit me harder. Tears mean pain, and not just the emotional sort. I outgrew the instinct my mother honed in me a little with my aunt, but I never got over it completely.

"I was a fucking mess watching her. Best thing I've ever done," he says, leading me to the couch and tugging me down beside him. "I thought I'd never top the Mia Malone concert, but I did."

He clicks into his messages and attaches the file for Kinsley before sending it. Then he hands me his phone before getting up and going to the kitchen.

I click on the play button, and at first, I think I'll be totally fine watching it. Her confusion over the dog being at the house is cute. But as the video progresses and Kinsley realizes what Nate's done, it's not her crying that makes tears spring to my eyes—it's how hard she's trying *not* to sob with joy. How often have I seen someone cry tears of joy? And for the person to be someone I love as much as Kinsley makes my heart feel too big for my chest.

Her excitement and happiness are clearly overwhelming her, and she's fighting to hold it together. She keeps asking Nate if he's sure, and every time he says yes, her control seems to crack a little more. Until she's on the ground, the dog clutched to her chest, crying so hard she can barely breathe.

A box of tissues appears in front of my face as the video ends, and I realize I am, in fact, crying. Tears are streaming down my face.

"Oh my god," I breathe out. "She really loves that dog."

"And honestly, that dog really loves her. You didn't see it, but he follows her everywhere. He's on her lap the minute she stops moving. He picked her as much as she picked him."

"How are you this good?" I ask, dabbing at my eyes. Now that I'm older, it makes even less sense that someone like Nate could share genetics with Jonathan and Celia. They're people who take, take, take, and Nate's someone who gives, gives, gives.

There's never been much I could give him in return. Once I've got my tears under control, I tug at the waistband of his jeans, drawing him closer. Then I'm undoing the button, drawing the zipper down while I stare up at him.

"I thought you'd be mad," he murmurs.

"I was," I say, releasing him from his boxer briefs.

"I thought you might kick me out." His hands sink into my hair as I hover over his hard length.

"Of your own house?" I grip him, moving my hand up and down.

"Yeah," he says with a strained chuckle, his gaze locked on the movement of my hand.

"Considered it," I say even though I didn't. Then I lick a line up his shaft. "Decided I'd rather fuck out my frustrations."

"That's an A-plus in conflict resolution." He groans as I take him into my mouth, rotating my tongue around his head. "Fuck, Hols. That feels... so good."

"Might be a bit of gratitude mixed in with my frustration," I say before I suck him in deep again.

"Gratitude?" His voice is hoarse.

"I've never seen my sister so happy." I swirl my tongue around and around.

"It was... it was my pleasure."

"It's about to be," I say, meeting his gaze before taking him deep again.

Then I let myself get lost in the pleasure I'm giving him, in the sounds he's making, in the way he's barely maintaining control. Sex was one of the only times in our relationship where I felt like I had the upper hand when we were younger, where he was content to let me lead, set the pace. The imbalance I often felt between us out in the world—whether it was about money or social status or even just our upbringing—became nonexistent in the bedroom, or wherever we chose to be together. It's the same heady sensation now, to know I have the power to make him lose control, to beg for more, to plead for release.

So much time has passed, and yet so much hasn't changed between us. All these years, I talked myself into believing that we'd have grown apart, that the intensity would have faded, that there was no way two people who were raised so differently could have worked out.

And I know why I had to tell myself those things, why I had to convince myself that the path I took was the only one that could have possibly led to anything good—but not one of those things has felt true since we moved into this house together.

Nate and I get along just as well, understand each other just as completely, want each other just as much as we always did.

The snake oil I drank at the time made other people's lives better, but it didn't make mine better, and I'm coming to terms with the fact that it didn't make Nate's life better either.

While I might have wondered whether my leaving would actually be a blessing for Nate—if he'd get over me and find some suitable socialite—part of me knew there was a chance I was damning us both.

That's a hard reality to face, and I'm not sure I'm ready to take the full load.

"Hols," he says, his voice thick, and I know he's close. His hands are deep in my hair, but I don't let up. I need this. I need him. "Hols, I'm gonna..." I appreciate the warning, and then he lets out the groan of satisfaction that I love the hear. I swallow, and I try to force the stickiness of my conscience down with it.

Chapter Thirty-Seven

HOLLYN

With Kinsley gone for the night, we order dinner, and we eat it at the kitchen island while talking about the show's episodes and Kinsley's incredible progress at almost every single skill in adventure racing. She's discovered numerous new loves, and I'll have to figure out how to make at least one of them work when we return to New York. A blessing and a curse.

After dinner, Nate checks with Owen to see whether the security company's employees can do puppy pee breaks. There are lots of people on the island who do pet visits, but Nate is paranoid about giving anyone who could possibly have ties to my parents access to the house. He seems to think their net extends quite wide, and maybe it does.

My parents don't seem to be nearly as poor as they once were. While they look rough, as though life has been hard on them, they don't appear to be struggling financially. I know them well enough to assume someone else is now suffering on their behalf, hustling to pay whatever debt they owe Mick, making good on whatever scam my parents are running on the island. Any wealth they've accumulated hasn't been earned through legal means.

Given how small Bellerive is, it always amazes me that my parents are capable of finding new people to draw into their webs.

At the kitchen island, Nate mixes himself a gold rush, and my lips tingle at the thought of tasting the bourbon later. While I still don't drink much at all, there's been something about the smell and taste of bourbon that's appealed to me from that first night I met Nate in the bar. At least with me, he was never one to overindulge, and for the first time in my life, alcohol wasn't linked to a negative experience. Teenage Nate, when he'd had a couple drinks, only became more loving, more gushy, more bright happiness illuminating my life. And so that smell, that taste, is intrinsically tied to goodness, to a period in my life when I felt his warmth shining on me.

"You're thinking deep thoughts," Nate says as he slides a glass of sweet tea, that he special orders every week from the hotel, across the kitchen island toward me.

"Am I?" I give him a little smile and take a sip of my drink.

"It's probably about how much you love Bellerive." A teasing glint is in his eye. He hasn't gone so far as to outright ask me to stay, but he frequently dances around it. "Off the top of your head, what's one good thing about your native land?"

"You," I say without even a second of hesitation.

He meets my gaze, surprise clear in his blue-green depths, and I wonder if I should have said it. Sometimes, given how things ended between us the first time and my refusal to stay this time, he gets frustrated when I make comments that he thinks should mean something they can't. I understand, so I've tried to be careful, to keep my reemerging feelings buttoned up more than I want to as we've lived together the last few weeks.

Even if I love him, even if part of me truly believes now that I'll never love anyone the way I love Nathaniel Tucker, I also know that the deal I made with Celia Tucker means right now is all I can have, all I'll ever get.

"Me?" he says, his voice hoarse.

"It's always been you, Nate. *Always.*" It's the closest I'll ever come to telling him the truth.

He steps around the island, closing the space between us and sweeps me into a passionate kiss, the maple and vanilla notes of the bourbon he drinks sweet on my lips. I wrap my arms around him, and I savor the pureness of this moment, where I can confess something without ruining anything.

"If you never admit to any other feeling," he murmurs as he kisses me again, "that's enough."

"What do you mean?" I draw back and frame his face with my hands. A little frisson shoots along my spine.

He searches my gaze for a beat and then he shakes his head. "It's nothing."

"It's obviously not nothing." I follow him around the island so we're on the same side again.

He swirls his drink and takes a long sip, then he sets it on the marble top. "I never asked you when we were kids, but what does love mean to you, Hols? Like if you had to describe it to someone, what is it?"

Strings that strangle you. Sacrifices you don't want to make. Losing things you want to keep. Nothing good comes from love.

"Why?" I ask, and I can feel myself closing off. Even though the love I feel for Nate right now, the love I felt for him back then, wasn't initially negative, those thoughts are my instinctual reaction to his question. Except for him, anyone who's ever said they loved me or pretended to has wanted something, has needed me to give up something for them. Love has always come with conditions.

"When we were kids, I said it to you all the time. And you never said it back—"

I open my mouth to protest, and he holds up his hand.

"Which was fine. I *felt* it, and I don't know that I needed you to name it. But it feels like you've got one foot here with me and one foot on the threshold of leaving. And I guess I'm still..." He picks his glass up again and takes another drink. "I'm trying to figure out what *enough* I need to give you to get you to stay with me." His tone is measured, and I can tell he's holding himself in check. "Love, money, protection, kids, no kids, house, no house, Bellerive, no Bellerive—there's literally nothing I won't give you or do for you or sacrifice for you, but I don't know how to make *myself enough*, I guess. I guess I just wish *I* was enough."

My heart constricts in my chest, and I know I'm about to damn us both again—that once I cross this line, he'll make it impossible for me to ever consider crossing back, and I'll have to. I have to leave—the island and him.

Messing up my own happiness all those years ago was a given, but it guts me to realize I have so thoroughly destroyed his too. And not just his happiness but also, somehow, his sense of self-worth. And he is literally everything. *Everything*. There is no other man on the planet who is as good, who loves as hard as Nathaniel Tucker.

"You are enough," I say, my own voice thick with tears. I want to tell him that he's always been enough, but it'll ring false when I threw so much away last time. "You were right. I loved you then. So much that leaving the island, leaving you, made me feel like I couldn't breathe." My voice catches. "And god help us both, I love you now. I love you. I love you so much." My chin trembles, and I can hear the shakiness in my voice. I've only ever said those words to Kinsley and my aunt, and even then, I guard that emotion closely, use the words sparingly.

Maybe New York is far enough that Celia's wrath won't touch me. Maybe we can run away and hide from the fallout together in a way I couldn't when I was eighteen.

And as he closes the distance between us a second time, telling me over and over again how much he loves me, how he's not letting me go, I let myself believe *this* is possible, that there's a corner of the earth we can journey to where Celia's long tentacles won't constrict me or Kin, that there's a reality where she won't force me to pay the same price or worse, again. I want a different reality so badly that I refuse to let any other thought in as we strip off our clothes, as he makes my body come alive in ways only he's ever been able to do, as we fuse together, two hearts and bodies straining toward the ending we both want.

"I love you, Hols," he says, one hand on my hip, the other cradling my head as he rocks into me. "To the ends of the earth," he murmurs before he scoops my lips into another kiss, angling his head to get deeper, closer.

But I can't tell him that I'm capable of the same commitment, as much as I want to, because my heart is too busy breaking and reforming in my chest, desperate for an outcome I'm not sure we'll get.

Chapter Thirty-Eight

NATHANIEL

She won't leave. That's what I keep telling myself for the rest of the weekend and for the next week as we get closer to having filming for six of the eight episodes completed. There's still a lot of behind-the-scenes work to be done before it lands on Bellerive's network for public consumption or before Interflix officially picks it up, but I'm feeling good about what we've done, where we're at.

A second season would mean Hollyn and Kinsley would be less likely to leave, and so I've been applying a little bit of pressure on people to make the call early, to invest in the series, to guarantee the show is a success. Under other circumstances, I might be content for the show to live or die on its own merits, but anything that gives me a slight advantage over a return to New York, I'll take.

She hasn't said a word about leaving since she told me she loved me, but she also hasn't made a single mention of staying. And the phrase "I love you" hasn't crossed her lips again.

It's like we're in a holding pattern, and I need to figure out how to tip the scales in my favor. If the fact that she loves me, that I love her, that Kinsley loves Bellerive, isn't enough to keep her here, her reluctance must have to do with her parents. That's the only thing that makes sense. She wouldn't want to live in Bellerive with that cloud over her and Kinsley.

Last I spoke to Owen, the police were doing their due diligence on the surveillance and other information he brought to them, and so I'm just waiting for Mickie to take her final bow and be escorted straight to hell.

Patience has never been my best skill—I grew up too privileged for that. So much of my life, I've been able to mold or bend to my desires, and so it's hard to wait for things to fall into place. Especially when those things might determine the course of the rest of my life.

With Mickie in jail, with a second season on order, with us in love and happy, I don't see how Hollyn could deny that staying on the island makes the most sense.

And if she leaves but she asks me to do long distance or move to New York, then I'll do that. It's not my first choice—staying on the island makes the most sense with the path I see for us. But she's had a life in New York for almost fifteen years, and I can't deny that she may have some ties she might not want to abandon. But in my mind, like always, every way the details shake out ends with us together, but I'm still not one hundred percent sure Hollyn believes that.

Tomorrow night, there's a charity auction and gala at the palace for Bellerive's Strays, the organization Maren became connected to as a passion project. Hollyn reluctantly agreed to attend, but Kinsley's acceptance was much more enthusiastic. A trip to the palace is not to be missed, apparently.

Bellerive Stays is also the reason we have Henry in the house. And I have to admit, the pitter-patter of puppy feet has become a favorite sound in the morning or when I arrive home at night. He's the embodiment of joy, and watching Kinsley love on him through training videos, research about food, and every other aspect that's caused her to rapid-fire questions my way—as though *I'm* some kind of expert—has been adorable. No matter what the outcome is between me and Hollyn, I'll never regret giving her this opportunity with him.

When I get home, Hollyn's in the kitchen baking what smells like strawberry cinnamon rolls. The Steckle family, which was the third home we worked on for the show, made the rolls for the crew, and Hollyn fell in love. She's been making them once a week since, trying to get them to taste exactly like Martha Steckle's version.

Other than her banging around with the dishes, it's eerily quiet in the house. I approach her from behind and slide my arms around her waist, nuzzling her neck.

"Where are Kinsley and Henry?" I ask as I trail a line of kisses down her neck.

She leans into the contact, pressing her ass against me. "Outside teaching Henry some leash manners."

"No sleepovers?"

She gives a throaty laugh and turns in my arms. "I could suggest it, but she might catch on."

The oversize sliding door creaks open, and Henry comes bounding in just as I step away from Hollyn to grab a glass from above her.

"I saw you," Kinsley says. "I'm not stupid, you know. The two of you are always staring at each other like no one else exists. It's kinda obvious."

I lean against the counter and give her a slow smile. "I don't know what you're talking about." But it's probably not the first time Hollyn and I haven't separated quite quickly enough, or my hands have found some part of Hollyn's body when they shouldn't have, or hers have grazed some part of me in passing. We have gotten quite comfortable with each other, and I'm sure that *is* obvious. When we're all over each other whenever Kinsley isn't around—which is a lot between her training, the friends she's made, and her long walks around the property with Henry—it's hard to remember to lock our connection down when she's around.

Or at least it's hard for me. Frequently hard. *So fucking hard*.

"I'm just saying," Kinsley says, "you don't have to pretend. No one's fooled."

"I was thinking I should get back over to Aunt Verna's place to finish cleaning it out soon," Hollyn says, directing her comment to Kinsley. "What works for you?"

"No, thanks," Kinsley says. "Can't you just hire someone to finish that?"

"Kin!" Hollyn's expression is dumbfounded.

"I'm not like you," Kinsely says. "I can't pretend to be fine when we're deciding what parts of Aunt Verna's life go in the garbage."

My breath comes out in a huff at the sharpness of Kinsley's tone, which I so rarely hear directed at Hollyn anymore. Some middle ground between the two has to exist. Hollyn's emotional defenses were well-earned, even if Kinsley doesn't understand them. The scars are literally still littered across Hollyn's body.

"I'll help," I say. "I don't mind helping."

"You shouldn't have to," Hollyn says. "Aunt Verna was *our* relative." Her focus is lasered on Kinsley, who won't meet her gaze. "Sometimes, we have to do hard, painful things for people we love, Kin. That's just life."

"Next Sunday, after training," Kin says, sweeping Henry into her arms and heading for the stairs.

Once she's gone, Hollyn turns back to the dishes in the sink. "I really hate that she just gave such an entitled response."

"I mean, I *could* hire someone, if you wanted. She's not wrong."

"If she really thinks we're deciding what aspects of my aunt's life to put in the trash, that's even more of a reason it should be a family member who cares, right?"

"I also see your point."

"Don't be diplomatic. Just tell me I'm right," Hollyn says, puffing out an annoyed breath.

"You *are* right," I say. "If I died tomorrow, I'd want someone who cared about me to go through my things—even if it was just to remember who I was."

"Don't..." Hollyn turns and faces me. There's anguish in her expression. "The idea of anything happening to you. Don't ever use that example again, okay?"

I draw her into a hug, and she clutches on to me, pressing her face against my chest.

"How about I help you next Saturday and Kin can help next Sunday? That work?"

"Yeah," she says against my shirt. She rises on her toes and presses a kiss to my cheek. "I love you," she whispers into my ear. "Truly. So much."

When she goes to step away, I tilt her chin and kiss her, cupping her jaw as I deepen it. On two occasions, I've heard her admit the depth of her feelings, and I'm really praying that I keep getting to unearth them for years to come.

My phone buzzes in my pocket, and I step away, knowing we can't do much more with Kinsley in the house.

On my home screen is a text from Owen.

They just picked up Mickie and Niall. They got him as an accessory to some of her charges. Should be enough to ensure she's gone for a good, long while, according to Stephen.

I stand staring into space for a beat, relief flooding through me. At least that hurdle will be gone now.

Should I keep security?

I would until after the various trials. She's vindictive. If she knows you led this, there might be problems.

Okay. Thanks, Owen.

"What's going on? Something wrong with production? We've only got two episodes left. What could possibly be inspiring that expression?"

"It's, uh... Owen just texted me. Mickie and Niall have been arrested."

"They'll get out of it. They've never once gotten what they truly deserved."

"They'll get *exactly* what they deserve this time."

She stares at me for a beat, assessing. "Did *you* do this?"

"They did it to themselves. I didn't uncover anything that wasn't there."

"What'd you find?"

"A lot. Too much. Obviously, the police weren't putting enough effort in. I just sped the process along. Owen says they should end up in jail for a long time." I hold her gaze. "Long enough that maybe you could consider Bellerive your home again."

Color leaves her face, and she turns back to the sink. "I'm not talking about that."

"Hols."

"Reyes and Cruz gave me the extension on my leave for Posey's wedding, and then... and then we'll see."

That's not a no, which is as close to a yes as I've gotten so far. "I just want you to consider that you *can* be safe here."

She bites her lip and turns away from me. Something I can't name is heavy in the air.

"Even if they tried to come for you or Kinsley through some of their associates, I'd protect you both, Hols. If I have to keep security on us forever to make you feel safe, I'll do that."

"I know you would," she says, but she's still turned away from me. "I don't think that's necessary, though."

My phone rings, and I can see it's the video chat I've been waiting for from the other two producers and the director to discuss the network feedback and the specifics of the final episodes.

"I have to take this."

"It's okay," Hollyn says, nodding but not looking at me. "I'm okay."

But it doesn't feel okay, and I'm stuck for a moment, indecisive. Even if I pushed right now, I don't think she'd tell me what's holding her back, what's making her unsure we can go the distance.

With her parents behind bars, I don't see any other barriers we can't leap over with ease.

"Get the call," she says over her shoulder. "I need to take Kin to get some things for the gala tomorrow night anyway."

"You're sure? There's a weird vibe..."

"I'm sure," she says, turning to look at me, a slight smile on her face. "I was just surprised about my parents. They've been such a cloud over my life. To think that might be gone is... it's good, but it's a lot."

I search her face for one more beat before swiping into the call. She comes over to me as I say hello and plants a quiet kiss on my cheek, her hand trailing across my middle as she makes her way toward the stairs, where the faint sounds of Kinsley training Henry echo.

Chapter Thirty-Nine

HOLLYN

While I got used to being around excessively rich people in New York and pretending I understood their extravagance, their lifestyle, galas like the one at the palace tonight only drive home how much of an outsider I still am in my own country. My parents' arrest yesterday hasn't helped that feeling. Everyone in there will know. The news will have spread like a wildfire across the country, and anyone who got screwed by whatever lucrative games my parents were playing isn't going to be happy.

The last time I was at the palace was the night of Nate's prom, and that night is a rocky memory, just like I'm sure this one will be.

Much like tonight, I felt beautiful, but I'd also felt unlike myself. I was pretending I was capable of being the partner Nate needed. While I'm now confident we could have grown in similar directions in the years between then and now, I'm not sure I ever would have felt like I fit into his circles, into the wider aspects of his rich upbringing. The wealth gap between us is still big, even if Posey thinks none of that should matter now. But maybe we were always meant to be a couple who could thrive in a house but struggle to survive in the world.

In our house, surrounded by what we've created together, we're great. Better than great. I love who we are and what we are to each other between those walls.

If it was possible to live in that space forever, I'd never have to wonder if we *truly* fit.

But already as we enter the palace gates, I'm keenly aware that I'm the criminal's daughter and he's a Tucker. The Celia Tuckers of the world are never going to accept me, welcome me, believe I belong on the arm of someone like Nathaniel Tucker.

"I can't believe we're going to a gala," Kinsley practically squeals from beside me in the limousine.

Even the fancy car and driver are an upgrade from the everyday existence we've been living, and unlike Kinsley, who seems to love the opulence, I hate it. In New York, these events were part of my job, not part of my life. Here, all the trappings of wealth remind me that Nate came from this and I came from nothing.

Across from me, Nate catches my gaze, and he holds it, as though he's capable of wordlessly pouring from his glass full of certainty into my half-empty one.

Everything inside me that has been winding tighter, slowly unravels back to some semblance of normal. For right now, I've got him. He's *mine*, and I refuse to let my doubts and my regrets ruin our time together.

When we get to the palace, the driver helps Kinsley out of the car, but when he tries to help me, Nate steps in to take my hand instead. As I rise out of the back seat, he says, "You okay? You seemed preoccupied."

"I'm not sure I'll ever fit," I say, staring at the palace entrance that Kinsley has already wandered toward with confidence. There's a line of people waiting to be greeted by the royals before entering, which I've heard about but didn't experience at the prom.

His jaw tightens and then relaxes before he says, "If you don't want this life, then we won't have this life. I don't *have* to do *any* of these events."

"That's not practical," I say, taking a step toward the line to join Kinsley.

"Practical is the furthest thing from my mind," he says, shoving his hands in his suit pockets to walk beside me. "I'll become a hermit. Live in a hut. Never again experience the sweet taste of a gold rush at one of these events as long as I get the sweet taste of you instead."

"I'm at the level of a gold rush, am I?" I ask, charmed despite the worries brewing under the surface.

"*Far* superior."

We take a few more steps and then he says, "I know you're still not sure—"

"I'm sure about you," I say. "I'm so, so sure about you. Truly. But the rest of this?" I wave my hands at the palace, which probably already houses his mother. "Shouldn't we be realistic?"

"Fuck realism," he says keeping his voice low. "I had that for fourteen years, and it was a slow march to death. If you want to fit in, I will *make them* accept you, and if you want to be outside all the bullshit, I'll stand there with you. The *only* reality I want is the one that features you."

I'm so tempted to ask him, right now, to run away with me. To come up with some place in the world where his mother would never be able to find us. But I genuinely don't know if such a place exists. She's got unlimited resources, a vindictive nature, and legal paperwork that could, if she chose to wield it, rip my heart out.

Before I can think of what to say, we're at the front of the line, being greeted by King Alexander, his wife, Queen Aurora, and their toddler daughter, Grace. It surprises me that they both know who I am, that they're able to ask questions about the production, acknowledge my aunt's passing, and ask about my job in New York at Reyes and Cruz.

It's clear from Kinsley's conversations ahead of me that she's met them both before, that they're aware of her training, and even that they've somehow met Henry. The warmth, particularly from Queen Aurora, doesn't even seem forced.

"It surprises me," I say to Nate as we walk away, "that people who seem so tuned-in can't see the massive wealth gaps across the country."

"They see it," Nate says. "But the gaps are a systemic problem. It's not something that can be solved permanently overnight. And I will say"—his hand lands on the small of my back, guiding me through the crowd toward where his siblings are gathered—"that since Queen Aurora came into King Alexander's life, the palace has become a place where a wide range of backgrounds and socioeconomic statuses are welcome. Your bank account is no longer your ticket onto the grounds."

"Everything seems so expensive," Kinsley breathes out. "This ballroom is..."

I'm trying really hard not to clock and total all the high-end pieces scattered around. Name brand after name brand dominates all their interior choices, from paintings on the wall to the wood on the floor. Kinsley's probably heard me talk about work often enough to have some sense of the money involved in creating this atmosphere.

Once we're close enough to Nate's family, I brace myself, expecting Celia and Jonathan to be among them. But I don't see either of them.

Sawyer looks stunning in a high-neck pale-lavender dress with long sleeves. I'd almost put money on her having lost weight, but Kinsley did say Sawyer had started training with the adventure race groups. It's probably my own bias poking through, but worry is my default when I notice someone has lost weight.

"Do we get to meet Dalton?" Nate asks Sawyer before he signals for a waiter to bring him a gold rush and an iced tea for me and Kinsley. Nate told me that Dalton grew up in Rockdown on the other side of the island, so the Tuckers don't know him that well.

"He's in the crowd somewhere campaigning," Sawyer says, her lips tilting slightly. "Only a few weeks until the Advisory Council selections." She glances around. "He's asked me to talk to some people for him too."

"Are you going to?" Nate asks.

"She shouldn't," Maren says, and Brice loops his arm around her and kisses the side of her head. "She's known him for five minutes, and implying that she's voting for him, and they should, too, seems a bit off to me."

"He's my boyfriend," Sawyer says with a hint of annoyance in her tone. "Brice likes him, right?"

"Well, he's hot," Ava says then sips her glass of wine. "Total age-gap-Daddy vibes. He's got my vote."

"I thought Gage was coming?" Nate asks, sliding his phone out of his pocket to check it.

"Nova had a fever, so he delayed his flight back from California to make sure it was nothing," Sawyer says. "He should be arriving any minute."

"I hear he got roped into helping Dad with the hockey team?" Nate says.

"Gage charmed a few people," Ava says, as though that's the easiest job in the world. "Is that really helping? I charm people all the time."

"Nate told me you might be doing some of the team's physio?" I say to Sawyer, seeing a chance to jump into the conversation.

"That's a plan my father and King Alexander have," Sawyer agrees. "I'm not sure I'm interested. Dalton doesn't think it makes professional sense."

"Why's that?" Maren asks, eyebrows raised.

Sawyer gives a little shrug.

"He grooming you for wife number three already? A Tucker would be quite a coup for a someone on the campaign trail," Maren suggests.

"Tucker," Brice murmurs beside Maren, his tone not quite warning.

"I know you think he's great," Maren says to Brice, "but I think that man has an agenda."

"I'm old enough to know when a guy is leading me down a path I don't want to go," Sawyer says.

"Did Mom stay home?" Ava asks, looking around.

"Mom didn't show up?" Gage says, coming up behind us.

"Wasn't feeling well," Sawyer says. "The last treatment knocked the shit out of her."

"Is it working, though?" Gage asks, a drink in his hand. He eyes me and offers his hand. "Gage. I think we probably met when I was a rambunctious little shit."

"That is exactly when we met," I say, laughing a little. "You and Ava."

"Oi," Ava says with a huff. "I was an angel. *He* was the ringleader." She takes another sip of her wine. "And to answer your question, Gage—no, the treatments aren't working yet."

"Do you think they'll let me be in the operating room when they slice you open to give Mom one of your kidneys?" Gage asks, a teasing glint in his eye. "Imagine the scar."

"It won't be me on that table, and we all know it. My heroic big brother would never allow it."

"We're a long way off kidney donation," Nate says, his hand coming to the small of my back again.

I should probably move away, but I've gotten used to having him close. On set or in the office, we're pulled in different directions, so it's easier to pretend we're merely colleagues. Tonight, even though I shouldn't, I feel like his date.

Gage introduces himself to Kinsley, and then the two of them get sucked into a conversation about dogs. He's been thinking about getting one for his daughter when they return from California.

Between nerves and the large glass of iced tea, I need the bathroom. I excuse myself from the group and head for a hallway that seems the most likely source of toilets.

"Hollyn Davis?" a female voice calls behind me.

My step falters, and I turn back to face whoever it is. She's blond, thin, and extremely pretty—the sort of delicate pretty that reminds you of a doll. There's a vague familiarity to her, but I can't place it.

"Do we know each other?" I ask with a hesitant smile. "I've been off the island for years, and I'm terrible with remembering anyone I met in passing as a kid."

"No, I..." She takes in a deep breath and releases it. "We've never formally met. I, um..." She tucks strands of her hair behind her ears. "I was one of the girls in the hallway at the prom party. Maybe you don't rem—"

"I remember," I say, bracing myself for another callous comment.

"I've thought about that night a lot—the things I said and the things I let other people say." She swallows. "I've actually spent a lot of time talking to my therapist about how ashamed I was of myself that night. Especially once I got older and I looked back on it."

"You think I'm here tonight literally raising money for my relatives?" I cross my arms. That comment has been burned into my brain for years, and I remember how hot the shame burned. At the time, these charity events *did* benefit me and my family members. A Band-Aid that never stemmed the financial bleed.

"We were cruel, and while we didn't know you were standing there, it doesn't excuse how we behaved. No one should have said that to you or about you."

"I don't know what you want me to say." In New York, I faced my fair share of people, particularly women, who enjoyed talking about others when they weren't around. It wasn't a behavior I ever participated in, since I fully understood what it meant to be on the other end.

"All these years, I was waiting to hear you were back on the island or even that Nate had finally left the island to reunite with you."

I swallow, and now I *really* don't know what to say.

"I just wanted the opportunity to apologize. The expression on your face that night—it's weighed heavy on me, and I hope what we said, what we implied, didn't have anything to do with why you and Nate broke up."

"It didn't." At least that I can say with certainty, even if women like her are why I'm not sure I could ever be comfortable in Nate's inner circle.

"A lot of us have grown up since then." She gives a self-conscious laugh. "Of course we have, right? But we're trying to raise our kids better."

"Kinsley's felt quite accepted here," I admit. Even with the wealth gaps, she hasn't felt excluded from anything or singled out. But I've never been quite sure if that's because Kinsley's on the fringes of the glow from the Tuckers and Summersets. Would people on this island dare to make enemies with someone tied so closely to such big families? I doubt it.

"I was glad to hear you and your sister were back," she says. "Nate was never quite the same after you left. Some of the spark dimmed, but I can see it again in him tonight. He even looks lighter, as though he's not carrying some invisible weight anymore."

Every word is a paper cut across my consciousness, and I struggle not to visibly flinch at each one. The damage I did to Nate when I left causes a sharp ache across my chest. Celia must have seen the impact on Nate. She couldn't have been blind to his suffering.

"If you decide to stay on the island, I'd love to see whether we'd mesh as friends. If you're willing. I think there are ways into society that maybe weren't there before. If your sister has found that to be true, then I hope it really is."

"Sorry," I say, only half listening, still processing. "What's your name again?"

"Sienna." She visibly swallows. "I've known Nate a long time."

The girl who was crying at prom, the one everyone was consoling by talking shit about me. "Are you still friends with the girls from prom?"

"Some of them," she says. "But as I've gotten older, I've become better at figuring out what's good for me and what and who should be left in the past."

That is a lesson I'm still trying to navigate. "And you were able to do that?"

"Leaving the toxic behind is hard," she says with a sigh. "Toxic clings, doesn't it? Makes you feel like you're the problem." She lets out a little laugh. "But I've been much happier since I let those influences go."

"We can get lunch," I say on impulse. Maybe Sienna and I have more in common than I ever might have thought. High school was a long time ago, and maybe it's time I moved beyond everything that happened back then. Maybe I need to let some of my preconceived notions and past feelings about those in Nate's circle go too.

This conversation just solidifies the truth I've been putting off seeing. I can't leave the island again. Knowing what I did to Nate, what I can't do again, means I have to take some risks. He can't be the only one putting himself in emotional danger. It's not fair.

Despite the consequences, I need to find some way to tell Nate what happened all those years ago, find the strength to betray the help Celia gave and still gives to me. Maybe Nate won't understand. Maybe he won't forgive me for trying my best during an impossible situation.

My only hope is that, once he knows it all, he still loves me too much to let me go, and I realize that depending on that is its own kind of cruelty.

Chapter Forty

NATHANIEL

During the last week in the office and at home, Hollyn has been on edge. Filming is the only time where she seems able to settle into some version of herself that I don't find concerning. The one time I tried to ask her what was going on, she said she was working up the nerve to talk to me, but she wasn't quite there yet.

I wasn't sure how to take that when she said it, and I'm still not sure how to respond as we drive to her aunt's apartment on Saturday. Whatever is going on in her head is obviously causing her a lot of anxiety, and I just wish she'd spit it out. But I've also learned that patience goes a long way with Hollyn. When I push too hard, she backpedals, so I can pretend to be cool, calm, and collected, while the opposite emotions rage inside me.

"Do you have a plan of attack for this?" I ask as I park in the lot behind the apartment building.

"I'll do all the personal stuff—the rest of her clothes, knickknacks, sentimental pieces I haven't dealt with yet. She kept a lot of old bills and whatnot that need to be shredded. It's mindless work, but if you don't mind...?" She opens her car door and climbs out.

"I can feed paper through a shredder, no problem. Just point me in the direction of whatever stack I can tackle." I hold out my hand for hers as she rounds the vehicle.

A man and a woman climb out of Owen's security car and follow us toward the building. To make sure their focus is on the right place, we're supposed to pretend they aren't there. I find that much easier when they're in the car, but I know this building is a hotspot of potential activity against me or Hollyn. I haven't said anything to her, but there have been a couple of attempted break-ins at the building. The area is rough for Bellerive, so it could be a coincidence, or it could be Mickie Davis at work. Hard to say.

When Hollyn uses her new key to unlock the door, I step through first. The living room is covered in clothes, papers, old seasonal decorations—more stuff than it feels possible for this apartment to hold. Verna never seemed like a pack rat.

"Did it look like this when you left?" I ask. "Where did all this come from?"

Hollyn sighs behind me. "I'm going to try not to take that personally. Kinsley wasn't keen to help, so I was cleaning out the mess on my own. There was a storage unit in the basement that I cleaned out and brought up here."

"I wasn't judging. I was assessing. You left because your parents broke in, so I wanted to make sure it looked ransacked before you came to live with me."

She lets out a little laugh and slides her arms around my waist. I slip my arm over her shoulders.

"Yes," she says, "this chaos was all me. I'm surprised you don't remember from the other times you visited."

"Too focused on other things." And I'm sure it wasn't *this* bad then.

"Do I need to make you focused on other things this time too?" She glances up at me from under her lashes.

"Unless you want Kinsley to think we did nothing today but have sex on every conceivable surface, we should probably do some of *this* first." I gesture to the piles of papers, clothes, and other items strewn around the living room. "Are the bedrooms clear?"

"Sort of," Hollyn says, stepping away. "At least of papers and clothes. Pictures, souvenirs, letters, and stuff like that, I'm going to try to handle."

"Can I clear out some of these decorations? Take them to the bin outside?"

"Sure," she says with a decisive nod. "Unless there's any you want to keep for your house?"

I *don't*, but if she needs me to keep some, I will. I slide her a look, and her lips quirk up as though she can read what I'm thinking.

"That was an offer, not an expectation," she clarifies.

"I'm good." I grab a garbage bag from the box near the door.

"If you can shred her old tax returns and bills and whatever else is in the filing cabinet when you're done, that would be such a help."

"As you wish, my love," I say, and I bow with a flourish.

She laughs and gives me a quick kiss before heading to the back bedrooms. I spend the next little while making several trips to the dumpster with decorations, occasionally stopped by neighbors who are appalled that I'm throwing out stuff that's so useful. In the end, I agree to pile some of the stuff in better shape at the entrance with a Free sign on it.

When the living room starts to look livable again, I take in the filing cabinet tucked into a corner near the window and try to remember whether her aunt had it when Hollyn was a teen. I grab the shredder from the center of the room, and I drag a chair over to the cabinet.

Hollyn is still in one of the two bedrooms, and I start taking out files, giving them a cursory glance, and feeding them through the shredder. I'm not very far when I start to second-guess myself.

"You don't need any of this?" I call to Hollyn. "This tax return is from last year."

"Oh," Hollyn says, appearing in the doorway to the short hall that leads to the bedrooms. "I do have to file one more return, I think. Keep that. And maybe anything else that might be important for her final tax return?" Her voice grows thick at the end, and her chin wobbles. She has a stack of photos in her hand.

I leave the filing cabinet to cross the room, and I drag her into a firm hug. She clings on to me, and I run my hand along her hair, smoothing it down.

"I really hate this," she whispers.

"I'll make a stack of any papers I think you should keep, and I'll hold my questions until the end to make it easier on you. Then you're not making constant decisions for me as well as whatever you're working on."

"Thanks," she says, pressing her cheek firmer against my chest. "It feels like I'm erasing her, and there's just so much history in this place."

"You're not," I murmur. "She'll live on in all the stories we'll tell our kids. All the photos we'll keep. Love means we'll always hold space for those people in our heart. The physical and material things might be gone, but the person they were, what they meant to us, they're still here. I really believe that."

"Oh my god," Hollyn says, her voice thick. "Nate, you need to go into business mode, or I'm going to be sitting on the floor, bawling my eyes out instead of getting this done." She sniffs and steps away. "I need you to be the objective, detached one. Because I don't know if I can."

"I can do that," I say, rubbing her back. "If you're undecided about something, come set it next to me, and I'll make the choice. I'll activate practical, business-minded Nathaniel."

She rises on her toes and kisses my cheek before wrapping her arms around my neck. Her fingers weave through the short strands at the back of my head, and she releases a contented sigh next to my ear. "You are literally the best."

"You're not alone in any of this, Hols. I'll be whatever you need whenever you need it. Say the word, and it's done."

"I love you so much it's ridiculous."

I squeeze her tight and savor the feel of her pressed against me. Those words are so rare that every time she lets them out, they settle over me like the warmest, softest blanket. Maximum comfort, even if what happens after Posey's wedding is still very much up in the air.

"Back to work?" I murmur.

"Thirty more seconds of this," she says, holding me close, "before I'm ready to go back to that."

A few hours later, I've cleared out the top two drawers of the cabinet, but when I tried to move the cabinet toward the door, something heavy was still in the bottom, somehow. No documents predate Hollyn leaving at the end of high school, so I'm pretty sure she must have added this organizational system after Hollyn left.

I tip the cabinet from side to side. There has to be a way to get into the bottom section, but I don't see how.

I go through the empty top drawer and second drawer again. Feeling around the edges, I snag on something. Over the edge, I see a mound of tape, and I gently pry it off with my nails. A key pings on the metal of the middle drawer, and a sense of foreboding settles in my stomach.

The only reason I can think of that Aunt Verna would need a locked compartment would be for secrets she was either keeping *for* Mickie or *from* Hollyn. I'm tempted to call Hollyn, get her to sit with me while I figure this out.

I glance toward the hallway that leads to the two bedrooms. Hollyn has been back and forth a few times while she sorts clothes to donate, knickknacks to keep, random photo books, or piles of stray photos. Last time she was out here, she said she'd stumbled on some letters her aunt had been writing to a man in England when she was younger.

Biting my lip, I take the key, and I examine the filing cabinet, looking for a place to slot it in. Maybe it's not even for this filing cabinet?

When I slide the cabinet forward, I see the lock at the bottom. Tiny. Easy to miss if you don't know it's there. I drag the cabinet out more, and I slot the key into the space.

The connection is stiff, as though it hasn't been used in a long time, and with a strong flick of my wrist, it clicks open.

The bottom of the cabinet springs open, and I'm momentarily dumbfounded by what's there—cash. So many large bills, disorganized and scattered, as though someone threw them in. When I push them back, there are manilla folders, several of them, but I feel that same hesitation.

I *should* call Hollyn.

But if it turns out that Aunt Verna wasn't as squeaky clean as Hollyn always thought, it'll ruin the memories Hollyn has of her aunt, destroy the image she grew up with.

Aunt Verna wasn't perfect—far from it—but she was the only family member Hollyn ever had in her corner in any way. I can organize the money, shred anything incriminating, and Hollyn would never need to know.

The stiffness of the drawer makes me wonder, though.

Whatever is in here has to be old enough to cause a bit of friction.

I tug out the first manilla envelope and slide out the contents.

Legal papers. I scan the typed documents and discover that they aren't linked to Mickie, like I expect, but to Aunt Verna.

When I check the date, my chest feels like it's about to cave in.

Holy shit.

Instead of reading any more, I reach into the drawer and pull out the other manilla folder. One after another, I slide papers out—legal documents, court cases, contracts—a picture starting to form.

A sharp queasiness is sloshing around in my gut, urging me to read more, making me wish I could read less.

"Hols," I call, the raspiness in my voice unmasking the torrent of feelings spiraling inside me. "Hols!"

"Is something wrong?" Hollyn's in the entrance to the hall, a frown marring her gorgeous face.

"I don't understand what all this is," I say.

But I do. It's betrayal of the highest degree.

She crosses the room, and when she sees the documents—contracts, NDAs, court documents—in my hands, all the color drains from her face. Her hand lands on the arm of the chair I'm in.

"Oh my god," she says. "Where did those come from?" Her knees seem to give out, and she starts to collapse.

The papers fall from my hands, scattering across the floor as I catch her and draw her onto my lap, cradling her close.

"What the fuck is that, Hols?" I ask, searching her face, my palm on her cheek, forcing her to look at me while I try to determine what I should be thinking or feeling.

"I can explain," she whispers, and she closes her eyes. "I've been trying to figure out *how* to explain."

Chapter Forty-One

HOLLYN

Fourteen years ago

When I turned eighteen, my aunt made me her emergency contact. At the time, I was honored to be given the responsibility, honored that in at least one area, I was a better option than my mother. In a crisis, I could come through.

But the reality of that decision doesn't fully hit my head and my heart until the night the police call to say they've arrested my aunt.

On the way to the station, I just know my mom has something to do with this. Somehow, she's pinned her crimes on my aunt, or my aunt's taken the fall for another mistake Mickie's made. Everything in me hums with anxiety. The timing couldn't be worse.

Tomorrow, I'm supposed to be on a flight to New York, but I can't leave if my aunt's in trouble. I also can't afford to change my flight or miss any of the transportation I've already paid for to get me onto campus from the airport. Everything was prebooked and prepaid.

At the station, the police direct me to a waiting area. In the chair beside me is a tall, hulking guy whom I vaguely recognize. Maybe from school? Though I think he's already graduated.

"You get picked up?" he asks.

"No." I shake my head. "My aunt."

"Who's that?"

"Verna Davis."

"Verna Davis?" he asks, seemingly surprised. "Heard them talking. Something about money laundering—does that make sense?"

Not even a little. "You were here when they brought her in?"

"Didn't see her. Just heard them all talking," he says. "I'm supposed to have a ride-along. Thinking about becoming a cop."

As far as I'm concerned, the cops in Bellerive are all crooked. None of them has ever been useful to me. Not one stopped my mom from hurting me or put her in jail long enough to keep her from ruining my life over and over. Now she's ruining my aunt's life too.

"You're going to need a lawyer."

"We don't have any money for a lawyer." I run my hands along my thighs and try to think about how I can fix this. There has to be a way. There has to be something.

A crushing weight is pressing down on my shoulders. My aunt can't go to jail. Then I remember I was supposed to see Nate after my shift. My heart aches, and I consider calling him. But he told me he had some important things to do today. I glance at the clock on the wall.

Maybe this is all a terrible misunderstanding and I'll still be able to meet Nate at the campground later tonight. We'll get to see each other one last time. My heart thumps in my chest.

No part of me believes that.

The piece of toast I ate earlier sloshes around in my stomach. I'm supposed to be going to work in an hour for my final shift. I text Franny to tell her I'm not going to make it in. It feels like the one thing I can do, something I have some control over.

Stupid. Silly. The last thing that matters is my last shift.

What if tonight isn't my last? If I need to pay for a lawyer for my aunt, I can't go away to college tomorrow. I likely can't go at all. All the plans I had to get off this island, get out from under the crushing pressure of poverty, are going up in smoke, burned down by my mother—just like always.

I put my head in my hands, and I try to keep myself from losing the tenuous control I have over my emotions. Crying isn't an option, but I can feel panic creeping in.

A *thwack* sounds from the front door, and then a clatter of other noises followed by excessive swearing. I'd know that tone anywhere. My pulse jumps, a reflex where Mickie Davis is concerned. Fight-or-flight activated, though if I'm honest, I'm much more likely to freeze.

Whenever I've been faced with my mother's viciousness, I've never been able to fight back in any convincing way.

"Get your fucking hands off me," she screams. "I wasn't washing anyone's money! I'm innocent. Someone else did this."

"Let my wife go," my father yells from behind. "You can't manhandle a pregnant woman like that. It's not right."

Pregnant?

A chill runs through me at his words, and as the two of them round the corner, in handcuffs, bracketed by police, the bump in my mother's midriff is outlined—small but distinct.

"No," I whisper. My father would be the type to lie about her condition to get sympathy or better treatment, but the last time I saw my mom, she was rail thin.

The two officers at the front desk shake their heads in my mom's direction. "You just know," the one says, "that Mickie will sell Verna out for whatever has happened. Shame, really."

"True," the other officer says with a laugh. "Mickie's Teflon. Shit slides off her. It would take an act of God to make something stick."

Fear has me gripped so hard I can't move.

"How sure are you that your aunt's innocent?" the guy beside me asks.

I'm not. Not really. She's done so many things for my mother that I can't be certain she wouldn't cross a few more lines if she thought it would keep Mickie safe, even if it put my aunt's life in danger. And if Mickie's pregnant... I close my eyes, overwhelmed by the implications.

"Can women have babies in prison?"

"Sure," the guy beside me says.

"But they wouldn't be able to keep them if they get out?"

"I don't see why not, as long as their crime wasn't tied to children. But I'm not a lawyer or a cop—yet."

I shake my head, and I can't stop shaking it. The idea of my mother and father being in charge of another human being is enough to make me want to scream. They cannot have that baby, and they cannot drag my aunt to jail with them. I *won't* let them.

"If I was you," the guy beside me says, "I'd be thinking of how I could get that money for the lawyer. I can't see Mickie Davis taking the fall if there's anyone else to pin it on."

"I don't have any money." The answer is a dazed reflex. I have some—a little. I'd intended to use it to help me at school until I could find a job on or off campus to keep myself completely afloat. There's no way it's enough for a decent lawyer.

"There's always a way to get money. A loan, maybe?"

I can't ask Nate. Besides, his mom keeps him on a tight financial leash. She holds him accountable for every dollar he spends, which Nate says she didn't used to do. He never adds, "before we got together," but it lies between us, unspoken. Asserting her control over Nate is the point.

Celia.

My brain has just clicked on a solution that's so terrible, I almost can't stomach it. The conversation we had on the back porch the first night I met her rises to the surface.

The Davis family have always had a price. When you've got yours, you know where to find me.

My chest is tight with the implications, and I can barely breathe. Rising from my chair, I go to the counter. Someone. Anyone. There must be another option.

"Excuse me," I call out.

"What can I do for you?" An officer ambles over.

"I need to see Verna Davis."

"No can do. Lawyers only."

"There's free ones, right?"

"Legal aid?" He raises his eyebrows. "If I can give you one piece of advice, sweetheart, it's this. Those charges against your aunt are serious. Real serious. If you've got the money for a better lawyer, I'd spend it. Mickie will have a good one, which'll make it even harder for Verna to get out from underneath this without legal aid."

Money. I need it, and I need it now. Nate would help me if he could, but I know there's really only one option.

I can't let Mickie raise another child, doomed to suffer the same abuse as me. I can't let Verna rot in jail for whatever Mickie and Niall have done. There'd be no relief for my brother or sister without Verna around, no one to temper Mickie's emotional swings.

Since I met Nate, my deepest desire has been him. Just him. But I can't let that life be what I desire now. It'll come at the expense of too many others. Turns out my deepest desire, the one Celia warned me would have a price, is to keep my sibling safe, to keep Aunt Verna out of jail.

I stand at the desk, numb. The kind of numb that used to take over whenever my mother sliced into me one time too many is settling across my consciousness. Bile rises in my throat at what I know I have to do, the only choice that guarantees the outcomes I can live with. I can't save us all.

I swallow down the idea of Nate, the future we hoped for, the one I'd almost started to think we could have, and I take out my phone to name my price to the one person I know who can pay it.

Chapter Forty-Two

HOLLYN

"So you went to my mother?" Nate prompts after I tell him about Aunt Verna's arrest and my limited options. His tone is neutral, like he's processing everything in slow motion.

Maybe it's my tears, the fact that I'm barely getting the words out, but he's being incredibly gentle. I'm still in his lap, and he's been listening intently, a crease between his brows.

"Yes," I say, my voice barely above a whisper. The next part makes my heart feel like it's being ripped from my chest, and I'm not sure if I can get the words out. "I... I... bargained our relationship for my aunt's release, for my sister's life."

Nate sucks in a deep breath, and he releases it slowly, the air hissing through his teeth. His reaction is what I've been dreading since I returned, the reason I've been guarding my secret so closely. He won't be able to forgive me, and I can't blame him. He's blameless in all of this.

I went to Celia willingly. No one forced me. No gun was put to my head. I knew what I had to offer, and while I understood some of what it would do *to* me, what it could do *for* me, I know now that I didn't consider Nate enough during the process. His feelings weren't on my radar the way they should have been. My aunt, my sister, and me—I didn't have mental or emotional room for anyone else that night.

Even now, I'm not sure I can bring myself to regret my choice. Maybe I should, but I kept me, my aunt, and Kin as safe as I could. That's worth something. The years we had together, shielded from the chaos my parents brought, meant something. Even if I broke my heart and Nate's in the process.

"I think I need..." He covers his face with his hands and seems at a loss for a minute before dragging them down. His expression is haggard. "I think I need you to sit somewhere else while I process this."

"Okay." I scramble off him, chest heaving, and I sink into the couch, running my hands along my thighs in quick motions. "Okay." I can barely contain my sob. "I don't expect you to forgive me. I know you won't forgive me."

"I need you to explain to me what you mean by you bargained for your aunt's release and your sister's life, because that can't be all of it. You fucking *disappeared*, Hollyn. I need you to explain to me very clearly what this deal entailed." He flicks his hand toward the pile of papers and the manilla envelopes on the floor. "Because everything I just read makes me think this betrayal goes really fucking deep."

"I don't know what you read." But more importantly, I had no idea my aunt had copies of the paperwork between me and Celia. *I* do, of course. In my apartment in New York, I've kept everything Celia gave me, made me sign from that night and the years in between. Why would Aunt Verna have copies?

Then I catch sight of the open bottom drawer for the first time, and I can't get over the amount of cash. We were always paycheck to paycheck. Why would she have that much stashed away?

Is the drawer Nate unlocked what my mother was looking for? Hadn't that been what Mickie said, Aunt Verna had her papers and some money?

Tears streak down my face faster than I can wipe them away. Confusion is swirling through me mixed with something akin to regret, but I don't even know if regret is the right emotion. I did what I felt I had to, and part of me is desperate to cling on to the sense of rightness that's been my constant companion for years.

The choice was impossible, and I went in the direction that incurred the least amount of damage to everyone I loved.

But all of it feels really fucking wrong when I'm sitting across from Nate, and seeing, knowing, *understanding* the impact my choices had on him. He didn't get to choose his future. I knowingly ripped the one he wanted right out of his hands.

"The deal has a lot of parts," I say, struggling to keep my voice steady. "I knew that night that she'd likely ask me to ghost you." Saying it out loud makes me feel a thousand times worse, and my stomach is threatening to revolt. I swallow down the bile caked around those decisions.

Nate stares at me, his expression devastated, his blue-green eyes haunted. I understand now what my deal cost him, and he doesn't encourage me to keep talking.

My breathing is shallow, and I lick my lips. "Celia said..." I take a couple of deep breaths, trying to calm my out-of-control nervous system. "She said she could get the charges dropped on my aunt. Said if I stayed away from you while my parents were in jail, that she'd help me get custody of Kinsley before they could get her back." My voice wobbles, and my chin is shaking so hard I'm barely holding myself together.

"You disappeared," he says, and I can hear the anguish in his voice.

"I said... I said you'd look for me." I meet his gaze. "She said she'd take care of that. New school. New program. A bit of distance. I wasn't that special." And at the time, I'd let myself believe that because I was young, because I wanted it to be true, because I wanted to believe that Nate wouldn't be devastated by my choices. It was easier if the only person being ruined was me.

Nate slumps back into the chair and stares up at the ceiling, an air of defeat around him. "And?"

"Just before I finished my degree, your mom contacted me to say she could get Kinsley out of foster care and to New York with me. Which is... which is what I wanted." My voice has grown thick again with tears. "Celia didn't want me on the island. Said she'd take care of the custody arrangements." I take a couple of deep breaths because this next part stings. It's how Celia has kept me over a barrel. "I didn't realize what that would mean." That letting her handle the details, staying off the island until the last moment, would only give her more room to screw me. "Technically, your mom has legal custody of Kinsley. I have temporary physical custody."

Nate shoots forward, his elbows landing on his knees. "*My* mother is Kinsley's legal guardian?"

"If I broke our agreement, I'd have to repay any money Celia gave me during my transition to a different college. I forfeited the scholarship I earned, and Celia paid for my degree instead. She also said she'd remove me as the temporary guardian if I didn't stick to our terms around contacting you."

"But you haven't stuck to the terms. Not since you've been back."

"Right." I swallow. "So, I went to see her after we started living together, and she made it clear I had to leave the island when the show was done filming. That part of our agreement was nonnegotiable."

Nate's expression morphs into something I don't recognize, and he whispers, "She makes and ruins lives." He presses a hand to his chest and stands up. "Jesus. I just never thought it would touch me. So fucking naïve. I can't stay here. I have to go."

"Nate," I say following him.

His hand is on the apartment door, and he keeps his back to me. His shoulders are slumped and tense, but he's listening, waiting for me to say something. I wish I could say anything that would make what's happening between us better. But there's nothing. Words don't change what I did.

My instinct is to run my hand along his back, and for the first time in weeks, I'm afraid to touch him, can't imagine that my touch, the sight of me, is any kind of comfort. I betrayed him in the worst way.

"I'm sorry," I say, my words garbled by the sobbing that's threatening to return. "I'm so sorry."

Nate glances at me over his shoulder, and when our gazes connect, I see a tiny glimmer of the man who loves me. Hope stirs in my chest.

"You should read what's in those papers. It's a lot more than you know," he says. "We both deserve the whole truth."

W. MILLION

Then he opens the door, and he's gone.

Chapter Forty-Three

HOLLYN

When the door closes, I collapse against it, my chest heaving with the sobs I've been barely holding in while talking to Nate. Of course he needed to leave, couldn't bear to look at me for very long before going. He must be disgusted with the choices I made, the way I threw his love away.

I didn't have to go to Celia that night. I could have given up my dreams of leaving the island, and I could have tried to save up enough money to get Aunt Verna a decent lawyer. At the time, it felt impossible to leave my aunt's fate up in the air, to trust that the truth would come out, to be sure that the truth would vindicate her and not damn her further. On top of that was the pregnancy—the idea that my parents would be in charge of a second human being. And fighting Mickie and Niall for custody would have taken more money, more time, more resources that my aunt and I didn't have.

Aunt Verna and I never talked about the deals I made once she was released. I never asked if she was innocent, and she never tried to tell me I made the wrong decision. What happened lay between us, unspoken, even when Kinsley was being handed over to me to take to New York.

When I've cried all the tears I have left in me, I crawl over to the papers scattered on the floor. The first one I find is the court document I already saw Nate holding. It's not new. I have a copy of it myself in New York.

But as I sift through the other loose pages, a chill runs through me.

Oh my god. Nate's right. There's so much I knew nothing about.

I pour over the contents of the pages, reading every word, every concealed document. I've watched enough movies, read enough books, seen enough TV shows to understand that parents are supposed to protect their kids. That has never been my reality, but for all of Celia Tucker's faults, teenage Nathaniel thought she came from a place of love, and even adult Nathaniel seems resigned to the kind of love Celia can give.

But nothing on these pages looks like love to me. Not the kind of love Nate's given me so freely. Celia's love is centered on power and control. And now that I'm older, I don't think that's any kind of love at all.

I shove all the papers back into one of the manilla envelopes, and I check my watch. I'm not on the visitation list—have *never* been on the list—but I think she'll see me. If for no other reason than curiosity. I've never sought my mother out before.

Like most things in Bellerive, the jail is more upscale than you'd expect. Leather sofas in the front waiting area, high ceilings, tasteful décor. God forbid anything on the island seem less than idyllic for tourists and the rich people randomly hauled into jail to sleep off one too many drinks. I've heard the prison—the place dominated by the lower classes in Bellerive—is much less comfortable.

When my mother struts into the visitation booth, I'm not even surprised that her outfit for jail resembles hospital scrubs more than regular prison attire. The branding around the Bellerive blue runs deep.

She drops into the recliner, nimble despite her age and the rough life she's led. She motions to the switch on the wall, and when I glance over, I see it is labelled with Sound On and Sound Off. I flick it to On.

"My eldest, finally lowering herself enough to visit her dear mother in jail." Her voice has a harsh edge to it. "You're just like me, you know. Only turning up when you want something."

"I came for the truth."

"Did you?" Her laugh seems like genuine amusement.

"Why is that funny?"

"Truth is subjective. Whoever is telling the tale is in charge of the truth."

"When the truth is documented, it makes the details a little firmer, I think." I hold up the manilla envelope I brought.

"Does it?" She lets out a derisive chuckle. "Maybe. I guess we'll see." She leans forward and gestures to the envelope I'm holding. "You found my stuff?"

Everything I uncovered is clearly my mother's, but I don't understand why my aunt had it stored in a secret compartment that Mickie didn't know anything about. The pieces are all around me, but I can't make them fit.

"When you went to jail last time," I say, slowly, "what were the circumstances around that?"

"If you found my stuff, you fucking know, Hollyn." She gives me an unimpressed look.

"I'd like to hear your version of the truth."

"That's a first."

I don't say anything in response, because it's true. Instead, I just wait for her. She's always liked to tell a story. Loved the ring of her own voice in a room. The only sound I think she liked more was my high-pitched cry as I begged her not to hurt me again.

"I'm always getting fucked over by a Tucker. You should watch your back. If your guy can do this to me, he can surely do it to you. He has it out for us Davis women, you know."

"Cut the shit, Mom," I say, exasperated. There was a time when I would have frozen up, been unable to speak back or fight back. Whether it's the years that have passed, the wall between us, or the fact I was actually able to find the courage to rise up against her last time we were face-to-face, I'm done taking her lies as the truth. Now I want the real thing.

"Just like last time, I've been framed by a Tucker," she says, pointing her finger at me.

No matter the depth or scope of Nate's anger at how Mickie treated me, I can't see him bending the truth that far. He's not that kind of person. Whatever Mom's been arrested for this time, I'm sure she's done it. Maybe she even did it last time, too, and she's just bitter she got caught.

"Who framed you?" I ask, seeing an opening.

"Celia Tucker. But you already know that if you found my papers."

"I read it all, and I don't feel like I know *anything*."

"That fancy fucking school she sent you to not teach reading comprehension?"

"Mickie," I say, exasperated again.

"I'm not Mickie to you. I'm your fucking mother. You came shooting out of *my* vagina. You don't get to treat me like I'm some stranger. I gave you life. You're full of my genes."

I'm not arguing with her over what I call her. In my head, I call her both. But naming her Mickie when I was younger helped a lot with separating the things she did to me with what I knew a mother should be.

She gives me a hard stare. "I didn't know who framed me and your dad when I went to prison last time. A mountain of evidence, and I knew I hadn't done shit. Other things, sure. If they'd picked me up on something else, maybe. Your dad and I were careful. Did we clean money? No. Not me. And sure as shit, that wasn't Verna either."

At least that answered that. My aunt hadn't been involved in what my parents had been arrested for.

"It wasn't until I got out that I decided to do some digging. Figured out how the whole thing went down. Phenomenal scheming, I have to admit." There's a hint of admiration in her voice tinged with anger. "Celia Tucker fucked us over good, didn't she?" She looks at me as though I should be nodding in agreement.

I mean, yes, but it feels wrong to agree with anything my mother says.

"Once I connected the dots, I went to Celia with the picture I'd formed. I told her I'd tell Nathaniel, tell you, about all the scheming she'd done behind the scenes to set you up. The whole thing would blow up in her face."

"You're lucky she didn't have you killed." Saying it feels like an exaggeration, but part of me believes it.

"She had enough money to make us both happy. No need for extremes." Mickie shrugs. "Of course, when I told Verna, she got all up on her high horse. You'd sacrificed so much to keep her safe and blah, blah, blah. Said I couldn't prosper off your heartbreak. I went to fucking prison, and I'm not entitled to anything?" She gives me a petulant look. "Guilted me into giving her the money. She said she'd tell you everything, give you the money, when the time was right. But she never did, did she?"

"No," I admit. But there'd been another document in the pile that makes me wonder whether she *could* tell me.

"I don't feel so bad about keeping half that cash, then. If it was just sitting somewhere in that apartment the whole time. Leave it to Verna to only do half a job."

"You kept some of the payoff?"

"Tuckers got deep pockets." Mickie's expression is unfazed. "Your dad and I needed something to get us back on our feet, get us up and running after prison. She sent us there to benefit herself. Least she could do was pay for our time."

Hot and cold keeps rushing through me in waves. At eighteen, I thought life and circumstances had backed me into a corner, were forcing my hand. Or maybe I thought Mickie was forcing my hand through her poor choices, but I never, not once, suspected that Celia was both my executioner and my savior. Celia gave me impossible choices, but this whole time, I'd thought they were *my* choices to make, that I'd gone to her of my own free will.

"She knew what I'd do," I whisper.

"That's what hunters do. They stalk their prey. Learn their weaknesses. Then they go for the jugular. Aunt Verna was your biggest weakness."

But if it had just been that, I might have held strong. Forfeited college. Stayed here and tried to make enough to pay for a lawyer. The true tipping point was

Kinsley. I couldn't stand the idea of my parents having her, of her growing up in the poverty and violence I'd been raised in. I wasn't even sure my aunt and I *could* afford to raise her.

Now, I was left with a different set of *if onlys* to mull over. If Aunt Verna hadn't been arrested, I'd have caught my flight to New York. I'd have stuck with my scholarship, and I think, with a clearer head and more life experience, that I would have stuck with Nate too. We would have made it, I think. So when it came time to get custody of Kinsley, we'd have done it together. A whole alternate life laid down, impossible to achieve after I'd veered onto a different track after one night, one set of choices.

"She told me that if I didn't take the deal on the spot, she wouldn't help me," I say.

"Of course," my mother says with a bitter laugh. "The ticking clock always works in the favor of the person holding the power."

A familiar trick, one I'd used at Reyes and Cruz to provoke an answer to a product we needed to order or a plan I wanted to execute. Apply pressure in just the right way. I understood the psychology behind it now, but at eighteen, my vision was clouded by my love for Aunt Verna and my terror over Kinsley being forced to walk the same path I had. I couldn't see the forest—the big picture if I made a different choice—because my vision was filled with those trees right in front of me, the two problems I felt like I had to solve *right now* in that moment. Aunt Verna couldn't spend one more minute in jail, and I couldn't allow my parents to have custody of Kinsley. But maybe neither of those choices had to be made *that night*.

Nate must think I'm such an idiot for making those choices. I cover my face with my hands, and I try to hold back my tears. I was so foolish and naïve.

Now that I have all the pieces, the puzzle doesn't look the same.

"Sometimes life fucks us over," my mother says, hands splayed. "You just gotta ride out the fallout."

For years, I've thought I understood what that fallout looked like. The complete and utter loss of Nate, of the kind of love and security he gave me. Being seeped in those feelings again, learning all this truth, has only made me question everything.

Even if I was pushed to the brink back then, I still made the choice. If I was in Nate's shoes, I don't know who I'd forgive, if anyone. My world might feel like it's teetering, but I can't imagine how he must be feeling right now. Everything flipped upside down.

Chapter Forty-Four

NATHANIEL

It's taken me longer than I would have liked to end up outside my parents' mansion. Even now, I'm in the car crawling up the long driveway, trying to wrap my head around everything my mother has done.

The anger is still there, bubbling, waiting to hit a full boil again, but it's been doused with a shot of sadness. She watched me suffer for years. It was completely in her power to end that suffering, and she did nothing. What kind of person does that? What kind of *mother*?

There's a good chance I've lost the element of surprise by storming all over Tucker's Town, intent on setting things right. But I can't worry too much about that.

Instead, I need to focus on letting my anger loose. Sadness can gnaw at me later, but for now, anger is the only emotion I'll feed.

After I park the car, I enter the house without waiting for one of the butlers my mother employs. They change so often that I have trouble keeping track of who is who anymore. Celia Tucker is hard to work for.

"Mother!" I yell, my voice reverberating around the mostly empty house.

"Sir," the newest butler says from the top of the stairs. "I didn't hear you come in."

"Where's my mother?"

"In the main living room, I believe," he says, descending the stairs in a rush to follow behind me. "I need to announce you."

"No need," I say. "I'm her eldest son."

"Oh, Nathaniel," my mother says, setting down her tablet when I enter the huge open plan room. "What a pleasant surprise. Gerrard, it's fine," she says to the man behind me.

I slap a sheaf of papers down on the coffee table in front of her, and I drop a pen on top. "I need you to sign this."

"What is it?" she asks, picking up the stack.

Her color isn't good—a bit gray—and I try to ignore my instinct to care.

"A custody agreement. You're turning over full custody of Kinsley Davis to Hollyn Davis, effective today. Caitlin and I are taking it to the judge as soon as it's signed." The handy part about having a cousin who's a well-respected lawyer is how quickly some things can be done.

She drops the pen without scrawling her signature. "I don't know what you're talking about. Why would *I* have custody of Kinsley Davis?" Her tone is shocked, but I'm not letting her play me this time.

"I know what you did. I know it all," I say. "You tricked Hollyn. I read all the legal documents, the contracts, the nondisclosure agreements. Verna kept every piece. I even know about the deal you struck with Mickie when she found out you'd framed her and Verna. The NDA you had Verna sign, so she couldn't tell me or Hollyn the truth. I'd ask what you were thinking, but I know. You were only thinking of yourself."

"I'm not signing anything." My mother sniffs. "If Hollyn Davis can't separate fact from fiction, that's not my fault."

"If you sign this, maybe there's a chance someday, a long, long, long time from now, that you and I might be on speaking terms. If you don't, I'll never see or speak to you again."

"You don't mean that. I'm your mother."

"What's that old saying? You can't pick your relatives."

She tosses the pen away from the pages and gives me a defiant glare.

In my thirty-one years, I've only ever gone against her when it involved Hollyn. Today is no different. If she wants a war, she'll get it. "Sign it, or I will get Hollyn custody of Kinsley by dragging your name through the courts. I'll make our feud so public, so scandalous, that you'll feel like you'll never recover. Every borderline-illegal thing you've ever done will be brought to light. You'll be a social pariah. The Tucker name will be treated like a disease."

"Nathaniel!"

"Those are *my* terms."

She picks up the pen, finds the highlighted lines, and she flicks her name or initials across the spaces.

"Happy?" she asks, standing up to pass me the papers.

"Not even a little bit," I say, turning on my heel, prepared to leave.

"I did what I thought was best. They've had a good life—much better than they would have had otherwise."

I spin around, and rage is a living, breathing thing inside me. "What about *me*, Mother? Hiring private investigators that you must have gotten to, chasing my tail, desperate to find her. The years I've spent believing she left me by *choice*."

"Don't kid yourself. She *did* have a choice, and she chose my money and influence over your love. That's the kind of woman you want to be with? I saved you from another conniving Davis, who probably would have led you into legal peril."

"If this is your version of being a savior, your version of love, I don't want it. I don't want any part of it."

"Did she tell you I made her sign anything? Because I didn't. She came *to me*."

"After you backed her into a corner," I roar. "She was eighteen. Probably scared out of her mind that the one adult in her life who she could rely on might be going to jail. And you knew—you knew because you set it up—that Hollyn would fold under that kind of pressure. Do *not* take the moral high ground with me. All these years, I've ignored the things people have said or implied about you because in my heart, I *never* thought you'd hurt any of us. Certainly not deliberately. And with such blatant cruelty."

"You were seventeen, and you thought you were going to get married? Please." My mother throws up her hands. "Recipe for divorce, and those are expensive. You think I was going to let the Davis family get hold of our money?"

"But you did," I say, staring her down. "You did exactly that when you paid off Mickie Davis so she wouldn't tell me of your betrayal. The worst part is that even if Hollyn and I had gotten divorced, she'd never have taken a penny from me. Not even if I'd begged her to. You don't know her. You never bothered to know her. And from now on, you won't know me either."

"Nathaniel," she says, following me down the hall as I stride toward the front entrance. "Nathaniel! I'm sick. You can't abandon your sick mother."

"For all I know, that's also a lie," I say over my shoulder.

Then I hear a loud crash and thump behind me, and I close my eyes before I turn around. On the floor, my mother is face down. The butler comes racing out of the adjacent room, and he's at her side before I'm able to convince my feet to move.

"I'll call emergency services," I say, "but I'm not staying."

It takes everything in me to turn back to the door, to open it, and to step though. Once I'm outside, I pull out my phone, and I dial for an ambulance, rattling off the details of the Tucker estate. When the dispatcher asks me to stay on the line, I tell her that my mother isn't my problem anymore, and I hang up the phone.

After I texted the sibling chat that Mom was on her way to the hospital, I drove to my apartment. Slowly, I've been moving my things into the house I've been sharing with Hollyn and Kinsley. Part of me has been afraid to hope too hard that Hollyn and I can make things work. But it finally feels like all of the secrets and lies are rising to the surface.

In my apartment, I sit on the leather couch, and I drag my phone out of my pocket. I've been clinging on for far too long to a lie, and it's time I let it go.

Dialing my voicemail number, I listen to the message Hollyn left me the night her life blew up. And for the first time in years, I let myself hear the anguish and the steely resolve. I'd heard those things that night, too, but when I couldn't solve it, I'd let the voicemail become a symbol of my rage, my frustration at how she left me. A single voicemail. How dare she.

But I don't want to cling on to any of that anymore, and I hit the delete button, then, knowing the instructions I gave to the phone company, I navigate into my deleted items on the web, and I delete it from there too.

I'm only dealing in truths now.

I rise from my seat, and I go into the principal bedroom to sort through one of my dresser drawers I often use for junk—odds and ends that don't quite have a home but that I can't bear to part with. At the very back, I find the small box that fits in the palm of my hand. I haven't let myself think of this thing in years. Truthfully, I'm not sure why I kept it.

When I flick open the lid, I can't help a little laugh. The tiny diamond is pitiful compared to what I can afford now, but this fucking thing meant the world to me that night, in the weeks leading up to that night. For months, and behind my mother's back, I'd tucked away every dollar I hadn't spent on looking after Hollyn and Verna. I'd bought this ring with intention and certainty and so much hope for the future.

And for the first time since then, I feel exactly the same way.

Chapter Forty-Five

HOLLYN

Unsure of what to do, I sent Kinsley to Indy's house with Henry for the night. We can't stay here, in this house, when Nathaniel probably can't stand the sight of me. I've packed as much of Kinsley's and my things as I could into the suitcases we had when we arrived.

Tomorrow, I'll have to pick up some boxes to pack everything else. Assuming Celia lets me leave the island with Kinsley, even though Nate now knows everything, we'll be gone as soon as I can get our things shipped.

It's late, so I can only assume Nate's gone to stay at his apartment. I close my eyes and take some deep breaths. Every time I think about how much I've hurt him, I want to burst into fresh sobs. I haven't had the courage to text him. If he wanted to see me, he would.

I don't hear the door open and close, but I do hear Nate's voice reverberating through the house when he calls my name.

"Hols? Where are you?" There's a hint of panic in his voice, and I hurry to the top of the stairs.

"I'm here," I say, a rush of relief washing over me that he came back. Maybe it's only to say goodbye for real, but he's here.

"Can you come down? We've got a lot to talk about." His voice has gone from slightly panicked to weary.

I descend the stairs one at a time, as though walking to my execution. Internally, I try to brace myself for whatever he might say about my choices, now that he's had time to process what I did.

When I enter the oversized living room, dining room, and kitchen, Nate is over by the fireplace mantel, a drink already in one hand and a manilla envelope in the other. After today, I've seen enough of those long brown envelopes to last a lifetime.

"I see you've packed." He gestures toward my suitcase and other things strewn by the front entrance, waiting for me to get boxes tomorrow.

I meet his gaze, but I'm not sure what to say. His tone feels indecipherable.

"Here," he says, passing the envelope to me.

I brace myself for a notice to vacate his property, or a termination slip from the show, or anything else that clips the strings that tie us together one by one.

Wordlessly, I slide the document out, and as I scan it, understanding dawns.

"I have full custody of Kinsley?" My voice is hushed, barely above a whisper.

"You do," he says, and when our gazes meet, the toll that today has taken is obvious. He looks exhausted, probably as emotionally wrung out as I feel. "And I think, if I've put the pieces together correctly, that's the last hold my mother had on you."

Tears fill my eyes, and I will them not to fall. Technically, she could force me to pay back all the money she spent to finance my college degree, but I have a feeling Nate would just take it out of one bank account to put it back in another, even if I told him not to.

"That was the big one, yeah," I admit, my voice thick. Maybe Celia would never have taken full custody of Kinsley, but she could have made our lives extremely difficult if I didn't play by her rules. I knew the risks when I made the deals, but I never expected Nate to come so fully back into my life, to make me question every decision I ever made. "Thank you." I can barely get the two words out. "You didn't have to."

"I did," he says. "Because when I ask you the next question, I don't want you bound to anyone but yourself. I need the truth, Hols. I need the complete and utter truth for my sanity. Do you understand?"

Tears have blurred my vision so much that I can hardly see him, and I nod.

"Do you want to be with me?"

"More than *anything* in the world." Tears spill onto my cheeks, and my words are garbled coming out of the tightness in my throat. "But I know... I know what I did is probably unforgiveable."

"What *you* did? Protecting your aunt and your sister is the *most forgivable* part of this mess."

"What?" I whisper, stunned. Maybe I could never bring myself to regret the choice I made—but I'd never expected Nate to forgive me for it, especially after I saw the damage I'd done.

Nate sets his drink on the mantel and closes the small distance between us. "You were eighteen. Manipulated and backed into a corner. Do I wish you'd been able to see that there were other choices? Yes. Do I wish you'd talked to me that night? Yes. But I also can't even imagine the panic you must have felt when you realized your aunt was in jail and your mother was pregnant. That's a one-two punch, and I can see how it would have knocked out eighteen-year-old you. I hate it, and I get it."

I shake my head, unsure of how to respond. Deep in my gut, teenage me thought Nate and I were doomed. He'd go off to college, and he'd find someone smarter or prettier or wealthier than me—his mom's words, those of his friends, got under my skin deeper than I thought. All those concerns seem silly now, shameful. None of that mattered. Our connection is so strong, and it's so rare to feel this way about another human being that all my past worries seem trivial.

"The only person I'm truly angry with is my mother," he says. "She could have helped you, made it all go away like she did, without asking you to sacrifice me. She didn't have to force you into that choice. And then she watched me want to cut out my own heart for years. I just..." He trails off, clearly lost for words.

"My aunt knew too," I say with a sniff. "You saw the NDA?"

"Yeah," Nate says with a curt nod. "After Mickie found out, my mom sealed that crack."

Although my aunt loved Nate once she got to know him, she'd never stopped being wary of what involvement with a Tucker might bring from Mickie and my dad but also from Celia. Even without the NDA, she might have believed that keeping what really happened a secret was protecting me. She didn't always make the right choices, but she tried.

Foolishly, I'd worked very hard to make it seem like leaving Nate behind hadn't been like being stabbed over and over again in the heart. She knew I'd given him up for her, and I didn't want her saddled with guilt that I was mostly sure belonged to my mother. Though, it seems I got that wrong too.

"I don't look at you and see betrayal, Hols. I did for a long time. Too long. But now that all the truths have come to light, it all just makes me unbelievably sad. I trusted my mother, and so did you, and she let us down, tried to run our lives for us. The audacity is... something else."

"I thought you were going to tell me to leave tonight," I say, my voice hitching.

"I've never wanted you to leave. Not for a second. This house, my life, my entire world is better when you're a part of it, and if I'd had a say, you'd never have vanished. I'd have kept you close forever." He hesitates for a beat. "I *have* kept you close, in here." He takes my hand and places it over his heart. "You've been in here the whole time."

I rise on my toes, and I kiss him. Part of me can't even believe that I get to kiss him again. That all the secrets have come out, the deals made in haste behind closed doors have all been brought into the light.

"I loved you then," Nate murmurs against my lips. "And I love you now, and I know with everything inside me that I'm going to love you forever."

And then we're kissing, and the sweet taste of bourbon is on my lips and tongue. He's walking me backward toward the bedroom we've been sharing on the main floor, and we're stripping each other. I'm frantic for the skin-to-skin connection, to know he's mine, to realize that everything I've believed about myself and him and us wasn't accurate. We might not be exactly the same people, but the love between us never died—I'm not even sure it truly faded.

"Fuck, I love the feel of your curves under my hands," he says as he guides my shirt over my head and then tosses it to the floor on our way to the bed.

It's not the first time he's said something similar. Since we've been together in this house, the compliments are constant and consistent, as though some part of him might have understood that underneath my confidence was a woman who didn't feel lovable. My weight gain has never held me back. The reluctance to sink into our connection has been based on my guilt—not that I *made* the choice but that my decisions hurt him—that hasn't allowed me to give myself to him completely, to move beyond our past to create something new.

With all the secrets and lies revealed, I have to learn to forgive myself. Nate's right—Celia could have taken a less hurtful path. I never expected her to go easy on me when I arrived at her doorstep, but she could have put Nate's feelings first. It wasn't her back against the wall or the lives of *her* loved ones hanging in the balance, but her cutthroat tactics hurt more than just me.

"Hols," Nate says as he kisses a line up my leg and inner thigh after urging me, naked, onto the bed. "Be here with me."

"I am," I say. "I'm right here with you."

He runs a finger along my core, letting out a groan of appreciation. "I love everything about you—have I told you that? But this pussy is exquisite."

My body tenses with eagerness, and at the first swipe of his tongue, I clutch the sheets, already anticipating how good he'll make me feel. There's nothing Nate won't do to make sure I'm completely satisfied, and it's been thrilling to be in a relationship with so much care and trust and love between us. I haven't felt this sexually free since we were together the first time.

In no time, he's got me panting and pleading, desperate for release and equally desperate to hold out for more pleasure, more time this close to him.

"Tell me what you want," he murmurs against my thigh as he dips a single finger in.

My breath catches, and I wiggle against him. "More," I say.

"Tell me."

"I want you inside me. Please. Please, Nate. I love the feel of you inside me."

Within seconds, I'm getting exactly what I want, his body pressed tight against me, filling me up in the most delicious way.

"Yes," I breathe out. "God yes."

His teeth graze my ear, and his heavy breathing with the faintest hints of bourbon is an aphrodisiac that I'll never get tired of experiencing. He cradles my head with one hand, and his other is on my hip, hitching my leg up to go deeper.

I curl against him, and the pleasure coming from the brush of our bodies is so intense that I might cry when my release finally arrives.

"Do you feel how connected we are? How perfectly we fit?" His breath is hot in my ear. "You're mine, Hollyn. You were always meant to be mine. And this time, you're mine forever. No one else will ever have you like this. Just me. Guiding you to the brink. Just me watching you come."

"Yes," I say, moving against him, in complete agreement with how possessive he is because it's how I feel about him too. Nothing and no one will come between us again. "Yes," I say again as he drives us over the edge together.

"I had a lot of time to think today while I was packing," I say, trailing figure eights on his arm. He's the big spoon to my little spoon.

"I hate that you packed. Those suitcases are going to be emptied back out and put somewhere that only I can find them." He kisses my neck. "What were you thinking about?"

"When we were younger—" I take a deep breath because I hate admitting this, but I vowed to myself that if Nate forgave me, I'd be more honest. "I used your wealth as a shield to protect myself from getting too deep with you. Money was the reason we wouldn't work, a reason I couldn't go all in, and I'm sure now that wasn't fair. You never cared, and I definitely cared too much. I did the same thing when I came back too. Another self-protection measure. If wealth was an obstacle, then I didn't have to admit the truth—what I did, what Celia did."

"I knew. And I was probably too dismissive then and now. But I've never wanted a socialite—someone who throws parties and manages charities. Maybe I didn't make that clear enough. I've only ever wanted you from the minute you pressed your hand to my back and I turned around. To be with you, the money, the status, didn't matter. I'd have given it all up."

I rotate in his arms, and I caress the side of his face with my palm. As tenderly as I can, I kiss him, and he wraps his arm around me, tugging me flush.

"I want to put all of it behind us. My parents are going to jail, and all the other secrets are out."

"I feel an 'and' here."

"I don't know how you're going to feel about this," I say.

"Okay," he says, slowly.

"I think I need to talk to your mom, clear the air." I don't say now that we're on equal footing, but that's how it feels. Like the weight she put on me that night is finally gone and I'm not being ground into the dirt under her will.

"I'll support that, but I'd rather not be there. She'll take it as a sign that I didn't mean what I said."

"What did you say?"

"I told her that it'd be a long, long, long time before we'd have anything to do with each other again."

"She *is* sick..."

"If she ends up needing a donor, she'll have to hope Ava volunteers. She doesn't deserve anything from me after what she did."

I can't blame Nate. After hearing Sienna describe the change in Nate after I left, I can't imagine Celia was oblivious. It must be deeply painful to realize she did this to me, but she knowingly did it to him too. Her son. I'd go to the ends of the earth for Kinsley, and she's only my sister. I can't imagine hurting a child like she hurt him, like my mother hurt me. It seems unfathomable.

"She's still got lots of treatment options," Nate says, and I'm not sure if he's soothing himself or me. The reality is that he's not the type to watch someone die, even if he hates them right now.

"You're okay if I talk to her?"

"If that's what you need, I can get Owen to find someone to escort you to the hospital tomorrow."

"Hospital?"

"She collapsed at the end of our fight. Family chat has been going off all night, but I've been ignoring it."

If this is how he needs to deal with Celia's betrayal, who am I to criticize him? This doesn't *feel* like him, but I also know that we make different decisions when our nervous systems are overloaded.

"If she was dead," he says, his tone flat, "someone would have called. They're probably gossiping about me in the chat, and I don't need to add to that noise right now."

That makes more sense. Seems more like Nate, and I breathe an internal sigh of relief. I've spent so many years with feelings in deep opposition to each other that it's hard to rewire my brain to place most of what happened on Celia's shoulders. She *could* have made different choices. Helped me and let Nate and me stay together, especially after she saw how miserable he was. I never expected her to be easy on me when I showed up at her house that night. She had a lot of leverage, but my feelings about the life she gave me are hard to pin down. I wish things had gone differently, but they also could have gone so much worse. What would she have done if I hadn't taken the deal? Let my aunt go to prison? Petitioned to have Kinsley returned to my parents' care when they got out? There's no doubt in my mind that she had that kind of power and vengeance.

"Tomorrow, we put all your things back where they belong—in my house, in my life, in this fucking bed—exactly where they always should have been."

Confronting Celia in the hospital wasn't the power move I needed, so I've waited until she returned home. At the Tucker mansion, I'm given much different treatment than the last time I was here. I'm shown directly into the main living room and announced with fanfare. It's a full circle moment.

"Come to gloat, have you?" she asks from the couch, where she's sitting with her tablet.

"Came to clear the air."

"Nathaniel did all the air clearing I think I can handle." Her gaze rakes over me with a critical lens, and she sets her tablet aside. "We really have nothing to say to each other. I gave you a better life, and *this* is how I'm repaid."

"The thing is," I say, "you didn't have to give me *that* life at the expense of your son. You had a choice."

"You and he are *not* a match."

In previous interactions, I've found her certainty to be hard to handle. Her tone and proclamations have put me on my back foot, unsure of where to step next. But I can't let her keep doing that to me. Maybe she's out of my life and out of Nathaniel's life, but I can guarantee she'll still be a crucial part of Bellerive society. That's just how the island works.

"We *are* a match," I say. "Despite the forced time and distance, we're just as in love as we were as teenagers. We're going to get married and have kids, kids you'll probably never meet except in passing."

"You threw him away, and *I* get punished."

"You set me up. Why can't you just admit that you set me up?"

"Your aunt was guilty, did you know that? Mickie and Niall weren't, but your aunt was. She was laundering money through the deli she worked at. I got her off. Made sure she didn't pay for her crimes. And this *betrayal* is how I'm repaid."

I have no idea if Celia is lying. My aunt kept all those documents, and there was nothing in there that would lead me to believe Celia is telling the truth right now. We certainly never had any extra money from these supposed illegal acts, so my gut says she's lying—one last-ditch attempt to hold something over my head. Or it's possible that Mickie was the one laundering through the deli and they're all lying to me. Maybe my aunt didn't know. Either way, I'm not letting her tarnish the good memories I have.

"The least you could do is speak to Nathaniel. Make him see reason. Tell him that I gave you and Kinsley—even your aunt—a good life."

"I won't tell Nathaniel how to feel about anything, actually," I say, straightening. "He's innocent in all of this. He can feel however he feels, and I'll support him completely."

"You're only saying that because he still wants you."

"I'm not. But I don't expect you to understand what it means to love someone like that—to want what's best for them, even when it's not what's best for you."

"You two will never make it long-term. Bellerive society might accept you while you're on television, but the minute that shine wears off, you'll just be another poor Davis girl."

"You can think what you like, Celia. The only person who needs to accept me is Nate. Took me a while, but I understand that now. Nate doesn't need Bellerive society to accept me." Talking to Sienna also reminded me how much people can change—both me and Bellerive's upper class. Seeing Kinsley thrive has taught me that this island, these people, don't have to represent what they once did. I need to fit into Nate's life, not Bellerive's harsh social classes. That's the important part, and I'm finally sure I can.

Celia gives me a grimace, but she doesn't contradict me.

"I just came to tell you that your hold on me is done. Your hold on Nathaniel is done. We're going to live our best lives together, without you, and I hope that watching it makes you realize how wrong you were then and how wrong you are now." I stare her down. "Because if you're not careful, you'll alienate *all* your children, and you'll die in that hospital you were just in, alone."

Then I turn on my heel and I leave before she can dismiss me. We don't need her approval for anything anymore. For the first time since I was a scared kid standing in her living room, I finally feel like I'm in charge of my life again.

Chapter Forty-Six

HOLLYN

I've never been to a wedding of one of Bellerive's elite before. Nate's prom was the closest I came to that sort of luxury when we were dating in high school.

To think, since Posey and I are trying to get our own company started, with tiers of service for different economic brackets, she's scaled *back* her wedding costs, and it's still this luxurious.

Securing a building, paying for branding, and being mindful of money is at the top of both of our minds with our new company. While I do have some funds from the TV show that I can use, Bellerive is an expensive country to live in and to source design materials. I'm also still reluctant to let Nate pay for anything that has to do with Kinsley, so sometimes my money feels tighter than it could if I wasn't so stubborn.

Even scaled back, there are a lot of people milling around the hotel's estate when we arrive. Rather than getting married at the royal palace, Posey's mom, who used to be the king's secretary, called in some favors, and Posey and Brent are getting married at the oceanfront resort that's been a celebrity hotspot the last few years. Posey said she wanted to get married by the ocean because it reminded her of how she and Brent met in the first place.

"This is nice," Gage says as he and Ember arrive outside the front of the huge white-and-black stucco hotel, a valet whisking their vehicle off behind ours.

"Nice?" Ember snorts. "A couple of years ago, I would have called this *insanely* luxurious."

"But not anymore?" Gage asks, and I can hear the hint of teasing in his voice. My favorite part of hanging around with him and Ember has become how clearly and dearly he loves her. He reminds me so much of Nate in those moments that I sometimes forget how much of a hellion he was as a little kid.

"No, it's still insanely luxurious," Ember says. "I've just gotten a bit more used to this ridiculous wealth."

"I don't know if you can ever really get used to it when you're coming into it from the outside," I say.

"I guess I'll find out," she says. "Got a few more years to see what I think." Now her tone is teasing.

"Or," Gage says, tugging her into his side, "the rest of your life. Remember, you're mine forever. Even the Bellerive courts agreed." He fiddles with the ring on her finger as a reminder, and she leans into him, placing a hand on his chest.

Nate seems fixated on her ring for a minute, and when I nudge him, he gives me a little smile. "Smug marrieds," he says quietly.

We've been watching old movies in the downtime we've had since filming ended. *Bridget Jones* amused him a lot, whereas I loved *Love Letters from Spain* with Wyatt Burgess and Ellie Cooper—gave me all the angsty longing now that I'm not experiencing it myself.

A car pulls up behind us, and Dalton Worthington and Sawyer are in it. Dalton hops out of the car and circles to open the door for Sawyer before the valet can get there.

"I hear he's going to make her wife number three," Gage says.

"Does Sawyer know that?" Nate asks, and I can hear an edge in his voice. He hasn't said anything bad about Dalton, but Nate's been reserved around him, as though he doesn't quite feel comfortable with him. If I didn't know Nate so well, I probably wouldn't even have noticed.

"Maren does," Ember says, "and she's big mad."

That elicits a chuckle from Nate. "For someone who's on the cusp of getting remarried, she's got big feelings about people who've been married more than once."

"I mean," Gage says with a little laugh, "you have to admit that having two divorces is a bit more than unlucky. I'm *never* getting divorced."

"It does take the gloss out of the old adage that 'you know when you know' if you've 'known' two previous times," Nate agrees.

"Sawyer told me," I say, "that he's driven and determined, and not everyone can handle someone like that."

"As long as he's not sacrificing her on the altar of his needs," Nate says. "And, I don't know... my dad and Alex have been trying to talk her into getting involved in the World Hockey League team coming to the island next year, and she keeps turning the job down, citing Dalton's distaste for it."

He's not wrong to be cautious. In the few months since I've been back in Bellerive, there's definitely been a change in Sawyer. She's gone from fairly bubbly to more reserved and serious, which I thought was tied to Dalton's increased political profile.

"Either way, I can't see marriage being something Sawyer would rush into," I say.

"Oh, that's me. Guilty," Gage says, partially raising his hand. "Very, very guilty on that one. To be fair, not all rush jobs are bad deals. I can't complain about how it's worked out."

"You'd better not," Ember says with a laugh. "I'm standing right here." He loops his arm around her and kisses her temple.

Sawyer and Dalton have finished talking to a few other people who approached them as soon as they arrived. I'm surprised at how covered up Sawyer is for such a hot day, but she told me that Dalton's vibe is sophisticated elegance. She certainly looks the part today in her high-neck pale-pink dress that covers her arms to the wrists. Her short dark hair is pulled back in a neat, low ponytail.

"Shall we?" Sawyer says, gesturing to the pathway that'll lead through the hotel to the outdoor seating. Posey's given me all the wedding details the last few weeks while we've been planning our company's launch. I could probably walk someone through every aspect of the day ahead of us without hesitation.

Nate takes my hand, raising the back of it to his lips as we walk toward our seats. My stomach flutters at the contact. It doesn't seem to matter how much time I spend with him—the smallest gesture still makes me swoon. Since Kinsley is at Ember and Gage's place with Henry, Nova, and Michelle, the nanny, we'll have the house to ourselves.

"I love you so much," I whisper as we find our seats.

Nate presses a kiss to the side of my head and guides me into my spot beside Ember. Sawyer and Dalton file in behind us so he's on the outside, able to stand up and talk to people as they find their seats.

The royals arrive and are seated near the front. Posey has told me that they're like family since she and her sister were raised on the royal estate. With her sister married to one of the princes, I suppose they're literal family now.

Soon everyone is settled, and the music begins to play for Posey to come down the aisle. When she emerges from the hotel, instead of looking at the bride, I focus on Brent. To me, the reaction of the groom is always the most telling for the success of a marriage. What's his expression when he sees her?

The absolute contentment on Brent's face is a good sign. No hint of nerves. No whiff of uncertainty. I've been around them a lot the last few weeks, and I'd have been surprised if there was, but I'm still relieved that what I saw before today is still there.

Posey is radiant as she walks past us in a gown that looks more princessy than I expected the first time she showed me a photo, gaze fixed on Brent. The rest of us are just decoration, really. The two of them probably could have gotten married in front of no one and been just as happy.

But Posey *does* love a party. And decorating. So the big wedding makes sense, and maybe the fairy-tale dress does too.

As we listen to their vows, Nate keeps squeezing my hand, and a few times, he brushes a kiss along my shoulder and my temple. It's funny how watching someone else get married can make you feel more connected to your own partner when what you're watching just *feels* right.

On the dance floor, Nate and I are swaying to the music. I have my cheek pressed to his chest, and his lips are close to my ear while he whispers all the things he loves about me. Bourbon swirls around me in the air. Our favorite game in close quarters or in a dark room is *all the ways that you're the one for me*.

His big hand is caressing my back, and I've never felt so safe or cared for. Every day, he sets the standard for this relationship higher, challenges me to rise to his level. Marriage and kids and a very long future stretch out before us, and instead of feeling anxious about any of it, I'm welcoming it with open arms. On a deep, soul level, we're meant for each other. Maybe that hypothetical Nate made up the first night we met is true—our souls have known each other across multiple lifetimes.

"What do you say?" Nate asks, lacing his fingers with mine. "Head home?"

The party is in full swing, but as usual lately, the thought of being alone with Nate is much more appealing. Even in a room this crowded, we seem able to create our own bubble of happiness.

Part of me still can't believe that we've ended up together. I keep waiting for an earthquake to hit and shake our newly poured foundation. But it really feels like we're unshakeable now, that no matter what comes at us, we can tackle it together.

"Going home with you is my absolute most favorite thing," I say, rising on my toes to give him a quick kiss.

"Let's get out of here," he says, and he takes my hand to lead me through the hotel to the main entrance. With his other hand, he's got his phone out, his thumb flying across the letters.

"Who are you texting?" I ask.

"Bill. He's driving the family around tonight. I've had too many drinks."

"Oh, okay." I hadn't been counting, but if he feels like it's too much, having a driver is exceptionally handy.

We slide into the back of the waiting car, and Nate draws me into a kiss, putting up the partition between Bill and us.

"What are you up to, Nate Tucker?" I ask with a little laugh.

"Soon," he says with a sly smile, "I'll be worshipping you at home. But I need to grab something from Cal's place first."

"It can't wait until tomorrow?" I ask, nuzzling closer.

"Definitely not."

"Boo," I say, kissing him. "What could Cal possibly have that you need to get right now?" I run my hand along his thigh, drawing close enough to tease before backing away.

"You're tempting me to postpone my visit, Ms. Davis."

"I can be *very* persuasive, Mr. Tucker."

"I made a promise," Nate says dropping kisses on my lips between words.

"Cal is very understanding."

Nate chuckles. "Only because I never break my promises."

"If I didn't appreciate that you're such a good man, I'd be a little bit pissed off right now," I say as his teeth graze my ear. "I just want to get you home and all to myself."

The car slows down and comes to a stop, and when I glance out the tinted windows, I find we're already at the campground.

Nate opens the door, and he urges me to climb out. "You want me to come with you?"

"Why not?"

"I'm all flushed and turned on. Cal will take one look at me and know what we've been doing."

"Pretty sure he already knows what we're *always* doing."

"Nathaniel Tucker, are you kissing and telling?"

"My level of happiness does not lie. What can I say?" He's walking backward, leading me across the campground toward the cliff.

"I thought we were going to Cal's house?"

"No, something was missed by the cliff a long time ago. I need to make it right."

It's such a weird comment, and I just frown while I try to puzzle out what he means. The campground is getting close to low season, and there are only a few spots taken by people in mobile homes. The whole place has a hushed, romantic atmosphere. It reminds me of the first time Nate brought me here—on the cusp of high season after he convinced me to give him one date. Four of the happiest months of my life.

And look where we are now?

Ahead, there's a trellis strung with lights and flowers. It's almost as pretty as the ones Posey had dotting the wedding.

"Oh gosh," I say, breathing out my surprise. "Isn't that pretty?"

As we get closer, I see there's a blanket and a bottle of something in a steel pot.

"We're going to interrupt someone's night," I whisper to Nate, clinging on to his hand. "We should go a different way."

"Nah, let's check it out. Just quickly. We won't stay long. There's no one here."

I glance around, trying to gauge whether we're ruining a romantic surprise. Once we're standing under the twinkling lights, Nate turns to me with an amused expression.

"The first night I brought you here, I wasn't sure I'd get a second."

"I think you knew."

"I hoped. I definitely hoped. From that first night in the bar, there was something about you that just spoke to me. I can't explain it. But I wanted you in a way I'd never wanted anyone before or since. Maybe my soul really did recognize yours. Just this, like"—he touches his chest—"*click click* inside me. The world finally made sense."

"Nate," I breathe out, touched by his love, by how in sync we are.

"And so, when I knew we were going to be separated by distance and college, I had hoped to bring you here one last time—get one last 'yes' out of you."

My throat closes at the implication, and I press the hand he's not holding to my chest.

"I didn't get to ask my question then, and maybe that's not a bad thing. Not as bad as I thought for so long, because I wasn't sure what you'd say then. Not really. Not truly. But I am now. I don't have to convince you or talk you into anything—we know where we're headed. Together."

Tears flood my eyes, and I step forward to run my hand along his jaw.

Out of his pocket, he removes a small box, and then he falls to one knee, flipping it open. "From the first moment I saw you, I knew what I wanted, and now I'm confident that you want it too. Hollyn Davis, will you marry me?"

"Yes. So many, many yeses," I say, launching myself at him, and we both fall backward onto the blanket.

He chuckles, trying to pluck the ring out of the box after keeping me from landing face-first on the ground. He takes my hand and slides the ring on, grinning.

The diamond is small, and everything about the ring seems right. "This is perfect, Nate. So, so perfect."

We're facing each other on the blanket, and he's looking at me with so much tenderness and love that my throat threatens to close up again.

"I'll get you a bigger one," he says. "But I needed to give you that one first."

"It's the same one?" My voice is thick with renewed tears.

"Kept it all this time. Don't even know why. But I'm glad I did. Getting to do this—I don't know—I think it finally set this fierce love I feel for you back in its proper place." He touches his chest. "Like everything in my life is finally where it belongs."

"I want this ring. I don't need any others."

"Then this ring stays."

"I cannot wait to live this life with you," I say, cupping his chin. "I've never looked forward to the future before, but I'm so excited to see where life takes us."

"I don't even care where it takes us. As long as I've got you, I know we can conquer anything."

Since the moment I saw the house on the cliff that we now live in, something inside me *knew*. This life with him has been calling to me since I was a teenager, but I didn't know how to grasp it, how to trust it. It's as though everything that went right between us as teenagers was in a holding pattern, waiting for us to find the path back to one another again.

And this time, I'm going to protect this life, this love, with everything I've got. No one will ever manipulate me into giving up what I've got with Nate again. This time, we'll last forever.

Want more of Nate and Hols? Sign up for my newsletter to read their deleted chapters and bonus chapters here: https://BookHip.com/SGSRTVL

Sawyer's story is coming in early 2026. Join my newsletter or follow me on Amazon or Goodreads for updates.

Wondering about the Bellerive Royals? Start with Posey and Brent, the first book in the series, here: https://mybook.to/FakeCrown

What else have I written?

Bellerive Royals Series

Fake Crown

Scarred Crown

Heavy Crown

Fallen Crown

Tucker Billionaires

Temporary Love

Fierce Love
Colliding Love
Reckless Love

New Adult Sports

Saving Us

Fake Crown

Donaghey Brothers Mafia Series

Retribution

Resurrection

Redemption

Little Falls Series

Rival Hearts

Mending Hearts

Healing Hearts

Guarded Hearts

First Date Challenge

W. MILLION

Adult Contemporary Romance

When Stars Fall

Miss Matched

Acknowledgements

First of all, thank you to any readers who sent me a "when will be get the next Tucker Billionaire novel". I know it can be a bit of a controversial thing with authors to have that pressure, but I like knowing readers care and are invested. The other books in the series shouldn't take so long to arrive.

A special thank you to Jenny Tryansky Faba, who was a TV producer in a former life, and she was kind enough to talk to me about her experiences on the phone. Any errors or creative license with the role of a TV producer is all me!

Thank you to my beta readers: Karen Flood, Jen Ragsdale, Serenity McClure, April Lawhorn, Lisa Kremnitzer, Rohini, Hayley Canigiani, Jordyn Suschanke, Andrea Gilbert, Emelia, and Megan Begin. Your keen eyes for plot holes or other relevant details along with your enthusiasm for Nate and Hols was a joy to read. Your comments and input was invaluable in shaping the narrative.

Thank you to Shannon at Shanoff Designs, who is always so creative and patient while we figure out series ideas and looks. I also appreciate Red Adept Editing who looks after the final product that lands on your Kindles.

A special thanks to Becca, who has become my blurb writing expert. I've learned a lot in our sessions about finding the emotional core of the story, presenting the stakes, and making it all hit the right tone for the book I've written. You're a rockstar.

Thank you to Hambright PR, who helped me get the word out, and to my PA Amanda Walker, who has taken the social media load the last few years, so I could focus on writing.

Lastly, a big thank you to my kids, who continue to support my writing dreams with a lot of patience, and to my dad and my husband who help carry the load when I'm deep in writing mode.

About Wendy Million/W. Million

Wendy Million is a high school teacher whose award winning contemporary romances about strong women and troubled men have captivated her loyal readers.

Writing as Wendy Million, she is the author of the romantic suspense series *The Donaghey Brothers,* as well as the contemporary second chance romances, *When Stars Fall*, and *Miss Matched*.

Writing as W. Million, she's the author of the *Bellerive Royals* series, the *Little Falls* series, and the *Tucker Billionaires* series.

When not writing, Wendy enjoys spending time in or around the water. She lives in Ontario, Canada with two beautiful daughters, two cute pooches, and one handsome husband (who is grateful she doesn't need two of those).

Made in United States
North Haven, CT
07 September 2025